Raging Skies

by

William Hallstead

International Standard Book Number 13: 978-1-60452-082-8
International Standard Book Number 10: 1-60452-082-5

Library of Congress Control Number: 2013914284

BluewaterPress LLC
52 Tuscan Way Ste 202-309
Saint Augustine Florida 32092
http://www.bluewaterpress.com

This book may be purchased online at -

http://bluewaterpress.com/ragingskies

Acknowledgment

My sincere thanks to the Sanibel Writers for their helpful review of the text as it developed--and especially to Peter Hilger for his experience-based insight of wartime Germany.

Prologue

Johannisthal Airship Field, October 17, 1913

At the airship field a few kilometers north of Berlin, the October breeze held a chill, an ominous chill Kapitän zur See Erwin Kottenhoff thought.

He shifted uncomfortably on the viewing stand's hard board seat. Had I not received a personal invitation from my old shipmate, he told himself, I could be enjoying a warm dinner at a plush Berlin restaurant instead of waiting for that ungainly hydrogen filled monster out there in midfield to get off the ground and show us what an "asset" it will be to the navy. But Bittendorf talked me into this. And after the times he corrected my navigation aboard our old Deutschland-- and said nothing about it-- I owe him.

I'm surrounded by fellow battleship Kapitäns, every one of them eager for this test to succeed. Graf von Zeppelin's ponderous gas bag, the navy assures us, could extend a battleship's scouting radius by hundreds of kilometers, well beyond the horizon's curve. A persuasive selling point, and I suspect I am the only officer on these buttocks-numbing boards who is not enthralled with the idea of depending on a fragile, explosive-filled aerial contraption for military scouting.

Gas bags as the eyes of the fleet? Just weeks ago, the navy's very first Zeppelin scout had gone down ignominiously in the North Sea. All hands had drowned, including the Kommandant of the fledgling Naval Airship Division. A disaster for the navy, but a career break for a young Fregattenkapitän-- a mere 37-year-old named Strasser-- fortuitously catapulted to Naval Airship Division Command! Would wonders never cease? The navy's first airship a fiasco. A lowly Fregattenkapitän rocketed to Division Command. And now, to follow today's test flight, another risky gas bag for the fleet.

Kottenhoff's uneasiness lay well beyond the promise of extended scouting. My gnawing concern is funding. The glamour of the new, I'm convinced, threatens the funding of the fleet's still most powerful arm, our aging battleships. We have not one modern replacement even in the planning stage.

That chills my soul. Just relieved of the 40-year-old second class battleship Deutschland's helm, I expected an eventual command on the bridge of a new first class battleship-to-be. That would be years away, even if funding would permit. But now the craze for Graf von Zeppelin's fragile bags threatens to drain more and more of the navy's allocations.

"Herr Kapitän! Old friend!" Hans Bittendorf had greeted him an hour ago, now a florid, graying man in his fifties, but with eyes still youthful at the challenge of doing something out of the ordinary

"Hans, my friend, you've come far."

"Official observer, Erwin. Practically an honorary assignment" the stocky former navigator burbled, his short, reddish hair standing straight up, seemingly mirroring Bittendorf's excitement. "I appreciate your coming, Erwin. After the flight, we will talk of the old days. I know a fine restaurant back in the city-- Ah, they are calling me."

He pushed back down through the tiers of navy brass and civilian technical specialists, strode across the intervening turf to climb the short ladder into the control gondola beneath the looming Zeppelin.

"Kottenhoff!" a voice suddenly grated two tiers above him. "I would not expect to see you within a hundred kilometers of this event."

Even before he swung around, Kottenhoff knew that raspy bray. Kapitän zur See Felix Graber. Among the battleship fraternity, Graber was the foremost Zeppelin proponent. Kottenhoff lost no love on the man, gave him a curt dip of the head and turned back to the afternoon's anticipated spectacle.

The packed stand fell silent. Then from the open, boat-like control gondola, the airship commander shouted, "Up bow!" The ground crew released their holds on the taut forward lines. Blue-white exhaust burst from the three engines, its acrid tang drifting into the rows of spectators. The muttering idle grew into hard drumming. The big propellers on their outriggers flanking the control gondola's engine compartment and the propeller on the engine gondola whirled into shimmering discs.

"Up stern!" the Kommandant shouted above the mounting roar. The aft ground handlers let go the stern lines. The huge airship rose in a slow climb, its 150-meter length appearing invincible. But Kottenhoff's research had told him how fragile the Graf's impressive airships were. Fragile frameworks of light metal girders supporting massive cells of hydrogen, highly inflammable hydrogen. Just weeks ago, the navy's first airship, L-1, had been lost at sea with all hands. Yet Graf von Zeppelin still had his hold on the public through his commercial airships of the airline Delag-- and now he fascinated the military. The army had already acquired six airships for scouting. Today L-2 would pass this final acceptance test and would put the navy back in the airship age. Yet another Navy Zeppelin, to be designated L-3, was scheduled for delivery next year.

A crucial waste of funding, Kottenhoff muttered to himself as he peered skyward. L-2 had completed a circuit of Johannisthal air field and now headed upward at perhaps 500 meters. It shoved through the air at a speed of-- Kottenhoff consulted the information handout given each guest-- a speed of 40 knots. Hardly faster than a motorcar's best--

A gasp from the crowd shocked his gaze back the circling Zeppelin. Mein Gott! His heart seemed to stop.

Bright flame stabbed aft from the forward gondola's engine compartment. The fabric it touched split and carried the fire around the airship's fat underside. With the rest of the crowd, he leaped to his feet, staring.

A flat detonation shivered the air. The stricken Zeppelin lost way. With a gut-quivering roar, trailing a broad gray scar against the sky's blue, the doomed airship sank toward the airfield's far side turf. Raging fire exposed the framework as it buckled amidships. L-2's jumble of girders, tumbling engines and blazing fabric slammed back into Johannisthal. The impact jarred the viewing stand.

Through 38 years of service, Kottenhoff had seen men die. Seven drowned in a Pacific hurricane in 1888. Three crushed in an ammunition loading accident two years later. But never had he witnessed a tragedy like this. Good men roasted to ashes in a pyre of flaring hydrogen and boiling engine fuel. The breeze shifted to bring the crowd the ghastly smell of disaster and death.

Oh God, Bittendorf...

In the grip of uncontrollable fury, Kottenhoff whirled on Kapitän Graber, his voice shaking. "Now, Graber!" he shouted. "Now what do you think of your precious gas bags? A waste of money! A waste of lives! Two down. One yet to be. How soon will we see that one in a pile of ashes?"

"You have no vision!" Graber shot back. "You are mired in the past."

"I have vision, all right. Vision that this madness must be stopped."

"Try telling that to Tirpitz."

Behind Graber, Kottenhoff noticed a fat little man with a drooping mustache frantically scribbling in a pocket notebook with a fountain pen.

God forbid. A reporter?

"That was a private conversation!" Kottenhoff shouted at him.

As Kottenhoff was to learn to his dismay, the chubby man intent on his note making, was a reporter, all right. Chief of the Berlin Bureau of Syndicated World News.

1.

KIEL, GERMANY, 1914

U p and out, that's what the navy has done to me. Up one face-saving grade, then exile here in the stodgy, isolated Procurement Division. My Elba.

Konteradmiral Erwin Gunther Kottenhoff, squarish, of middling height, fingered his bushy muttonchop sideburns and glared out the window behind his desk. From his remote perch high up in the Naval Procurement Building he enjoyed this small favor: a grand view of a large portion of Kiel's sprawling Baltic Naval Station and the dark waters of the Kiel Fjord beyond.

Aging, distraught – but far from broken, despite the drastic consequences of his public outburst at the Johannisthal calamity – Kottenhoff seethed in frustration. Among the dozen warships anchored out there lay two of Germany's First Class battleships: Kaiser Friedrich III and slightly newer Kaiser Wilhelm II, both built in the last century. Except for Kaiser Wilhelm der Grosse, all the Fatherland's battleships had been built in the last century. That was the root of Kottenhoff's concern. The need to upgrade Imperial Germany's first line of defense was being eroded by the most mundane of military set-backs: the diversion of funds. And to an unproven flash-in-the-pan invention that had beguiled "experts" who commanded influence far above the meager remains of his own once formidable clout.

He loved the old navy, the battleship navy, his former life on steel decks challenging the restless sea; but he hated the new breed and its futuristic idiocy. Damn them! Damn them for stranding me up here in luxurious near-exile, smug in their assumption I am powerless. Powerless indeed! Today – this moment – I will initiate the action I have been planning through the past six months of brain-deadening procurement minutiae.

He swung away from the window, seated himself firmly in his high-backed leather chair.

"Fräulein Tammler! Come in here. You are needed."

Kottenhoff tented his gnarled fingers and pondered. How would she react?

"Herr Admiral?" Alexia Tammler, tall, slender in a lacy white shirtwaist and ankle-length dark green skirt, strode into the Admiral's inner office, notepad in hand. Striking woman, he reflected. Were I thirty – no, forty years younger…

"Close the door, please. Sit."

She perched demurely on a hard-backed chair in front of the imposing oak desk. "Yes, Herr Admiral?"

He leaned forward and flattened his palms on the gleaming desk top.

"I am a worried man, Alexia. An old sailor devoted to the fleet, to the formidable power of the fleet – specifically to the future of the battleship. Our unsinkable fortress of the sea."

She offered a disarming smile. "I am fully aware of that, Sir."

"Are you also aware that while the fleet must have increased funding just to maintain its strength, major appropriations are being diverted to a project so damned flawed it is a total waste of money – and men. And despite the losses of its first two, the navy has purchased another one. The L-3, delivered just days ago." He felt his face flushing. He was unable to restrain his utter frustration.

"The airship program, Admiral."

"I knew you were an exceptionally smart woman. Which, of course, is why I accepted your father's suggestion that you be employed as one of my non-military aides. An unusual position for a woman, but you have always impressed me as an unusual woman. How is dear Otto these unsettled days? And Tammler Zeugmaschine Fabrik?"

"My father is well, Herr Admiral. Our factory is doing very well. I thank you for asking."

He dismissed her unnecessary thanks with a casual wave; regarded her in silence. Frowned.

"Herr Admiral?"

"My concern, Alexia, is this. The damned Naval Airship Division. That spell-binding Graf and his hydrogen-filled flying death traps have finally captured the full attention of the navy's highest echelon. Graf von Zeppelin's bone-headed dream is draining money that should go into upgrading the fleet."

Kottenhoff made an effort to get hold of himself. His discussing such a technical situation might puzzle Alexia. He peered at her closely. "You do understand my concern?

"I do, Herr Admiral."

Whether or not she truly understood, he could see she was intrigued by his frankness. Excellent.

"The situation, as you can see, Alexia, is that those dumbheads authorizing naval appropriations refuse to see. The count's misguided claim that his fragile gas bags will somehow revolutionize sea warfare has blinded them to rational thinking."

He paused, looked her straight in the eye. "What I need, Alexia, is evidence beyond the possibility that the first two Zeppelins were lost due to preventable mishaps. I must have first-hand proof the airship is fatally flawed as a potential weapon of war."

"I will be glad to collect every publication available--"

"I'm sure such publications have already been reviewed and refuted by the dunderheads involved in the airship program. No, what we need is someone trustworthy, someone loyal to this office, who will become part of that program and who will report directly to me. I must have such a person!"

He had risen as his voice rose, turned to gaze again through the window. Up and out. Up in rank one notch then dumped in this shore-bound backwater. He couldn't get past it.

"Herr Admiral?" Alexia prompted with a little smile, "surely you are not proposing that I somehow become a… an informant against the airship program."

Kottenhoff turned to face her. "Of course not, Alexia. But I do need someone within that program."

"I don't understand how I might have any part in--"

He returned to his chair, offered her a disarming a smile. "I need you to help me find a completely trustworthy person, Alexia, who agrees with my position. To be truthful, I may have already found such a person, but I need a face-to-face evaluation – your insight."

"Herr Admiral, I'm not sure I--"

He raised a silencing hand. "Alexia, I have a confession to make. I know I can trust your discretion." The little smile remained, but he waited for her response.

"Admiral Kottenhoff, after all you have done for me, you needn't ask such a question."

"My apologies. Well, some time ago, I prevailed upon an old friend of mine, an instructor of military history at the Naval Academy, to conduct a little test among his students. An essay with the title, 'The Military Importance of the Airship.' The responses were almost uniformly favorable toward the rigid airship as an observation platform and even as a potential offensive weapon. There were a few vague exceptions, but only one truly excellent analysis of the glaring weaknesses of the airship as a weapon. That exceptional evaluation was written by a senior Kadett named Reinhart. Peter Reinhart.

The admiral fingered an ornate letter opener. "What I need now is an evaluation of now Leutnant zur See Reinhart. I know no one more qualified to make that evaluation than you, Alexia."

He tented his chunky fingers and locked his pale gray eyes on hers.

She met his steady gaze. "An evaluation."

"A character evaluation, Alexia."

"I'm not sure I'm as qualified as you believe, Herr Admiral. Might not a psychologist better serve?"

"No. I need a perceptive woman, not some observer bound by professional protocols. A woman I can trust. You."

"And if I find this Peter Reinhart to be a man of dependable character?"

"It is not your place to ask," Kottenhoff snapped. Then he relented. "But I will answer. He will become my sub-rosa personal representative in the airship program."

She offered him an enigmatic little smile of her own. Then with the candor he so admired in this fearlessly outspoken young woman, she said, "You are asking me to help you recruit a personal spy."

2.

Admiral Kottenhoff had arranged for Alexia's arrival at the Emperor's Yacht Club with Kapitänleutnant Hermann Krause in his clattering old Benz. Her midnight blue satin evening gown and the fox fur stole were her own decisions. The stole had been her mother's, lovingly given to Alexia when she had graduated from secretarial training.

As a civilian aide in a backwater department, she seldom wore the stole. But when she did, she recalled her father muttering – with a degree of admiration, she thought, "At twenty-two, most girls would be thinking of marriage, not work in some office." Maybe she was something of a rebel, but she was determined not to languish in some dreary domestic existence determined by a husband. She had discerned no acceptable prospects of marriage anyway, certainly not among the dull sons of her father's friends.

So Alexia had ventured into independence, though at the outset, not entirely on her own. She talked her father into prevailing upon his long-standing friendship with Admiral Kottenhoff, and Alexia, feigning surprise at the Admiral's subsequent offer of employment, accepted.

Now intent on her mission this pleasant June evening, she was bemused by the evident hand of the admiral in the arrangements. Escort

Krause seemed a pleasant enough young man, excruciatingly polite, even quite decent looking despite his startlingly heavy eyebrows and unusually thin lips. That odd combination gave him a look, she thought, of craftiness.

At the yacht club entrance, he braked the cloth-topped Benz, handed it over to one of the valets and hurried around to open Alexia's door. Low clouds hung over Kiel. A sudden breeze ruffled her auburn curls. She defied the convention of women's neatly arranged hairstyles and hated ornate hats; near-scandalous rebellions she knew her mother deplored, but sensed her father secretly admired.

With her fingers light on Krause's arm, they swept through the ornate entrance. She shrugged off her stole and handed it to the checkroom attendant. At the auditorium doorway, a uniformed enlisted man frowned over Krause's tendered invitation, then nodded. They walked into the swirl of newly commissioned naval officers and their formally gowned ladies, all fast-stepping to the accelerated waltz rhythm of a small but determined orchestra on the far side of the big room.

"I hope Peter Reinhart will be here," she said as they joined the celebration. "His father was an old friend of the family."

"I know Reinhart. I'll introduce you."

She gave him a curious look. So much for her little deception. Krause obviously had the admiral's confidence. Did he know why she was here? That could make things a bit easier. She had wondered just how well she would play for Krause the role of an awed low-ranking aide at this academy graduation soirée. Now she suspected she didn't have to play it at all. She and Krause were on assignment.

"Leutnant Krause!" The call came from a group of three Leutnants zur See at a nearby refreshment table. "How are things at the pulse racing Department of Procurement?" All three laughed.

With a good-natured smile, Krause introduced Alexia as a department colleague. That drew wry smiles, including one from Krause, himself, as they joined newly commissioned Leutnants zur See Becker, Schmidt and Müller.

"Can you believe this man?" short, blond Leutnant Becker asked. "From teaching military tactics at the Academy to riding a desk at Procurement. Still a student of Army maneuvers, Kapitänleutnant?" He turned to Alexia. "Your escort taught land tactics to naval kadetts. A rather unusual – "

"I remind you again, gentlemen, wars are – "

" 'Won on the ground'!" all three chorused.

The orchestra struck up a bouncy version of what normally would have been a stately waltz.

"Shall we?" Krause asked Alexia, opening his arms toward her.

"I'm afraid I'm out of practice, Leutnant, but…"

She shrugged and they whirled into the crowd with more enthusiasm than grace. After a few moments, she surprised herself by managing to keep in step with his deliberate clomping. He seemed more intent on scanning the dancers than dancing with any discernible skill.

"Ah," he said abruptly, and they swung toward a table laden with refreshments dominated by a huge cut glass punch bowl.

Oh, dear, she thought. The evening was already complicated enough.

But Krause was not interested in punch, or even in offering her a cup. He headed toward a tall, blond Leutnant zur See standing at the end of the table in conversation with a short officer who had a decidedly froggy and aggressive look.

"Peter Reinhart," Krause called above the music's din.

She held her breath. Frog-face swung toward them. Oh, damn.

Then he nudged the blond officer. "You're being paged, Reinhart."

Alexia let a little gasp of relief.

"Oh, hello there, Hermann." Reinhart said without much apparent interest. "How are things in the accounting world?" He turned to Alexia. "Imagine a Navy Kapitänleutnant making a career of checks and balances." He grinned. "I'm just joking. Hermann and I are old friends. And you are?"

"May I introduce Fräulein Alexia Tammler," Krause interposed smoothly. "A colleague of mine. Alexia, this is Leutnant Peter Reinhart, Academy Class of 1914."

"Fräulein," Reinhart offered her a little bow, then glanced at Krause. "A colleague?"

"An acquaintance, " Krause said,

Alexia smiled. "A fellow worker in the Procurement Department." This is pleasant, but not what I'm here for, she thought. How am I to –

Krause, more adept than he appeared, touched her shoulder. "Oh, there's Fritz Niemeyer. I have a message for him. May I leave you in Leutnant Reinhart's care for a few moments, Alexia?"

"You certainly may," Reinhart agreed. "Say hello to Fritz Ritter, Fräulein Tammler." He nodded at his chunky fellow officer. "Now, if you will excuse us, Fritz." He turned back to Alexia. "Dance, Fräulein?"

She frowned at the spirited piece the orchestra had just launched. Several couples were executing a series of intricate steps that had already attracted a growing circle of onlookers.

"What on earth are they doing?" she wondered.

"It's a new craze imported from America. I think it's called the Castle Gavotte."

"I think I'd rather sit this one out with you. Perhaps in a quieter location?"

"The veranda," he suggested. "If you don't mind a little night air."

As they walked from the auditorium onto the auditorium's broad porch, she wished she had her stole, but her eagerness to get on with this now-fascinating assignment quickly overcame the evening's chill.

They stood at the porch railing in the glow of an overhead string of Japanese lanterns. He peered into the night. "How long have you worked for the navy?"

"Not quite a year, Leutnant."

"So formal. To you, I'm Peter. We both are green navy. I've been a Leutnant zur See all of ten days."

"Do you get a choice of where you will serve?"

"No, Fräulein, you get a hope."

"So formal," she mimicked. "To you, I am Alexia. And what do you hope for?"

"I hope for battleships."

She took a quick breath. *Here I go.* "I thought the glamor service was Zeppelins."

"I didn't join the navy for glamor. I joined to do something of value."

Compared to the navy men she knew in the Department, he sounded naïve. Charmingly naïve. Or perhaps truly dedicated?

"Let me guess," she teased. "You hope to be a captain of battleships."

"Well, yes. Someday."

"So you are going to the battleship fleet."

"I am going where they send me."

"And what," she said, with what she hoped was a disarming little grin, "if they send you to the Airship Division?"

"They won't."

"Why not?"

"Everyone in Zeppelins is a volunteer."

"A volunteer? Is it that dangerous?"

"It's foolhardy. Do you know what those things are filled with? Hydrogen. Explosive hydrogen. All it takes is a spark to set it off. I've heard Zeppelin crews have to wear special shoes so they won't..." He turned away from the darkness, leaned back against the railing and faced her. "I'd rather talk about you. Obviously, you're no starry-eyed farm girl. Big city?"

"Northern outskirts of Hamburg. My father's factory is in the city."

"So, an industrial family."

"Making machine tools. Not very exciting."

"Unless you are a machinist. You went to school in Hamburg?"

"Of course. And also in Hamburg for secretarial training." I'm supposed to be interrogating him, she reminded herself.

"Perhaps to work in the family factory?"

"Oh, no. Father would have approved, but Mother still doesn't want me to work at all."

"But here you are, far from Hamburg. What brought you to Kiel?"

"Typewriter training. But I'm a mere clerk.'

He gave her a playful grin. "And your mother doesn't think – "

"She is, well, a traditionalist. Mother hopes I will marry someone who – " She stopped, embarrassed at slipping into family matters.

"Someone who – ?" he prompted.

"You don't want to hear such trivial stuff, Peter. Tell me where you are from."

"Hannover. Down in Lower Saxony. Full of history but not much else for me. I had to get out. I was expected to follow my father's career in the army, but I chose the navy."

"Your father is in the army?"

"He was. He retired in 1904 as an Oberst on the General Staff representing Saxony. Thanks to his memory, I qualified for an appointment to the Academy."

"Oh, I'm so sorry."

"That I qualified?"

"That your father died. You said, 'in his memory.' "

"You're very perceptive, Alexia. Yes, he died six years ago. Dreamed of my going to one of the military academies, and then following in his bootsteps. I did join the military, as he had wished. But the navy instead of his army. Water is more appealing than mud."

"So," she pressed, hoping he wouldn't consider it as such, "water is also more appealing that air?"

"I don't – Oh, clever. To be specific, battleships are where I want to be. In a calamity, you can hope for a lifeboat."

"And in a Zeppelin?"

"Two Navy Zeppelins have already gone down. The L-1 was shoved into the sea by a strong downdraft. Six aboard survived. Then L-2 caught fire in midair. Nobody got out of that one alive. I'll take battleships, thank you. Floating fortresses – with lifeboats."

Both hands on the damp porch railing, she peered into the darkness. "Sounds as if you were in something of a revolt, choosing the navy over your father's army."

Silence. Have I gone too far?

Then he chuckled softly. "I've never thought of it that way. I think you're right. Father, a career army man, couldn't help himself, I suppose. So it was to be the army for me. After he was gone – I was fifteen then – I compromised. The military, but not the army."

Beyond the dark shrubbery edging the lawn, she could see pinpoints of light glimmering on the other side of the firth's dark expanse. Accordingly, his was a military family. Would that deter him from the Admiral's proposed little intrigue? Or make such an assignment even more appealing?

She let the conversation drift away from the navy, a bit apprehensive, in fact, that she may have been too inquisitive concerning the subject of airships. A few minutes later, Leutnant Krause appeared in the porch doorway.

"There you are. Isn't it cold out here? Should you care to thaw out a bit, coffee is being served."

"Excellent idea," Peter agreed. "Alexia, a pleasure to meet you." He clicked his heels, took her hand and raised it toward his lips. Was he mocking her?

On the drive back to her apartment, Krause asked, without taking his eyes off the road, "Did you get what you came for?"

"I came for the party, Lieutenant."

"Of course." He concentrated on the dimly lighted roadway. Then he said, "I assume everything went well."

Well enough, she hoped. She was already concentrating on her report to Admiral Kottenhoff.

3.

"Good morning, Fräulein," Admiral Kottenhoff said cordially as Alexia responded to his summons. "I assume you enjoyed the dance?"

"Leutnant Krause was most... helpful, Herr Admiral."

His rampant gray eyebrows rose as a trace of a smile played at the corners of his wide mouth.

"Very perceptive, Alexia."

"Well, he didn't try to hide it. I assume he works for you."

"Leutnant Krause is – you could say – a facilitator." Kottenhoff drummed his fingers on a file folder centered on his otherwise barren desktop. "And your impression of Leutnant zur See Peter Reinhart?"

"A personable young man, devoted to the navy – the battleship navy."

"How do you believe he would react to assignment to the Naval Airship Division?"

"He would not like it, but he would accept it. His is a military family."

"His father was an Oberst. Retired in 1904. Died four years later."

"You have already--"

"I have a copy of his Academy file." He tapped the folder. "A thoroughly reliable kadett, Reinhart ranked in the upper fifth of his class. No discipline problems. Followed orders promptly and fully."

She frowned. "If you already knew all this, Herr Admiral, why was I at the dance?"

"Because," he said with a smile that she felt showed no mirth at all, "I needed to know how you relate to him personally."

She peered at him. How utterly peculiar. No doubt, Krause had turned in a report of his own. But based on what? He hadn't been present when she and Peter had their veranda conversation.

"I don't quite see how my opinion can be nearly as important as the records you already have, sir."

"Your observation is the most important aspect, Alexia. I want you to be entirely frank."

What was happening here? She hesitated, then chose her words carefully. "I found Leutnant Reinhart to be an honest, likeable, self-controlled and devoted naval officer."

The Admiral nodded in apparent satisfaction.

"But if you will permit, Herr Admiral, I still do not understand the purpose of your--"

"You will, Alexia," he said with no trace of a smile now. "You will."

The chilly morning air swirled past the windscreen. Patches of sunlight between cloud shadows dappled the roadway, but Peter sensed rain before the day was through. On the sparsely populated outskirts of Kiel, he had gunned the borrowed automobile to its maximum speed of 40 mph. So read the foreign speedometer. A rattling rate of about 65 kph, he calculated. Former classmate Karl von Roemer had implored Peter to "keep it under thirty," but this straight stretch of level gravel roadway was too much of a temptation to pass up.

When Karl's overgenerous bachelor Uncle Ludwig had arranged for delivery of the Ford to his nephew at the Academy, Karl had taken a ribbing.

"Crude American engineering, if you can call it that."

"Can't Uncle Ludwig afford a Daimler?"

Then the tune changed. Indeed a far cry from meticulous German craftsmanship, the mass-produced Ford Model T had already served its inexperienced young driver for two full years with only the most minor repairs.

A hundred meters ahead, Peter spotted the grove of elms described in

Konteradmiral Kottenhoff's personally signed note. He carefully pressed the rightmost of the three-foot pedals. The machine slowed to a jouncy clacking.

Early this morning, the note – a summons, to be accurate – had been slipped under the door of the tiny apartment he was renting by the day, pending his expected orders to the fleet.

> ESSENTIAL YOU REPORT TO ME AT 10.00 HOURS
> THIS DAY AT MY RESIDENCE.

The address followed, with the mention of the elm grove landmark, all this over the cramped signature of Konteradmiral Kottenhoff.

Peter was initially stunned then elated by this personal summons from an admiral of the fleet. This could be the battleship posting I've been hoping for. I'd be happy enough with an assignment to one of the third or fourth-class battleships, but now with a konteradmiral summoning *me* to his residence... Perhaps a first class ship? Dare I hope: even a posting to the *Kaiser Wilhelm der Grosse*, the newest first class battleship in the fleet.

Upon receiving the admiral's summons, he had contacted von Roemer for the loan of the Ford, readily agreeing to refill the fuel tank on the auto's return. Now with his mind racing as the auto slowed past the elm grove he had been told to look for, he swung into a half circle graveled drive and scuffed the Ford to a rocking stop at the carved oak front door of the admiral's looming house.

As he reached for the big iron doorknocker, the door swung open.

"Leutnant Reinhart? The admiral is waiting." As Peter entered, the elderly butler – Peter assumed he was a butler despite his tweed trousers and open-collared tan shirt – held out his hand for Peter's visored cap.

"I am Albert. Follow me, please."

Peter trailed the stooped, balding old man down a broad hallway, past a darkened parlor and sunroom to a doorway across from an unlit dining room, its door ajar. A house, Peter felt, lingering in fading Victorian grandeur.

At the door opposite, Albert discreetly knocked.

"Reinhart?" a gravelly voice called.

"Yes, sir."

"Join me, Leutnant zur See Reinhart." An invitation with the overtone of an order.

As Peter entered the large library, Admiral Kottenhoff pushed out of his fireside armchair. In dark trousers and a heavy black turtleneck sweater, the stocky, heavily side-burned admiral appeared almost combative.

"Precisely on time. Excellent. I insist on promptness. Albert, we will have coffee. Agreeable to you, Leutnant?"

Peter had the impression it had better be. "Certainly, sir."

He glanced around the paneled room with its towering glass-fronted bookcases and hand-hewn ceiling beams. A modest fire simmered in the imposing stone fireplace.

"An impressive house, Herr Admiral."

"Too big since Mathilde passed away. But I refuse to spend my final years in a sterile flat down in the city's smoke and clamor. Clare Brass, my cook, has stayed with me. And housemaid Eva Bitzer continues to find her employment here more appealing than work on her family's Thuringian farm. You've already met Albert, my orderly."

All this pleasantry, Peter felt, was designed to put him at ease. But for what?

"Sit, Reinhart. Here by the fire. I like a fire, even when the weather is only moderately chilly."

Sunk into the overstuffed leather armchair opposite Kottenhoff's, Peter found his attention drawn to the lovely model of a battleship, easily a meter long, centered on the low table between the two armchairs. Intricately detailed, it was protected by a glass case.

"This is beautiful work, Herr Admiral. The old *Delag*, is it not?"

"You have an excellent eye, Reinhart. The model was presented to me on my last day of command." He leaned back, arms on the chair's arms. "I presume you wonder why you are here."

"Yes, Sir." Peter almost vibrated with anticipation. What an incredible way to begin his naval career. A personal recommendation perhaps, from one of the fleet's best-known battleship Admirals. Almost all of Peter's class had already received postings, notified through daily listings on the Academy's Common Room bulletin board. Peter checked the board every morning, but his name was always missing.

"I have considerable respect for your record at the Academy, Reinhart. I was particularly impressed by the paper you wrote in your senior year, the overview of the navy's airship program. You are an officer obviously devoted to the service, a man with the potential for outstanding accomplishment."

"I am honored, Herr Admiral." That damned paper. I know now I wrote it as a rebellious reaction to my strict boyhood as a high-ranking officer's son. Then all that tight discipline through four years at the Academy. The paper was a chance to buck navy thinking for once. A protest of a sort, to be graded then forgotten. Now it's haunting me.

"I need an unusual man, Reinhart." The admiral smiled briefly. "I need a man I can trust, absolutely trust, for an extremely sensitive project. One that offers risk but that in the final analysis, could change the entire direction of our navy's defense planning."

Kottenhoff stroked his muttonchops, studied the battleship model for a long moment, then raised his eyes to Peter's.

"Are you such a man, Leutnant?"

Peter felt his heart thud. How many just-graduated Leutnants zur See are presented with an Admiral's "sensitive" project? Careful, now. Careful.

"I would hope to be of service, Herr Admiral."

Kottenhoff nodded in satisfaction. "I'm sure you are aware of my deep concern about the condition of our battleship fleet."

"I am, Herr Admiral." What is this man driving at? That report I wrote. This odd conversation.

Kottenhoff's intent gaze shifted to the doorway. "Ah, thank you, Albert."

The aged orderly in his gamekeeper garb, had returned to wheel in a laden coffee service cart. As they watched in silence, he poured.

"Will there be anything else, Herr Admiral?"

"No, you may go, Albert. But leave the door open."

As Albert quietly withdrew, Kottenhoff leaned toward Peter. "The navy offered me an enlisted rank to serve as my personal orderly, but I felt more secure hiring my own man. Albert is from Flensburg, up the coast." He sat back, sipped his black coffee.

Felt more secure? Peter felt a little twinge of apprehension. What is this?

"In simple terms, Reinhart, I must have information I can bring to the attention of the proper office, specific information on the liabilities of the airship as an offensive weapon of war."

The liabilities? Then it hit him. Kottenhoff had to be the rumored käpitan zur See who had been "kicked upstairs" and isolated to shut up his anti-airship rants. Careful not to rattle the cup on its saucer, Peter set it back on the service cart and braced himself. Elation died as a worm of apprehension began to gnaw.

"I need a reliable and confidential representative to collect that information and report it to me. Leutnant Reinhart, I want you to be that representative.

Peter let out a long breath. "You want me to make a study of the airship program and prepare a confidential report, Herr Admiral?"

"I want you to enter the program, Reinhart. By becoming part of it, you will become thoroughly familiar with its problems and flaws."

Peter struggled to keep his voice steady. "You are asking me to volunteer for airship service."

"That is a gentlemanly way of putting it."

Christ Almighty, I'm being ordered to become a part of an admiral's vendetta against the navy's most publicized project. What do I really know about airships? From a distance, I've seen the commercial airships of Delag – *Hansa, Sachsen,* possibly *Victoria Louise.* But I've never seen one up close. I wrote that damned paper from news clips, not real research.

As if Kottenhoff had read Peter's mind, the admiral handed him an envelope. "Your orders, Lieutenant. I am sorry you will have to miss the annual celebration of Kiel Week, but this is of prime importance to me. And to the navy. You are to report to Nordholz by the fifteenth."

"Nordholz, Sir?"

The airship base just south of Cuxhaven on the North Sea coast."

My God, Peter realized in shock, I'm being – what was the term? Railroaded.

"You will provide your reports to an intermediary who will relay the information personally to me. An intermediary we both can implicitly trust. So, with your agreement to become a vital part of this little counter project of ours–" He turned toward the doorway and raised his voice: "Please join us now."

From the darkened dining room across the hall stepped a tall woman with auburn curls.

Peter scrambled to his feet. "Alexia! I should have guessed." But how could he have guessed even ten minutes ago, that – with the contrivance of a konteradmiral – he and Alexia Tammler were about to spy on a sister service?

4.

Jouncing back toward the city with Peter in his borrowed Ford, Alexia found the morning depressingly dark. When Albert had driven her out here two hours ago in the admiral's big Daimler, patches of sun had dappled the roadway. Now she rode beneath lowering skies. But the threat of a downpour did not lessen her excitement. Imagine! A secret assignment from an admiral!

She stole a sideways glance at Peter. He drove with his eyes never leaving the road. He had readily agreed with the admiral's suggestion, to motor her back to Kiel – suggestion, she wondered, or contrivance? She and Peter were becoming increasingly involved in Herr Admiral's hatred of the Zeppelin program – she in anticipation of a fascinating adventure. But Peter...? His face seemed frozen.

"You are not elated with our assignment?" she asked over the engine's rattle.

"I follow orders."

A kilometer from the admiral's residence, rain began to pelt down.

He pulled off the roadway, brought the Ford to a stop, and leaped out to yank loose the fastenings of the folded top.

"Let me help."

"You'll get soaked."

"Peter, until the top is up, it is just as wet inside as it is outside."

Together, they managed to latch the unfamiliar top in place then scrambled back under its shelter. As rain drummed on the waterproofed cloth, he turned toward her. "You've been a part of this all along, haven't you?"

"I've done what the admiral asked of me, yes. And now so have you."

"What was the point of your appearance at the yacht club? Some sort of evaluation?"

"Yes. But now I know it was an evaluation of me as well as you - of us. Potentially working together."

"I think there's a difference. For you, this may be wonderfully exciting. For me? Like the admiral, I consider myself a battleship man. Unlike the Admiral, I'm not eager to spy on another naval division"

"Does it matter? We both seemed to have met the admiral's requirements."

He stared through the rain-spattered windscreen. "It's not what I expected to be doing as a naval officer."

"Nor I as an admiral's aide," she said with a lot more enthusiasm than he seemed to be feeling. "But what does it matter? The orders are simple. You are to get information to me, and I am to deliver it to him, and we are not to be caught at it."

"For our sakes as well as his. You would probably lose only your job with the Procurement Division. I could lose my navy career."

"But we will not be doing anything that can be considered -" Her voice faltered. Then she managed, almost in a whisper, "- treacherous."

"Ask a Zeppelin captain that."

It's only an old admiral's game, she told herself. Their real problem was how to play it.

"You are ordered to Nordholz," she said. "I am in Kiel. How do we -"

"I go to Kiel, or you come to - what town did the admiral say was close to Nordholz?"

"Cuxhaven. Thirteen kilometers."

"- Or you come to Cuxhaven. Easier for you to move about, than for me as an assigned military officer. So you come to Cuxhaven."

"Surely not every day," she teased, and she saw the first trace of a smile from him this entire morning.

"Surely not," he agreed. "But on a weekend. Let's try two weeks from now. A test run, unless I have something of immediate importance before then." He peered at her. "You just lost that confident look I admired on the yacht club veranda."

"Is this –" Her mouth was suddenly dry. "Could what we are about to do be act of... of military disloyalty?"

"What we are doing is an act of military politics."

"Politics," she echoed without conviction.

"The rain's stopping." He adjusted a lever on the steering column, swung down to the roadside grass, walked around to the front of the Ford and bent down for the crank to restart the engine.

"I have a problem," lanky Karl Roemer announced when Peter returned the Model T to the Naval Academy parking area. His close-set eyes met Peter's then swung away. "Fortunately it's a problem anyone would enjoy having."

"You've lost me."

"Uncle Ludwig has gone overboard. See that Mercedes behind you? That's my graduation present from my ever-doting uncle. Now I have two cars. What am I to do with two cars?"

"Keep the new one, sell the old one."

Karl's narrow face broke into a sly grin. "I accept your offer, Peter." He thrust out an envelope.

"What's this for?"

"Title and a sales agreement. You pay me each month the moderate amount I've listed. It will not eat too much of a bachelor leutnant zur see's pay."

"The Mercedes just arrived? What a fortunate coincidence."

"Well, not exactly. It was delivered two days ago, but your borrowing the Ford today gave me the idea of –"

"You have a future, Karl, but more likely in some salesroom than aboard a ship."

A day of manipulation. First the admiral. Then, to a degree, Alexia. Now Karl. I know damned well I'm being maneuvered, but there have to be some benefits in all this.

At least my go-between is a pretty woman. How many green leutnants fall into this kind of strange assignment? On balance, it could be a huge plus, but one with a potentially huge risk.

He would drive to Hannover, spend two days with his housebound, aging mother, then arrive on June 15, as ordered, at Nordholz – in his own automobile. Ready to begin the admiral's confidential assignment.

5.

In his short time home, Peter managed to coax his mother into the Ford for a drive into Hannover, a look at the Herrenhäuser Gärtan then the Marketplatz. But despite his best efforts at diversion, the depression into which Erika Reinhart had fallen after Peter's father's death persisted. He left early on the 15th, confident he had ample time to reach Nordholz – until he hit a stretch of unusually rough road some 15 kilometers south of Hamburg. After one unusually hard jolt, he heard the hiss of escaping air. The Ford lurched to the left. He forced it straight, but the steering wheel wobbled in his hands. Flat tire.

As he stood in the roadway wondering what to do, he heard another auto approaching. A dusty Benz pulled in behind him.

"Need help, son?" a booming voice called. "I'm an expert in the bad tire department." The driver, a strapping middle-aged man, stepped out of the Benz, switched it off and peered into the Ford unbidden. "I see you have a repair kit. Let me give you a hand, Leutnant." He stuck out a meaty paw. "Emil Kinder. Have a shop in Harburg, up ahead.

Built like a wrestler with arms as thick as his neck, the fellow opened the emergency kit Karl Roemer had included in his sale arrangement. "Ah, spare inner tube. Sehr gut!

"Sir, I can't let you –"

"Have you ever done this, Leutnant?"

"No, I –"

"Then just stand back. After three hours bouncing on the road, I can use the exercise."

In the middle of the tire repair, Peter heard the rumble of engines. He looked up and shaded his eyes to watch the long, white cigar shape of an airship drum past, a kilometer or so north, low and rumbling eastward.

"Quite a sight," his roadside Samaritan said from his crouch by the front wheel.

Straining his eyes against the sky's brightness, Peter made out the prominent black lettering on the airship's forward section: VIKTORIA LUISE. "One of Delag's commercial flights."

"Coming from the airship field near Wilhelmshaven, I'd guess. Maybe heading for Berlin. I'd like to get aboard one of those things, but it's too rich for this mere butcher's blood." He burst out laughing. "Sorry, bad joke." He turned back to the tire repair. "Where you heading?"

"Nordholz."

"You a gas bag man? You're going to be waiting a while. The place is still being built."

Still being built? Peter was taken aback. Was the admiral aware he might have to wait awhile for this – uh – reporter of his to find anything worth reporting? "All set," the smiling butcher finally announced, reaching for the jack handle.

Should I offer to pay this helpful guy? Peter wondered, as Kinder let the front end down and stowed the jack. He reached for his wallet. "Herr Kinder –"

"Ach, nein, Leutnant. My pleasure to help one of our navy men." He shouldered back into his Benz, pulled around the Ford, waved and jounced on north.

Well, that certainly was a spot of luck, Peter marveled. But my next problem is fuel.

Not until he had made the westward turn at Harburg just south of Hamburg did he spot a small inn with a benzin pump nearby. He embarrassed himself in front of a pimply-faced attendant who grinned at Peter's search for the fuel tank, ultimately discovering it directly beneath the front seat. That seemed ominously appropriate for a Zeppelin "volunteer" – sitting right over a tank of explosive. He paid for the tankful of benzin and stepped into the inn's small dining room.

After a quick meal of herrings and jacket potatoes, he set out on the final leg of this trip to the increasingly flat and bleak west coast.

Late in the afternoon, in the haze along the flat horizon, he spied a pair of long, low humps. The Zeppelin sheds of Nordholz?

Peter made a quick scan of the sky all around him. Not a hint of an airship. No flying today? Twenty minutes later, he gasped in disbelief. No wonder there were no Zeppelins in the air. As Herr Kinder had said, the airship base was still under construction – the dual hangars in their final stages, from the looks of the skeletal hangar doors, but still under construction.

As he pulled up to the guard post at the entrance road, a solitary seaman emerged, saluted.

"Leutnant zur See Reinhart." Peter offered the typed orders Konteradmiral Kottenhoff had given him.

The big-shouldered guard, who looked to be in his mid-40s, waved an arm at the empty expanse of scruffy grass broken only by the looming pair of partially built hangars, the foundations for several more, and a collection of smaller frame buildings some 800 meters from the hangar site.

"Welcome to Nordholz, Sir. Or what will be Nordholz when it's finally built. Officers' quarters in the building to the left." He pointed and Peter thrust his shuddering auto back into gear.

"What is that, Sir?" The seaman jerked his head toward the motorcar.

"An American Ford."

"American," the guard sniffed. "Noisy."

Was that a bored sentry's not-so-subtle effort to engage this officer half his age in a political discussion? Peter was having none of that.

"It got me here."

"Yes, Sir. That building on the left."

That building, a good quarter-kilometer from the entrance, was a two-story frame structure with a tarpaper roof. It looked temporary, as did the several other frame buildings nearby. Peter noted the considerable open space between those and the hangars. Aha. They had been located a safe distance from future hangar tenants charged with their thousands of cubic meters of explosive hydrogen.

He parked near the entrance at the near end of the barracks-like structure, signed in at a desk presided over by a disinterested enlisted rating who directed him to Room 3 on the upper level.

He toted his meager luggage up the narrow wooden steps. A short distance down a barren, linoleum-floored hallway, he heard voices and found the door to #3 ajar. He pushed it open and stepped into the sparsely furnished room. Double bunk along the right wall, single on the left. Two officers already here, one blond and sassy looking, the other slim and trim with a neat little mustache. Both in their mid-twenties, I would think. I'm last in, so last served, Peter knew. My bunk will be the disdained upper.

The room offered three chests, a single desk and a couple of chairs. One window, with its window seat occupied by the blond leutnant zur see while the slim-trim Oberleutnant zur See leans against the double bunk. Someone's got to say something.

"Gentlemen?"

"Aha, Ernst," the blond fellow lounging on a window seat said to the other officer. "I believe we are about to welcome the third occupant of our cozy little domain."

Blouse unbuttoned, knees splayed, he looked like a country farmer trying a new occupation.

"Leutnant zur See Reinhart, gentlemen" Peter said.

"First name?" the blond asked. "We're not exactly high brass here."

"Peter." He set down his bag. "I thought this was an airship base. Where are the Zeppelins?"

"Excellent question, Leutnant zur See Peter Reinhart. The whole Naval Airship Division asks it." Ernst, an intense looking fellow with deep-set dark eyes, smiled without mirth, the ends of his prissy little mustache twitching upward. His uniform was crisply fresh, all buttons secure. "You are not aware the entire complement of naval airships at this moment is exactly one? There were three. Then L-1 went down in the North Sea last year. Everyone aboard lost, including Korvettenkapitan Matzing, who knew something about airships. His replacement, Leutnant – a mere Leutnant! – Peter Strasser, who knew nothing about airships. His own admission. Then last October, L-2, Leutnant Peter, L-2 caught fire on a test flight over the Johannisthal airship base."

"Meet Oberleutnant zur See Ernst Wolff," the blond officer broke in. "Ernst the Lecturer."

"Thank you, Leutnant zur See Franz Schuster the Duelist." Ernst was obviously not pleased with the interruption. "Why don't you tell Reinhart about that famous scar on your cheek?"

"How about telling Reinhart about the L-whatever it was?" Peter suggested.

I know the details of L-2's demise; I even included the incident in that damned class paper that got me into all this. But I'm the new guy here, and considering why I'm here, I'd rather be as unremarkable as possible.

Ernst regarded Peter with a look of superiority. "L-2, Peter. It blew up on a test flight at the Johannisthal airship base near Berlin last October. No survivors, but a real break for Strasser. In just hours, he determined the cause. Vented hydrogen trapped in the forward car, ignited by sparks from engine exhaust. His stock went up from there."

"So with L-2 gone, that leaves only L-3."

"Good math. L-3 was delivered to the navy just last month. It is stationed at Fuhlsbüttel. But the army is way ahead of us with six airships already operational."

"That leaves me with just one question." Peter turned to Franz. "What about that dueling scar?"

The grinning blond fingered the prominent white scar on his left cheek. "Heidelberg."

"I didn't know they still dueled at Heidelberg."

"Heidelberg is what I tell the girls, Peter. No lies here though. I got this falling off my tricycle when I was five."

"I'll tell you Franz's real claim to fame," Ernst put in. "His brother Kaspar is a member of the Kaiser's advisory staff in Berlin. It is through Cousin Kaspar that our roommate escaped the Daimler factory's grease pits and is now a lordly leutnant in this airshipless Airship Division. It is also through Brother Kaspar that we –"

"Ernst," Franz cautioned, with a touch of resignation, "you're aware I like to keep my source confidential. Like a newspaperman. And, you, you ass, know damned well my commission stripe came from a year on a miserable little torpedo boat before I got tired of bouncing around the Frisian Islands."

He turned to Peter and aimed a thumb at Ernst. "Even that beat our oberleutnant's past as a dockworker."

"Dockworker?"

"I was an inspector in the Department of Naval Depots in Wilhelmshaven. The Airship Division sounded like a lot more fun than that, so I volunteered." Ernst gave Peter a speculative look. "You asked where are the Zeppelins? They are under construction, five of them to be delivered before Christmas. To four new bases, likewise all under construction. Hage, Seddin, Tondern and here at Nordholz. Enough to make an airshipman salivate."

"Actually, I'd hoped to be a battleship man," Peter blurted. He felt his face flush. A terrible slip. And Ernst caught it.

"Then why," the now unsmiling Lecturer asked, his dark eyes narrowing, "have you volunteered for the airship service?"

Stupid, stupid. Peter held Ernst's gaze as his mind raced. "Because," he finally said, "the battleship fleet is mired in the traditions of the past. I decided a new service could offer more opportunities."

"Peter the Eager?" Franz quipped, pushing himself off the window seat. "There's a passable imitation of an officers' mess in that gaggle of buildings behind this one. Let's eat."

6.

Phew! Hell of a morning. Evaluation by training officers. Filling out forms. Then a dreary and seemingly endless orientation lecture by an oberleutnant obsessed with military deportment. Finally having met these requirements, Peter ambled across the stubbly airship field to take a close look at the hangars under construction.

As he neared the twin sheds, Peter was struck by their hugeness. Two mammoth barns, side-by-side, housing for two Zepps. The twin structures were astride a giant turntable, their wheeled ends riding its circular perimeter track. And now, shading his eyes against the midday sun, he noted more hangars were beginning to rise from the widely disbursed foundations on the immense airship base's flatlands.

He walked closer to the nearly completed twin sheds on their great circular base.

"To permit the Zepps to emerge heading directly into the wind," his roommate, the Lecturer, had informed him. "The sheds at other airship bases are being built facing the prevailing wind. Only Nordholz has the turntable. It will make ground handling far more efficient here. A Zeppelin in even a moderate crosswind becomes nearly unmanageable by its ground handlers."

Careful not to impede the rattle bang of construction on the gigantic sliding doors of the nearest shed, Peter edged past the scaffolding and peered into the cavernous interior.

"Quite a sight, is it not, Leutnant? Nearly two hundred meters long and over eighteen meters high." The man in workman's rough garb was built like a wrestler with a voice to match. He thrust out a meaty hand.

"Bruno Zimmer, construction foreman. You find this interesting?"

"I find it fascinating, Zimmer. Hell of a piece of work."

The building's metal sheathing clanked and rumbled in the late summer heat. Peter aimed a thumb at a series of holes that stretched along both sides of the flooring. "What are those for?"

Zimmer chuckled. "I can tell you're a green Zeppelin man. Those are for the hydrogen hoses. Efficient charging of the airship lifting cells."

"You're right. I've been in the airship service not quite two weeks."

"Well, it's new to a lot of my guys, too. Not to me, though. I put in eight years with Delag. Construction down in Hamburg, hangar maintenance, even a ground handler at times. Finally got an offer from the company building these two big barns."

"Any idea when they will become operational?"

"Peacetime pace, Leutnant, though they tell me the new kommandant of the Airship Division is a real ball of fire."

He peered upward. "No! Not that way," he shouted. "Hold up on that. I'm on my way. Sorry, Leutnant," he said over his shoulder. Then he began the long climb up the scaffolding ladder.

Peter walked clear of the construction, turned back and stood with his feet spread, hands behind his back. A picture of certainty, perhaps, though I'm anything but. Exactly what can I report to Alexia?

He had received her telephone call last evening; rather Leutnant zur See Lehman had.

"Damn!" Peter had heard him shout as the phone halfway down the hall jangled. "That cursed telephone is outside my room so I'm secretary for the whole damned hall!" Lehman snatched up the receiver anyway.

"Leutnant Reinhart," he shouted as he dropped the receiver and stomped back into his room. "For you."

"Thanks, Lehman," Peter called as he picked up the receiver. "Leutnant Reinhart here."

"Oh, so formal," Alexia chided him. "I have only a moment. I will be near Cuxhaven tomorrow. At the Blauer Adler Inn, south of the city along the coast road. Can you meet me in the afternoon?"

"The training day is pretty much over by noon here. It should be no trouble."

"Look for a sign with a big blue eagle, so I'm told. I'll see you then."

Now out here at the hangar site in the warm early afternoon, he was torn. He would do the job Konteradmiral Kottenhoff had ordered him to do. But he could not shake the feeling he was somehow betraying... what? The navy? Did not the admiral have at heart the navy's best interests? Or, Peter wondered, was he simply betraying – no, not that ugly word. He was evaluating a service arm built around the fragile, fire-prone invention of charismatic but aging Graf von Zeppelin. Both navy versions had crashed, killing everyone aboard.

Why had he let himself become involved in this confusing situation? The only bright spot was Alexia. But, he reminded himself, she had been part of Kottenhoff's scheme to put him here. His pass had become effective at noon. He pulled out his watch. 13.20 hours. Time to be on the road.

He shoved the watch back in his pocket and hurried to the administrative buildings.

The road from Nordholz to the Cuxhaven-Hamburg road angled through monotonous flat country. He settled back in the Ford's high seat and forced himself to concentrate on his driving. But the challenge of the lumpy roadbed failed to divert the doubts that had closed in on him the moment he cranked the Ford.

Just where did his ultimate responsibility lie? To the admiral who had sent him on this mission? To the navy? To both. But what Kottenhoff had ordered him to do was intended to affect the very project Peter was now part of. At the least, to impede the airship program; or, surely deep in the admiral's heart, cancel it altogether.

The navy or the admiral? A subject for philosophical debate, no doubt. But he knew his career depended on his value to Konteradmiral Kottenhoff, undoubtedly at this moment impatiently awaiting Alexia's report.

And exactly what of any value had he to tell her?

Some eight kilometers north of the base, the road intersected with the Hamburg-Cuxhaven road. He turned left into that wider, smoother roadway, rumbled through a stand of windblown, salt-air stunted trees, passed several farms, and then a sign seemed to leap out of the scant shrubbery on the right. Stark white, surmounted by a large, elegantly carved blue eagle.

"And so," Peter muttered uneasily, but with an undeniable tingle of anticipation at seeing Alexia again, "it begins." He turned into the wide gravel drive.

A valet at the entrance to the rambling Bavarian-style inn parked the Ford, trying, Peter thought, to disguise his disparaging look at the dusty American import. He climbed the wide entrance steps, walked into a large rustic-style lobby and approached the registration desk.

"Leutnant Reinhart to see Fräulein Tammler," he told the apple-cheeked desk clerk. The dumpy, middle-aged man in something of a tan uniform coat continued his noisy chalking of the day's guest activities in a slate notice board behind the desk.

"Leutnant Reinhart to see –"

"Oh, sorry, Sir." The well-fed clerk laid down his chalk. "Fräulein Tammler is on the east veranda. That way." He nodded toward the French doors at the far end of the lobby.

She stood at the end of the porch railing overlooking the expanse of the nearby Elbe River's estuary behind the inn. Tall and slender in an ankle length, long sleeved green dress, she turned toward him, auburn hair in carefree curls. A pendant on her silver necklace glittered in the waning sun. She offered a small smile, not one of surprise. No doubt, she had watched him drive in. Could she also, he wondered, be looking forward to this "reunion"?

"How have you been, Peter? You are looking well."

"So formal? You are looking well; I am looking dusty."

"Come, sit." She touched one of the two wood slat chairs on this isolated end of the broad porch.

"How did you get here?" he wondered.

"Leutnant Krause. He was sent to a conference in Cuxhaven. He offered me a ride here then went on to the conference.

"And he takes you back to Kiel also?" Obviously the fine hand of the admiral. Peter sank into one of the uncomfortable chairs. "Is Krause to be your personal chauffeur for our report meetings?"

"I plan to get an auto of my own."

"I didn't know you could drive."

"I can learn." She leaned close. "Would you recommend a Ford like yours?"

"Only if you like cranking the engine to start it."

"Oh. Then maybe a Rolls-Royce?"

"If you like to arrive with all eyes on you." He grinned.

She was teasing him.

"What have you to tell me?"

He looked down at her empty hands. "Shouldn't you take notes?"

"I have an excellent memory, Peter. Depend on it."

He shrugged. "At this point, I'm not sure I have anything that is not general navy knowledge. Nordholz is still under construction and probably will not be finished for another month. The hangars may be of interest. The two almost finished are side-by-side on a giant turntable to take advantage of wind shifts. I saw dozens of fixtures in the flooring for hydrogen hoses that will permit rapid charging of the lifting cells. But charging the cells under cover apparently will be dangerous. There were already 'no smoking' signs posted. And construction of several more hangars is getting underway."

"You have nothing on the Zeppelins themselves?"

"There are none there. The navy has only one, the L-3. Delivered just last month to the Fuhslbüttel airship base. Surely the admiral knows that."

He stared out to sea, then turned back to her. "Surely the admiral knows all of this, Alexia. Why are we here?"

"I suppose you might call this a test meeting. I don't question him. You should not, either."

He frowned. A test meeting, with her again the cool, efficient administrator of the test. He felt a touch of resentment being used this way. But, he realized, anyone in uniform is being used. It is called military service.

"How is the morale of those at Nordholz?" she asked.

Her question or the admiral's?

"In the peacetime doldrums everyone easily adjusts. I attend evaluations, discussions for about half the day. Nobody seems yearning to get on with the airship program. Nobody but Peter Strasser –"

"The kommandant of the Airship Division."

"The driving force, but by the time his drive works its way to Nordholz, it's more like a walk. And some of this...well, lack of urgency could be the result of the L-2 crash eight months ago. A Zeppelin blowing up in midair all by itself is not much of an inspiration."

"That I certainly can understand."

"She sat silent for a moment. "Tell me about the telephone service."

"The telephone service?"

"Yes. How were you told I was on the line?"

"There is one telephone on our residential floor, midway down the hall. When it rings, the nearest officer answers then calls the name of who is wanted – and who the call is from, if he's told that much."

"So it is probable some of your fellow officers will become curious over the same woman calling frequently."

"To hell with what they think."

"No, it is important what they think, Peter. To keep them from thinking too much." She pondered. "Any suggestions?"

"If the phone answerer asks, tell him you are my fiancée."

"Your fiancée?"

"Professional 'cover,' I believe it's called."

"You may wipe that smirk off your face, Leutnant. No privileges are implied."

Was she teasing him? He could tease too.

"Oh? The very word –"

"Peter!"

"Sorry. I'll try not to get carried away by all this."

She consulted the pendant on her necklace, a small watch. "Will you stay for supper?"

"I'm sorry. I have to get back to Nordholz."

"Such a rush. It's only a short drive."

"I want to get back before dark"

"A brave leutnant zur see doesn't want to drive in the dark?"

"I don't want to be fixing a flat in the dark, Alexia." He stood. "It is nice to see you again. Sorry I didn't have anything earth rattling to report." What a scintillating way to end this first, presumably secretive get-together.

"Next time perhaps."

"May I walk you back to the lobby?"

"I think I will stay to watch the sunset."

Was she a bit piqued over his lack of real information? His turning down her supper suggestion?

"As you wish." He strode away toward the lobby.

Behind the reception counter, Apple Cheeks was again clicking his damned chalk on his bulletin board.

"Excuse me."

"Sir?"

"My auto. I would appreciate the valet's bringing it out front."

"Immediately, Sir."

Peter nodded at the board. "What's so interesting this time?"

"Phone call from a newspaper friend in Cuxhaven. He gives me news the guests might find interesting. I'm not so sure this will be exactly earth shaking. Some fool duke has got himself shot to death in … I think he said down in the Balkans, wherever that is."

As he drove south in the fading afternoon, Peter wondered who the hell would bother to assassinate a duke?

7.

Because he's tall? Is that why I'm so fascinated with this assignment? So many attractive men are too short for a tall woman. Or am I so willing to work with Peter Reinhart because I was dreadfully bored with the admiral's office work?

Alexia gazed through the Blauer Adler's dining room window to the rippling estuary beyond. She liked Peter's eyes, deep brown eyes that implied sincerity – and offered a sparkle of unexpected fun at his suggestion that she call herself his "fiancée. But that had not been a frivolous idea. They both knew her phone calls and their meetings, were they to become frequent, would be sure to prompt curiosity among his fellow officers. Such curiosity could lead to –

"Fräulein Tammler? Fräulein Tammler?

Now why, Alexia wondered, would I be paged at breakfast at this remote inn? Or paged at all? This was supposed to have been a confidential assignment.

She motioned to the young bellman.

"A telephone call, Fräulein. The booth at the end of the desk."

She left her boiled egg reluctantly. Who could be calling me here? Only Peter, Leutnant Krause, and, of course, the admiral knew –

"Alexia?" The urgent voice on the lobby telephone belonged to Krause. "The conference has been cut short. Because of the situation."

"What situation?"

"I'll tell you when I get there. Can you be ready to leave in an hour?"

Well, damn. Krause was supposed to pick me up late today, and I've been looking forward to a few hours with nothing to do but enjoy the seacoast. What is happening?

"I'll be ready, Leutnant." She bolted the rest of her breakfast and rushed to her room to pack then check out.

When Krause pulled up in his assigned navy staff Mercedes, she was waiting. He trotted around the front of the auto to open the door for her while a bellman strapped her traveling bag on the rear luggage rack.

"My apologies." Krause plunked back in the driver's seat. Thick eyebrows knitted in concentration, he rammed the car into gear and they lurched forward. "The conference was abruptly cancelled this morning. We're all ordered back to our stations."

Was his expression one of concern or exasperation?

"This is ridiculous!" he burst out as he swung them eastbound into the Cuxhaven-Hamburg road.

"What's happened? I did hear some talk this morning in the dining room about an assassination. Some duke, but –"

"Austrian Archduke Franz Ferdinand, successor to Emperor Franz Joseph, shot dead in Sarajevo. Ferdinand was next in line to head the Austro-Hungarian Empire. I don't see--" Alexia caught her breath as Krause swerved wildly to avoid a dog that had trotted into the roadway. "I don't see why that would be enough to disrupt a conference in Cuxhaven."

"Nor do I, Alexia. But I'm only a naval leutnant. It's affected more than the conference. What remained of Kiel Week has been cancelled."

"With the Kaiser there?"

"The Kaiser left when he got the news. Got it in an odd manner, by the way."

"Oh?"

"Some admiral commandeered a launch and raced to the royal yacht in Kiel Harbor. He threw his cigarette case aboard. Kaiser Wilhelm opened the case, read the note inside, and that's the way he learned of the 'earth shaking' event."

"You don't think it is?"

"It was to our kaiser. We heard he turned white when he read the note, and raced out of Kiel. But whatever he heard, he didn't go back to Berlin. He went on his planned vacation. What do you make of that?"

"I don't know what to make of any of this, Leutnant."

"Nor do I. All I know for sure is Kiel Week is over. The British ships are heading home. Confusion reigns."

But, Alexia was certain, in such an apparently chaotic sea, Konteradmiral Kottenhoff will remain an island of calm purpose, though he won't be exactly overwhelmed by my hangar construction report. My real problem at the moment is how in the world can I get an automobile?

Following the event in Bosnia, Peter felt Nordholz to be a half-built military base in a state of indecision. Everyone seemed to be waiting for someone else to take some initiative. The result: a stand-down. In Room 3 of the officers' quarters, Franz the Duelist had supplanted Ernst the Lecturer as the man with the inside word. Franz's brother, Kaspar, had called just hours after the details of the assassination had become known, and spent almost a full half hour on the phone with him. Now Franz was gleefully full of it.

"Kaspar says Berlin is like here. Everybody waiting for the kaiser's next move. We have an alliance with Austro-Hungary, so what happens next is anybody's guess."

"That took Kaspar a half hour to explain?" Peter asked from his perch on one of the room's hard chairs.

"Oh, that was just the beginning."

As Franz began to pace the room, obviously bursting with whatever Kaspar had told him, Ernst gave Peter a roll of eyes from the window seat. "It's just another one of those Serb flare-ups. They've been fuming for the past six years, ever since the Austro-Hungarian Empire grabbed Bosnia and Herzegovina. That lit the Serbs' fuse because they'd wanted those provinces to become part of the Serb Empire."

"And they've been sizzling ever since," Franz broke in. "So when they got word Archduke Ferdinand was to visit Sarajevo, a group of wild-eyed Serbs saw their chance to kill the next in line to lead the hated empire to the north."

"Franz," Ernst reminded him, "I'm the Lecturer. Anyway, it's time for lunch."

"I know, I know. But I want to tell you this story while I remember the details."

"Next time, tell your brother not to call you just before lunch."

"He calls when he has a chance to call. Do you want to hear the rest of this or not?"

"I want to hear it," Peter said. "Ernst, let him get on with it."

"You'll love this idiocy," Franz persisted. "Aside from the tragedy part, it's like a comic opera."

"An assassination is like a comedy?"

"Just listen, Ernst." Franz plunked down the room's other chair and hunched forward eagerly. "According to Kaspar, the drama begins with the motorcade of six automobiles on an avenue along the River Miljacka, heading for a reception at Sarajevo City Hall. Archduke Franz Ferdinand, his wife, Sophie, and a general are in the back of the second automobile, with its top down.

"The plotters, a half dozen Serb fanatics, are strung through the crowd along the route. When the archduke's auto passes the first would-be 'hero,' he does nothing. The next one, though, pulls a bomb out of his pocket, bangs it against a lamp post to arm the thing, then throws it at Franz Ferdinand." He paused, apparently enjoying Ernst's obviously contrived look of disinterest.

"And?" Peter prompted.

"And now the comedy begins. The owner of the car, riding in the front with the driver, hears the bomb smack the lamppost and thinks it's a flat tire. 'We'll have to stop!' he yells. But the driver sees the bomb coming and rams down the accelerator. The archduke spots the bomb heading straight for his wife and knocks it aside. The thing bounces into the street and goes off, knocking out the third car. Now the first and second cars race ahead. Then they stop to check damage."

"Where's the comedy in all that?"

"Try this, Ernst. The bomb thrower has a cyanide pill. He gulps it down and jumps in the river. The cyanide is old; he only throws up. The river is only ankle deep, so he's dragged out and arrested. The motorcade, minus the damaged third car, goes on to City Hall with more would-be assassins along the route not doing a thing as the archduke's auto rolls past."

"So the City Hall ceremony--"

"Goes on as planned, Peter. Then the motorcade takes the same damned route back along the avenue paralleling the river. And there wait a half dozen assassins – minus the one with the wet feet – spaced along the return route."

"Damned casual security," Ernst said. "If any at all."

"The assassins are pretty casual, too. While they're waiting for the motorcade to show up, one of them wanders away from the river road and walks up Franz Joseph Street looking for something to eat. Next, the motorcade turns into that same street so the archduke can keep a promise to visit a city museum. Now –"

"Hold on, Franz." Ernst gave him a scowl. "Are you sure you're not making all this up?"

"That's what I asked Kaspar, but he swears it happened this way. So now, the general riding with the archduke and Sophie yells at the driver, 'This is the wrong way!' The driver hits the brakes – right in front of the store where the hungry assassin is standing and chomping on bread and cheese he just bought. He can't believe his luck. He yanks out his pistol and fires two shots. The crowd mobs him and he's rescued by the police who arrest him. Now he swallows his cyanide, which is from the same batch as the cyanide the other guy took. And this one gets sick, too. But he's alive."

"And the archduke is not."

"Well, yes, he is, Peter. He sees his wife slump down. Then she's gone, shot in the abdomen. The archduke is shot in the neck, but he lives through the rush to the governor's residence, then he dies. The whole thing is an unbelievable mess of errors and coincidences."

"And it means… what?" Ernst wondered.

"Well, the one they caught, some Serb named… What did Kaspar tell me? Princip, I think. He says all the plotters are Serbs. So Austria is not very happy with Serbia. And, according to Brother Kaspar, that's where it stands at the moment."

"Lot of fuss over not much, in the grand scheme of things," Ernst grumped, miffed, Peter suspected, at having been a mere auditor of the most compelling lecture he had yet heard delivered in Room 3.

Ernst stood, stretched, and yawned. "I'm going to lunch."

As Ernst's footsteps faded down the hall, Peter buttoned his uniform tunic. "Did your brother have an idea all that is going to amount to anything?"

Franz shook his head. "He gave me what he said was a quote, which kind of threw me since Kaspar is not given to quotes. He said, 'Leave things of the future to fate.' Does that mean anything to you?"

"It could mean the kaiser and his people are... I'm not sure a naval officer should say it."

From the doorway, Ernst said it for him. "Indecisive. In the meantime, we do not have to be so affected. Time for lunch."

8.

From her father's glassed-in office, Alexia and Otto Tammler peered down at the factory's bustling expanse of manufacturing operations. A full acre of whirring lathes, whining drill presses and machines she couldn't identify roiled beneath her buttoned shoes. Muffled by the observation window's heavy glass, though, the clangs and wails and bangs sounded oddly distant.

"I thought you were making machine tools, Pappi. Do I see gun barrels?"

"You are a very perceptive girl, Alexia. Tammler Zeugmaschine Fabrik is now in the machine gun business." A usually jolly man, stocky and beardless in this age of beards, he walked back to his desk and picked up a sheaf of papers. "Army contracts, Alexia. God knows I would rather be making the machines of peace, not war, but these contracts came through only a few days after that incident in Serbia. Some in high places are nervous."

She walked away from the broad window overlooking factory operations to perch on the sofa near Otto Tammler's big oak desk. "I'm delighted by your visit," her father said, "but I sense you're getting a view of the work floor is not its real purpose." His eyes probed hers. "It's not some sort of problem with our friend, the admiral? Other than his outspoken attitude about matters military. A refreshing attitude for an admiral, but heedless, I'm afraid." He gave her an indulgent smile. "Please don't tell me it's any sort of personal problem between you and him."

"Pappi! It's nothing at all like that. The problem is... I need an automobile."

"An automobile?"

He flattened his pudgy hands on the desktop and pushed himself out of the high-backed chair to join her on the sofa. Now we are going to get down to business, she thought. How many contracts has Pappi sealed by yielding the formality of the desk for the informality of this sofa?

"A woman your age should be more concerned with the possibility of starting a family than bouncing about in an automobile, Alexia." He always says this with a smile, his standard comment when I make what he considers "unwomanly" requests. I remember Pappi's very same words when I told him I was intent on a career. But then he reached for his telephone and called his old friend, Konteradmiral Kottenhoff. I know he is quietly proud I'm trying to find a career more compelling than that of a hausfrau.

"I need an auto, Pappi, for navy business."

Pappi Tammler's bushy eyebrows rose.

"Truly," she said.

"What 'navy business'?"

"I cannot tell you, but it is extremely important to the admiral."

Pappi sat back and smiled again; this time, she hoped, in fatherly toleration of her cheekiness. "I am going to confess something, Liebchen." He took her hands in his. "If I had a son, I would want him to be like you. Purposeful, direct, yet somehow – and I don't know how you manage this, Alexia – somehow all the while charming."

She knew she had the auto.

"I will pay you back, Pappi. An amount each month."

He held up a silencing hand. "No, no. That will not be necessary. You happen to have timed this well. We are replacing some of our older company automobiles. They have been well serviced by our own mechanics, and I will arrange to transfer one of them to you."

He paused, and his piercing blue eyes gave away his bemusement. "You can't possibly have known about the automobile replacements."

She smiled back at him. "Of course not, Pappi," Fun to let him speculate. "It is just a lucky coincidence."

"Sure it is, my so-well-organized daughter." He crossed his legs, leaned back and peered at her over the top of his horn-rimmed glasses. "And, of course, you already know how to drive an automobile."

"Actually no, Pappi. I will have to find someone to teach me. Starting promptly, I hope. I must be back in Kiel at the beginning of next week."

"I am giving you an automobile, now you must learn to drive it? What kind of planning is that?"

I was hoping you might know of some way I could –"

Otto snapped his fingers. "Rudi Mott. Our chief mechanic and a former test driver for Daimler. I will tell him you will be at the factory garage first thing tomorrow morning."

She kissed him on the cheek. "You are a marvelous manager, Pappi. I can't thank you enough."

"Somehow I find myself glad you are not one of my business competitors, Daughter." He stood. "Now I must briefly get back to business I know I can control. Then we will head for home."

A Daimler, she marveled. Was it possible?

"I will never understand your generation," her tall, stylishly slender mother burst out when she learned the real purpose of Alexia's surprise visit. "A young woman of your age should be preparing for marriage and children of her own. Certainly not driving an automobile like ... like a female chauffeur."

"Ingrid," Otto muttered from behind his evening paper, "it is Alexia's life, not yours. Times are changing."

"For the worse, if you ask me. She should be thinking of a career of marriage to a proper, respectable young man of substance." In the well-furnished parlor, she perched forward in her high-backed chair, her dark blue French serge dress and lack of any jewelry giving her a look of severity "Oh, I miss so much of the past. Everything now seems so... industrial."

Otto peered around his newspaper. "You married an industrialist, my dear. Forget your pangs for days long gone. Enjoy the sweetness of success."

I love them both, Alexia reassured herself. But there's no question. I am my father's daughter.

"Have you heard anything more, Pappi?" she asked in the silence. "About the assassination?"

"According to the paper, Kaiser Wilhelm has lunched with the Austrian ambassador and assured him Germany will stand with Austria, even if – and this I find unsettling – even if Austria were to go to war with Serbia's defender. Which is –"

"Russia?"

"Ah, my daughter, you are even more worldly that I imagined. So in effect, the kaiser has told Austria to deal with Serbia any way it wishes. Ominous, to say the least. But here's something not in the paper. I heard it from 'high places.' After that lunch, our kaiser went from the dining table straight to his motor yacht for a North Sea cruise."

"A cruise, while Germany waits for him to do something?"

"Perhaps to assure us with his calmness, Alexia."

"Or perhaps he simply doesn't know what in hell to do, Pappi."

"Alexia!" Ingrid burst out. "Watch your tongue!"

"Our daughter has a point, my dear. I agree our kaiser seems to be adrift while a fuse is burning. I pray to God all this tension will dissolve in diplomacy. But in the meantime, I'm afraid I must continue to produce machine guns."

Rudi Mott turned out to be a spidery little man, ineffectively trying to hide his surprise that the driver-to-be that the boss had sent down was a woman. How many women drivers were in Hamburg, she wondered? Rudi looks as if he's dead certain women have no place behind the wheel of an automobile.

Which, for her, turned out not to be the Daimler she had briefly hoped she was destined for, given Rudi Mott's former Daimler connection. The machine was a French Panhard. "A 1904 'Berline,' " Rudi told her, "with a six cylinder Sans Soupapes engine."

But after 10 years in Rudi's care, the ungainly auto looked to her as if it were a recent showroom graduate. Its rigidly squared bright blue enclosure for the driver and passengers and red spoked wheels, glittered in the early morning sun.

"Not a real beauty, but she's well made," Rudi assured her.

"I'm not after beauty, Herr Mott. I need transportation."

"That, Fräulein, is what you are going to get. Now watch me closely."

For the first half hour, he drove the Hamburg streets while she tried to remember every move. Then on a near-deserted road on the city's outskirts, she took the controls, clashed the gears, rabbit-hopped in the starts and oversteered in turns. "Damn!" she muttered in frustration. "Not as easy as I expected."

Rudi's pixie face wore a grin. "You are letting the auto control you. You must be in control. Treat it not like a wild dog needing taming, but like a child needing guidance."

Be in command, be in command. But gently.

Two lessons later – and after two more tense nights at home – she finally felt she had the upper hand on the obstinate, clunky Panhard. To her surprise, Rudi agreed. "She's yours, Fräulein. She knows you are her mistress. And," he added, scuffing the garage floor with his battered work shoe, "you have any trouble with this Frenchy, bring it to me. If you cannot, I will come to it. A promise." His face reddened. "From an old mechanic to a young and now very good driver."

He peered at her. "You are surprised I say that?"

"I am thunderstruck."

"Myself, I am… relieved. Imagine if you had turned out to be otherwise."

She laughed and touched his sleeve. "Otherwise, you would be upstairs now, with father demanding –"

"I hate to think." He gave her rare grin as he patted the fender of the looming Panhard. "On your way, Fräulein Alexia. The fuel tank is full. The oil has been changed. For further instruction, an owner's booklet is on the seat. I know you will treat this old lady with respect."

A half hour later, Alexia left the outskirts of Hamburg behind and thrilled at the rush of independence that coursed through her. Independence? A short-lived illusion. Had not Pappi arranged for the Panhard, and the driving lessons? And he had handled all the documentation. Am I not due back in the office of Pappi's friend, the konteradmiral, Monday morning, "Without fail." Independence?

Bouncing along the narrow road through the tiny town of Bad Bramsted, she was passed by a half dozen military trucks rushing the other way. *I pray to God all this tension will dissolve in diplomacy*, Pappi had said. But when she kissed him goodbye, she knew she would not forget the deep lines of worry that creased his forehead.

9.

In Nordholz's wood-framed, bare-walled assembly room, conversation was hushed but anticipation was high. Peter Strasser, the controversial and peppery kommandant of the Naval Airship Division, was about to make his first appearance here. Named to his new post to replace Korvettenkapitän Friedrich Metzing after Metzing was lost on the L-1, Strasser was already noted for his near fanatical faith in the military value of airships.

Peter was sure he was the only officer of the two dozen officers present who felt he was trapped. *Everyone else is a volunteer; I am the only one here "volunteered" by an anti-airship admiral. My orders were signed by some Fregattenkapitän I never heard of, because Kottenhoff's name on the orders would have finished off this risky business before it started. Whoever signed the papers, I am now a volunteer for aircrew training in airships that don't exist on an airship base still being built.*

Peter's chair creaked as he shifted uncomfortably. *I hope to hell I can quickly send the admiral what he hopes for, then get out of this place and onto the deck of a battleship – or any ship with water under it.*

"Are you aware," said Ernst, seated on Peter's right, "Our esteemed visitor was a mere leutnant of gunnery until the L-1 went down last September and took Korvettenkapitan Matzing with it?" Ernst Wolff the

Lecturer spoke out the side of his mouth. "Replacement Strasser has been commanding officer of the Airship Division for all of nine months, and that also happens to be his total Zeppelin experience. I heard they drew his name out of a hat because no career officer wanted to touch such an experimental program."

Franz, on Peter's left, leaned forward. "Come on, Ernst. That's nothing more than a stupid rumor. Just like the story he was only a leutnant when they handed him the Airship Division. You want the truth? Strasser was a korvettenkapitän of gunnery in a Berlin office assignment when he was appointed kommandant of the Airship Division, but he volunteered for aviation years ago and managed to go through airship officer training."

"All this from your usual source, I presume."

Franz shrugged. "Better than yours."

Peter glanced around the austere assembly room. Most of the officers, in full uniform by order of the base commander, are trainees, as are Ernst, Franz and myself. The others are the few experienced Zeppelin men now serving as ground instructors. We are a skeleton force. All bones, no flesh. A half dozen bases in various stages of construction, hundreds of men in training. One airship, but right now, it is stationed elsewhere.

"All this preparation is a pain," Franz grumbled. "I, for one, would like to get my dead butt in the air. All this classroom work and ground duty has me bored out of my mind."

Ernst preened his little mustache. "We're all suffering from inertia of the brain, except you, Peter. What's your secret?"

I'm trying to comply with the training and serve Konteradmiral Kottenhoff at the same time. That's my secret. But he said, "Navigation study may be more compelling than the observer and engine work you two are training for."

"*Attention!*" barked the base commander, portly Fregattenkapitän Weitzel, in the front of the room. The scrapes of chairs and thuds of shoes were followed by dead silence as the entire gathering waited at rigid attention.

Through a door to the left, an officer strode in, flanked by two aides, kapitänleutnants, both noticeably taller that the man preceding them.

"*That's* Strasser?" Ernst whispered. "That little skinny officer with –"

"–With four fregattenkapitän sleeve stripes," Peter whispered back.

The two flanking kapitänleutnants stood back. The fregattenkapitän stepped to a temporary dais.

"At ease, Gentlemen. Be seated." When the scraping of chairs subsided, he surveyed the gathered officers, small head held high. His intense glare beneath heavy brows and his precise mustache and narrow goatee gave him, Peter felt, the look of a zealot.

"I am Fregattenkapitän Peter Strasser." His voice, deeper than Peter had expected, added to this short, wiry officer's intensity. "As kommandant of the Naval Airship Division, I address you this morning to impress on each of you the urgent need for your absolute dedication to the military airship." He paused, a long pause. And here Peter was surprised by Strasser's wry little smile. "The future 'eyes of the fleet.' That is the admiralty's current thinking. To be sure, an airship at altitude can impressively extend the eyes of the warship. But I am convinced such passive use of our potentially great weapon would turn us into eagles without talons."

Another pause. He strode back to the speaker's stand. "Gentlemen, I propose to offer – to fight for – the employment of the Zeppelin for something that has never been done in the history of warfare."

Despite his long-standing doubts concerning the Naval Airship Division, Peter found himself caught up in Strasser's forcefulness.

"Never before has any military service of any nation had the potential to bombard the enemy's factories, military bases – even the enemy's cities – from the air. The Zeppelin gives us the means to do just that. To attack at altitude, invisible at night. To fly slowly or even hover over a target. To rain high explosives accurately upon it. Gentlemen, we are at the dawn of a new chapter of military history."

Peter heard exclamations all through the room. Can't deny it. This man is a gifted leader.

Then Franz muttered, "So where are the airships?"

As if Strasser had heard that near-whisper, the dynamic little fregattenkapitän's eyes swept the room. "At this moment, new naval Zeppelins are under construction. In the next few months, I will give you, here at Nordholz, the very first of these improved airships. Zeppelins designed, gentlemen, for far more than serving simply as 'eyes of the fleet.' They will be the first airships designed to take war to the heart of an enemy and destroy that heart. Until those Zeppelins arrive, I have arranged with Delag for a series of familiarization flights in that firm's commercial airships. Nordholz is on their schedule."

Again, his burning eyes swept through his fired-up audience. "From this day on, you must dedicate yourselves to your training. If war comes – *when* war comes – we are destined to make history."

His audience leaped to attention as Strasser turned toward the exit and strode out the side door, followed by his two stone-faced aides. "Dismissed!" the base kommandant ordered, and followed them.

"So endeth the lesson," Ernst said with a tight smile, "And with his solution to the Austro-Hungarian mess."

"His solution?" Franz asked. "He is not a politician."

"His solution is war," Ernst told him. "And in military politics, he is a master. He's getting exactly the Zeppelins he wants."

"War," Peter said, as they walked into the blinding afternoon sunlight. "And he's counting on our being in it."

"Well, that telephone call should please our bellicose leader," said Franz, returning to their room from the telephone station in the hall as he plunked down into a chair. His eyes flicked from Peter to Ernst then back to Peter. A man burning to talk.

"Care to release the details?" Ernst urged. "Your Berlin brother is our only dependable source. Everything else is ninety percent rumor."

Franz leaned back, crossed his legs, linked his fingers behind his head, and gave them a smart-assed look.

"Come on, come on," Ernst shook his head and sighed. "You want us to beg?"

"You are begging."

"You want us to pry it out of you?" Peter said. "All right, we will pry it out."

"Such impatience. The two of you. Ah, well, it's like this. The big player now, Kaspar just told me, is Count Leopold von Berchtold."

"Who is…?" Ernst prompted.

"Who is Austria's Foreign Minister. According to what Kaspar has learned, 'sources in Vienna' say Berchtold wants Emperor Francis Joseph to send Austrian troops into Serbia. Vengeance for the assassination."

"I gather that if the emperor has to be pushed, he's not so eager to do that," Peter said from the window seat.

"You could be right, but Berchtold, after a private little meeting with our kaiser, is certain Germany will back him up. I'm just a green leutnant zur see, but it all sounds to me like an Austrian excuse to grab off part of Serbia, and have us help them do it. I don't see why we have to be part of that."

Ernst glanced at Peter then at Franz. "Did you ask Kaspar what *he* thought?"

Franz nodded. "Sure I did, but he said his opinions must be reserved for the advisory council. Or maybe he just doesn't want to admit he doesn't know what to think."

"And what do you think, Franz?" Ernst's little grin had a hard edge.

"A war over the death of an archduke?"

"An archduke is equal in rank to a prince. And he was next in line for the throne."

"Even so, I can't believe Austria wants to go to war to get its hands on a slice of Serbia."

"Or all of Serbia?"

"Any of Serbia, Ernst. So what do I think? I think it's all a ridiculous game of fist shaking. War over the assassination of an unfortunate touring archduke would be crazy."

"So, no war."

"Right, Ernst, no war."

"Peter?"

"Doesn't it all come down to the ambitions of the men who make the decisions? From what Franz has told us, Berchtold – for whatever reasons – sounds like he's hell bent on goading Emperor Franz Joseph into a show of force against Serbia. If he succeeds, and if the kaiser does back him up, we could soon be doing a lot more than flying training missions."

"So you predict...?"

"Austria sending some kind of force against Serbia, Ernst."

"With Germany along for the ride?"

"Depends on the kaiser's frame of mind."

"His frame of mind?"

"My father knew the kaiser, or at least met him several times. In Father's opinion –"

"Your father knew the kaiser?" Franz broke in. "How?"

"Father was an adjutant to General von Waldersee, Army Chief of the General Staff back in the eighteen nineties."

"With a father like that, why did you choose the navy?"

"Do you want me to go on, or not?"

"Shut up, Franz."

"Yes, Sir!" Franz threw Ernst a mocking salute.

"In my father's opinion," Peter said, "Kaiser Wilhelm is not a man of real self-confidence. He was born with that withered arm. Imagine how that affects a boy as he grows up – and now, as the head of a nation."

With their eyes intent on him, Peter realized, for once I have the full attention of these two.

"You think," Ernst said, "our kaiser could be talked into sending Germany into Serbia to prove his manhood."

"Yes."

"My God."

"Fraulein Tammler does have a reservation for today," the apple-cheeked desk clerk at the Blauer Adler said, "but she has not yet arrived."

"Then I will wait for her on the south veranda." Peter tried to keep his tone offhand, but sudden apprehension knotted his chest. Ridiculous. She was simply late.

He strolled onto the wide porch. Had the admiral again recruited the intrusive Leutnant Krause as her driver? Or might she have taken the train from Kiel to Hamburg? Was there rail service between Hamburg and Cuxhaven? A taxi from Cuxhaven to here? All that would take time.

He paced the porch's south end overlooking the parking lot. Why am I worrying? Alexia can take care of herself. Why worry about her at all? She's just an aide dabbling in a konteradmiral's anti-Zeppelin obsession.

Why should I worry about myself? Hell, I was ordered to do this. And I happen to agree with Kottenhoff's distrust of the Zeppelin program. I'm doing this for the Fatherland. Am I not? And Alexia? She is just a part of the arrangement.

But where is she?

He sank into one of the uncomfortable wood slat chairs. This would be much simpler if I could telephone my information to the admiral. But the phones at Nordholz are not private. And at his end, perhaps not so private either. By mail, then? Aside from the delay, the admiral made it clear he does not want anything written to arrive at work or at his home. Or does he not trust the postal service?

As Peter scanned the parking area, a sleek Daimler pulled in. A corpulent man in black trousers and a garish orange sweater emerged. Still no Alexia.

Where is she?

Long minutes later, an ugly blue Panhard with an exceptionally smoothly running engine rolled up to the entrance. A tall woman in beige with a jaunty blue scarf stepped out. The scarf matched the car.

"Alexia!" He was so surprised, he spoke her name aloud.

She hurried into the entrance as he shoved out of the chair. They met in the lobby.

"You're late!" Then he realized how callous that sounded.

"Ground fog. South of Kiel. We had to crawl for miles "

"Oh. Sorry. I thought maybe you had... I don't know what I thought. Who's your driver this time? Some Frenchy? That's a French Auto."

"Driver?" She peered back at the car. "I don't see anyone. Where do you suppose my driver got to?" Her grin seemed to be making fun of him.

"You said 'we' ran into fog."

"The Panhard and me."

She's teasing. Maybe she told her driver –

"Peter, you're talking to the driver. I am the driver."

"*You're* the driver?"

"I took driving lessons while I was home last week." She looked at her pendant watch then peered over his shoulder toward the dining room. "It's almost 14.00 hours. Have you eaten?"

"*You're* driving?" he persisted.

"I'm starving, and I see the dining room is open."

She walked toward the entrance then looked back, auburn hair disarrayed, green eyes sparkling. "Are you coming?"

Now Peter was grinning. "Alexia..."

"I'll tell you all about it after we order."

They chose a table in a secluded corner.

Should he pull out her chair, help her – opportunity lost as the obsequious, gray haired host did that honor. He was replaced by an equally aging waiter, stoically indifferent as they pondered their menus. Pork for him, a salad for her. A salad for mid-day dinner? The waiter departed with eyebrows raised.

That persistent little smile, Peter thought. She's still teasing me. "All right," he said. "You are the driver. Where did you borrow the car?"

"I didn't borrow it, Peter. It is mine. A delightfully ugly Panhard, vintage 1904. A retiree from my father's factory. His gift to our cause."

"My God, you didn't tell him –"

"No, of course not. He knows only that I work for the admiral."

"And how did you learn –"

"To drive? Lessons, thanks again to my father."

The waiter returned with Peter's Schweine Kottlett and her Kartoffelsalat. She took a sip of water. The waiter strode away. "Now that we're up to date, she said, "What have you to report?"

He glanced around the nearly deserted dining room. The only other late luncheon customers were a couple of chuckling middle-aged businessmen at a distant window table, apparently exchanging jokes, and well out of earshot.

"Strasser visited Nordholz last week. A hard driver, that man. He's convinced the Zeppelin is more than just a scouting platform. He sees it as a bomb dropper, a maximum weapon. He's pushing big expansion of airship bases. And he has arranged for the temporary use of Delag airships for navy flight training. The man is a dynamo." He frowned. "I think you should be taking notes."

"The admiral insists I put nothing in writing. I have a very good memory, Peter."

She patted his hand, then quickly pulled back.

He seemed not to notice. "What does the admiral do with this information?"

"I don't know. Perhaps he works it into conversations with fellow admirals at the Kiel Officers Club. Maybe he sends confidential memos to those he believes might have some influence on the Zeppelin program. I really have no idea. But he is interested in any negative information you can uncover."

She looked at him closely. "Peter?"

"What you just said made me feel like an enemy agent. Is that what we're doing?"

"No! We are following a konteradmiral's orders to report on a project he is convinced is a threat to the navy's future." She looked down at the table. "I'm sorry. I sound like a recruiting poster for some sort of –"

He held up a quieting hand. "What does our admiral think of all the political rumbling?"

"The Serbian thing? He doesn't confide in me, Peter. But I did hear him say he was afraid the kaiser could be talked into joining the Austrians if they go into Serbia."

He set down his fork. "Could be 'talked into' that?"

"I thought that was odd, too. I remember the admiral saying he suspected the kaiser might do it 'to prove he is a man of decision.'"

"Our Kaiser would go to war to prove he's a man? I find that close to incredible."

"I, too." Her frown dissolved into a smile. She touched his hand again, this time without hesitation. "Come, finish your dinner. Then let me introduce you to Monsieur Panhard. He's an old man, but he has a stout heart."

10.

In the rear seat of his navy-supplied Daimler, Kottenhoff knotted his fists and gritted his teeth in apprehension. Relax, Admiral, he told himself. In a few minutes, I will find out why I am here.

Two more impressive residences rolled by the automobile's windows. Then Albert, in chauffeur's livery at the wheel, nodded to himself. He swung the big Daimler through the next break in the lush roadway shrubbery. The automobile crunched up a wide gravel drive to stop at the broad steps of the Bremmer family mansion.

Kottenhoff opened the rear door before Albert reached it. "I hope to be no more than an hour, Albert," if that long, he thought to himself. I dislike formal functions, but the surprise invitation to this most exclusive of Kiel's society balls stressed need for my appearance. Why, for Heaven's sake?

As Kottenhoff mounted the steps, Albert returned to the driver's seat and the automobile rolled away toward the rear of the looming mansion. A parking area, no doubt, where his orderly would pass the time with other waiting drivers.

At the top of the steps, a brief concrete walkway between precisely pruned terrace hedges took him to the mammoth residence's entrance. Its double doors stood open. A formally garbed butler stood just inside. The chatter of a large crowd drifted into the cool air, nearly drowning out the music. A piano, thank God. An orchestra would have prompted dancing and I am no dancer.

"Konteradmiral Kottenhoff," he murmured to the stone-faced butler, and offered his invitation. Which the man actually perused.

"'And guest'?" The butler peered down the walkway then back at Kottenhoff with a hint of... disdain?

"I am alone." I was tempted to ask Alexia to join me. She would have jumped at that. Invitations to Bremmer Haus were known to be select and coveted. But this aging admiral escorting a lovely woman less than half my age would prompt tongues to wag, no matter how innocent my intent. And I don't need to add social gossip to my other problems. So here I am, Herr Gatekeeper. Alone.

And mystified. The widow of legendary Hugo Bremmer, the 'ship builders' ship builder," is known for her magnificent and highly exclusive soirees. Counterpoint, I'm sure, to her and her late husband's origins – he a dry goods merchant's son; she the daughter of a schoolteacher.

In common with myself, Kottenhoff thought. He handed his emblazoned uniform cap to the attendant of the cloakroom near the entrance and walked through the marbled foyer. I'm a carriage maker's son, or so I say when I'm pressed. That has a better ring than the exact truth: a carpenter's son.

At the top of three steps leading down to a vast, marble-columned ballroom, Kottenhoff paused. The place was jammed with gentlemen in eveningwear, naval officers in formal uniform—Thank God mine is just out of the French cleaners—and ladies in elegant, colorful evening gowns. At least a dozen servers weaved among them offering trays of apéritifs and canapés.

At the foot of the steps stood a woman as imposing as a battleship among lesser craft, her prow magnificent. A lacy frill at her neck was the highlight of her otherwise drab brown evening gown. A waiter approached, she snapped an order and he scurried away. Has to be our hostess. Yes. I recall her being pointed out to me during Kiel Week.

Kottenhoff swallowed his uncertainty and descended. She smiled and thrust out her hand. He bowed, raised the pudgy fingers toward his lips, but knew one was not expected to actually kiss proffered hands.

"Good evening, Frau Bremmer. Truly a grand party."

"So pleased you could join us, Herr..." He caught her glance at his sleeve stripes.

"Konteradmiral Erwin Kottenhoff, Frau Bremmer. So good of you to invite me."

I recognized her, but I can see she hasn't the remotest idea who I am. I remain mystified. Why have I been invited?

"You will find refreshment in all four corners of the ballroom, Herr Admiral." He was being dismissed. "And I trust you will have a most pleasant evening."

As he ambled into the crowd hoping to find at least one familiar face, he heard a voice behind him. "Admiral Kottenhoff?"

He turned toward a starchy young oberleutnant. An oberleutnant here? Surely someone's aide.

"Your presence is required, Sir, in the east library."

"Required?"

"Yes, Herr Admiral. By Grand Admiral von Tirpitz."

He felt a flash of heat. Von Tirpitz here? Calling for me? Oh my God. Now I know why I was invited to Bremmer Haus! If von Tirpitz had summoned me from my office, that would have thrown the entire Procurement Division into a whirl of speculation. Here though, in the cover of party confusion, I am being ordered to appear before the Grand Admiral of the German Fleet.

And I know why. The surge of nervous heat abruptly congealed into ice.

"If you will follow me, Herr Admiral?"

They forged through the crush of partygoers, then up the steps at the far end, along the perimeter hallway to a paneled door. The aide knocked discreetly.

"Herein." A muffled voice, but one with authority.

The aide swung the door wide. Kottenhoff squared his shoulders, and walked into the surprisingly austere room. The aide withdrew, shutting the door behind him.

Bare parquet flooring. Gray painted walls. Floor to ceiling glass-fronted bookcases to the left. To the right, a few framed pastoral scenes in murky oils. And facing me in front of a mahogany desk stands Grossadmiral Alfred von Tirpitz.

"Ah, Kottenhoff, good to see you again."

Again? Kottenhoff drew a blank. Should I salute or should I –

Von Tirpitz solved the quandary, stepped forward to thrust out his hand. "We met briefly when your ship returned from protecting German interests in the Philippines, after the Spanish-American War. You were a kapitän zur see at the time, burdened with international cooperation responsibilities. I'm not surprised you do not recall our brief meeting in the dockside confusion at Manila."

Von Tirpitz stepped aside and indicated a leather-clad chair oddly isolated some distance from the room's right side.

"Be seated, Admiral."

Signs of an informal chat? But Von Tirpitz remains standing, an imposing presence; tall, his epaulets on broad shoulders, five narrow and three broad golden sleeve stripes gleaming in the drawing room's subdued light. Eyes wide-set in his chunky face, his beard forked into a pair of graying pennants, the grand admiral towers over this seated konteradmiral.

A maneuver: I'm seated, he's standing. I hope I appear composed, but my guts are jelly. Von Tirpitz has pulled this damn uncomfortable armless chair away from the wall to isolate me out here like a suspect about to undergo interrogation.

Kottenhoff forced himself to settle back. In a show of equanimity, he crossed his legs.

Von Tirpitz again leaned against the desk front, arms folded. "I am here in Kiel unannounced to inspect the Baltic Naval Station, Admiral, and I'm taking this opportunity to discuss a matter with you that is causing me concern. You understand to what I am referring."

Ach, the memorandum I submitted to him, based on Reinhart's report of Strasser's Nordholz comments. "My memorandum was submitted in what I believed – still believe – to be the best interests of the fleet, Herr Admiral."

"Yes, the memorandum." Von Tirpitz began to stride around the room, one closed fist behind his back, the other hand stroking his beard. "I must say I found it offered considerable insight into the Zeppelin program. Rather impressive for an admiral assigned to the Procurement Division."

"Thank you, Herr Admiral."

"That was not a compliment, Kottenhoff, An observation. What disturbed me – continues to disturb me – is the intent. I trust you follow me?"

Kottenhoff fought rising dismay. Von Tirpitz, in the most gentlemanly manner, was handing him a personal dressing-down, the navy's dreaded "black cigar."

With effort, Kottenhoff kept his voice steady. "If I may speak frankly, Herr Admiral?"

"Please do."

"The concept of the airship – and I personally witnessed the L-2 disaster, so my view is far from hearsay – the concept of the airship itself is flawed. A huge machine lofted with thousands of cubic feet of explosive hydrogen? And now with Strasser's inspiration of the airship as an offensive weapon, we face a catastrophe in the making. The navy is investing a major allocation in a so-called weapon too fragile, too dangerous to be considered at all. Those funds should instead be allocated –"

With a wave of his hand, von Tirpitz silenced him. "I'm well aware of your objections, Kottenhoff, but you are missing a few salient facts. Delag has used Zeppelins for years without mishap. And I'm sure you are aware our battleship captains – all of them – are highly favorable toward the Zeppelin as a scouting asset?"

"I am, Herr Admiral. A few airships for that purpose might suffice."

"Thank you for that much." The grand admiral's aggressive striding persisted, his shoes clacking on the hardwood flooring

Kottenhoff decided to press on. "I am far more concerned with Fregattenkapitän Strasser's insistence that the airship will be a viable offensive weapon. I understand he is actively planning the use of Zeppelins to bombard enemy cities."

Von Tirpitz stopped, peered almost impishly at Kottenhoff. "You cannot bombard an inland city with a battleship."

"You agree with him, Herr Admiral?"

"I agree in theory, if we ever were to reach such a desperate possibility. There is an important point you are overlooking. To build a ship – even a cruiser – requires two years. To build an airship requires a mere six weeks."

"But a Zeppelin could never sink a warship, Herr Admiral."

"And a warship could never bomb Paris, London or Moscow."

Kottenhoff held von Tirpitz's intense eyes. "Do you truly believe, Herr Admiral, it might come to that?"

Von Tirpitz took three quick strides to the door. Which he tested, apparently to make certain it was tightly closed. Then he returned to lean against the damned desk. He seemed suddenly weary, a man with more than his share of problems.

"I assume you are aware, Kottenhoff, of the news this past Thursday. The Austrian Ambassador to Serbia delivered an ultimatum: that Serbia permit Austrian officials to operate in Serbia to counteract anti-Austrian publicity."

"Yes, I am."

"Are you also aware that in the Serbian premier's absence from Belgrade, the Serbian Minister of Public Information reacted to that ultimatum – reacted in public? 'There is nothing to do now but die fighting' the idiot announced. Then, in the premier's name, he appealed to Russia for help."

"Do you believe, Herr Admiral, if he gets that help, Austria and Serbia will actually go to war?"

Von Tirpitz sighed. "I did not believe that, until today."

"Until today?"

"It is not yet widely known, but Tzar Nicholas has ordered that thirteen army corps be 'readied' – his word – in the Russian districts along the Austria-Hungary border. Our sources in St. Petersburg believe it is only a matter of days until the tzar orders full mobilization."

Kottenhoff's mouth went dry. "And that," he managed, "that would –"

"That, as one of my staff members put it, 'would seal the fate of Europe.'"

"And Germany?"

"The kaiser has already sworn to support Austria." Von Tirpitz pushed away from the desk front and stood frowning at Kottenhoff. "At this hour, we need the full support of every branch of the Imperial Navy, Admiral. Now consider this: your objection to an established navy program very nearly resulted in your forced retirement. But in view of your outstanding record as a senior battleship kapitän zur see, I was able to advance you one grade and arrange for your serving as a department head. I spared you from the ignominy of a disciplinary proceeding. Consider yourself extremely fortunate, Konteradmiral. Whatever you think of the Zeppelin program shall remain your private opinion, damn it. I trust I am fully understood?"

Kottenhoff, eyes still meeting the grand admiral's hard gaze, nodded. "Understood, Herr Admiral."

"Excellent. Come, we will rejoin the party."

Riding home a half-hour later, Kottenhoff tried to swallow his anger at Von Tirpitz's warning. Warning, hell, it was a threat. Keep on with this anti-Zeppelin agitation, Admiral, and you are kaput. But there's a lot more at stake here than my career. I know I am right! The airship program is a colossal mistake. Funds pouring into hydrogen-filled flying disasters. The unacceptable risk of Strasser's high cost experiment is being overlooked in the excitement of possessing a futuristic weapon – a means of destroying the enemy from a platform thousands of meters overhead. No wonder Strasser is able to sell his program to the high command and the public.

I cannot dismiss a terrible foreboding. All that hydrogen up there. All that hydrogen waiting for a single spark. Somebody has to head off this lunacy.

11.

In the shade of the twin rotating hangars, twenty-four trainees, each holding a helmet and goggles, stared into the sky. Twenty-three of us eager for what is about to happen, Peter thought. The twenty-fourth, me – not so eager. These other guys are carried away with the spirit of adventure while I'm supposed to be looking at this through Admiral Kottenhoff's critical eyes.

The announced time of arrival was 11.00 hours. Nearly that now. Peter shaded his eyes. The sky to the southeast was a blinding late morning glare. Nothing yet out there. Then excitement rippled through the crowd.

"There it is!" someone shouted.

Low on the horizon, he made out a silver bead. A bead suspended in space, seemingly unmoving. But slowly growing larger. From the twin hangars rushed dozens of construction workers, pressed into service as ground handlers.

Minutes later, the silver bead had grown into a silver globe, now becoming huge. The muted rumble of engines swept over the airfield. The approaching craft swung into a ponderous westward turn and slowly lengthened into the nearly 200-meter-long commercial airship *Viktoria Luise*.

"It's a disgrace the navy has to borrow Delag's airships for training," Ernst muttered to Peter, "But in this case, we're honored, I suppose. This particular one is named for the kaiser's only daughter."

"Umm," Peter muttered. Both my roommates are becoming more friendly. A not altogether reassuring development, considering what I'm supposed to be doing here.

Silvery in the sun's glare, the airship chased its long shadow across the flat land west. Then it came about in a slow 180-degree turn to head into the light easterly wind. Moments later, *Viktoria Luise* nosed down to begin her descent into Nordholz.

Some 20 meters above the field, the airship leveled. The engines subsided to a rumble, the four big propellers barely turning on their fore and aft outriggers. Like tentacles from a great aerial octopus, the handling ropes unreeled downward. The improvised ground crew seized the dangling lines. With a hiss of venting hydrogen, *Viktoria Luise* settled until she rested on the big bumpers beneath the forward and aft gondolas – open gondolas suspended on vertical struts from the Zeppelin's underside.

A V-shaped ventral extension to the hull, running bow to stern, gave the otherwise sleek airship a "drooping drawers" look, Peter thought. From his classroom training, he knew it housed the hull's catwalk, and bulged midway between the two gondolas to form the passenger cabin.

"At least that part is closed in," Ernst said. "Real luxury."

"Only for paying passengers. The control car and the engine gondola aft look like rowboats hanging there with that big open space above them. Must be just wonderful at a couple hundred meters altitude in the winter."

I've got to avoid the risk of close friendship with either Eric or Franz, Peter told himself. They are becoming eager airshipmen. And no one devoted to this flawed cause would be pleased to discover a fellow trainee is here for another purpose: helping to undermine the program. That is Admiral Kottenhoff's intent. To have me observe the program from within, on the prowl for weaknesses. Could be dangerous. Face it. No matter what kind of justification Alexia has tried to sell me, I'm a damned spy.

The doorway of the passenger cabin popped open. A square-faced kapitänleutnant in his forties stepped to the ground.

"Trainees aboard," he ordered.

With the airship's engines idling in the control gondola forward and the engine gondola aft, and their outrigger propellers slowly flipping over, the aircrew officer trainees filed into the passenger cabin.

Peter was surprised at the luxury inside. Mahogany paneling and twin rows of polished wood columns edging the ranks of stylish wicker chairs along the port and starboard rows of big windows.

He settled into one of the portside chairs forward, relieved that Eric was seated well aft. This is a real challenge, Peter thought. I'm supposed to be looking for airship weaknesses. Now that I'm aboard one of the things, I'm stunned at how impressive it is. And I know Delag has carried more than 10,000 passengers without so much as a scratch on any of them.

I can't deny the excitement I'm feeling. I'm actually going up in an airship. Through all those years at the Academy, I looked forward to sea duty, a career aboard an Imperial Navy battleship. Flying through the air had never crossed my mind – not even after Kottenhoff pressured me into serving his anti-airship drive. Now I'm about to leave solid ground and rise into thin air.

He gripped the chair arms with apprehension. Yet he found himself intrigued with the prospect of… of floating free.

The two dozen trainees settled in the narrow cabin's chairs, peered through the rows of windows lining each side of the compartment. The kapitänleutnant instructor slammed the door shut. Through the open windows, Peter heard a cry from the control gondola forward.

"Up bow!" The airship's nose began to rise. "Up stern!"

The fore and aft engines howled. The ground handlers ringing the ship released their holds on the dozens of lines.

Peter felt as if the airship were standing still while the ground slowly fell from beneath it. Up… Up…When the airship finally leveled off at what he guessed to be at least 500 meters, they could have been standing still – except for the slipstream pouring through the windows.

He felt an odd sensation in the pit of his stomach, a lightness. Apprehension or exhilaration? *Viktoria Luise* rose higher. He peered down. What a sensation. The buildings of Nordholz look like a haphazard collection of toys. That patch of smoky haze to the east has to be Hamburg. Imagine being able to see such a distance! No wonder the battleship kapitäns were pressing for Zeppelins as scouting platforms.

Beneath my shoes, the floor feels solid. The airship has a surprising feel of dependability. As if it belongs up here. Their instructor strode forward between the rows of chairs, swung around to shout, "Secure windows!" The engines' rumble and the rush of air faded as the open ports slid shut.

The wooden-faced instructor pointed to a carton on the floor near the hatchway behind him. "Felt boots. To prevent any chance of sparks from shoe nails. You will put them on over your shoes as you leave this cabin. Four at a time. Follow me to the control gondola."

He pointed at the trainees seated forward in the portside row. "You and you." He swung toward the starboard row. "And you and you. Boots on, then follow me."

Peter, the second man on the starboard side, stepped into the narrow aisle, pulled on a pair of the felt boots and, now second trainee in line, followed the instructor through the forward hatchway.

A catwalk offered a narrow footway through V-shaped duralumin formers and their stringers. Above the fabric-walled keelway passage, Peter made out the bottom arcs of several of the hull's shaping rings and the immense fabric undersides of the nearest hydrogen cells. The longitudinal duralumin ring-to-ring stringers visible from the catwalk looked too fragile for the massive hull.

In the eerily dim light penetrating the hull, the interior smelled of oil, engine fuel, and a faint chemical tang. Or was that Peter's imagination? They all had been warned hydrogen was odorless, colorless and tasteless. Which made a leak insidious and all the more dangerous.

The engines' muffled thrum was punctuated by an occasional clank or squeal of flexing aluminum connections. Peter found that unsettling, but their instructor took no notice. Apparently, such creaks and groans were part of a Zeppelin's standard behavior. Peter tried to disregard the disturbing sounds, but he couldn't ignore the dank coldness of the hull's interior on this sunny summer afternoon.

When they had walked well forward, the instructor halted, then pulled open a hatch in the catwalk floor. Even colder air rushed in, and the racket of the forward engine surged through the opening.

"Goggles in place," he shouted. "First man, climb down."

The trainee in front of Peter eased gingerly into the opening.

"Firm grip on the ladder. Place feet carefully."

As the trainee, a young, white-faced leutnant zur see, sank out of sight, the instructor motioned Peter forward.

Now comes the real test. I'm staring straight down into the control gondola. And past it, open air then the ground damned far below. From up here, the open gondola looks even more like a boat scudding along on its suspension struts and wires. And it's already crowded. The kommandant, two crewmen, the first trainee, all in the skimpy forward area, with the engine and two mechanics behind a bulkhead two-thirds of the way aft. An overloaded whaleboat of the air.

"Down, Leutnant. Others are waiting."

Grip the edge of the catwalk's floor. Ease down to the top rung. Down two more. Let go the walkway edge and grab the top rung. My hands are sweating. The chilling slipstream has to be a thirty-knot gale at least. My coat's glued flat against my back.

The descent through open air was not more than two meters, but he felt a surge of relief when his felt-booted shoes found the control gondola's floor. A deceptive solidity, he thought. The gondola's wall is only chest high. The slipstream rushes right through. And I can't forget this whole aerial monster is held up here by nothing more than bags of hydrogen.

Above him, the third trainee of his little group began the wind-whipped descent.

The heavily bearded airship commander, in the trim uniform of Delag, shouted something at Peter, his words distorted by the howl of the engine behind the bulkhead in the control car's aft section.

The civilian kommandant motioned him forward and shouted again, this time right in his ear. "Rudder control." He pointed at the Delag man handling a large vertically mounted wheel forward.

The kommandant then nodded at a similar wheel on the port side of the narrow control car, this one handled not so confidently by the first trainee in Peter's group of four, while the Delag elevator man stood by. "Elevator control," the kommandant shouted at Peter. "Your turn, now. First, the rudder wheel."

Wind blasting his face, Peter pushed through the crowded forward section. I'm supposed to be Kottenhoff's observer. Now here I am, about to control one of these things.

"Rudder wheel, Leutnant!" the kommandant insisted.

The Delag man stepped aside. Peter wrapped cold fingers around the spoked metal wheel. He peered forward, then down. What a view! Like an immense Christmas garden. A great spread of open fields dotted with tiny houses. And over there on the murky horizon, Hamburg again.

The Delag rudder man moved close, his flowing mustache almost in Peter's ear. "Always allow for the lag. That's the secret."

"Five degrees turn to starboard!' the kommandant ordered behind him.

"That's you," the rudder man prompted.

Peter moved the wheel a quarter turn. It took some muscle, he discovered.

"Give it more than that," the rudder man directed. "Check the compass on the console there. Couple of full turns then back to counter the lag. Remember the lag."

Sweating now, Peter managed to nurse the lumbering airship to the right and stop its travel just past the ordered five degrees. He felt a surge of accomplishment.

"Sehr gut," said the kommandant. "Now to the elevator wheel."

Peter shouldered his way to the port side. Why such tiny space for such a huge airship? Even with a normal crew of four or so, it must feel crowded.

The ruddy-faced young elevator man motioned the first trainee aside and nodded to Peter.

He grasped the big metal wheel firmly, confidently. Just a matter of keeping us level.

"Bow up, five degrees!" the kommandant called over his shoulder. Peter whirled the wheel. The Zeppelin nosed upward, reluctantly at first, then eagerly.

"The lag, the lag," the elevator man said with a nudge.

"Level off," the kommandant barked.

Peter reversed the wheel. The nose began to come down. Remember the lag... He backed off a few degrees, and *Viktoria Luise* settled nicely level.

I've done it! When I tell her I have actually flown an airship, Alexia will be stunned.

He glanced aft, past the gondola's crammed aft compartment housing the forward engine, past the portside bulge of the passenger cabin to the isolated rear engine gondola and its port propeller outrigger. How long could engine crews' ears hold out against these yammering engines?

Beyond the aft engine gondola, the hull tapered sharply, but he could see the curiously Victorian-like box kite arrangement of the portside tail planes. It struck him as symbolic of a 19th century dream of weightless flight dragged into the 20th century's whirlwind of aeroplane development. He had mentioned this in a Nordholz class on flight progress. "Small matter," the smug instructor had fired back. "There is no aeroplane capable of reaching the maximum altitude of airships."

As the control gondola's kommandant shouted the functions of various knobs and dials on his control console, Peter realized this cannot truly be "training." At best, it's a familiarization cruise. Almost recreational. If only it were not so damned chilly. And, I thought as I climbed up the ladder back to the catwalk, if it were not for the possibility of a long, long fall if I lose my grip.

***

With the sun low on the horizon, Nordholz drifts into view through the portside windows of the passenger cabin. The airship tilts down, but the approach appears to be Nordholz rising to meet us. There go the handling ropes. Engines throttle back to a burble. Feel a thump. We have landed.

"So what is your impression of all that!" Eric asked behind him as they stepped down to solid earth and walked toward the administration area.

"I felt as if…" His words trailed off. Across the field, milling groups of station cadre seemed to be in a state of agitation.

"What the hell is bothering them?" Eric wondered as they strode toward the obviously excited crowd.

"There's Franz. Hey, Franz," Peter shouted. "What's –"

Franz cupped his hands and shouted something.

Ernst shook his head. "What did he say?"

"I couldn't make it out – here he comes."

Franz rushed toward them. "Wa –" He gasped for breath. "War, guys. We're at war!"

Peter felt a wave of ice wash through him. "Did you say –?"

"Ja, ja. Germany has declared war."

"On *Serbia*?"

"On Russia, Peter. We are at war with Russia."

12.

In a secluded corner of the noisy Nordholz Officers Club, away from the boozy shouting and off-key singing around the bar, Peter and Ernst quietly nursed their beers. Franz, well into his third, incessantly pumped his two roommates about the training flight. Peter's effort to avoid further closeness with either of them had collapsed again. When Ernst and Franz urged him to join them for an evening at the club, he realized he could not refuse without appearing a consummate snob at best, raising questions at worst. Franz was panting to hear every detail of the *Viktoria Luise* flight.

"Come on, Peter, what was it like?"

"Comfortable in the passenger cabin, spooky on the catwalk, cold in the control gondola."

"And hair-raising on the ladder," Ernst added. "You'll find that to be a 'high point' on your flight tomorrow."

"So what's it *really* like?" Franz insisted with a beery grin. "Up there with the –"

"For God's sake, Franz, sober up," Ernst broke in. "We're *at war*. You were all fired up over that this afternoon. Now you haven't said a damned word about it.

"Well, after the shock of actually being in a war, it hit me that we're dealing with Cossacks on horseback and peasants with pikes. We have machine guns. Who do you think will win that kind of battle?"

"You sound like Napoleon of the Airship Division," Ernst said as he hoisted his glass for a quick sip, then fingered a line of foam from his prissy little mustache. "'Home by Christmas?' I wonder if the Crusaders said that when they set out for the Holy Land?"

"What's the word from Kaspar?" Peter wondered. "He must have some inside word by now."

Franz moved his chair closer to their table. "Brother Kaspar –"

A roar of laughter erupted from the officers at the bar. "To the tzar!" someone shouted. "Bless him for the Iron Crosses we are about to win!"

Ernst leaned toward Peter. "And, inevitably, wooden crosses. Have you heard the decision on parachutes? Feldman, the equipment kapitänleutnant, told me just after the landing today. No parachutes for crews. The powers-that-be claim the weight of the parachutes would require a decrease in bomb loads."

"Strasser," Peter assumed. "He's hell bent on bombing."

"Seems so. Or, just between us, the high brass may be afraid we will panic at a sight of an enemy aeroplane and parachute over the side."

Franz took a long drag on his Löwenbräu. Shrugged. "No aeroplane can come close to a Zeppelin's service ceiling. Even if one could, tests show the only damage from bullets is a bunch of minor little leaks. It would take hundreds to have any effect on lift. Besides, aeroplanes are for observation, not attack."

"How about artillery fire, straight up?"

"A hit would be just plain luck, Peter, even if the Russians have any artillery like that and their peasant gunners could figure out how to use it. Anyway, Kaspar tells me our general staff has been getting ready for war for the last ten years. So, you two gloom-meisters, this little scrap with the borscht slurpers will be what the guy at the bar just said: our chance for a little glory."

"So you *have* heard from Kaspar." Ernst nudged Peter. "Full attention, Leutnant, Franz is about to give us a report on Kaspar's insight."

"I am? Oh, yes, I am. He called just before you two came back today. I almost missed the landing, but I was the first one here to get the news of war. Beat the official word by five minutes."

"Franz, for God's sake, get on with it."

"Sorry, Ernst. He told me the kaiser demanded the Russians call off their mobilization. They refused – three times, then our ambassador handed Foreign Minister Sazenov our declaration of war. The general staff is celebrating. After years of getting ready for war, now they have one."

Ernst fingered his still nearly full glass. "A war between cousins. Tzar 'Nicky' and Kaiser 'Willy.'"

"It won't last long. Kaspar told me we are about to put pressure on Russia's most important ally –"

"France?"

"Very good, Ernst. By the way, say nothing about this next thing to anyone." He motioned them closer. "We are about to insist France hand over to us the fortresses at Verdun and Toul. A sort of guarantee France will stay out."

Not a chance, Peter thought, but he said nothing. Let Franz have his moment.

"So when France agrees…" Franz shrugged. "All we will have to is flatten Russia. And we lucky few will soar above it all, radioing Cossack positions to our artillery." He grinned and raised his glass toward the bar. "As our friend over there said, Iron Crosses all around."

Ernst caught Peter's eye. He, too, Peter noted, appeared to be thinking beyond Franz's eagerness. A comment by then-retired and disillusioned Oberst Viktor Reinhart – Peter's father – sprang to mind: "Wars always start with a call to glory, my boy, but they soon become nothing more glorious than old men ordering young men to die."

"Oh, one more thing." Franz gave them a smug look. "It's unofficial but Kaspar has heard Strasser is moving the Division Headquarters out of Fuhlsbüttel."

"To where? And should we care?"

"We should, Ernst. He's coming here."

With the chair behind his desk swung around to let him stare at the sprawl of Kiel's Baltic Station, Konteradmiral Kottenhoff found himself in a dilemma. I can rationalize my little scheme involving ever-so-disciplined Leutnant Reinhart and compliant Fräulein Tammler as legitimate. I am simply gathering information "for the good of the service –" the surface fleet. I honorably forwarded my opinions, bolstered with Reinhart's observations, in that memo to Tirpitz. Now Tirpitz has ordered me to cease. That's the dilemma. Or part of it.

Kottenhoff rested an elbow on the chair's arm and cupped his chin. The other part is the kaiser's declaration of war delivered to Russia last Saturday – actually, a decision I suspect was made for him, but nonetheless a state of war now exists. Another memo to Tirpitz would finish me. But before more navy Zeppelins go down in flaming ruin, I've got to find a way to publicize the stupidity of the program. Publicize... Directly to the public? Possibly through a trusted newspaper reporter who would never divulge his source?

Ingenious. But not without risk. In peacetime, such "leaking" to the press could be considered in the best interests of the Naval Service. In a country at war, it could be considered treason.

Kottenhoff absently fingered his beard as he gazed unseeing across Kiel Harbor. Do I really need all this tension? My best move at this point could be to drop my whole anti Zeppelin effort. Release Reinhart from his Nordholz commitment and arrange for his reassignment to the surface fleet. I could thank Alexia and continue her assistant status. As for myself, I could comfortably complete the remainder of my navy career as an over-rated paper pusher.

He gripped the chair arms in sudden anger at himself. No! The project continues. I must find a way to use the information Reinhart will surely acquire as an airship crewmember. He stays in place. Alexia as well. And I will find a way. The war with Russia could help to point out airship deficiencies, should hostilities even last long enough for Zeppelins to see service at all. Russians, for God's sake. Even the Japanese beat them. Now we have the chance to –

A fist thundered on his office door. Then the door burst open. In rushed Leutnant Krause, eyes wide, waving a piece of paper.

"Krause!" Kottenhoff snapped. You are aware I insist on –"

"Telegram from Berlin sir. Just received."

"What's so important that you burst in here like –?"

"We have –" Krause swallowed noisily in an attempt to get control of himself.

"Herr Admiral," he gasped. "The kaiser has just declared war on France."

13.

Kottenhoff scanned the urgent memorandum Krause handed him. Then, with no change of expression, he set it on his desk. "Not unexpected, Leutnant. Not at all unexpected. We demand French neutrality. We demand the occupation of two French forts. We demand free passage through Belgium to the sea. How can the French possibly accept all of that?" He peered up at Krause. "You will, of course, not repeat that opinion to anyone."

Eyes somber beneath his heavy brows, Krause nodded. "Of course not, Sir." He clicked his heels and turned to leave.

"Stay a moment," Kottenhoff blurted.

What am I doing? Do I need the wisdom of a mere kapitänleutnant? Am I that isolated? God knows I've found no warmth in those hard faces at the Kiel Naval Officers Club. One drunken vizeadmiral even labeled me "Herr Hoch und Raus." Mister Up and Out. That slur, reaching me roundabout through a retired cruiser kapitän sur see.

"Herr Admiral?" Krause waited, eyebrows raised.

"Sit, Leutnant. I recall you were an instructor for several years at the Academy."

"Several semesters, Sir, until the navy decided my course in land tactics was a nonessential subject for future naval officers."

"Probably an unfortunate decision. A rumor claims we already have troops at the Belgium border."

"From what I have gathered from certain army friends, Herr Admiral, at this moment we have a million and a half men moving westward, and another half million mobilized to challenge Russia."

"And do your army friends have information on the French forces?

Potentially some sixty divisions to face our nearly ninety, Sir."

"Armed with?"

"No specifics yet, Sir. But we have the most formidable armament industry in Europe. Krupp alone employs more than forty thousand workers. And our divisions are armed with heavy howitzers and the new weapon, the Maxim machine gun."

"So, if you were a betting man, Leutnant..."

"A short war, Herr Admiral."

Kottenhoff sank back in his chair. *And I will be pushing paper while our navy stands at war stations and needs every mark being squandered in the damned airship program.*

"A short war," he echoed.

"We have been preparing for war since the turn of the century, Herr Admiral."

"And now we challenge Russia, France, surely Belgium. And, undoubtedly, the British."

Krause responded with a derisive laugh. "The British. They are dithering. And at best, my studies –"

"Your studies, Leutnant?"

"My Academy classes in army logistics and tactics were cancelled, but my interest has grown. At best, the British could muster a mere dozen divisions. Not a balance tipper by any means."

"But they are a stubborn people, Krause."

"As are we, Herr Admiral. And we are prepared. They are not."

"With the exception of their fleet."

"With all due respect, sir, the final outcome – in my opinion, of course – will be decided on land."

Interesting attitude for a naval officer. Our land forces will be of little use against the English fleet. Only battleships, Leutnant, can cope with that.

"I suspect," Kottenhoff said quietly, "the British will declare war on us within the week."

Krause said nothing, too well trained to contradict his superior.

"Thank you for your views, Leutnant. That will be all."

Three days later, Kottenhoff congratulated himself. The demands France could not possibly agree to resulted in the sudden invasion of Belgium. Then England's foreign secretary lamenting, "The lamps are going out all over Europe" as the British Empire slid into war.

Kottenhoff's concern refocused, far more acutely now, on the accursed airship program. Strasser's wild dream of Zeppelins serving far more than auxiliary eyes of the fleet was infecting the entire naval service. What made the navy's urgency even more acute was the startling news that Delag was about to turn over to the army its commercial airships *Sachsen, Hansa* and *Viktoria Luise*. With the three Delag airships, four new military Zeppelins and three older airships already in hand, the army would possess 10 of Germany's 11 airships. The navy? Just one. Fine. Let the army prove the airship's vulnerability. But, Kottenhoff knew, that's a vain hope. Strasser has managed to mesmerize the Naval Cabinet, even Kaiser Wilhelm II himself. New navy Zeppelins are already on order. A further squandering of navy funds. And only God knows how many more could be authorized.

Kottenhoff sighed and plucked the next requisition form from his overflowing in box. One glimmer of hope. Reinhart and Fräulein Tammler. Good choices, yet even there, a regret. Reinhart is expendable. But Alexia? Have I put the daughter of an old friend in danger as well?

At their "usual" table in the Blauer Adler dining room, Alexia realized the dark-beamed ceiling, the varnished maple floor, the smoky tang of roasting meat had become almost as familiar as her family's kitchen in Hamburg.

It's way past noon. Where is he? She glanced toward the entrance again. For Heaven's sake, Alexia, stop worrying. He – Oh, at last!

Peter strode to the table and dropped into one of the armless chairs. "Sorry I'm so late. My second flight took longer than I thought it would. *Viktoria Luise* again. Last training trip before she is turned over to the army. This time I was sent aft, to the engine gondola. Miserable back there, too."

He signaled. The white-haired waiter rushed to them, but they ordered without much thought. The waiter pursed his lips and ambled away toward the kitchen. Fewer young men everywhere, Alexia had begun to notice. The war.

"What really gets to you," Peter said, "is the noise. The cold air is bad enough, but – Alexia, what is it?"

She looked straight into his eyes. "I've got to say this. It has gnawed at me since all the war talk began." She took a deep breath. "Peter, is what we are doing, or trying to do, of any use at all now that we are at war?"

He sighed. "I've asked myself the same question, but I have no answer, except that an admiral has ordered it, and I am required to obey orders."

"How dangerous do you think this is?"

"Dangerous?"

"The secrecy. The information you get and I take to the admiral. This is spy work, Peter, even if it's for our own side."

"It's orders, Alexia. From a naval officer much higher ranked than I am."

She glanced around the almost empty dining room. "This seems so strange. The sense of urgency in Kiel, yet such a lack of it here."

"We're in a country inn, Alexia. People come here to get away from the war."

"Or to exchange secret information about the war." She gave him a flicker of a smile.

"Oh, so that's why we're here." He smiled back. "All right, hear this: the army is racing through Belgium. The fleet is on station. Army airships are already flying missions. The navy's airship program bumbles along."

"The admiral will no doubt be pleased to hear you confirm that, but you sound disappointed."

"Shh," he warned. "Here comes our dinner."

The waiter plunked down their plates as if, she thought, he was disappointed in their unimaginative orders. Then he ambled away.

She nibbled at her potato salad. Then looked up. "What else might you have to tell me?"

"Parachutes. There will be none for airship crews. The official word is the weight of parachutes would force a reduction in the airships' bomb loads. The rumor, though, is the higher-ups suspect that having parachutes, we will all go over the side at the first sign of trouble."

"Trouble?"

"An engine fire, perhaps. Or enemy aeroplanes attacking, though we are told Zeppelins can fly higher than any aeroplane."

"But I thought the Zeppelins were intended for scouting."

"Not if you listen to Fregattenkapitän Strasser, and he is the one in charge. To me, a big problem is the open gondolas, at least on *Viktoria Luise*. I told you it is cold up there, but I can't imagine anyone jumping out with a parachute because he's cold."

"The admiral will be pleased to hear that."

"Pleased we won't jump?"

"Not about the parachutes. In his mind, I imagine, the effects of cold on the crews will make the airship that much less promising."

The wrong thing to say? He appeared uncomfortable.

"Peter?"

"You're right, of course. But I don't think he has much to worry about. The Nordholz revolving sheds still are not finished. The new sheds are barely begun. In fact. I've heard the only fully operable shed on the whole North Sea coast is at Fuhlsbüttel north of Hamburg. A rented hangar, at that. The navy's mighty Airship Division boasts exactly one airship. One! To patrol both the North Sea and the Baltic."

He finally paid attention to his sausages. For just a moment or two, then he put down his fork. "And there's this. At Nordholz, construction has also begun on more barracks and other buildings. The headquarters of the Airship Division is to move from Fuhlsbüttel to Nordholz, but there has been a construction problem. Workers quit, new ones wander in. No one seems in charge. Another draw-back is no work at night."

"Why not?"

"The Army Kommandant at Cuxhaven has ordered nighttime blackout for his entire distract, and that includes Nordholz."

He sounds as if he almost resents all those problems, she thought. But hasn't Admiral Kottenhoff selected him for this assignment because of Peter's distrust of the Zeppelin program? I wonder… Let it go, Alexia. You have doubts of your own.

"Peter, has it struck you that perhaps all our information gathering –

even the whole airship project – will be all for nothing anyway. Admiral Kottenhoff told me the kaiser has said, 'When the leaves fall, we will be back home again.'"

"Do you believe that?" he asked.

"I don't know what to believe. Going to war because some archduke was shot by a madman in Serbia? That's crazy."

"Oh? I thought women were expected to concern themselves with fancies and fashions, not world affairs."

"Not this woman."

His deep blue eyes had softened. "Oh. You are teasing."

She was delighted. He had seemed never to offer any lightness. "Eat," she commanded with mock sternness. "It's getting cold."

Instead, he flushed and leaned close. "If I may say this, I really admire you, Alexia."

"Admire?"

"I detect a bit of daring under all that seriousness. And I'm beginning to think you are a bit of a rebel."

Well, that's unexpected. And... endearing? "My turn, Peter. I have found you to be –"

"Reinhart! Peter Reinhart!"

The booming shout came from across the room. A squat leutnant zur see with a remarkably thick neck and closely cropped blond hair leaped to his feet and rushed around several tables toward them.

"Ah, Fritz," Peter rose to greet the chunky officer with a handshake. "You remember Fritz Ritter, Alexia. You met him at the Kiel Yacht Club dance. Fräulein Alexia Tammler, Fritz."

"How nice to see you again." But not at this particular moment.

"Will you join us?" Peter asked, the soul of disciplined courtesy.

"No, no. Sit, Reinhart. I'm here on official duty. From Cuxhaven ten kilometers up the road. Naval liaison officer to the army base kommandant."

"What brings you here?"

"Precautions, Reinhart. The possibility of British shelling of this area. The blackout. The army has given this navy man a make-work job. I'm evaluating compliance of all public places in the Cuxhaven District." He glanced at Alexia then back to Peter with a little smirk. "And you?"

"Obvious, isn't it? We manage to steal a few hours together from time to time."

"All the way from Kiel? That's where I last saw you."

"I'm based at Nordholz."

"That's an airship field. As I recall, you never were much of an enthusiast for gas bags."

Peter shrugged. "The inexplicable military, Fritz."

"You're assigned as a ground officer."

"I'm a navigator trainee."

"But I thought airship crew service was voluntary."

Oh, God. Alexia held her breath.

"I find myself obsessed with the need to discover first-hand whether my aversion was justified."

Ritter's sandy eyebrows shot upward. Peter's eyes held his. Alexia tensed.

Then Ritter said, "I guess I should commend you for such conscientious research. Good to see you again, Peter." He bowed courteously to Alexia. "Enjoyed seeing you again, Fräulein. I hope you both have a pleasant afternoon."

And he strode away.

"I hope he is as dense as he looks," Alexia murmured.

He was staring at departing Ritter. "Guess it works."

"What works?"

"My 'cover story' suggestion, 'fiancée.'" Then he said seriously, "Do you plan to make a life's work of serving as an admiral's aide?"

"My father asks me the same question. Someday I hope to find a more challenging position. But now with Germany at war? I will stay with the admiral as long as I am useful."

"As, apparently, will I."

She gave him a long, sharp look. Was his tone a touch bitter? She couldn't be sure. Now he attacked his plate as if he suddenly realized he was ravenous.

She sipped her coffee and watched him eat. *I can't help being attracted to this man. His face, almost boyish when we began this odd liaison, now appears years older. Windburn has seared his cheeks. His eyes are more* penetrating. Those sea blue eyes. That determined jaw. I've found all this remarkably appealing. Could I possibly be falling in love with Peter Reinhart? Do I even know what love is?

Stop it, Alexia. You know so little of men a mere smile can spark too much imagination. Stop this. You are here on business.

"Another thing the admiral should know." Peter sat back and set his napkin on the table. "Zeppelin L-3 is to be assigned to Nordholz next month. For training and patrol flights. At the same time, he'll no doubt be glad to know, the blackout is slowing down airship base construction."

He shoved back his chair and signaled the waiter. "I should get on the road. I was lucky to get a pass at all today. If I'm not back before six, I won't be lucky again."

On impulse, she placed her hand over his. "Oh, stay a bit longer, Peter. Nordholz is less than an hour's drive, and it's only mid-afternoon."

Their eyes met. He grinned, actually grinned. "That doesn't sound to me like an assignment-obsessed admiral's staffer."

"Is that how you think of me? Hah!"

"Hah?"

"To the porch, Leutnant. Let us talk of anything, everything but the airship service and the damned war."

On the broad east porch, they settled into unyielding slat chairs on the secluded north end, overlooking the estuary's leaden water. Clouds hid the lowering sun. Everything seems to be waiting, silently waiting for – she shuddered.

"You're cold out here, Alexia?"

"No, I'm... Oh, look, Peter. Sea gulls."

He gave her a curious look.

"Talk to me," she urged, "talk about anything but Zeppelins and the war. Tell me where you went to school."

"You know I went to the Naval Academy."

"I mean before that."

So he told her about his early school days, the privileges and problems of growing up as the son of a prominent then disillusioned army general staff officer. And she recalled her upbringing as the only daughter of a successful manufacturer, an easier childhood than his, she decided. Because she was female or because her father was not preoccupied with her future?

"Now though, Pappi is much more interested in what I'm doing and how well I'm doing it. Because he and the admiral are old friends. That's how he knew the admiral needed an office aide. I'm sorry. I'm rambling."

"Not at all. But –" He pulled out his pocket watch. "Uh, later than I thought."

He stood, clicked heels and gave her a little bow. "From Leutnant zur See Reinhart, his thanks for an afternoon far more enjoyable than he had anticipated."

He turned away stiffly, then relaxed and turned back, placed his hands on her shoulders. "But from Peter Reinhart... this."

His lips softly brushed her cheek.

She closed her eyes and felt a surge of delicious warmth. *God, I want to wrap my arms around him, but I dare not.*

He trotted down the steps and strode toward his American Ford.

Her eyes never left him as he cranked the automobile, bounded into the seat and chugged out of the parking lot. His arm raised in a farewell wave as he turned into the Cuxhaven-Hamburg road.

That totally unexpected gentle kiss, she knew, had just changed everything.

14.

"Just what is your problem, Ernst?" Peter demanded as they walked toward the waiting airship, the navy's only airship, Zeppelin L-3.

Ernst Wolff, helmet and squarish goggles dangling from one hand, fiddled with his little mustache. "My problem, your problem – all of ours – is those army airship losses. The rumors are true. Heard it this morning from a friend at Köln."

Peter stopped short and faced him. "The rumors say three were lost. *Three?*"

"Unfortunately, yes. Three army airships lost in these first days of the war. One had just bombed the fortress at Litetia near Paris. Cloudy weather forced it to make a low altitude attack and shrapnel chewed it up so badly, it crashed near Bonn."

"And the crew?"

"My friend didn't know. The next one also was forced low by clouds and taken down by artillery and small arms fire near Saint-Quirin in Lorraine. No word on the crew there, either."

"You think the army may be withholding information on the –?

Ernst shrugged. "I don't know. Crew losses this early surely would not be a real morale builder."

"God. And the third?"

"Unfortunately, first shot at by our own troops. It swung clear of them, but right over a French unit armed with machine guns. They damaged the steering gear and riddled the gas cells. The crew brought it down smack into a French cavalry charge. In all the confusion, though, most of them got away."

"Well, thanks a lot, Ernst." Peter headed for the waiting airship. "A great morale boost just before our first real patrol. I assume those easily gunned-down army ships were their wooden-framed Schütte-Lanz glue potters."

Ernst shook his head. "No. All three were Zeppelins." He nodded at the airship looming ahead. "Like this one."

Sweating in the late August heat in their sheepskin jackets and flying pants, and soft leather flying boots, they trudged across the sandy turf behind the rest of the crew. Wearing his helmet with the goggles pushed up on his forehead, Peter carried his leather navigator's case in one hand, his flying gauntlets in the other.

The L-3 had finally arrived at Nordholz for combined training and North Sea patrol missions. The 158-meter-long Zeppelin loomed over the ground handling crew like an ominous grey storm cloud. Compared to this thing, Peter decided, my *Viktoria Luise* flights probably have been carnival rides. No plush cabin on this one. That midships space in the L-3 was the "bomb room." And atop the hull, well forward, I see a small platform ringed by a handrail; a machine gun emplacement. "No aeroplane can fly as high as an airship," we have been told. Why a machine gun up there?

The boat-like control gondola, like the aft engine gondola, was open to the wind, of course, except for a semi-circular windscreen forward. Does Count von Zepp believe the crews need a constant blast of frigid air to stay alert?

Peter followed obviously more eager Ernst through the gondola's entry door. A burly, bulldog-faced instructor greeted them with a brief nod then kept eyeing them while stroking his thick beard with a sour "look what the hell they're sending us now" expression. The instructor ranked equally with the airship commander, a big man in his mid-30s with a face like that of a battered prizefighter. He lacked a beard and, Peter thought with some apprehension, also lacked a look of confidence.

"Kapitänleutnant Hugo Kellner," the instructor informed Peter and Ernst, "our airship kommandant. And I am Kapitänleutnant Grauel, flying today as executive officer." He pulled a form from a pocket of his sheepskins, studied it and noted Peter's leather case. "Navigation table aft, Reinhart, just forward of the engine compartment. Wolff, you report to the engine compartment."

Peter, with Ernst close behind him moved aft, past the portside elevator wheel and the hull access ladder starboard in the cramped gondola. The so-called navigator's station turned out to be a tiny shelf crammed between the ladder and the engine compartment bulkhead.

Ernst edged past him, opened a narrow door in the chest-high bulkhead and stepped into the engine compartment.

As Peter opened his case, pulled out pencil, ruler, protractor and a map of northwest Germany and the adjacent North Sea area, Grauel appeared at his elbow.

"Wind is four knots from the northwest, Herr Navigator." His little smile seems a touch mocking, Peter thought. The light breeze drifted the map to the corrugated metal floor, and Grauel's eyes rolled upward.

"Try to keep your materials on the desk, Reinhart." He strode forward.

With the sides of the gondola only shoulder-high, this was like going aloft in a clumsy, cluttered dory. So much for the glamor of the airship service. L-3's first "engagement" of the war, Peter had heard, had not gone well. The failure was not Kellner's. Kapitänleutnant Hans Fritz had been kommandant when L-3 flew over a flotilla of German cruisers and destroyers off Wilhelmshaven. The destroyers opened fire on L-3, which swung east to escape – and missed sighting British Admiral Beatty's approaching ships. While the British sank three of the German cruisers, L-3 flew homeward in ignorance, an abject scouting failure of the Naval Airship Division.

Up forward, Grauel and Kellner appeared to have fallen into a spirited discussion, with Kellner's voice rising above the mutter of the now idling fore and aft engines.

"...damned student navigator! This is supposed to be a combat patrol. Do you know how many flights I've logged in these things? Over twenty with Delag and already six with the navy. Never once lost. I am my own navigator."

"The radio, Kommandant. He could help."

"I am my own radio operator, as well." He motioned toward Peter. "Surplus weight. Get him off my ship!"

"Strasser's orders, Kommandant," the instructor said patiently. "I have no doubts of your navigational skill, but this is a training flight as well as a patrol mission."

The airship kommandant threw Peter a hard-eyed glance. "Keep him out of my way."

The rudder man and elevator man waited at their stations. To the rudder man's right, Kellner studied a map on his console. Grauel hung over Peter's shoulder. In the engine section, two mechanics and Ernst. Eight of us in this cramped sky-going boat, Peter marveled, and I'm already tagged as surplus weight.

"Up bow!" Kellner shouted. The bow rope handlers let go. "Up stern!"

Kellner grabbed the funneled end of the speaking tube to the engine men. "Full power."

Peter heard the engines in the aft gondola rev up, then the engine in the compartment just behind him. A pungent stench of exhaust swept through the gondola. The propellers on their fore and aft outrigger struts whirled into shimmering discs.

Peter watched the ground fall away. L-3 began to climb, its bulk angled steeply upward.

As he turned back to his map, the instructor appeared at his elbow.

"Plot a course to a point twenty kilometers west of Sylt," he shouted over the engines' blare. "We will be patrolling along the North Frisian Islands."

"Yes, Sir." Peter bent over his little table. He determined the course as 350 degrees. Adjust for magnetic variation and a four-knot wind from the northwest. Since wind velocity usually increases with altitude, he would adjust for that when they reached cruising height.

He gave the instructor his finding. Grauel nodded, but made no move to inform Kellner. "An exercise, Leutnant. With such good visibility, navigation will be by visual landmarks."

A decidedly cool twenty minutes later, Kellner ordered the elevator man to level off. Then he reached for the valve handles above the Kommandant's station to vent enough hydrogen to stabilize their 1500-meter altitude.

For the next several hours, they drummed north-northwest along the North Frisian Island chain, hazy blue on the eastern horizon. No navigation challenge at all, Peter realized. Not with the constant presence of the islands out there a consistent 20 kilometers distant.

As they passed Anrum Island, The instructor's heavily jowled face hung over Peter's shoulder. "Another revised bearing, Reinhart? Ah, I see you increased the wind effect. Good guess."

"An observation, sir, based on our longitudinal angle compared to our actual direction. The wind up here has to be at least ten knots from the northwest."

Grauel nodded. "Not much of a patrol, is it? We haven't sighted a single ship. All I've noticed is that darkening to the west, but our kommandant says nothing about any radio reports of changing weather conditions."

Peter stood to peer past the elevator man. Grauel was right. The sun had slipped behind a long grey smudge low obscuring the western horizon.

"We are fifteen minutes from the point of return," Grauel told him. "I hope we can beat that mess back to Nordholz, but at our forty-knot top speed..."

Forty knots. That's only five knots faster than my old Ford's top speed, and it's no racing car.

At 15.18 hours, Leutnant Kellner ordered a 180-degree turn. At last, Peter noted with relief, they were heading back. By now, the dark wall to the west loomed close, a fast-approaching fog bank.

Minutes later, the first misty tendrils whipped past the gondola. Peter peered down at the white caps speckling the black water below. He plotted a new line on his map, the return course to Nordholz. Then he stepped forward to glance at the compass at the rudder man's station. The reading was ten degrees easterly of the course he had just plotted.

Now I have a problem I can surely do without, he realized. In fact, I didn't want any of this, but like it or not, I'm supposed to be the navigator on this flight.

"What is it, Reinhart?" Grauel asked behind him.

"I... have a course correction, sir," Peter called over the engine and slipstream racket. "If the kommandant would –"

Kellner whirled around from his control board. "If the kommandant would what, Leutnant Reinhart?"

Peter stepped forward and said close to Kellner's ear, hoping the rudder man would not hear, "According to my calculation, sir, we should be heading ten degrees more westerly."

They flew into the fog bank. The airship was swallowed by dense, moist vapor. Visibility zero.

"Return to your station, Reinhart," Kellner snapped.

Peter returned aft, but Grauel stayed at the commander's side. He said something that was drowned in the engines' yammer. Kellner threw a sour look in Peter's direction and shook his head. No change of direction, Peter knew. Certainly not one recommended by a trainee.

Aside from his arrogance, Kellner's insistence on maintaining his own heading was understandable, Peter decided. The change he had recommended would have taken them deeper into the swirling fog.

Two and a half long, chilly hours later, the fog had diminished. Up forward, heads were swinging, obviously looking for Nordholz. Kellner grabbed the speaking tube, shouted, and the engines' racketing faded.

"Cuxhaven's damned blackout order," he heard Kellner tell Grauel. "Where in hell is our airship base?"

"Leutnant?" said a quiet voice near Peter. The elevator man, a non-commissioned master's mate, caught his eye and nodded to port. Peter stepped to his side. Through the now thinning fog, he spotted lights faintly glowing through the darkness. A lot of lights. Apparently, the Cuxhaven coastal blackout did not apply this far inland.

The instructor appeared behind him. "What do you make of that, Reinhart?"

"Hamburg, Leutnant. The only city that large our present course would intersect."

Grauel gave him a tight smile. "And your recommendation now?"

"Give me a minute." Peter returned to his workspace, picked up the protractor and consulted his map.

"Two six-five," he told Grauel, who strode forward, his broad face still wearing his bemused expression.

His back to Peter, the instructor spoke quietly to Kellner. The airship commander looked as if he had been struck by lightning. He stared to port, glanced over his shoulder at Peter, scowled, then reached for the speaking tube. Seconds later, the idling engines' mutter swelled to a roar. Kellner shouted at the helmsman who spun the big rudder wheel. The airship's nose swung slowly to starboard, a full 90-degree change of course.

An hour later, an apprehensive hour for Peter, a dim light glowed in the darkness ahead. The Nordholz locator light, turned on at the sound of their approaching. Zeppelin. He bent over his work shelf to hide his grin.

Fifteen minutes after that, the L-3 was safely on the ground, secured to a temporary mooring mast near the still incomplete rotating hangars.

As the engines fell silent, Peter packed up his kit and followed Ernst out of the control gondola. As he and Ernst walked toward the administration and barracks area ahead of the rest of the crew, he could feel Kellner's eyes on him.

"What the hell was going on up there?" Ernst asked. "Back in the engine compartment, we felt we were all over the map."

"Navigation without landmarks isn't an exact science, Ernst."

"In other words, we were lost."

"We're here."

Behind them, Peter heard footsteps. "Reinhart!" The instructor's voice.

"Yes, sir?"

"Good work. Have a pleasant evening – what's left of it." Grauel strode on past.

"So you weren't lost," Ernst deduced. "Kellner was. When word of that gets around –"

"He was our kommandant, Ernst," Peter said quietly. "Are you or are you not a loyal crewmember?

15.

With his orderly, Albert Walther at the wheel, traffic light, and the late August morning gloriously bright, Admiral Kottenhoff tried to relax in the cushioned rear seat of his Daimler. Even a pigeon-holed, aging konteradmiral at odds with the Zeppelin-hungry fleet had a few privileges left. This chauffeured morning ride to Kiel's Naval Procurement Division building – and the evening run back home – were among those remaining.

His ride to work usually was a relaxing part of Kottenhoff's day. But this morning he found himself mulling grim facts. Five German armies had cut through Belgium and Northern France like a bayonet through lard, following the vaunted Schlieffen Plan to ram through to the Channel. Then just days ago, General "Gloomy Gus" von Moltke abandoned the Plan and ordered the armies to swing south to counter heavy French resistance. The Fatherland's massive attack was disintegrating into what Kottenhoff suspected would be stagnated trench warfare.

And on the Russian front, the Eighth Army under Colonel General Max von Prittwitz und Gaffron was hugely undermanned. Defeated by the Russian rabble at Gumbinnen in East Prussia, von Prittwitz had already been replaced as Eighth Army commander by General Paul von Hindenberg. An old man, for God's sake, recalled from retirement. The situation down in Galicia was no picnic, either. The Austrian Army was already stalled along the Carpathian Mountains by Russian forces.

Too many fronts. Germany expected a quick, slashing victory, but with the war less than a month old, Kottenhoff sensed a stalemate.

Near the access road turn-off to the Procurement's office annex, Albert slowed the big automobile, rolled down his window and thrust out his arm to signal a right turn. Though few vehicles were on the street, trust Albert to follow procedure.

As the Daimler began its ponderous swing into the side street, a hard jolt thrust Kottenhoff sideways.

Albert rammed down the brake pedal.

"Someone just ran into us, Herr Admiral."

Kottenhoff reached for the door handle.

"No need, Herr Admiral. I will attend to it." As the bony manservant stepped out of the automobile, a chubby, almost cherubic face appeared at the admiral's window. Startlingly like the face of that American buffoon, Arbuckle, in the new fad, "moving pictures."

Albert hurried aft to assess the damage. Kottenhoff rolled down his window. The man touched the brim of his gray Homburg.

"I am deeply sorry, Sir" The careless driver wore an expression of abject contrition "I'm afraid I let my attention wander, and as you slowed for the turn... Well, I'm afraid I drove right into you. My fault, of course."

"I agree with that," Kottenhoff grumped. This was not the way to start a day, even a tedious one behind the swarm of official forms I know are awaiting this morning, every morning. Some of them inevitably would concern allocations for the Zeppelin program, not so subtle "touchés" via Tirpitz.

Kottenhoff peered past the bulky culprit at his window. "Albert, what is the damage?"

"The rear bumper is bent into the right fender, sir. Easily fixed. I can take the automobile to the repair garage after I drop you off. Shouldn't take more than an hour or two."

"And damage to this man's vehicle?" Kottenhoff asked, his burst of anger subsiding into a touch of concern.

"His Benz also needs a bit of work."

Kottenhoff's attention refocused on the man at his window. "You, Sir, are you all right?"

"Only my pride is damaged." He thrust a meaty hand through the window. "Max Moellendorf. My sincere apologies for my woefully inattentive driving this morning."

Kottenhoff shook hands without much enthusiasm.

"I will, of course, reimburse the cost of the repair," Moellendorf added.

"Not necessary." Kottenhoff yearned to get off this avenue and away from the small group of onlookers that had begun to gather. My reputation is shaky enough without the public spectacle of a stupid automobile accident.

"No, no, I insist, Herr –" Moellendorf glanced at Kottenhoff's sleeve stripes.

"–Herr Admiral. As soon as you have the invoice, I will reimburse you in full"

For expediency, Kottenhoff relented. "Very well. If you will follow Albert to the shop after he delivers me to my office."

Moellendorf shook his head. "I would be pleased to do that, Herr Admiral, but unfortunately, I am already late for an unavoidable appointment." He offered a little smile. "I could meet you later in the day, perhaps in your office?"

"No, no." Kottenhoff did not relish the idea of this thick-necked fellow appearing in his office to settle an automobile accident liability. I don't need such attention to the automobile the navy has somehow failed to reclaim after my fall from military grace.

"Coming to my office would not be convenient today." Or any day.

"But the accident was entirely my fault. I insist on paying. Perhaps, if the vehicle is registered to the navy, I could submit the damages payment to the Procurement Division?"

That, Kottenhoff realized with a twitch in his stomach, could be the spark to light the fuse that would sizzle straight into the Transportation Section. Look at this, Gustav, some high-minded minion could say. Admiral Kottenhoff still has the missing Daimler!

Moellendorf looked distraught. "There has to be a way to settle this debt that has already begun to haunt me, Herr Admiral. Perhaps this evening, I could bring the reimbursement to your residence?"

Anything to get free of this obsequious peasant – and the ever-growing crowd out there. Albert could take Moellendorf's reimbursement at the door, and the matter would be quietly closed.

"That will be acceptable," Kottenhoff agreed. "Albert will give you directions."

"What time will be most convenient?"

After supper, surely. "Twenty-one o'clock."

"Agreed." Again, Moellendorf thrust his hand through the window. "I shall be there."

After a brief discussion with Albert, the hulking driver of the errant Benz chugged past and disappeared into the increasing traffic.

At the end of his dreary workday, with Albert and the repaired Daimler waiting near the Procurement annex's entrance, Kottenhoff found himself feeling a touch contrite. The accident had, after all, been a minor one. No one injured, and the man – what was his name? Mullenhorff? Moellendorf, that was it – the man had insisted on going to considerable inconvenience to pay for the minor damage – if, in fact, he did live up to his promise to repay the repair cost this evening.

And, Kottenhoff realized when his door chime broke the silence at precisely 21.00 hours that evening, apparently, the man had kept his word. In his library, out of uniform in a rumpled gray smoking jacket and corduroys, Kottenhoff heard the mutter of conversation at the distant front door. Then Albert appeared, expressionless as always. But with nothing in his hands.

Aha. As Kottenhoff had suspected. All talk.

"Herr Moellendorf asks your permission to speak with you, Herr Admiral."

"A complication?"

"He says he realizes you and he have an interest in common, sir."

"An interest in common? Other than settling the accident?"

"So he claims, Herr Admiral."

"Well, I cannot imagine what the man is talking about." Such effrontery. This stranger, daring to call on me in my own home after such brief acquaintance. It just is not done.

Albert cleared his throat. "Should I send him away, Sir?"

"Of course."

Albert turned toward the library door.

"Wait, Albert." 'An interest in common'? Whatever the man had in mind, it could serve to break the monotony of another lonely evening.

"Show him in, Albert, but stay nearby in case I need you."

"Good of you to see me, Herr Admiral," Moellendorf boomed from the library's doorway moments later. He strode in, nodding toward the fireplace. "A fire is certainly welcome this blustery evening." He grasped Kottenhoff's hand. A big handshaker, this fat comic.

"After our unfortunate –" Moellendorf began, then bent down to examine the intricate battleship model on the low table in the sitting area. "The *Deutschland*, is it not? A beautiful piece of work."

"My old ship, Herr Moellendorf. I am pleased you recognize her."

"I'm pleased I recognized you, Herr Admiral. Unfortunately not until I drove away this morning. Then it hit me. My God, I've just collided with Konteradmiral Erwin Kottenhoff, the man who had the foresight to criticize the navy's pet project, the airship program."

"That," Kottenhoff asked with a frown, "is what you have termed our 'interest in common'?"

"It is, indeed. But first, let me make good my promise. Your man –"

"Albert."

"Yes, Albert told me the cost of the repair." He pulled a wallet from his jacket, counted out the amount and handed the marks to Kottenhoff with a flourish. "Now my conscience is clear, Herr Admiral. Again, my apologies for the inconvenience."

Critics of the Zeppelin craze were few and far between, and this rotund fellow with the skin of a baby might be one. Kottenhoff found himself offering the man a chair.

"My card, sir." Moellendorf offered a business card that had materialized in his pudgy hand. "Maximilian Moellendorf, industrial counselor," he announced with a self-deprecating little twitch of his lips. "Translation: I am retained by clients seeking to build their businesses – and who isn't? Case in point, certain armaments manufacturers who are, as you are, concerned that the vast investment in the navy's airship program is seriously misplaced."

In his black leather chair across the low table from his visitor, Kottenhoff tented his fingers. "Just who are these enlightened clients of yours?"

"A proper question, Herr Admiral. But unfortunately, I have been asked to keep their identities confidential. I am in a delicate business, but I can assure you that my clients' concern is identical with yours."

"Albert!" Kottenhoff called.

"Yes, Herr Admiral," came the reply from the hallway. Albert appeared seconds later.

"We will have Dornkaat, Albert." He turned to Moellendorf. "Agreeable with you?"

"Of course, Sir. Dornkaat indeed."

"So you represent clients who believe, as I do, the funding for the damned gas bags would be of more value to the Fatherland were it invested in proven weaponry."

"Well said, Herr Admiral. And I am aware you have been doing everything you could – within the limitations of your rank and situation, of course – to further that conviction. Unfortunately to the detriment of your career, if I may be forgiven for such frankness."

Kottenhoff waved a hand. "Public knowledge, Herr Moellendorf."

"Max, please."

First name basis? I think not. "It seems we do have a common interest, Herr Moellendorf. I have done what I believe has been in the navy's best interest, but it has not met with a tantara of trumpets."

"That, Sir, is why I believe we can help each other toward our common goal."

"Ah, Albert. Set the tray here on the table, please. Good German brandy, not that Dutch stuff." Kottenhoff poured two liberal portions and handed one to Moellendorf as Albert faded into the hall. "Prosit."

Moellendorf raised his tumbler in salute.

Kottenhoff gave him a nod. God, it is good to have someone to drink with, even if you aren't entirely convinced you can trust this man.

"I have repeatedly brought to the navy's attention the risks – the dangers – of the airship, Herr Moellendorf. All that accomplished has been the curtailing of my access to those in positions to affect the project."

"It happens," Moellendorf said with an engaging smile, "that as a consultant, I do have that access. You can get the information I need; I have the contacts."

"I forwarded much information on the perils of the Zeppelin as a war machine, and now the army has lost three airships in the first few days of combat. Nobody listens."

Moellendorf held up a hand. "I am aware of that, Admiral. What we must make painfully obvious is the poor cost effectiveness of the airship even as scouting vehicle and, if that firebrand Strasser prevails, its limitations as an offensive weapon. High command expects to lose lives. What truly alarms them is the squandering of funds."

"You are a cynical man."

"I am a practical man, Herr Admiral."

You are, indeed, Kottenhoff found himself agreeing. And so am I. Here, in this clumsy looking fellow with a shrewd mind, may lay my path to success in curtailing the airship program after all. Can I trust him?

He poured another splash in Moellendorf's tumbler and raised his own.

"May the vaunted gas bags deflate!"

Max chuckled. "I certainly can drink to that." When he set his tumbler back on the table, he got to his feet. "I thank you for your hospitality, Herr Admiral. I will contact you shortly."

A remarkable conversation, Kottenhoff thought as his possibly useful visitor drove off into the clear autumn night.

And, he thought, stroking a bushy sideburn, what a remarkably fortuitous coincidence...

16.

A lexia tapped the paneled office door, and then slowly pushed it partway open.

"Pappi?"

"Eh? Oh, Alexia! Come in, come in, my favorite daughter."

"Your only daughter."

"You would still be my favorite daughter if I had a dozen."

"God forbid!"

Otto Tammler laughed. "Precisely. What brings you here this fine September day?"

Trimly efficient in a dark blue wool crepe jacket and skirt, she walked into the glassed-in office. The floor vibrated beneath her shoes. She glanced down at the bustling assembly lines a floor below. As many women as men.

"Come, sit down." Otto patted the sofa. "Such a nice surprise to see my career-driven daughter in Hamburg."

"I was just passing through and stopped to say hello – and to have Rudi Mott make a quick check of the Panhard." That is not actually why I am here, but the admiral told me to keep that to myself. Keep it from my own Pappi, one of the Admiral's good friends? From everyone, the Admiral told me.

Beside her on the sofa, Otto draped an affectionate arm over her shoulders. "Knowing Rudi's surgeon-like preciseness, you surely will have time to join me for lunch."

"I wish that were so, Pappi, but I am expected by friends at Cuxhaven this afternoon."

"Cuxhaven? Is that wise? The disgraceful loss of our cruisers took place not so far west of there just a few days ago. Who knows where the Royal Navy may try to strike next?"

She smiled. "No need to worry, Pappi. If a British warship appears, I will quickly disappear." All a fiction, but she was not about to tell her father today's destination was yet again the Blauer Adler Inn to meet *her* leutnant zur see – her leutnant? How far her impression of this strange liaison had progressed, built on one fleeting kiss on the cheek.

"Any problems with the Panhard? I could arrange--"

"It is taken care of, Pappi." By Admiral Kottenhoff, whose deft manipulation of certain paperwork made maintenance and fuel available to her in Kiel – and to Peter at Nordholz.

"I am sorry my time is so limited today, Pappi, but I did want to stop just to say hello."

With a little sigh of disappointment, Otto reluctantly withdrew his arm and stood to grasp her hands. "A treat to see you, my daughter, even for a moment. Now, be sure to drive carefully. The roads are full of military vehicles."

"I will. And please be sure to tell Mother I am well and most sorry my time is so limited."

She kissed his pudgy forehead, stepped toward the door then turned back, a forefinger to her chin. "I almost forgot. Do you know of a man named Moellendorf? Max Moellendorf, I believe his name is." She felt a pang of duplicity. This was her real purpose in stopping in Hamburg today.

Otto chuckled. "Fat Max? Wherever did you run across him?"

"Someone in the office mentioned him." I hope that isn't as unconvincing to Pappi as it sounds to me.

His shrewd eyes were intent on hers. Then he stepped back behind his desk and sat down.

"Maximilian Moellendorf is an influence peddler, Alexia. For a fee, he will represent your company. 'Industrial coordination,' I heard someone call that questionable line of work."

"But what do you think of him personally?"

His eyebrows raised. "You cannot be entertaining any sort of personal relationship with –"

"No, no, of course not. I've never met the man. Just curious."

Another small deception to her indulgent father. But Admiral Kottenhoff had asked her to do this, hoping prominent industrialist Otto Tammler would have encountered Moellendorf. Why the admiral was concerned about such a man, Alexia had no idea.

"I can tell you I know the man does what he claims to do. And has for several years. I just don't have much faith in 'industrial coordination' as a business practice. What I do have faith in is that." He gestured toward the assembly floor. "Production is business. Talking about it, Moellendorf's forte, is mere busyness. End of lecture." He gave her a disarming smile. "Drive carefully, daughter."

She waved her father a cheery goodbye, hiked her skirt to knee level and rushed down the office access stairway. Fashion's lengthy skirts were an inconvenient bore, but lingering prudes still felt exposing a woman's calves was an affront to their purity. The same kind of bluenoses, no doubt, who were distraught to see a woman behind the wheel of an automobile.

To hell with them. Fifteen minutes later, she drummed out of Hamburg, eager to meet her Leutnant zur See Rinehart again.

By the time she pulled the Panhard to the Blauer Adler's entrance and turned it over to the valet, the afternoon had mellowed into a golden haze over the dark waters of the Elbe Estuary. She walked up the steps and into the lobby thinking, we always meet in the inn or on the east porch. This is too nice an afternoon to spend our time together in the same old places.

BIG BATTLE AT MARNE RIVER EAST OF PARIS, read the chalkboard at the registration desk. "A mere stumbling block on our way to Paris, Fräulein." The desk clerk's grin in his round flat face gave him the look of a vaudeville comedian about to tell a knee-slapper. "Your leutnant has not yet arrived."

My leutnant. The desk clerk seems to have become a player in our "trysts." If this game Peter and I are playing ever became the subject of a navy investigation, just what would this leering little man be able to "reveal" to the investigators?

"Tell him I will be down by the water, Helmuth..."

"Be careful of the steps, Fräulein. They are quite steep."

She strode onto the all-too-familiar porch, then down to the lawn that ended on the brow of the bank of the Elbe River where it broadened into the Helgoland Bight.

Helmuth was right. The wooden steps down to the beach were breathtakingly steep. Twenty-eight, twenty-nine, thirty of them, she counted as she gripped the weatherworn wood handrail. Not an easy descent in her confining long skirt and stumpy-heeled shoes, the lowest heels a tall girl was able to find in Kiel.

The narrow beach was soft sand, though hard-packed along the edge of the lapping waves. The inn's beach frontage had been widened to about 10 meters, no doubt at high cost.

The breeze, warm for late summer, carried a sea salt tang. A capricious gust threatened to flip off her narrow brimmed hat until she slapped it back in place – then pulled it off to let the sea breeze ruffle her auburn curls. I hate the stupid hats women are supposed to wear. I put up with only the most insignificant ones I can find. A small rebellion of its own. Like trimming my hair into natural curls. No buns or rolls for this girl.

Except for a distant solitary figure to her left, the beach was deserted. Beyond that lonely fellow – was he in uniform? – she could make out hazy gray lumps along the landside of the horizon, no doubt the buildings of Cuxhaven some eight to 10 kilometers distant. Just above the horizon, a gray streak smudged the sky, probably the smoke trail of an invisible ship.

The breeze ruffled her hair. The salt-scented air seemed purifying. Too beautiful a day to realize we are at war. This is a seascape for a painter.

Then behind her, she heard footsteps descending.

"Alexia!" Peter's voice. "Our friend the desk man told me you were out here. What a good idea. No prying eyes anywhere."

"Except him." She pointed up the beach.

"A sentry, I think. One lone sentry to warn all of Lower Saxony, if a marauding British fleet were to appear. Should make us all feel wonderfully secure. Especially after the two aerial attacks in the new Zeppelin sheds at Düsseldorf."

She gave him a curious glance. "You sound cynical this fine day."

"Sorry. It's just that – Let's walk."

On the harder sand near the water, they strolled northwestward.

"It was only a few kilometers out there where the British sank three of our light cruisers."

"I know," she said. "The *Mainz, Koln* and *Ariadne* just a week ago. Lots of talk in Kiel about that sad debacle."

"Was there also talk about L-3's pathetic performance?"

"Not that I've heard. What –"

"The navy's first sea battle of the war, and the Airship Division failed miserably." He kicked a sand lump. "On routine patrol, L-3 was fired on by our own destroyers and escaped east, thinking it was enemy fire. The Zepp returned to base, but if it had kept going west, it would have spotted the British attack force early, and there would be a different story gassed about at Kiel."

She swung toward him. "Peter, were you on that flight?"

"Me? No, Lexie. By then L-3 had been returned to its base at Fuhlsbüttel near Hamburg. While it was at Nordholz, I flew on a few more patrols since we last met, but nothing much happened. I'm not sure I have anything our admiral might find useful."

Lexie. He's never called me that before. It's quite... endearing. "The admiral told me he especially needs information on the Zeppelins as offensive weapons. I think he's realized they really are useful for scouting."

"When flown by crews that know what the hell they're doing."

"You know what our admiral wants, Peter. He told me 'crew risks, technical problems.' Obviously, he wants any negatives. 'Bomb capacity compared with cost' was another of his specifics."

"An easy one. The L-3 can carry about five hundred kilos of bombs. Twenty-two thousand cubic meters of hydrogen, four engines and a crew of sixteen to deliver a mere five hundred kilos. Not even equal to a truckload of artillery shells. Tell him that."

"You sound resentful, Peter. You don't like what we're doing?"

He turned to face her. Wind-burned, lean cheeks clean-shaven, his intent brown eyes searching hers. "Do you, Lexie?"

"I like seeing you," she murmured.

"And I, you."

To her delight, he linked his arm with hers. She found herself resisting a girlish impulse to skip.

The other beach stroller had ambled close. Peter had been right. A sailor carrying a rifle. As he passed, he snapped a crisp salute. Which Peter returned without enthusiasm.

"I'll never make it as a career officer," he said as the sentinel seaman strode out of earshot. "Here on the beach, I'd be happy with a friendly nod from the man, instead of a salute."

She gave him a curious look. "You have doubts about yourself? But haven't you chosen a military career to honor your father?"

"To honor him?"

"To honor his hopes, Peter, while I hope to have a business career in spite of my mother's hopes."

"Her hopes?"

"Every mother hopes for a daughter to become a socially respected Hausfrau."

"Not for you?"

"Not now. I want to prove a woman can succeed in business. My work with the Procurement Division is a start."

"*This* work?"

"Mainly the office work. But even this is business of a sort."

He gave her a curious look. "Well, then, back to business. In a few days, Strasser is scheduled to move the Airship Division's headquarters to Nordholz. His new administration buildings are finished, but none of the hangars is ready for use. I'll bet that will change in a hurry. Strasser is an absolute stickler for getting as many Zeppelins as he can for attack weapons."

He fell silent. "I'm sorry. I'm talking too much."

"Isn't that why we're here?"

"You're right. The battleship kapitäns want airships for scouting. Strasser wants airships for bombing. Kottenhoff has put himself in the middle of all that, so things are bound to get seriously sticky, at best."

She felt a little ripple of apprehension. "And what will happen to you?"

"I am stuck, Lexie. Aircrew service in the Airship Division is supposed to be volunteer, but I was ordered to join. I don't know of anyone unvolunteering, but it would be a calamity. Aside from the assumption of cowardice – and I don't think I'm a coward – my naval service would be in the trash bin. Third officer, perhaps, on a fleet coaling vessel?"

I've never heard him talk this way. A chill rippled across her shoulders. "I'm sure everything will work, out, Peter." *But I'm not sure at all.*

"You haven't told me how you feel about all this."

She stared out to sea. *How* do *I feel about Admiral Kottenhoff's demands? I only know how I feel toward, you, Peter.* "Like you," she finally managed, "I'm only following orders."

"But you really don't have to. You're not in the navy. You could simply change jobs."

"Would you want me to?"

"That would be up to you, not me."

"But would *you* want me to?"

"We would find ways to see each other."

"Well, we have a way to see each other now, Peter. I wouldn't want to change that."

"Even if it were to get you into serious trouble?"

"Even if."

He slipped an arm around her shoulders. *Oh, God,* she prayed, *let him kiss me before I embarrass myself and throw my arms around him.*

"Lexie –" He swung her toward him, drew her close and kissed her so intently she was gasping when they parted.

"I think I love you, Lexie," he whispered.

" I *know* I love you, Peter."

Then she felt a stab of apprehension. *Am I crazy? I'm in love with an officer who is not only a confidential informant for an out-of-favor admiral. He is also sure to be assigned to an airship combat crew, one of the navy's most dangerous assignments.*

17.

Hands clasped behind his back, Fregattenkapitän Peter Strasser, the Airship Division's Kommandant, paced back and forth across the front of the big barnlike assembly room. Goatee jutting forward, eyes fiery, he turned to face his audience. He was fuming.

Peter felt what surely they all felt – shock at Strasser's frustration to the point of venting in front of his personnel.

"Finally," Strasser said after a pause for breath, "We are about to have a Zeppelin permanently based here at Nordholz. And in two weeks' time, October 14 to be exact, this will be the new headquarters of the Airship Division."

""But," Strasser pressed on, "The twin revolving 'Hertha' sheds still lack one of their doors. The 'Nora' and 'Hindenburg' sheds will not be of use until January. And now, here at what is about to become the heart of the Airship Division, we will have one airship. One. And which is it? That dated workhorse, L-3, and that one is here temporarily, for only two months. The new L-4 has already been assigned – not here but to Fuhlsbüttel. L-5 is to be delivered there, also. With luck, we will accept delivery of L-6 here in November. So a month from now – three months into the war – the headquarters base of the mighty Airship Division will have all of two – count them, gentlemen – two Zeppelins, and one of them temporary."

He rammed his hands to his hips and thrust his head forward, a little rooster of a man who electrified the room.

"Any questions?"

More of a challenge than a request, Peter felt. Who would have the nerve to –?

"With all due respect, Herr Fregattenkapitän?"

Peter craned his neck to see who had the temerity to toss a question at this fire breather. Good Lord, it was none other than Kapitänleutnant Hans Fritz, back in command of L-3 after Hugo Kellner's brief command of L-3 as a training ship. No doubt still smarting from his August 28 scouting fiasco, Fritz could be a man with guts after all. It took guts to question Strasser. Now for an explosion.

"In view of the Zeppelin production lag at the Friedrichshafen works," Fritz asked tentatively, "might the Division Kommandant consider the temporary use of Schütte-Lanz or even Parseval airships?"

"No. Not temporary. Not at all. As you are surely aware, the Schütte-Lanz design uses a laminated wood frame. With even moderate humidity, laminated wood weakens. The Schütte-Lanz is not dependable for extended combat use."

"That wasn't so bad," Peter muttered to roommate Ernst Wolff, seated to his left.

"He's not finished. Here comes the balloon puncture."

"As for the Parseval," Strasser snapped, hands still clamped on hips, "They have no framing at all. They are small, cheap, and operate at low altitudes highly susceptible to ground fire. One serious puncture of the supporting gasbag and down they go. Parsevals belong back in the last century, not in the Airship Division."

He glared around the room. "More questions?"

"If I may, Herr Fregattenkapitän?" A hesitant voice in the back of the room. Peter craned around to pick out a white-blond leutnant zur see who looked all of nineteen.

"You may," Strasser grated.

"After the British aeroplane attack on September 22 on the Düsseldorf sheds, and with Nordholz about to be Division headquarters, should we expect such an attack here?"

"We should, Leutnant, and we do. I have already ordered machine gun emplacements around the base perimeter."

He paused and again asked, "Further questions?"

No one dared.

"Very well. We proceed with patience as best we can manage. But I promise each of you, we will soon prove the military Zeppelin to be the ultimate weapon of this war." The Division commander's sharp eyes swept the room. "Dismissed!"

"I'm surprised Strasser refrained from biting off Fritz's head for that question of his," Ernst said as they emerged into early autumn's mid-morning sunlight.

Peter clapped on his visored cap. "His impatience is not with us. It's with everyone but us. With that loosely managed work force out there *still* banging away on the hangars. With the Zeppelin works for not turning out airships faster. I'm sure he's impatient with our hesitant kaiser, himself."

"Strasser at odds with the kaiser?" Ernst sounded incredulous.

"You haven't heard that rumor? Strasser intends to bomb London. It will be history making. The world's first attack on a city from the air. He's convinced Zeppelin attacks will panic the English to demand an armistice, even surrender. But the Kaiser is wobbling."

"You believe that?"

"It doesn't matter what I believe, Ernst. According to Franz, by way of his brother's call just after you left for your barracks inspection detail this morning, the kaiser seems not to believe it. He has banned any airship attacks on England."

To Peter, Strasser's performance had seemed a bit hollow. The man was, at the moment, all fire but no fuel, so to speak. Nordholz, about to become headquarters of the entire Naval Airship Division, had only a single airship on base – and that one to be here only two months. Four hangars, all still incomplete, yet with more about to go under construction. "We're not an airship field," Ernst had muttered at breakfast. "We're in the real estate development business."

For the balance of September and well into October, Peter felt Nordholz was at a standstill. The Airship Division's headquarters transfer from

Fuhlsbüttel produced a flurry of vehicles lasting only a few hours. Then the base reverted to frustrating inaction. When not attending to the launch and recovery of an occasional L-3 scouting flight, the men of the ranks were ordered to practice close order drill almost daily. Much of this, Peter knew, was the result of the assumption that enlisted ranks deteriorate through idleness. No such worry about commissioned officers. He, Franz and Ernst were mostly left to their own devices to occupy the dragging hours.

The worst part of all this idle time, he found, is it produces nothing I can report to Kottenhoff. No excuse at all to make my brief trip to the Blauer Adler – to Lexie. I could arrange to meet her just to be with her. But her drive to the inn from Kiel and back is a two-day grind. But God, I would love to see her... to hold her –

Franz burst into their room. "Off your arse, Reinhart. Time for an Officers Club beer."

"A beer." Peter dragged himself off his bunk. "Some way to fight a war."

Then, in mid-October, Peter "lucked out," as Franz put it, with an assignment to an L-3 scouting flight. Peter wasn't sure whether that was good luck or bad. Yet, Peter recalled, Fritz had mustered the courage to confront volcanic Strasser at that September meeting.

At any rate, this flight with blond, narrow-faced Fritz in command, grim and apparently resolute, appeared to Peter as an effort on Fritz's part to put the dismal August 28 performance well behind him.

"Look sharp, Leutnant," he barked at Peter just before liftoff. "I do not need to find your eyes anywhere but on the sea. Not only to the west. The sea all around us, understand?"

"Perfectly, Kapitänleutnant." Peter understood more than that simple order. He realized all his navigation training had been pushed aside. Airship commanders had urged the powers-that-be to let them handle the navigation. What they needed were observers armed with powerful binoculars and the stamina to spend an entire patrol staring into the monotonous expanse of the open sea. No longer – so went the assumption – would British warships be able to slip in close enough to bombard coastal targets. "The lesson of August 28," Franz's Berlin brother had termed it in a recent phone call.

By early evening, L-3 settled back into Nordholz, its control gondola and engine gondola crews shivering from nine hours in the damp North Sea air. Peter's eyes felt they would pop right out of his head if he had to stare at empty water one more minute. He had seen nothing, nothing at all.

"Did either of you check the bulletin board this morning?" Peter asked Ernst and Franz as they walked toward the Officers Mess.

"There's never anything on it worth reading." Franz raised his collar against the chilly November wind.

"There is today. The full report of that October 25 scouting flight we heard was such a fiasco.

"What about it? Ernst asked.

"It was a mess. L-4's this time, flying out of Fuhlsbüttel. Rain, fog. So they came back from the Frisians reporting nothing."

"We heard they missed some British ships south of the Helgoland Bight," Ernst reminded him, "So what's new in the report this morning?"

"What's new is a German intelligence report. The ships L-4 missed spotting were carrying seaplanes for a raid on airship hangars they thought were at Cuxhaven. A rain storm kept them from taking off, so the whole thing was a bust."

"Hangars at Cuxhaven?" Franz laughed. "It would have been a bust even if they had taken off."

"Not funny," Ernst snapped. "I'd bet a month's pay the hangars they were after are right in front of us. We are already a target while we sit here waiting to join the war."

"Not exactly waiting," Peter reminded them. "We've all seen the machine gun emplacements out there around the base."

"And they, too, sit and wait. Sit and wait."

"Maybe we shouldn't do so much complaining, Franz," Peter cautioned. "I'm sure a couple million poor bastards slogging through French and Russian mud would sell their souls to trade places with us. 'Home before the leaves fall,' but the leaves have already fallen."

"And the only ones returning home are the dead," Ernst muttered.

Silence. Then Peter heard a distant drumming. "That can't be L-3 back so soon."

Franz peered south then shrugged. "Looks like L-3."

Peter squinted against the cold morning sun. "Except for the tail assembly, Franz. Freidrichshafen has dropped the box kite idea for straight up-and-down rudders and horizontal stabilizers."

Then it hit him. "That has to be L-6. More than two months into the war, gentlemen, and we are finally getting our first new airship."

18.

"A truly lovely place you have, Herr Admiral."

Kottenhoff watched Max Moellendorf's sharp little eyes in that oddly boyish face flit along the shelves of leather bound books, the library's dark paneling, the crackling fireplace. Then back to the focal point of the sitting area: the exquisite model of the battleship *Deutschland*. "A lovely place indeed."

"Thanks, as a matter of fact, to my late wife, Frau Kottenhoff. This home was in her family for generations. She was the remaining survivor, so when her mother passed on…"

Why am I telling Moellendorf this, a man I've met under less than auspicious circumstances? An automobile collision. Then only once since that clattering encounter, when Moellendorf realized we share a "common interest."

He focused on the little smile that dimpled the man's plump cheeks. Might he think I am explaining how a low-ranking konteradmiral can afford such accommodations?

"It is a strain sometimes, to keep the place at peak operating order." Again, he paused. Might Moellendorf mistake that as a hint for some sort of financial accommodation? "But," Kottenhoff quickly added, "Albert is a gem, and with Clara in the kitchen and Eva, my housemaid, we manage." Shut up, you old fool. The novelty of having a guest is prompting me to babble.

Moellendorf smiled and raised his eyebrows expectantly, an apparent invitation to Kottenhoff to continue his prattling. A moment of awkward silence was broken by Albert's entrance. His skinny hip nudged the library door, and then he swung his laden silver tray inward.

"Ah, Dornkaat," Kottenhoff gushed. "To your liking, I know, Herr Moellendorf."

"Max, Herr Admiral. Please."

Kottenhoff ignored that. I'm not on a level with the aristocratic "Monokelfritzen," Herr Moellendorf, but though you are a pleasant fellow, I still do not know you well enough for first name relationship. And there is no chance in hell you will ever be invited to call me Erwin.

In his gray tweed trousers and white shirt, buttoned at the neck this evening, Albert set the tray on the low table near the ship model.

"Thank you, Albert. You may retire, if you wish. I will see my guest out."

Albert bowed slightly. "Thank you, Herr Admiral. Goodnight, gentlemen."

Kottenhoff poured a moderate tipple into each of the crystal snifters. Moellendorf raised his in a little salute. "To an officer of resolve."

"Thank you," Kottenhoff nodded "My best wishes to you this Christmas season."

Together they swirled the brandy, sniffed its bouquet, sipped. Kottenhoff kept his eyes on Moellendorf. That we share concern over the airship's future in the navy seems quite a coincidence after our "coming together" by accident. Accident? Hell, it must have been planned! This man is one crafty son of a bitch. No wonder Otto was so guarded in what he told Alexia about Moellendorf. Yet Otto did tell her the man was what he said he was, an industrial consultant.

And now, Kottenhoff thought, here on this chilly mid-December evening sits Herr Max Moellendorf eagerly awaiting whatever it is I am about to reveal. Should I go ahead with this? I am about to hand him what could put the torch to what's left of my career. Yet, if he does what he claims he can do...

Kottenhoff turned to pick up an unsealed envelope from the desk behind him and handed it to Moellendorf. The self-styled industrial consultant looked at him, eyes questioning.

"Yes, yes. Open it."

Moellendorf perused the two hand-written sheets, nodded, refolded them carefully and tucked the envelope into a pocket of his green corduroy jacket.

"Written on a typewriter. Good."

"No handwriting. I cannot take that risk."

"But have you not taken the risk of including in our arrangement whoever transcribed these notes?"

"I trust that person completely."

"I meant the risk to that person."

I've put Alexia at such risk already, Kottenhoff realized, how can this make it any worse? Impassively, he sipped his brandy.

"So," Moellendorf settled back in the overstuffed leather armchair, legs comfortably crossed. "The power now is a mere fregattenkapitän named Strasser. I've seen his picture. A small man with big ambition. Now at Nordholz with three Zeppelins, but more coming. All of L-3 class, though, with only a new tail design. And he is hell-bent on bombing England."

"Impressive. You are quick at absorbing details."

"I have to be. Documents on desks are not always so conveniently handed to me."

He chuckled, took a long drag of his brandy. "In fact, I've made something of an art of reading upside down."

A little chill skittered across Kottenhoff's shoulders. Just who were this man's clients? God forbid, am I making a tragic mistake here?

Moellendorf appeared to sense his discomfort. "Has it struck you, Herr Admiral, that the British have tried – and apparently failed to this point –" He chuckled. "–have tried to demonstrate just how vulnerable our airships are on the ground?"

"You refer, I assume, to the several attacks on our airship fields, attacks by British aircraft based in Belgium?"

"Specifically September 22, when a lone British aeroplane dropped two bombs on the Düsseldorf Zeppelin sheds. Bombs that fortunately did not explode."

"Certainly I'm aware of that attack on the Dusseldorf installation – and you surely are aware of the second attack there October 8. Again a single aeroplane, but more effective this time. Its lone bomb did explode and destroyed a Zeppelin that had just been delivered."

"The L-9, to be exact, Herr Admiral. So the British have realized airships make tempting targets on the ground. Clumsy elephants at tether. But the Englanders are not yet overly adept at such hit-and-flee tactics, are they? The November 21 attack on the Zeppelin works at Friedrichshafen? Good target selection, but again, just one British Avro biplane. Flying out of France, this time. Only two small bombs. One new Zeppelin destroyed by a lucky hit. However, that appears to have been no deterrence to the Zeppelin program. I have heard bits and pieces of a report that the Count is already working on an improved design. I believe it is called the L-10 class. More hydrogen, more horsepower."

Rolling the brandy snifter between his palms, Kottenhoff studied his partner in this risky liaison of theirs. For a non-military businessman, Moellendorf seemed exceptionally well informed.

Moellendorf appeared to read his mind. "I have many contacts, Herr Admiral, all in my line of work."

Kottenhoff paused. *I hope to hell all those contacts are on the east side of the North Sea.* "The point," Kottenhoff said, "is what happens to the airship program when the British finally discover how to go about bombing the bases with real effect."

"Precisely, Admiral."

Ah, there goes the honorary "Herr," Kottenhoff noted.

"Even bumbling around through lousy weather," Moellendorf went on, "three aeroplanes and fewer bombs than you can count on one hand have destroyed two Zeppelins and part of their production works."

"And what do you think the British response will be if our kaiser overcomes conscience and agrees with Strasser to send our Zeppelins against England?"

"I would be on my knees with thanks I am not a Zeppelin crewman, Admiral."

"May God help us both to bring our navy's Zeppelin-dazzled fanatics to their senses."

Moellendorf raised his snifter. "Prosit, Admiral."

"Prosit." Kottenhoff suppressed a sudden chill. *If this man turns out to be a spy, that will make two of us.*

"Know what I think it is?" Franz Schuster straightened from his perusal of the Ford's engine. "Ice in the fuel line. That was a hard freeze last night."

"Sounds logical," Peter agreed. "But it's finally beginning to warm up now."

"So eventually, this cranky American wonder-wagon should start and chug its way through the condensation in the fuel line and be fit to travel."

Together they gazed across the flat expanse of Nordholz airship base.

"Ernst may be the lucky one, after all, Peter. Straining his eyes as observer on L-6 beats our spending Christmas morning here, waiting for ice to melt."

"I'm not giving up hope. Even with a late start, there will be time to make it to Hannover for Christmas dinner with my mother and her mysterious Herr von Storch. You're free to make it a party of four, Franz."

"I thank you, but I have been asked to join friends in Hamburg – if I can find a way to get there."

"You know I go right by Hamburg on my way. That's how you will get there."

Now they stood in the Nordholz motor yard waiting for the balky Ford to recover from the day-before-Christmas temperature plunge.

Franz slapped the Ford's hood. "Ernst is having all the fun this morning."

A flurry of reports from L-6 had stuttered in by Morse, the sighting of various unidentified vessels ten kilometers off shore in the Cuxhaven area.

"You sure you want to be out here in the open?" a grizzled old rating had asked when they arrived at the motor yard shortly after breakfast – a man with a grin and apparent disdain for their ranks. They disregarded the affront, and the cynic, no doubt a veteran reservist unexpectedly recalled to duty, sulked back into the motor yard shed behind them.

"Already nine in the morning and I'd hoped to be on the road an hour ago," Peter lamented.

"How about a small fire under the engine?" Franz grinned, but Peter thought he might actually be serious.

"After we splashed fuel all over the place trying to prime the carburetor? A fire? Not under my auto we don't!"

"Ach, look at that." Franz pointed northwest, toward Cuxhaven. "A damned fog bank rolling in. Sure as hell not my idea of Christmas weather."

The swirling vapor crept over Nordholz, misting their view of the hangars, the administration and operation buildings. It shrouded the base in a clammy silence that made the morning's disappointment even more depressing.

Then deep in the swirling vapor to the west, Peter detected a faint ripping sound.

"Airship engines?" Franz cupped his ear. "Circling in the fog. Maybe L-9 looking for Nordholz."

"It sounds like a single engine, not an airship's four Maybachs. It's got to be –"

"An aeroplane. And it's coming closer."

"Heading for us!"

The fog had cut visibility to a quarter kilometer. The hangars loomed as dark hulks in the ghostly white mist.

The engine yammer grew louder. Its pitch increased."

"He's diving!" Franz yelped.

To the north, they heard the sudden stutter of a machine gun on the western perimeter. Then leaping out of the mist, a biplane with floats rushed toward them. Beneath the bottom wings outboard of the clumsy pontoons, Peter spotted black objects.

"Bombs, Franz! He's carrying bombs for the Zeppelin sheds."

The seaplane raced low over the twin Hertha sheds and aimed straight for a low building some 300 meters northeast of the motor yard.

"My God!" Franz cried. "He's after the hydrogen generating plant. "There are almost a thousand cubic meters of hydrogen in there!"

Two hundred meters above the turf, the seaplane roared past them, its bulls eye cockade clearly visible aft of the empty rear cockpit. No gunner. To enable a heavier bomb load, Peter wondered? Or a show of disdain. He caught a glimpse of the helmeted pilot, crouching forward, concentrating on his target.

"There go both bombs." Franz sounded as if he were strangling.

The black missiles arched downward, sailed over the hydrogen building and slammed into the pine trees at the edge of the airship base. An instant later, a double boom jarred Peter's stomach. Against the bleak morning sky, black smoke boiled upward.

"A clean miss!" Franz whooped.

Belatedly every machine gun around the perimeter cut loose. Behind them, a bullet whined off the roof of the motor yard shed.

"We're going to get killed by our own guns," Peter gasped as they both hit the ground behind the Ford.

The aeroplane flew out of sight beyond the woods. The wild machine gun bursts stopped. In the stunned silence, they stood to peer across the field. Then they heard shouts around the field's perimeter.

"Listen to that, will you?" Franz shook his head. "Sounds like they're celebrating a victory, as if we've been saved by all that panicky shooting."

"Let's try to start this balky Ford again. If more seaplanes are on the way, there's nothing we can do about it but get out of here."

The engine chugged, choked, ran raggedly then smoothed out. Success at last.

"On our way," Peter announced. Franz jumped in beside him, and they bounced down the service lane to the connecting road to Hamburg.

Four hours later, they were to learn, L-6 with Ernst aboard and well-shaken, loomed into Nordholz from its coast patrol. Commanded this time by Kapitänleutnant Horst von Buttlar – who had been radioing warnings since 8.30 – L-6 dropped one bomb at a British seaplane carrier but missed by 30 meters. As it passed overhead, the crew of the carrier fired rifles at the Zeppelin – and missed, so the crew thought as they fired back with their new on-board machine guns.

L-6 returned to Nordholz at 13.30, her crew not proud of their missed target but jubilant the volley of rifle fire from below had also missed. Then repair crewmen found a scattering of bullet holes in the airship's big gas cells.

With L-6 damaged in battle, the smoke of British bombs lingering in the pinewoods and the machine gunners around the perimeter still peering nervously skyward, war had finally come to Nordholz.

19.

As they neared the intersection of the Cuxhaven road with the Hamburg-Hannover road, Peter glanced at his passenger. Does Franz really have friends in Hamburg, Peter wondered, or is he ashamed to admit he has no one to spend Christmas with? He never speaks of family, friends, schoolmates. Only his brother Kaspar, who – so Franz claims – is too involved in Berlin's high political circles to have Christmas with him.

Peter slowed the Ford. "You know you're welcome to stay aboard to Hannover, Franz. Come on, join my mother and me.

"Thanks, but no. My friends are waiting."

Peter pulled the Ford to the side of the road and stopped. Franz stepped down to the rough turf shoulder.

"Happy Christmas, Peter."

"And to you." Peter put the auto back in gear and turned southward. Over his shoulder, he saw Franz begin to trudge toward Hamburg.

Pushing his tough Model T to its limit through the long drag of often rough and winding roadway, Peter reached Hannover's outskirts as the sun's last rays faded into dusk. Stiff and chilled, he pulled to a stop in front of his mother's modest, out-of-place Bavarian-styled Reinhart home.

He shut off the engine. Took a long breath. *This is not going to be easy. Trying to ease Mother's endless gloom with a show of lightness is going to be as exhausting as the drive down here.* Traveling bag in hand, he crunched up the gavel walk, reached for the door handle –

The door flew open. "Peter, my Liebling!" Erika Reinhart, smiling hugely, eyes sparkling, threw her arms around her startled son.

From gloom to euphoria, he marveled. *What has happened?*

He embraced her then stood back in further surprise. Gone was the drab gray she seemed obsessed with during his stopover here on his Kiel-Nordholz trip. Now his mother wore bright blue. Pink cheeks replaced her former gray pallor. She had put on weight and no longer looked like a forlorn waif.

"A happy Christmas Eve, Peter. How wonderful to have you with us."

"But so late, Mother." *Had she said, us?*

"No matter. When you telephoned about the problem with the automobile, I decided we would forget tradition and have Christmas dinner in the evening. In wartime, everyone must adjust."

"After I called, there was an attack on Nordholz that held me up even longer."

"Attack? Oh my God, Peter! Are you all right?"

"Not a scratch, Mother. "But it was –"

"An attack on Nordholz?" A man's voice boomed from the hallway behind Erika.

"Peter, I'd like you to meet Horst von Storch. *Professor* von Storch," she added with obvious warmth.

"Come on in, Herr Leutnant," von Storch offered.

Invited into my own family's house, Peter thought, *not in resentment; in bemusement.* He stepped into the delightful aroma of Christmas dinner cooking.

"Professor?"

"Of history, Herr Leutnant. Retired last year from twenty years of teaching in Hannover. Three months of leisure were less than fulfilling, so I –"

"Now Horst is curator of our state museum," Erika interrupted.

"Assistant curator, Erika. Respectable title, but in truth, a jack of all museum trades. I'm too old to fight, so I tell myself I'm serving the Fatherland by keeping its artifacts alive."

Von Storch appeared to be in his early sixties, Peter judged. A tweedy, apple-cheeked, rotund fellow with a warm twinkle in his alert brown eyes, and a paunch that appeared to fit him comfortably.

"We were having a pre-dinner sip of sherry as you arrived, Peter – may I call you Peter? You are welcome to join us."

The professor was obviously at home here. Peter glanced at his mother. Her eyes were intent on Professor von Storch. Her mouth, so bitterly compressed when Peter had last seen her, now relaxed in a smile.

"A little sherry would be welcome," Peter agreed. "The drive from Hamburg was something of a contest."

"Contest?"

"A contest between the Ford's springs and Lower Saxony's country roads, Herr Professor."

"The attack you mentioned. Obviously you survived it unscathed."

"As did the airship base. A lone British aeroplane dropped its bombs late and blew up only a few pine trees. "If that's the best they can do, we have only to worry about our own gunners' wild shooting."

"I hope you aren't just making light of the danger for my sake."

"Not at all, Mother. That's exactly how it happened."

"My God, Peter, that's bad enough." She stepped toward the kitchen. "I had better attend to my stove. Dinner will be ready in a few minutes. Off with you, until I call."

"Let's go into the parlor, Peter. More comfortable in there by the fire."

Peter waited until he heard the clanging of pot lids, then he kept his voice low. "My mother seems much better than when I was here in June."

"Your mother is a wonderful woman, Peter, but she had lost her sense of... being needed. In truth, so had I. My wife had left me. We were two floundering souls depressed by the war when we found each other in the soothing silence of the museum's art gallery." He paused. "Enough of that. Suffice it to say we have discovered we are good for each other."

Von Storch sank into an armchair near the fire, pulled out a gnarled briar pipe and a tobacco pouch and proceeded to pack the bowl. "Sit, Peter. Tell me – if I'm not speaking out of turn – what effect do you think the airships will have on the war?"

Peter sat back and stretched his legs toward the fire's warmth. Well, that's getting right to the point, he thought. To date, if the truth were known, the airships have been floundering around the North Sea as great vantage points that weren't seeing much. But I'm not about to say that to anyone other than Admiral Kottenhoff... or Alexia.

"From several hundred or a thousand meters' altitude, we can see what no warship observer can ever see."

"With little effect on the war to date," von Storch said amiably.

A man eager to offer his own opinions, Peter decided with relief. "I'd like to hear an historian's view on the war."

"Ah, a man with depth." Was von Storch's smile a touch mocking or a compliment? "No great insights on airshipmanship?"

"All I know, Herr Professor, is what the navy wants me to know."

"All I know, Peter, is what the newspapers want me to know, but history often leads me to disturbing conclusions. And since you asked..."

He struck a match and sucked on his pipe, drew the flame into the bowl, then puffed out a cloud of bluish smoke, followed by a sigh of satisfaction.

"For one, I suspect the Army General Staff was riding a wave of optimism when war was declared against France. I can almost hear the great Moltke reminding the General Staff, "Remember, gentlemen, back in 1871, the Franco-Prussian War. France collapsed in a mere 180 days. Napoleon III lost his throne, and Germany became a united empire.' And, in truth, Peter, that was resounding success – then."

"And now?"

"Now we have a hesitant kaiser and an army that had intended to rush straight to the English Channel. But the much-maligned French forced a change of plan. The phlegmatic English stirred themselves into action. Now we have a stalemate. Fortunately, one not on our soil, thank God. On French and Belgian soil."

"Might not the stalemate give both sides time to –?"

"Come to their senses? You are a dreamer, Peter. If the men in the trenches were running the war, you could be right. But the men in Berlin, Paris and London are running the war from their desks. I'm afraid it will be long and as in all wars, the most costly casualty will be mercy."

He offered Peter a little smile, puffed in silence a moment. "You are among the fortunate ones, Peter. Lucky to rise – literally – above it all. In your truly impressive airships. Were I a young man that is the service I would choose. Away from mud and blood. Up there in clean air."

He peered at Peter expectantly. Did he await a protest against his implied denigration of the airship service?

Peter stared into the fire. Just where do I stand? I wanted sea duty, but Admiral Kottenhoff killed that hope. I'm well aware of the airship's weaknesses, but I can't help respecting the men who truly volunteered. And there is a thrill in a clear morning lift off, then soaring into the crisp air...

Professor von Storch peered at him expectantly.

"Thin air is better than thick mud," Peter finally said.

"Good man! Supported in that thin air, however, by thousands of cubic meters of hydrogen waiting for a spark to blow you into kingdom come. You have my respect, Peter, and my thanks. With the army going nowhere, we are depending on the Zeppelins to bring the English to their senses and end the war before it becomes an unstoppable cataclysm."

"The kaiser seems to be working against you, Professor, with his ban on bombing across the channel."

"Just between us, the kaiser is a soft-headed dallier. Even the children are ahead of the man. Have you heard what they are singing?" He fished a slip of paper from his vest pocket and handed it to Peter.

> Zeppelin, flieg!
> Hilf uns im Krieg...

> Fly, Zeppelin, fly!
> Help us in the war,
> Fly to England,
> England shall be destroyed with fire,
> Fly, Zeppelin!

Tight lipped, Peter handed back the paper. My God, even the children. Except for the kaiser's hesitation, the madness is complete.

"Gentlemen, dinner is ready," his mother called from the kitchen.

"Give us just a moment, Erika." von Storch called. "Peter, I have something for you."

He reached behind his chair and brought out a leather case. "Your mother tells me you are now an airship observer, and I suspect an observer can make use of this."

He handed the case to Peter. "Go on, open it."

The binoculars were new, glossy black enameled brass Leitz 7x50s. "Favorites of the U-boat service. Got them from a friend who knows the manufacturer."

"I don't know what to say, Herr Professor. Thank you seems inadequate –"

A shout rang out from the kitchen. "Peter! Horst! Enough talk. Come, eat."

"Alexia," Otto Tammler said in the doorway of their crowded kitchen, "I need you to join me in the study."

Why? Alexia wondered? She glanced at the milling guests who had wandered into the kitchen from the front room. Her mother gave her a resigned shrug. "It's all right. I already have more help here than I can use."

Isolated down the long hallway from the Christmas dinner crowd, Tammler sank into his big leather chair. Without a word, he gazed at his daughter, perched apprehensively on a ladder-back chair near his roll-top desk.

"I really should be helping in the kitchen, Pappi."

"There are already too many in the kitchen. I need to talk to you, Liebling. I have noticed one moment, you appear happy. The next, you seem troubled."

Am I that transparent, she wondered? Pappi is too perceptive. I am trapped in an obsessed admiral's effort to discredit his own navy's highest priority project, and now by my love for the admiral's leutnant assigned to discredit that project.

"When you mentioned Max Moellendorf at the factory, Alexia –"

"Only because I was curious, Pappi." I didn't fool him then, and I see by that little smile I haven't fooled him now.

"When you set your heart on a business career rather than early marriage and motherhood, your mother despaired. But I must admit I was – still am – proud of you, Alexia. I was pleased to be in a position to assist you through my friendship with Erwin Kottenhoff. Quite a long term friendship."

"Yes, Pappi. Since he was in a navy group checking into the factory's making tools for ships' machine shops."

"You do have an impressive memory, Daughter."

"I thank you, Pappi." And I wonder where you are heading with this.

"An impressive memory and an impressive woman. I would hate to see such promise run aground."

She stared at him.

"There are rumors, Alexia. I know Max Moellendorf as an opportunist. An ingratiating man, but no less dedicated to whatever client he happens to be serving."

"What rumors?"

"Surely you are aware of the admiral's recent history, bordering, I am told, on insubordination. You must know he was given his current post in order to – well, frankly, to isolate him, yet leave him a degree of dignity."

"The rumors, Pappi?"

"You're forcing me into a corner, Alexia."

Now she smiled. "But you built the corner."

He laughed. "So I did. So I did. The rumor that reached me through another friend in Naval Appropriations is that on the face of it, Erwin has desisted from his anti-Zeppelin fomenting. But, so said my contact, he has found another way to express his views. And when you mentioned Moellendorf… I must tell you, I'm no longer entirely comfortable about your working in that office."

"But, Pappi, you got me there. You pulled the strings with the admiral."

"I believed the admiral had learned his lesson and accepted his new station as a military bureaucrat in a non-critical backwater assignment. Please tell me, Liebling, that you are not part of this rumored –"

"So there you two are!" Tall, slender Ingrid Tammler burst out in the study's doorway. "We are about to eat."

Alexia jumped to her feet. "I'm so sorry, Mother. Here, let me take that tray."

She whisked the silver platter of bread and cheeses from Ingrid's hands and strode into the gathering crowd in the dining room. "Oh, Cousin Winifred. What a lovely gown. And Herr Graeber. How nice of you to join us."

In his shadowed library with only the fire for company, Erwin Kottenhoff toyed with the Christmas dinner Albert had wheeled in on the creaking teacart. Since Gretchen died, I hate eating alone in that drafty dining room. I never noticed its discomfort until she was gone. At least in here the fire is a touch of life.

He picked up his fork and toyed with the chestnut and apple stuffing. This bleak Christmas day, I almost asked Albert to join me. Barely caught myself in time. One does not dine with one's servants. Anyway, I need this time to think, to think about Otto Tammler's disturbing phone call three days ago:

"My apologies for this intrusion, Erwin," Tammler had said, "but I know you will want to be aware of certain... uh, rumors that have reached me."

Kottenhoff's heart had thudded almost audibly. Rumors?

"As a friend, I implore you to be most careful."

"With whom, Otto?"

Tammler hesitated, cleared his throat. "With anyone you deal with concerning... ah, sensitive matters, Erwin."

"Specifically?"

"That's the problem. Only the name Moellendorf has been mentioned, but with no particular reference."

Kottenhoff pondered. Might this cryptic conversation have been instigated by my own request to Alexia to subtly probe her father's knowledge of the too-personable "industrial relations" expert?

His tension eased, but only a degree. "Your concern is appreciated, Otto. And noted. My best wishes to you and your family this season, especially to my admirable assistant, Alexia. She is a gem."

"Ingrid and I are very proud of our daughter, Erwin. We would not –" Again, a hesitation. "We would not want her caught up in any –"

"I understand your concern, Otto."

But now my concern is just how much you – and God knows who else – have heard about this game of mine.

The phone conversation had ended amicably, but its import still reverberated here in the library's shadowed solitude this somber Christmas day.

20.

At the entrance to the assembly room, Franz craned forward to concentrate on the bulletin board.

"'January 10, 1915: Air attacks on England approved by the Supreme Warlord,'" he read aloud, and then grinned at Peter and Ernst behind him. "It's official at last." He turned back to the notice. "'Targets not to be attacked in London but rather docks and military establishments in the lower Thames and on the English coast.'"

"Not so easy to find in the dark."

"The coast is, Peter. At least our kaiser has decided to use his newest weapon to attack the English where they live."

"And that's how we will win the war."

Ernst's tone seemed a trifle sarcastic, Peter thought. "At least the children think so," he said. "'England shall be destroyed by fire.' My God, children."

"They could be a jump ahead of the 'Supreme Warlord,' Peter. You watch. The Zeppelin is going to win this war. Right, Ernst?"

Eyeing Franz with something of a supercilious smirk, Ernst stroked his little mustache, a gesture that always struck Peter as an affectation. Then he shrugged. "The Zeppelin is going to be in this war, Franz. That's all I'm sure of."

In pale morning sunlight, they strode toward the Officers Mess building. To Peter, the crisp air seemed to crackle with intensity. *The long wait is over. The destiny – or disaster? – of Graf von Zeppelin's aerial weapon is about to be decided, and I'm caught in the middle. I can't go into combat hoping for failure, but I'm here because the admiral is expecting failure.*

"Day or night?" Franz wondered.

"What?"

"Do you think we will attack in daylight or at night?"

"Haven't you been listening to Strasser's endless lectures?" Peter asked. "He plans to approach the English coast in daylight to locate coastal targets. As evening falls, we attack. Then we escape in the darkness, making it hard for defensive gunfire and any enemy aircraft to find us."

"You think they have any aeroplanes that can reach us?"

"At three thousand meters, Franz?" Ernst said. "So far, some low-flying airships have been brought down by ground fire. But not a single one flying low or high has been hit by enemy aircraft. Besides, haven't we already seen that rifle and machine gun bullets simply punch little holes in the gas cells? Most can be patched in flight. That's why the crews include sail makers. Right, Peter?"

"Everybody says it would take hundreds of bullet holes in the gas cells to bring down a Zeppelin. About Franz's wondering if any enemy aeroplane can reach us at three thousand meters, though, are we forgetting about the Fokker Eindecker? Its service ceiling is five hundred meters higher than that, well above that of L-3 class airships."

"But the Eindecker is ours, Peter. You think the English have a designer equal to Anthony Fokker?"

"I'm saying underestimating the enemy can be fatal, Ernst."

"Well, that's a gloomy outlook in the face of the go-ahead from the chief of naval staff. You are an enigma, Peter. I'm never quite sure of what you are really thinking."

"I'm thinking of breakfast." *An enigma? You're too damned perceptive, Ernst. Where* does *my loyalty lie now? To Konteradmiral Kottenhoff who sent me to help him prove the airship program is a waste of navy funds? Or to my fellow Zeppelin crewmembers? Those scouting missions haven't been much of a challenge. When I'm up there in a gasbag with anti-aircraft shells exploding, what then?*

* * *

"What irony!" Ernst blurted on a blustery January 13. "The kaiser makes the big decision three days ago, then the weather turns rotten, and now Strasser is off somewhere on an inspection tour."

He banged down his coffee cup hard enough to turn heads in the officers' mess.

"At this rate," he fumed, "we'll all be pulling inspection tours – like Franz this morning, checking the crew checking the engines on L-5. Make-work."

Peter shrugged. "Strasser's off touring bases, but he did leave Kapitänleutnant Mathy in charge while he's gone, and Mathy's not noted for patience."

"Not noted for patience on destroyers, Peter. He's been in the airship service exactly three days. Talk about –"

"Word is he ranked tops in the airship commander course – which he took while he was still a destroyer kapitän. And he's supposed to have a gift for accurate navigation."

"A destroyer man, for God's sake."

"Keep your voice down, Ernst. He's sitting right over there."

Heinrich Mathy, a crease of extreme concentration centered between his arched brows, breakfasted alone in a nearby corner. Looking older than his 31 years, he seemed to be searching distant horizons even as he absently set down his coffee mug.

"If you were Mathy," Ernst asked in a lower voice, "what would you be thinking at this moment?"

"If I were suddenly a temporary commander of the Airship Division, now with Zeppelins at every base at my disposal, I would be thinking God was telling me something."

"Ah, the damned weather."

"Precisely."

At that moment, a slim patch of sunlight blazed across the floor planking near the door. They both swung toward Heinrich Mathy. Abruptly on his feet, the temporary commander of airships rushed out the doorway and raced into the brightening morning.

"Now," Ernst said, punching Peter's arm, "something is going to happen."

For an airship base suddenly coming to life, it happened with lightning speed. Before noon, L-5 and L-6 rose steeply out of Nordholz into a wintry sky still struggling to clear. Mathy rode L-5's control gondola, not only as airship kommandant but also as acting Kommandant of the entire Airship Division. By now, word had reached every man on the base – from headquarters know-it-alls to the lowest ranking ground handler – L-5 and L-6 were headed west to join the Airship Division's first attack on England.

"Can you believe this?" Ernst, hands on hips, head jutted forward, stared westward as the drone of Maybach engines dissolved in the distance. "Franz lucks out just because he was already in the L-5 engine gondola on that damned make-work inspection!" He shook his head in disgust. "The first raid on England, and he's the one who gets to be a part of history."

"Oh, shut up, Ernst." Peter had heard enough of his nattering for one morning. "Let's get back to quarters. I've got a report to write on my tour yesterday of Nordholz anti-aircraft defenses."

"Another make-work project," Ernst griped as their boots crunched the wintery stubble on their way to the housing and administration complex.

"It beats freezing in the gondola on a raw day like this one."

"You're not exactly a tiger of the air, are you?"

"Not in an open gondola in mid-winter." Not in a hydrogen-filled flying target at all, Peter told himself. Yet had he not enrolled in the Naval Academy pledging to defend the Fatherland? Might he be the only Zeppelin "volunteer" faced with this gnawing uncertainty?

"Lucky Franz," Ernst muttered. "He won't be back until tonight, and what a story he'll have to tell."

But "lucky" Franz was back by mid-afternoon. To the west, the rumble of engines preceded the pair of airships looming through the light rain that now misted Nordholz. After the two big airships had been secured by their swarm of ground handlers, Franz emerged with L-5's debarking crew. Still shivering from the cold air at altitude, he was the picture of dejection.

"Right on schedule," he blurted, "over the offshore islands, L-3 and L-4 flying out of Fuhlsbüttel joined us, and we all headed for England. A pretty damned impressive sight – four Zepps with four bomb loads about to take the war smack into the enemy's homeland."

"But..." Ernst put in. "There has to be a 'but.' You're back much too early to have made a round trip to the English coast."

Franz nodded. "*But* we suddenly flew into some of the worst rain I've ever seen. A drenching so damned heavy it actually began to weigh us down. Mathy had no choice. We dumped all water ballast as we turned back, engines at full blast to get us some altitude. So our very first try at bombing England turns out to be a complete bust."

He wrapped his arms around himself and shuddered. "Damn, I need some hot coffee – or better yet, a good stiff drink."

Five days later, Peter found himself temporarily assigned as observer on what now was to be the first naval Zeppelin attack on England. Something of a shock, but undeniably thrilling, he had to admit to himself moments after the 09.30 lift off. Thank God I wore a full uniform under all this sheepskin. It is below freezing, and we've just begun to climb. All those hours of navigation training, and here I am as an observer. The airship kommandants wanted to keep navigation to themselves and they got their way. I hope our Kommandant is better at it than Hugo Kellner was.

He thought back to the flight plan detailed at the morning assembly. Thirty-three hours in this open gondola with a windscreen forward only. It will take a week to thaw out. A few hammocks slung along the hull's catwalk for relief of the rudder and elevator men. The rest of us?

Peter took a long look at the crowded control section of the gondola. Seven of us in here. Airship Kommandant Oberleutnant zur See von Buttlar, his executive officer, the rudder and elevator men, a radio operator crammed back here on the starboard side against the radio compartment bulkhead. Then me – and our revved up passenger: Airship Division Kommandant Strasser himself. I wonder how von Buttlar feels with Strasser hanging over his shoulder?

Ten 50-kilo high explosive bombs and 12 incendiaries back there in the bomb room. Eighteen gas cells full of hydrogen overhead... Target: the dock facilities east of London, on the River Thames.

Portside, aft of the elevator man, Peter raised his prized Leitz binoculars and began his hours of sweeping the misty horizon.

As L-6 left the Weser estuary behind and bore out to sea to parallel the Frisians west-southwestward at its unimpressive 45-knot cruising speed, Peter checked his watch. Only 11.15. A quarter hour ago, L-3 and L-4 were scheduled to have lifted out of Fuhlsbüttel to attack military installations along Britain's River Humber.

England shall be destroyed by fire? From three airships? This was the most formidable force two airship bases could muster for this history-making first attack on the enemy's homeland? High hopes in low numbers.

He crossed the narrow gondola. Time to continue his watch on the starboard side.

At 14.25 hours, just short of the sprawling Dutch island of Terschelling, he noticed what seemed to be a wave of consternation forward. Strasser shouted at von Buttlar as von Buttlar grabbed the speaking tube. Then Peter heard a lessening of engine noise, and he could see the aft starboard propeller on its spindly outrigger lose revolutions until it "windmilled" uselessly in the slipstream.

The elevator man shouted at him, "Port engine in our aft compartment just broke its crankshaft!" Forward, Strasser was throwing a tantrum. Von Buttlar shrugged and called an order to the rudder man. The airship's huge nose swung ponderously to port. They were coming about in an ignominious return to Nordholz.

Though he would never admit it to Franz, Ernst, anyone – well, perhaps one day to Alexia – Peter felt a surge of relief. Then, to his surprise, a pang of disappointment. Surely, that could be no more than a reaction to the obvious letdown that swept the whole gondola crew. A history-making opportunity had just dissolved in the clank of a failing engine part.

A reprieve from the inevitable, Peter told himself.

Five hours later, the return of L-6 to Nordholz in the early evening bitterly disappointed the entire cadre of the big airship base. The letdown became even more dismal when word came from Fuhlsbüttel of the successes of the other two Zeppelins assigned to that first attack on England. L-3 had dropped its bomb load across Great Yarmouth. "A far cry from installations along the Thames," Ernst pointed out. "Great Yarmouth is at least 150 kilometers north of London."

"It's still England," Franz said, shouldering into his greatcoat for the walk to dinner.

"And better than L-4," Peter added sarcastically. "Its kommandant admits he was totally lost, but did drop his bomb load on what he called "a big city."

Several days later, English newspapers available at Nordholz revealed – to Strasser's outspoken consternation – that L-4 had actually bombed the small village of King's Lynn a good 90 kilometers from where the kommandant thought he was. His seven explosive bombs and six incendiaries smashed several homes and killed a woman and a small boy.

"Three Zeppelins, 44 crewmembers and 58 bombs destroy a woman and a boy," Peter muttered to Ernst, as he handed over the paper.

"But the general staff assures us we have put the fear of God into the British."

"You think they will just sit tight and shiver?" Only God knew, Peter realized, what awaited the next Zeppelin attack – and all those Strasser planned in the uncertain future.

At 1,000 meters altitude in the late morning of January 23, slipstream rushed through L-5's open control gondola cold enough to make Peter's temples throb. With a mere 15-minute notice, he had been assigned to pink-cheeked, youthful Kapitänleutnant Klaus Hirsch's patrol flight when the crew's observer had suddenly taken ill just before liftoff.

I'm the stranger on the crew. Again, the only name I know is the kommandant's. Everyone else is just a face. Another sullen winter day. Another routine patrol, this one off the Denmark coast beneath a solid overcast.

Routine until the radio operator, who looked like an over-eager schoolboy, abruptly craned over his work shelf. He slapped a hand to his headset then scrawled on his message pad. He ripped it loose and handed it to the hawk-faced executive officer. The exec scanned it and rushed forward to hand it to Kapitänleutnant Hirsch. The kommandant thrust the message back to the exec and nodded to Peter standing on the portside of the gondola near the engine compartment bulkhead. The exec stepped aft and handed the message to Peter.

Am in action with battle cruiser squadron, 109 at 7. Am steering SSE 1/4S Hipper

A message from the kommandant of the High Fleet's scouting forces – Konteradmiral Franz Hipper himself! The position code, Peter noted, put Admiral Hipper's group some 200 kilometers west northwest of

Helgoland Island, in the area of Dogger Bank, an immense subsurface sandbar halfway between Denmark and England.

"The kommandant orders you to keep a sharp eye to the southwest, Reinhart," the executive officer shouted over the engine roar and the buffeting slipstream. His spade beard bobbed up and down in excitement. "You be damned alert, you hear me? We're about to be the first Zeppelin ever in a big battle at sea." He whirled around and rushed back to his station forward, not an easy feat in the middle of L-5's abrupt swerve to port.

Peter glued his binoculars on the gray horizon. Every man in the crowded gondola peered ahead. Nothing. Peter scanned his binoculars on the northwest horizon. Long minutes crept by. Nothing. Then he carefully refined the focus.

'Smoke, Herr Kommandant," he shouted. "Twenty degrees to port." He centered the glasses on the smoke smear as it grew larger. With L-5's top speed approach, Peter began to make out details of the burning ship's superstructure. "Battle cruiser," he called out. Then, to his dismay, "German!" A German battle cruiser, slowly underway but in serious trouble with thick smoke pouring from the aft section.

Where in hell is the rest of Hipper's force, Peter wondered? He rushed starboard, aimed the binoculars toward the coast. "Three more battle cruisers, four light cruisers and a destroyer screen," he called. "All German." And all carving wakes *away* from the limping German ship below. My God, they're running! Why in hell is Hipper running? He's still got seven cruisers.

Rushing back to portside, Peter swept the horizon from the north to the west – There! Directly west. "Four...No, five big battle cruisers, British silhouettes. Bearing about two-seventy," he called.

Hirsch nodded but seemed hesitant about what to do now. No course change?

Bomb the damned ships rushing toward the burning German cruiser, Peter urged silently. Hirsch and the exec were engrossed in what looked like a disagreement

Then, fifty meters dead ahead of L-5, a shell burst. My God, we're under fire. As they flew through the black smudge, Peter could smell the acrid aftermath.

Hirsch shouted into the speaking tube's funnel. Peter heard the forward engine rev to full power.

"Climb!" Hirsch shouted to the seaman at the elevator wheel.

The Zeppelin nosed steeply upward. He scrambled for balance, banged his elbow on the gondola's rim. Two more shell bursts, a hundred meters to port. Missed us again. He shuddered. Getting shot at makes you want to dive to the floor and curl into a ball. Getting missed, though... Now I feel, hell, exhilarated!

At 2,000 meters, L-5 leveled off and swung southeast, away from the melee below.

Apparently, Hirsch had decided to cover Hipper's retreat. There would be no attempt to bomb the aggressive English ships.

Skirting the ragged underside of a cloud layer, L-5 left the scene of what was to become known as the Battle of Dogger Bank. Peter kept an eye on the burning ship they had left behind. When he last centered his binoculars on that frustrating scene, he felt sick. Only smoke remained. The German battle cruiser had gone down.

He slammed his fist on the gondola's rim. What had been in Hirsch's head? He peered at the others. No man's eyes met his. The Naval Airship Division's first appearance over a sea battle had been of no consequence whatever. The return to Nordholz was without spirit.

Hours later, Peter hovered over his third mug of coffee in the Officers' Club, still trying to shake his numbing chill.

"So if you had been kommandant," Ernst pressed, "what would you have done?"

Peter banged down his mug. "At the absolute least, I would have shadowed the British force and radioed reports of its positions. That would have been worth a lot more than trailing along behind a retreat."

"You sound as frustrated as Strasser must be."

"Yes, I know I do," Peter agreed. "And, by God, I am!"

21.

As if God had sided with the English during the Airship Division's miserable performances, the worst of winter descended upon Northern Germany in general, and Nordholz in particular. Whipping wind – "Cold as a witch's breast," said Franz – blasted the airfield's snow-dusted sand into eddies that stung unprotected faces. Ground personnel slammed hangar doors tight, yet wind-driven grit penetrated everywhere. Idle flight crews were put to work cleaning and sweeping. Their officers sulked in the Officers Club.

In this period of inactivity, off-base passes were generously granted. On a bleak mid-February day with low-hanging clouds as gray as dirty sheets, Peter cranked the chilled Ford then bounced north on the winding roadway out of Nordholz toward the Hamburg-Cuxhaven road. Alexia, a note of urgency in her voice, had telephoned from Kiel. They must meet at the Blauer Adler Inn this weekend. He would have gone to almost any extreme to wangle a pass, but due to the pall of inactivity still gripping Nordholz, the pass was promptly granted

He was elated to be on his way to the Blue Eagle again and reveled in the freedom of the open road – except for two concerns: the strange note of apprehension in Alexia's voice, and – as he scanned the blackening horizon to the west – the damned weather.

No sun, bone-aching cold… And now, with sudden intensity, snow. Not the lazy flakes of a short-lived flurry. This was the fine, wind-driven stuff than warns of a blizzard in the offing. And maybe not so far off. In the next fifteen minutes, the roadway was blanketed and visibility closed in to only a few yards through the swirling screen that seemed intent on burying him out here in the frigid farm fields. Grimly now, he pushed the Ford on, praying it would not slither off the roadway into a waiting ditch.

Then to his relief, the intersection with the Hamburg-Cuxhaven road loomed out of the storm. He whirled the wheel left and rolled onto the far smoother roadway. Visibility, though, did not improve, and he swerved just in time to miss ramming an army truck rumbling past in the opposite direction. He gasped in surprise, tightened his grip on the steering wheel and craned forward to concentrate on the challenge of staying in his lane when he could barely see the road at all.

Tense minutes later, he squinted through the snow screen expecting to spot the blue and white sign of the inn. Nothing he could make out along the roadside looked familiar. Could he have already passed the inn's entrance? Might this road somehow be the wrong one entirely? Some by-road he hadn't noticed on his eager drives up –

There it was, the Blauer Adler's carved eagle, wings outspread in welcome. Thank God. He swung into the parking area, already submerged ankle-deep in snow. The young parking valet, his collar turned up and his knit cap pulled down, ducked under the Ford's raised top.

"Some afternoon, Herr Leutnant. Another hour of this stuff and I don't think you can make it out of here."

"Any chance of getting this machine under cover?"

"We do have covered parking for long term guests, and a couple are open. I'll see what I can do."

"That will be most helpful – and appreciated." He almost dreaded his next question. "Have you noticed whether a young woman has arrived? Driving a –"

"Bright blue Panhard? Who wouldn't notice that? She pulled in just before the snow began." He had to shout the last few words. Peter was already flying up the entrance steps, stamping snow from his boots.

She stood just inside the double doors, her hair haloed by the bright lighting of the registration desk across the lobby behind her. In her ankle-length dark blue dress, neatly belted at the waist, she looked every bit the serious admiral's aide – until their eyes met.

"Oh God, Peter! I've been so worried. They're predicting snow up to our knees. I was afraid you –"

He swept her into his arms, silenced her with a long kiss, not caring who in the lobby witnessed their sudden intimacy. After all, was not their cover story one of a young couple in love stealing hours together whenever Peter was granted a pass?

"Oh, I'm so glad to see you," she managed breathlessly. "I've been praying you'd come."

"You think a little blizzard could keep me away?"

She kissed him again and then reluctantly let him go. "Have you eaten?"

"I haven't even thought about eating, but now that you mention it –"

"Come. The dining room is nearly deserted but it's still open."

After the demanding drive up here, he found himself ordering a platter of Lendenbraten and dumplings.

"Only the lentil soup for you, Fraulein?" the graying, stooped waiter asked, considering Peter's contrasting order.

"Yes, just the soup. And apple juice." As their waiter returned to the kitchen, she murmured, "I'm sorry, Peter, but I'm too upset to be hungry."

"You sounded upset on the telephone. What is it, Lexie? What's happened?"

"I hope my imagination is working overtime and I got you up here for nothing, but I'm so worried, Peter."

He took her cold fingers in both his hands. "I never come up here 'for nothing.' Not since I first saw you. I would come here just to… to be with you, Lexie. But please, tell me what is so damned serious."

Her fingers tightened on his. "I have learned that Herr Moellendorf has been barred from the Naval Procurement building."

"Barred? Are you sure?"

Her eyes held his. "It was told to me in confidence?"

"By whom?"

"In confidence."

"In view of what might be about to fall in on us, Lexie, to hell with that confidence where I'm concerned. You can be certain I won't let it go a centimeter further."

She leaned close then pulled away as their waiter approached with their orders and placed them with slow precision. When he retreated again, she raised her apple juice with the fingertips of both slender hands, sipped, and set the glass down gently.

"It was Leutnant Krause," she murmured.

"The officer the admiral ordered to introduce you to me at the Yacht Club – and set this whole arrangement in motion. That Leutnant Krause?"

"Yes."

As Peter absorbed what she had just confided to him in this near-deserted dining room, he felt a flush of heat rise above his stiff uniform collar.

"You realize what this must mean, Lexie? You were under the impression Moellendorf had such a trustworthy reputation that he had access to just about any navy installation he chose to visit. And suddenly he's banned from the Procurement building – the location of Admiral Kottenhoff's office. Do you know if he has been shut out anywhere else?"

"Not that I'm aware of. What are you thinking?"

"I'm thinking it's possible somebody has knowledge of what Moellendorf's real motive may be. Or, Lexie, maybe what our admiral is up to."

She took a big swallow of her juice this time, setting down the glass with a clunk. "I assumed Herr Moelloendorf's intent was the same as the admiral's. To try to reduce appropriations to the Airship Program."

"And divert such savings where? I gather Max Moellendorf is not exactly an altruistic type. What's in it for him?"

Her eyes met his again, this time with apprehension. "Is that our real concern, Peter? Of much more concern to me is Leutnant Krause's warning. Isn't it an indication that someone--"

"That someone is talking."

"Yes. But who – and to whom? Concerning only Herr Moellendorf? Or the admiral as well. And maybe us, Peter?"

He forced a bite of his pork roast, his mind racing. "Surely Admiral Kottenhoff can't be talking. But could it be someone he works with in Appropriations? Someone he might have made curious enough to –"

"He works with me, Peter. And I can't think of anyone else in the department he has much contact with at all. He eats lunch alone. Others avoid him. All that aside, I cannot imagine the admiral making the slightest slip of the tongue that would put us in jeopardy."

"What about Moellendorf? A slip of the tongue on his part?"

She shook her head. "From what I've seen of the man, he carefully cultivates the appearance of a back-slapping, overly friendly business lightweight. But what I've heard of the man is quite different. Shrewd, perceptive. I doubt he would engage in loose talk about anything at all sensitive."

"He is perceptive – your word – but might he also be deceptive? Sent by, say, someone intent on finally sinking our admiral?"

Soup spoon poised halfway, she froze. "You sound like my father, Peter. I'll admit I hadn't thought of that."

"What about Leutnant Krause? The admiral entrusts him with an occasional chore related to what we're doing. Had him drive you to our first meeting here. Might the helpful leutnant have another master to whom he reports?"

"You will make me suspicious of everyone."

"At this point I am suspicious of everyone."

"Surely not me." She offered a hint of a smile.

"Never you, Lexie. I have much different feelings toward you."

She reached out to touch his hand. "And I, God help me, toward you." She pondered a moment. "We are considering only Kiel. What about Nordholz?"

"I keep to myself as much as possible, even concerning my two roommates. I'm certain Ernst and Franz believe my trips up here are those of a hopelessly smitten man seizing opportunities to be with the woman he loves. And," he added, looking straight into her deep green eyes, "they are right. Aside from the admiral's requirement, I am always eager to see you again."

"And even if the admiral were to abandon his obsession," she said softly, "I would still come to the Blauer Adler."

"As would I."

He had tossed off any thought of an anti-Kottenhoff informant at Nordholz, but how much did he really know about Ernst and Franz? Especially Franz. The "dueling scar" story and his brother with high connections – or so Franz claimed. Peter realized he knew almost nothing about either of his roommates.

He glanced down at his plate. "We've hardly eaten a thing. Let's hope the banning of Herr Moellendorf from your building is no more than the grating of his personality on some officer who was having a poor day."

* * *

He addressed the Lendenbraten seriously this time, and then peered through a nearby window. "I wonder if this snow will ever stop."

"Surely you don't intend to drive back to Nordholz today. The roads could be impassable. And you have yet to tell me anything I could report to the admiral."

"I thought you came up here on your own?"

"I did, but should he hear of it, I would like to be able to tell him you had information to give me."

"A cover story inside a cover story. All right. He may have gleaned some of this from newspapers anyway, but tell him navigation for attacks on England is so inaccurate, most airship kommandants who have found England at all had no idea what they were bombing. Fortunately, English defenses have been ineffective. You could add that the bombing results compared to the costs of getting those results would put any private business out of business in short order."

"That's the kind of information he delights in."

"It's the truth, Lexie. More coffee? Dessert?"

"Thank you, but I think we should check on the weather."

He signaled their waiter, settled the bill, and they returned to the lobby. Beyond its broad windows, the late afternoon had grown even darker. Now the swirl of wind-driven snow cut visibility to a few meters.

"You simply cannot drive in this, Peter." She sounded less than dismayed. So was he.

"I'll notify Nordholz. If the telephone lines are not down. I'm sure they will appreciate the situation."

"So do I," she said playfully. "Time to consult Helmuth."

"'Helmuth?' Oh, the desk clerk."

At Peter's request for a room, Helmuth's smile was not quite a leer, but Peter thought it came close.

"I have no luggage," he said.

"But you do have an auto we could impound in the event that you –" Now his leer became a grin. "A little joke, Leutnant. If I cannot trust an officer of the Airship Division, who can I trust? Your key, Sir. Room Four."

"Why, that rogue!" Alexia burst out when Peter joined her in the cozy lounge just off the dining room.

"Rogue?"

"You'll see."

* * *

As they walked together up the broad staircase, he felt unexpectedly awkward. Then he found his room was next to hers. An assumption on Helmuth's part? But logical, was it not, in view of the story they had settled on from their very first meeting here.

And now what? They stopped at the door to her room. He took her hands in his. "Good night, Lexie," he said abruptly. Then, to his own surprise, he kissed her only lightly, and on the cheek.

Her expression seemed to be one of... bemusement? Then she squeezed his hand.

"Good night, Peter. Sleep well."

He walked the few steps down the carpeted hallway to his room. That little smile.

And the unmistakable hand squeeze... What was that all about?

His quarters were larger than he had expected; the bed turned down, fresh water in the nightstand's ewer, clean towels in the nightstand rack. He pulled off his boots, loosened the top buttons of his tunic and stretched out on the bed. What a strange day this had turned out to be. Snowbound in a country inn with the love of his life in the next room...

Then he noticed the room's second door on the far side of the protruding chifforobe and realized not only were the rooms adjacent; they were also adjoining. He pondered. Then on impulse rolled off the bed, turned the door's deadbolt lock and hesitantly tried the door. It opened quietly, only to reveal another door, tightly shut of course. Double doors on adjoining rooms.

He stood there uncertainly. Should he knock? And possibly make a fool of himself when she held her silence or, worse yet, called out some crushing riposte.

False hope. Then as he started to turn away, he heard a click. The same click as his deadbolt had made. She had unlocked her door.

His heart thudded as the door slowly swung open. In a dark blue robe, neatly tied with a pink sash, she stood silent, still offering that little smile.

Behind her, shadows flickered in the darkened room.

"You have a fireplace."

"Thanks to our friend at the front desk and the fact I'm considered a frequent guest. Come in, enjoy the magic of a crackling fire on a snowy night."

"And a beautiful woman to share it with."

"Only in the eye of the beholder. I've never considered myself beautiful."

"That makes you more so." On impulse, he took her in his arms, kissed her gently then with more intensity. She pushed away and glanced down at her sash, now hanging loose.

"That's naughty, Peter."

He felt his face flush in embarrassment.

Then she pulled him close, locked her arms around him and whispered, "But I feel naughty tonight." And she began to unbutton his tunic. Suddenly they found themselves in a disrobing frenzy, giggling like children. He had never heard her laugh, really laugh, like this.

Her robe fell to the floor, then her nightgown. Her lithe nakedness glowed in the firelight, she squealed and dived for the bed to burrow beneath the down-filled comforter.

Can this really be happening? he marveled. Then he tore off the rest of his clothes and slid beneath the comforter. And she melted into his arms.

"I promised myself I would do this only with someone I loved," she whispered, her breath warming his ear. "And I have never loved anyone but you."

22.

How shocking! Alexia thought as she wrestled the unwieldy Panhard out of the inn's half-cleared parking area and skidded onto the Cuxhaven-Hamburg road. How incredibly impetuous of me. How utterly unthinkable.

But as she guided the bulky auto along the snow-blanketed roadway, she smiled. How exciting. Thrilling. What a magical night. How wonderful to wake up snuggled against Peter.

Then came the matter of returning to Kiel before dark on this dangerous driving day. "One hundred sixty kilometers at – if I'm lucky – maybe twenty-five kilometers an hour. A more than six-hour drive, Peter."

""What you're saying is you have to get an early start."

"Today of all days. I'm so sorry."

He had signaled the waiter and settled their breakfast bill.

Wearing a knowing look since they had appeared walking down the stairs arm-in-arm, Helmuth sent the parking valet into the sun-dazzled morning to bring both their autos to the entrance. Such an expeditious parting, she thought; the inn's doing, though, not Peter's. He looked as if he were eager to spend the day with her, Nordholz be damned. And what further pleasures that might have offered.

She took a curve a little too fast, recovered neatly from the skid. Keep your mind on driving, woman, not on last night. Last night... I never dreamed I could be so passionate No self-control at all. And... She smiled. It could happen again.

But the risk... A pregnancy would complicate my life beyond anything I want to face at this point. A consultation with wonderfully understanding Doktor Hoffman is a priority. From the sublime to the mundane.

Supply trucks to Nordholz had broken through the snow crust and made the road passable. The Ford slithered out of the broad ruts several times, but Peter forced the auto back on course. His mind kept returning to last night. I never dreamed such a thing could happen with prim, self-controlled Alexia Tammler. Now I know I'm in love with two women: one of them demure, reserved, devoted to her assignment; the other, capricious, adventuresome, eager to surrender to passion. Two women: Alexia and Lexie.

In the overcast early afternoon, he manhandled the skidding Model T onto the airship base. Back to reality. Nordholz is as bleak as Greenland must be. As chilling as Lexie's news of Max Moellendorf's ouster from Procurement. If she's right, someone, not a friend, knows too damned well what the admiral is up to. Who can it be? Could it lead to some kind of investigation? How far would it reach?

He turned into his parking space in the base motor yard. I should have rejected Admiral Kottenhoff's project. But how does a leutnant zur see turn down an admiral?

In Monday's blinding sunlight, Peter trudged through the snow toward the rotating hangars where he was to supervise an inspection of the hydrogen cells' fabric in L-6. "Make-work, make-work," Ernst had chanted derisively, but with persistent gusty wind, there was little to keep crews occupied other than inspections and an occasional brief North Sea scouting flight.

Peter raised his coat collar and pulled his cap low. The bitter wind burned his face. This, after a night to remember the rest of my life. Will she share that life with me? Or will it be shattered by whoever had Max Moellendorf barred from Admiral Kottenhoff's office.

Damn it. I'm right back to worrying about that. He yanked open the small access door in the double hangar's huge sliding door and stepped out of the wind.

* * *

"Now here," Franz told Peter and Ernst at dinner in early March, "is what happened to L-8. Got this from a mechanic who has a cousin stationed at Düsseldorf. On February 26, L-8 lifts out of there for England. But before reaching the North Sea, they run into headwinds that stop them dead in mid-air. Beelitz – he's the kommandant – orders a 180 and heads home. Doesn't make it. He does make it, though, into the army airship base near Ghent. Comes a break in the weather a couple days later, he tries to make a stab across the Channel to bomb Mersea Island."

Franz paused for breath. Took a quick swallow of beer.

"And?" Ernst prompted.

"And now it gets crazy. West of Ghent, Beelitz decides to check his position. Orders L-8 to fly low near Ostend – right into range of Belgian trenches they didn't know were there. L-8 is riddled with rifle and machine gun bullets. The Zepp struggles through an about-face and heads toward Düsseldorf. Beelitz dumps most of the fuel and all 70 incendiary bombs. No help. A hundred thirty kilometers short of home base, L-8 sinks to the ground and smashes into a row of poplars. The crew gets out, but the wind chews the Zepp into junk."

"'England,'" said Peter, "will be –"

"'–destroyed by fire,'" Ernst finished.

"Cynics," Franz muttered.

"Hard not to be," Ernst shrugged. "L-5 and L-6 sent from here to Fühlsbuttel. L-7 sent here from L-eipzig. L-9 due here this month. I wonder how Strasser gets anything done with all that shifting and shuffling. Think of the paperwork."

"And," Franz added, "I heard we are due to get still another Zepp in here in the next few days. Transferred from Hage. And if you believe the rumor, at Hage's request."

The transfer from Hage over on the North Sea coast near the East Frisians took place two days later. The L-3 class Zeppelin materialized out of low-lying scud, made a half circuit around Nordholz then began to settle in – crosswind.

"Why crosswind?" Peter wondered, shading his eyes against a sudden flare of sunlight.

Apparently the Zeppelin's commander had just asked himself the same question. The airship made a ponderous 45-degree adjustment and continued its descent. The dozens of ground handlers were forced to dash en masse to a newly anticipated touchdown site. With the Zeppelin finally secured, its crew debarked and pushed through the watching crowd.

Franz nudged Peter. "You see who's commanding that bumbling airship?"

Peter peered at the big kapitanleutnänt working through the crowd. Recognition dawned.

"That's Kapitanleutnänt Hugo Kellner, Franz. The airship Kommandant Ernst and I flew with on that training mission last fall."

"The arrogant kommandant you saved from a navigational fiasco."

Peter glared at him. "Where did you hear that? From Ernst?

I never told a soul about Kellner's confusion that day, Peter was certain. But Ernst had been aboard. Had he figured out what had happened?

"No, not from Ernst," Franz said. "One of the crewmen in the control gondola told me. You could have gotten Kellner a black cigar over that and given your own career a goose. Pretty damned loyal to a kommandant you had just met."

Loyal. Peter winced. I protected Kellner but kept right on serving Kottenhoff's clandestine project. How loyal is that?

Now the German Army was determined to have its try at bombing England. Four of its airships were transferred to forward bases in France and Belgium. On March 17, all four set out for London but lumbered into dense fog and failed even to find England itself. One of the ships, using a "Spähkorb," according to the intelligence report received at Nordholz, did succeed in dropping a few bombs on Calais but was damaged upon landing.

Three days later, the three remaining airships raided Paris. Ground fire downed one on the return trip. On April 13, the third of the ill-fated four was damaged by anti-aircraft fire and fatally crumpled in the ensuing forced landing. The single remaining airship of the original four Army "London bombers," a Schütte-Lanz "glue potter," was sent back to the factory for refitting.

Calamity for the army airships, Peter thought. If they had been navy airships, would Admiral Kottenhoff still be counting on me to send him reports?

"What in hell," Franz wondered when he finished reading the bulletin posted in the assembly room, "is a Spähkorb?"

"Ah, Franz," Ernst sighed as the three roommates settled into folding chairs to await Strasser's appearance. "A little more reading of technical bulletins would have told you about the army's 'spy basket.'"

"Which is?"

"Which is," Ernst said, "a little one-man observation car suspended on several hundred meters of cable below the airship. The purpose is to get an observer below a cloud layer. He identifies targets invisible to the airship above the cloud layer. The observer has a telephone to report target information up to the control gondola."

"Whew!" Franz shook his head. "Dangling at the end of a damned wire? That's a ride I wouldn't take."

"Especially when you hear the rumor they have an axe in the Zeppelin to cut the car's cable if they have to climb in a hurry. But you don't have to worry. It's an army project."

Thank God for that, Peter thought.

"Attention!" shouted an officer. With a rattle of chairs and scuffle of boots, everyone leaped to his feet as Strasser strode in. When they all were seated again, he faced them in silence, hands clasped behind his back. His periodic tours of navy airship bases had become something of routine morale boosts, but this morning he appeared grim.

"Gentlemen," he barked with a sour grimace as he began to pace. "I bring you the kaiser's latest determination of strategy concerning airship attacks on England. Namely 'Fetwa Zwei.' Effective immediately, London – with the exception of that city's docks – is no longer approved for attack."

A chorus of groans met that stunning announcement.

"We can barely find England," Peter murmured, "let alone the docks of London."

"I am pressing for clarification of this latest Fetwa," Strasser continued. "In the meantime, naval airships will concentrate on North Sea patrols with attacks on any sighted enemy vessels."

"'England shall be destroyed with fire?'" This time the sarcastic mutter came from Franz.

Konteradmiral Kottenhoff rested his elbows on his chair arms, his chin on tented fingers and regarded Alexia in the hard-backed chair facing his desk. A delicate matter, this; delicate indeed.

"I have reviewed your notes from your recent meeting with Leutnant Reinhart, for which you have my appreciation, of course. But I..." How to go about this? For an instant, I pictured her as the gawky thirteen-year-old I first met during an official tour of the Tammler factory. A girl too tall for her age, no doubt enduring taunts from her classmates. She had seemed remarkably self-assured even then. As an attractive and highly intelligent woman, she appears even more self-assured now.

"I do not intend to intrude upon your family's affairs," he said, "but I have...ah, reason to be concerned about your father's guarded reaction to your mention of Herr Moellendorf.

He watched her fingers touch her cheek and her eyes shift to the window behind him. A woman with a problem? Then she clasped her hands in her lap. Her eyes returned to his.

"May I speak frankly, Herr Admiral?"

"That is the purpose of this conversation, Alexia."

She said, "I have heard Herr Moellendorf has been banned from the building,"

Word surely gets around. "That is correct, Alexia, though I am surprised knowledge of that has reached you so quickly. What do you make of such an action?"

Her eyes never wavered. "I interpret it as a warning, Herr Admiral."

A warning. She was correct, of course. Whoever has instituted the ban against Moellendorf's presence here surely realizes such a maneuver by no means cuts off communication between us. There is the telephone, though I suspect my calls, incoming and outgoing, might now be monitored at the switchboard. There are out-of-the way restaurants and other remote meeting place possibilities. There is my home. But as a warning, I cannot deny the official action against Moellendorf has an impact.

"More than a warning, Alexia. It tells us someone is dangerously aware of what we are trying to accomplish, perhaps even how we are going about it. I can only assume that we –"

"–are being watched," she blurted, then reddened. "I'm sorry, Herr Admiral. I did not intend to –"

"Your perception is appreciated. The question is, watched by whom? Max Moellendorf's visits here should have been considered routine efforts to influence naval appropriations on behalf of whomever he represents. Nothing further. Someone has speculated or seen beyond that." He paused, stroked his sideburns with a gnarled hand. *How can I phrase what I know I must ask her?*

"You told me your father seemed distrustful of Herr Moellendorf, Alexia. Did he, by chance, express any opinion of the Naval Airship Program?"

"To my knowledge, Herr Admiral, my father has never offered any opinion of the navy's airships. Concerning the war, his sole interest is the manufacture of machine guns. Concerning me, he knows only that I am your aide. He *cannot* be the source of information on what we are involved in."

Her vehemence surprised him. He compressed his lips. *Should I remind her of my rank? No. She is a civil aide – and a personal friend.* He cleared his throat, pondered a moment.

"Sorry, Alexia. It was necessary to ask. Somewhere someone is apparently aware of what I am still trying to accomplish for the good of the navy – and the Fatherland. Such a person, or persons, can put us all in jeopardy." He held his eyes on hers. "I am counting on your excellent sense of perception. Can you think of anyone who could possibly know what we are involved in? Perhaps someone close to Reinhart at Nordholz? Might it be possible our Leutnant Reinhart has inadvertently..." He let his words trail off.

"No, Herr Admiral. It is not possible."

"You sound quite certain."

"I have discussed it with him."

"I see. And you think I may be looking too far afield? Perhaps here in Kiel there may be someone more perceptive than we realize?" Again he stroked his sideburns. "Just for conjecture, Leutnant Krause comes to mind."

"Leutnant Krause has never seemed interested in what I may be doing beyond my clerical duties here, Herr Admiral."

"A clever investigator would not." *But Krause,* Kottenhoff recalled, *was the man I appointed to introduce Alexia to Reinhart; the man I had drive her to the inn near Nordholz for Reinhart's first report.*

"No one else comes to mind, Alexia?"

"No, Herr Admiral. I am sorry."

"If anything at all pertinent to the situation does occur to you, I know you will apprise me immediately. You may return to your regular duties."

As she closed the door behind her, he stood and turned to gaze through his big window at Kiel's sprawling harbor. Problem – and my future, if I have one – unresolved.

23.

In baggy dark trousers and a black turtleneck sweater, Kottenhoff drummed the fingers of both hands on the arms of his fireside chair. Max Moellendorf had arrived, per the admiral's urgent telephone call, precisely on time at 20.00 hours on this blustery late March evening. Despite the fire's warmth, Kottenhoff suspected this would not be a cozy get-together.

Voices muttered in the hall, and then Albert appeared. "Herr Moellendorf, Sir."

"An invigorating evening, Herr Admiral," Moellendorf boomed, striding in. "Wie geht es Ihnen?"

"Disturbed, Herr Moellendorf. That's how I feel." He nodded toward the matching armchair on the other side of the low table before the fire. "Sit."

"Certainly, Herr Admiral," Moellendorf sank into the chair. "I assume this meeting is the result of the action concerning my presence in the Procurement Building." He offered a little smile.

A damned smile? "Apparently that seems to be a matter of minimum concern to you."

"But a major concern to you, Herr Admiral?"

"Absolutely. It indicates to me the disturbing fact that someone – and not a friend – has somehow discovered what we have been trying to accomplish. That, I am forced to conclude, puts what is left of my career in even more jeopardy. And I assume you face a similar dilemma."

"Do you have in mind anyone who might be this non-friend?"

Kottenhoff glared at him. "Do you?"

"You suspect me?"

"Or perhaps your client, whoever that might be. You've never had the courtesy to tell me for whom you are working."

"The only contact I have with my client is my monthly cheque, Herr Admiral."

"Then where do you apply the information I have been giving you?"

"I 'apply' it to a trusted individual with access to an influential audience."

"A trusted individual who is…?"

"Who happens to be a field correspondent for Reuter's."

"Your client is Reuter's?"

"No, Reuter's is my indirect access to a key percentage of the public."

Well, that was a revelation. Reuter's. "How trustworthy is your man?"

"He would not reveal a source even were his life to depend on it."

"And you have spoken to no one else concerning our effort?"

"No one. My word on that."

His word. The word of a professional information purveyor for hire. "I must tell you, Herr Moellendorf, I am not at all confident we should continue our arrangement."

Moellendorf chuckled. "I have the answer to that, Admiral. Our arrangement is no longer of use to me. My client has received full value and has no further need of my services. Therefore –"

"Your client. Your client. Who in hell is your client?"

Moellendorf's doughy face wore an irritating little smirk. He sat back, crossed his legs comfortably. A man at ease. "Now that my client has received major funding to proceed with development of his planned project, I see no reason why I cannot tell you that client has been Gothaer Waggonfabrik A.G."

"The seaplane maker in Gotha?"

"Richtig, Admiral. But with their new appropriation, due largely to our efforts – yours and mine – the company is developing a landplane, the Gotha G.II 'Bomb Dropper,' a very large two-engined biplane with a twenty-four meter wingspan. Five hundred kilos of bombs at twice the speed of a Zeppelin. An army crew of only three, not the Zeppelin's sixteen or so. And what the G.II will also lack will be a hull full of dangerously explosive hydrogen."

Kottenhoff stared at him. "I have put myself at risk so the army will get a contract?"

"Indirectly, Admiral. But think of it this way. The increasing interest in giant bombers may be helping your cause. Count von Zeppelin himself also seems to be concerned with his Zeppelins' limitations and is hedging his bets. I am told he will soon test fly the Zeppelin-Staaken V.G.O.I., a biwinged bomber similar to the Gotha design, but with three engines. As a point of interest, industry gossip holds that the military would abandon airship bombing in favor of the Riesenflugzeuge – the giant aeroplanes – were it not for one highly influential individual."

"Strasser."

"Precisely. Even our admirals falter in the vehemence of that remarkable airship man."

"Not this admiral."

"You are in confrontation with an unusually influential personality, Admiral. A martinet on duty, but – and this is little known – he can be ingratiating during his off-duty time, particularly with key members of the Old Guard Navy. A formidable man to oppose."

"Indeed. I am aware Zeppelin just received a major appropriation for his so-called 'height climber' Zeppelin development. But I was not aware his company has also been granted funding for development of a large bomber aeroplane."

So Magnetisch Max has used me to win funding for his client, Gothaer Waggonfabrik, Kottenhoff reflected bitterly. And Strasser remains undeterred in generating additional funds for his damned gasbags. Max wins. Strasser wins. I gain nothing and remain dangling in the cold political winds.

"Herr Moellendorf," he said, rising to his feet, "I suppose I should congratulate you for deft maneuvering. And rebuke myself for naïve expectations. Albert will see you out."

"No glass of Dornkaat tonight," Moellendorf said amiably. "I wish you well, Admiral."

"Albert will –"

"–see me out."

"Gute Nacht, Moellendorf."

* * *

"Ein verfluchter Zeppelin," Franz told Peter, "with a nachlässig crew."

They watched Kapitänleutnant Hugo Kellner's airship rise ungracefully into the calm April morning. Dead calm, though Kellner's ascent appeared to be a struggle with unfriendly elements. A cursed airship, manned by a careless crew?

Peter shaded his eyes as the Zeppelin plowed higher in its erratic climb. "How can you make that assumption?"

"One of the engine officers told me a lot of the crew is made up of men shucked off by competent kommandants. It is a dumping ground, Peter. The ship itself is a rebuilt old L-3 class, put back together after slamming the ground in a storm over at Hage."

"You're kidding me."

"No, I'm serious. Kellner's ship is a piece of flying junk with a crew of rejects. A disaster waiting to happen. "Düsseldorf gets Mathy, and we get Kellner."

With Kellner's airship finally leveling out and seeming to settle on a northwestern heading, Peter and Franz headed back to the officers' quarters and clumped upstairs.

Ernst, sprawled on his bunk and surrounded by newspapers, looked up as they walked in. "Just bought these Dutch papers. Takes a bit of work to translate, but there are some interesting revelations in there."

Franz plopped into a chair. "Such as?"

"How about this? Mathy didn't make landfall on the Tyne day before yesterday. He reported he bombed shipbuilding centers, but what he actually hit were a couple of mining villages about twenty-five kilometers north of the Tyne River."

"Mining villages?" Franz said. "We're bombing miners?"

"Mathy was bombing barns. A barn roof was charred by one of his incendiaries. An hour later, he did reach the Tyne at a town called Wallsend. Dumped the rest of his bombs, damaged a house and hurt two people. Apparently, that was the 'big success' that inspired three airships and Strasser himself to have a try at England again yesterday."

Franz shrugged. "The Brass in Berlin believes every airship attack is effective."

"Where'd you hear that?"

"From brother Kaspar, where else? High command is convinced the English are so panicked by Zeppelins over Mother England they will cave in and sue for peace."

Through their window, Peter watched Kellner's airship dwindle northwestward on another North Sea patrol. "Do either of you believe that? When the English seaplane bombed Nordholz on Christmas Day, did that make you want to surrender – or did you burn to pay them back?"

"Good point," Ernst said. "According to this Amsterdam paper, one of those three ships yesterday did manage to set a lumberyard on fire, but talk in the Officers' Club this morning was that all three Zeppelin kommandants had no idea where they were. Von Buttlar in L-6 took a bunch of ground fire but managed to limp home. You think that terrified people on the ground?"

"Just hearing Zeppelins up there at night, ready to dump bombs on you could –"

"Oh come on, Franz. One of the three didn't even get there – L-7 with Strasser aboard. A hell of a headwind forced it to turn back. I'll bet Strasser was a sight to see. He's getting a reputation as a bad luck Jonah. Lousy weather, engine troubles, who-knows-what when he's aboard."

"But Strasser," Peter said, "is... Strasser."

"That he certainly is, friends." Ernst stood, stretched. "And – I wouldn't want this repeated – I'm beginning to realize such hell fired determination could get all of us killed."

24.

"So now the glory belongs to the damned army!" shouted a stumpy, red-faced leutnant zur see at the Officers' Club bar.

"In his cups," Ernst muttered to Franz and Peter at their corner table, "but he does have a point. Army airships stole our thunder when they hit Bury St. Edmonds, Southgate, and Ramsgate all in one night at the end of last month. And now May is beginning to look like it belongs to them, too."

Peter nodded, took a quick swallow of Paulaner and clunked down his beer mug. "Right. They're getting the first three of Wilhelmshafen's new four-engined Zepps."

"With thirty-two thousand cubic meters of hydrogen," Franz said. "How did they get hold of those before we did?"

"We're due for our first next month. L-10 class. And more after that." Peter took a long pull of his beer. The faster deliveries of new Zeppelins would not please Konteradmiral Kottenhoff one bit. But, damn it, airship attacks are now the only offensive the Fatherland is able to mount. The Western Front is barely recovering from the miserable winter. The trench lines from the Belgian coast to Switzerland's northwestern border are a quagmire. Crouching in 640 kilometers of filthy, human-filled ditches, the armies are pecking away at each other across nightmarish strips of "no man's land." Stalemate.

He clunked down the mug. "I don't know what strings the army pulled to get those new airships, Franz. But you can be sure Strasser's blowing a gasket."

Peter was also sure the admiral had to be going through frustration of his own. The ships of the fleet had been embarrassingly ineffective. At the Battle of Helgoland Bight a British cruiser flotilla had sent three German light cruisers and a destroyer to the bottom of the North Sea without losing a ship of their own. At the Dogger Bank disaster, we lost a capital ship with 951 men, while the British could shrug off a mere 14 killed. At least our airships are accomplishing one thing: a boost of German morale. I'm freezing my ass off under 22,000 cubic meters of explosive hydrogen to raise morale.

"What in hell is eating you?" Franz asked him.

"It just hit me that the airships are the only military arm that seems to be doing anything, even if it's mostly appearance."

Ernst held up both palms. "Will you two shut up? Things are going to pick up. Strasser told us our first L-10 class Zepp is scheduled for delivery in the next few weeks."

"Hard to be optimistic," Franz grumped, "when it's the army's raids that finally inspired the kaiser to approve bombing London."

"'East of the Tower,'" Ernst put in.

"Enough to let the army dump more than a thousand kilos on northeast London," Franz said. "The first air attack ever on an enemy's capital city."

"Drama," Peter said.

"More drama," Franz countered, "than our patrols sighting nothing dramatic at all."

"I'll make a prediction," Ernst offered. "When L-10 gets here, things are going to change."

To their surprise, the promised new Zeppelin L-10 rumbled into Nordholz May 17, days earlier than expected. The reworked design was an obvious improvement over the now-discontinued L-3 class. Four engines instead of three. Forty percent more hydrogen that almost doubled the airship's lifting capacity over that of the L-3 types. And, Peter noted, a mostly enclosed control gondola. Thank God.

Days later, came disappointment.

"Nothing but familiarization flights since it got here," Ernst grumped.

Peter looked up from the note he was writing to Lexie. "Now who's the disillusioned one? You've haven't heard the rumor? The L-10 is supposed to head for London tomorrow."

The rumor proved to be true. Lifting off under the command of Kapitänleutnant Klaus Hirsch, L-10 noisily returned in the wee hours before dawn the following day. At a pre-breakfast assembly, a visibly excited Hirsch reported he had salvoed his nine explosive bombs and 11 incendiaries, "Smack on target, gentlemen. The Harwich Naval Base. The lights of Ipswich confirmed our position."

Nordholz morale soared – until the Dutch papers arrived. According to neutral Holland's reporters, L-10 had actually bombed the town of Gravesend 90 kilometers southwest of Harwich. What Hirsch had thought were the lights of Ipswich actually were the lights of London. What had appeared to be a major accomplishment by the first of the new Zeppelins at Nordholz turned out to be an embarrassing case of opportunity lost.

Ernst stabbed a morsel of Pichelsteiner stew. "I hear you're scheduled to fly with Bocker tomorrow."

"In rickety old L-5. Routine patrol," Peter said. "Not much chance of anything happening over the North Sea." God, I'm caught between Kottenhoff's obsession to kill off the airship program and my hope we might actually play a part in ending this damned war.

At 13.00 hours, L-5 lifted into the spring afternoon, but at altitude, the rush of air through the open gondola was cold. This old crock is one of the last of its breed, Peter thought, as he swept the empty horizon hoping for the sight of a ship – any ship – to break the monotony. The L-3 series is being chewed up. L-3 itself and sister airship L-4, both flying out of Fuhlsbuttel, were lost the same day in February. Forced landings in Denmark. L-3 hit hard and buckled. L-4, with two engines out, crashed into North Sea surf. Eleven crewmen got out before the airship went back up, taking four of the crew with it, then back down to drown. First wartime fatalities of the Naval Airship Division.

In the leaden sea, he spotted a narrow wake. "Small vessel to port," he called. "Looks like – yes, it is. A minesweeper. One of ours."

He rubbed his eyes, then raised the binoculars again. We're one big target up here. Three weeks after L-4 got it, L-8 was shot down by Belgian ground fire. Then just last month, L-7, another L-3 class airship, that one flying out of Tondern, was blasted out of the air by British cruisers near Horns Reef. Eleven crewmen lost; seven taken prisoner. Only two of the old L-3 class left, and I'm on one of them. This boredom is bad enough, but what's worse is not seeing Lexie for weeks. Not since the Admiral told us to stop the meetings at the inn until he can find out who the leak is. How long will that take, if he's able to do it at all? God, how I miss her.

As dusk began to dim the western horizon, Peter stood on watch starboard. His now obsolete navigation training told him L-5 was some 20 kilometers off the Belgian coast, flying unusually high. Radio reports of active British aircraft based in northern France had prompted Bocker up to 2,500 meters.

Early evening deepened into purple twilight. Almost enjoyable, Peter felt, except for the persistent air rush through the gondola. As L-5 rumbled northeastward at its plodding 45 knots, he stepped starboard and trained the Leitz lenses landward. In the murky distance, he spotted pinprick flashes surely marking the trenches' northern limits near Nieuport. What those poor bastards – on both sides – must be going through.

A brighter flash caught his eye. Further inland. Then another distant red flare. Not on the ground.

"Explosions in the air starboard," he reported.

A third flash. A fourth. He kept the binoculars glued to that distant invisible location. A fifth flash; another tiny red rose flaring then as quickly fading.

"What the hell is that?" the executive officer said in his ear.

"I don't know."

"Five flashes –"

Then a sixth, that one followed by an orange glow that burst into huge fireball, even from this distance.

"Inland, over the trenches," Peter said.

The mass of flame brightened the night sky. Then it sank out of sight leaving a reddish aura that slowly faded into blackness.

"Damned odd," the young, scraggly-bearded exec said above the yammer of the Maybach engine just behind them. "What in hell was that?"

Peter let the Leitz hang on its neck strap and gripped the gondola's rim with both hands. "I think..." His voice cracked. "I think we just saw an airship go down."

When the Naval Intelligence report was posted at noon the following day, Peter learned he was right. Army Zeppelin LZ-37, identical to the navy's new L-10 class, was attacked over the Belgian trenches by a British aeroplane. But not with machine gun fire. The aircraft, identified as a Morane-Saulnier monoplane, flew above LZ-37 to drop a series of small bombs. The sixth bomb, Naval Intelligence deduced, ignited escaping hydrogen from the previous detonations. LZ-37 crashed on a convent near Ghent. One crewmember survived.

"Not good news," Franz said to Peter. "Not good at all."

"So much for your theory their aeroplanes can't touch us. A Morane-Saulnier, can reach 4,000 meters. This one was flying above that army Zepp.

"They won't touch the height-climbers."

"We aren't flying in height-climbers, Franz."

"I wish to hell we were. But we got one good thing out of the loss of those poor bastards in the army Zepp."

Peter nodded and said, "Strasser's order to install a machine gun position on top of all navy airships."

"Right. Come on, let's get some lunch."

They stepped into the drizzly early afternoon. "No flying today," Peter said, "unless this stuff lets up."

Franz walked on in glum silence.

"What's eating you? I was the one who watched those poor souls go down on fire, not you."

"Got a call from Kaspar about an hour ago. What's not on the bulletin board is what he told me."

"I'm listening."

"The British are testing a combination of explosive and incendiary bullets. The explosive one is designed to blow holes in an airship's hydrogen cells. Then the incendiary rounds set it on fire."

"Well, that's a pleasant lunchtime bit of information."

"Maybe it's not as bad as it sounds, Peter. Kaspar said the newest British fighter, a Sopwith Type 9700, has only an estimated 4,000-meter service ceiling. That's way below where the Height-Climbers will be."

"But just about even with the new L-10 class and with our L-3 class crocks."

"Hey, wait up a second!"

Franz glanced over his shoulder. "Where in hell have you been, Ernst? By the time Peter and I got up, you were out the door."

"Saw a crowd around something by the Hertha shed. You'll never guess what's in there."

"A truckload of machine guns per Strasser's order for top gunners."

"No, Franz. The mechs are already working on those. What's over there is not something Strasser ordered. It's something he has been ordered to do."

Franz and Peter stopped. "Something Strasser has been ordered to do?" Peter marveled.

"By the Chief of Naval Operations."

"And?"

"And so, meine Herren, there sits over there, just uncrated, an ugly little sub-cloud car, as the army now calls it. An 'angel basket,' as the crews call it. Nordholz has been ordered to test the damned thing."

25.

Alexia stared at her bowl of Kartoffelsuppe and two slices of dark bread. Potato soup was all she felt she could manage. The scuffed floor and echoing pressed metal ceiling did little for her appetite, nor was stress much of a dining companion.

Such a terrible feeling of apprehension. Every day since I became the admiral's liaison with Peter. Now Herr Moellenhoff's ban has made it worse. I'm sure Peter is right, assuming Moellendorf is a part of Admiral Kottenhoff's anti-airship effort. Someone must have informed higher command – God knows how high. I'm terrified all this will crash down on Peter. And me. Is it possible we both will be considered guilty of… *treason?* That would be a disaster. For the admiral. For my family. For Peter and me, and any future we could have together.

She picked up her spoon and her hand trembled. The accusation itself would be devastating for Peter. A commissioned officer working against the navy's most dramatic effort to take the war to the enemy's homeland. God in Heaven, how had they both allowed themselves to become embroiled in this mess? And how on earth could they possibly--

"Guten Tag, Fräulein Tammler."

Startled, she looked up into the intense eyes beneath heavy black eyebrows of Kapitänleutnant Hermann Krause. He nodded at the crowded tables behind him. "You seem to have the only table with seats still available. May I join you?" The thin lips smiled, but the smile did reach his eyes.

"Certainly, Herr Leutnant."

She noticed an empty table near the kitchen door. Perhaps he had not seen it. More likely, she suspected, he had quite another purpose in joining her.

He glanced at her lonely soup bowl. "You don't have an appetite today, Fräulein."

"I don't eat much for lunch. A woman is always conscious of her figure."

"Yours, if I may say so, has no need for fasting," He accompanied that with what she felt was a bit of a smirk. Was he after information or was this a simple flirtation?

A sullen waiter appeared. Krause ordered Schwartenbraten with sauerkraut and dumplings, and a mug of beer.

"I see you have no qualms concerning your figure," she countered with a quick smile.

"I can't resist pork roast. By the way, it's something of a coincidence our dining together. Just a few minutes ago, I delivered a message to the admiral. A message from Berlin."

She peered at him. "From Berlin? Is that so unusual?"

"You know damned well it is, Alexia. Your paperwork admiral does not have much, if any, occasion to receive communications from Naval High Command."

Without taking his eyes off her, he took a long drag of beer, set the mug down, and added, "Might you have any idea why he would be honored with such a communication?"

"It is no business of mine, Herr Kapitänleutnant."

"Hermann, please. I took you to that yacht club dance. I drove you to the Blauer Adler Inn. Don't you think you know me well enough to call me Hermann?"

"All right. Hermann. But I still have no insight into the admiral's Berlin message." She absently stirred her soup. "Do you?"

"Do *I*?"

"You seem so intrigued by the message, I can't believe you did not... ah, perhaps steal a glance as you rushed to –"

"The damned thing was handed to me by our message center in a sealed envelope," he said, with a little laugh and a mischievous glance her way.

Perhaps he is more human than I assumed. Or, is he even more clever than I suspect?

"Eat your Schwartenbraten, Hermann."

A sealed message from Berlin. Her fragile appetite faded entirely. She forced herself to finish the soup, took a few bites of the bread, and checked her pendant watch.

"Oh, I'm running late. Sorry. I must get back to work."

She rushed back upstairs to the admiral's office. If he needs me – But she found he had abruptly left for the day.

Before dawn's first light, with Albert at the wheel and Admiral Kottenhoff sitting uneasily in the rear passenger seat, the Daimler rolled out of Kiel. Could not whatever was on von Tirpitz's mind have been transmitted to me by telephone? Telegraph? Even a note? Why subject me to a four-hundred-kilometer trip on uncertain roadways? Taking a stuffy, soldier-choked train was out of the question. But ten hours in this jouncing automobile is going to be no pleasure at all.

Some four hours later, near Boisenburg on the Elbe's east bank, he felt the right side of the automobile sag. Albert pulled off the road and stopped.

"A punctured tire, sir. This will take only a few moments."

With his deft handling of the spare, they were back on their way in fifteen minutes. At the next stop, this one for a quick meal at a passable restaurant in Perleberg, Albert took himself to a distant corner table. Kottenhoff was given a table at the front window. Should I have asked him to join me? he wondered. A man does not dine with his servants, but dining alone is no pleasure.

Back in the Daimler a half hour later, they rolled another 20 kilometers, when Albert called over his shoulder, "High oil temperature, sir." Again, he pulled off the road once more, saved the day. He tightened a leaking oil line connection and magically produced two spare cans of oil to put the Daimler back on the road.

In late afternoon, they wound through Berlin streets and at last pulled up in front of the Admiralty Building. Why, Kottenhoff, wondered, as he stepped out on stiff legs, does the Admiralty need such grandiose housing for directing its role in a deteriorating war? Our mission for glory is already a bitter killing contest. And why, he asked himself again, have I been summoned here?

He squared his shoulders, mounted the broad steps and pushed through the massive entrance doors. At a security check desk, he was directed down a broad and busy corridor to a stairway. His nervousness increased with every step upward. Guarding a towering oak door at the end of another corridor, a clean-shaven blond oberleutnant snapped to attention and clicked heels as Kottenhoff approached, approached, his heart beginning to thunder.

"Konteradmiral Kottenhoff, responding to Grossadmiral Tirpitz's... invitation."

"One moment, Herr Admiral." The crisply uniformed oberleutnant tapped the door, slipped inside and shut it behind him.

All the anxiety Kottenhoff had desperately tried to suppress last night and through today's miserable drive pervaded brain and body in a hot rush. He thrust a hand against the wall to regain his balance just as the door reopened.

"The Grossadmiral will see you immediately, Herr Admiral."

Kottenhoff's chest clenched. He drew a long breath, straightened his uniform with a quick tug, and stepped into the office of Navy Minister Grossadmiral Alfred von Tirpitz. I've been here before, he recalled, but under more pleasant circumstances. Now the dark paneled walls seemed threatening. The gleaming hardwood flooring, icy cold. Kottenhoff walked the echoing 12 meters to reach the massive mahogany desk at its far end. Behind that desk, looking too much like a stern schoolmaster observing the approach of a renegade student, sat von Tirpitz. The grossadmiral's bushy sideburns and two-pronged, graying beard give him the appearance of a benign grandfather, Kottenhoff thought. But there's nothing grandfatherly in that glare.

"Sit, Admiral." Tirpitz indicated an armless chair near a corner of the desk.

"My apologies for this late afternoon hour, Herr Minister," Kottenhoff perched stiffly on the rock-hard chair. "There were problems with the automo--"

Tirpitz held up his hand. He obviously did not intend to engage in idle chatter.

"I am sure you know why you are here, Kottenhoff."

"No, sir." But I have a sick feeling about this.

Tirpitz folded his arms. "I remind you of our conversation in Kiel some months ago. Just before the war broke out. At that time, I informed you that I had revised my early concerns of the airships' military value – revised it to an outlook parallel to that of the kaiser's."

"I recall that conversation, Herr Minister." Politics so easily corrupt military reality.

"But unfortunately, you have not heeded it."

Kottenhoff fought to keep his eyes on the grossadmiral's. Silence is the only way to respond.

"Well, Admiral Kottenhoff?"

"It is my… judgment, Herr Minister, that an officer must be true to his convictions."

"And it is my conviction that an officer cannot interpose his personal prejudices between his duty and his performance of that duty." Did Tirpitz's expression soften a bit? "I still do question, to a degree, the Zeppelin's efficiency as an offensive weapon. Yet it is proving its worth as a means of forcing the English to maintain an active anti-airship defense system. That demands artillery, a large number of men and several squadrons of aircraft to remain in England instead of reinforcing the enemy's front. For that alone, I have become increasingly convinced the airship program has military merit."

"In fact," the navy minister continued after a disquieting pause, "our airship program, plus that of the army, seem at the moment to be our only actively aggressive strategy of the war. The situation in France and Belgium has deteriorated into the gain of a few yards at the cost of too many good men, only to lose ground to a counter push. Or there is failure to capitalize on opportunity, such as the fiasco of April 22."

"April 22?"

"Yes, Kottenhoff. Our army's first use of chlorine gas. Against French infantry at Ypres."

"I was under the impression that attack was a success in that fifteen thousand French Colonial troops panicked and ran."

"The real failure belonged to our army in its total lack of a follow-up plan. When the French troops fled, they left a seven-kilometer breach in their line. But our army failed to capitalize on that opportunity. They handed the Canadians and British the time to close the gap. Opportunity lost. In contrast, our airships are pressing attacks on England whenever conditions permit. Opportunity exploited."

Not without loss of airships and the crews manning them, Kottenhoff reflected sourly, in what I firmly consider a dubious strategic effort. But arguing with a military superior leads only to humiliation. Or worse. He remained silent.

"I will accept your non-response as a tacit acknowledgement of my point, Kottenhoff."

Tirpitz stood, clasped his hands behind his back and began to pace the generous space behind his desk. His tall, brooding presence struck Kottenhoff almost as physically threatening. This interview could not end happily.

"Erwin," Tirpitz said in a surprisingly conciliatory tone, "after your outburst at the L-2 disaster, I effected your face-saving promotion and had you assigned to a non-political backwater. You could have easily coasted out the war. But now I am informed that, despite what I thought was an understanding we had reached at Kiel, you have been actively and, in my opinion, deceitfully engaged in trying to discredit the Naval Airship Program."

When Tirpitz reverted to his first name, Kottenhoff's chill warmed a bit. Now, though, he was desperately trying to steady his breathing. Moellendorf, you son of a bitch, have you done this to me?

"I have been devoted to what I consider the best interests of the Fatherland, Herr Minister."

"Unfortunately, Erwin, what you consider to be the Fatherland's best interests is in contrast to what the High Command is convinced are the Fatherland's best interests."

Tirpitz stopped his infernal pacing and towered over him. "In view of your underhanded obstinacy in this matter, I regret to inform you that 'in the best interests of the Fatherland,' it is my sad duty to request your resignation from the Imperial Navy. No more than thirty days from now."

Resignation. Thirty days. Mein Gott.

"That will be all, Admiral."

Indeed. Kottenhoff turned on his heel and strode out on quaking knees, hoping the oberleutnant doorman would not notice.

As Albert held open the Daimler's rear door, Kottenhoff felt his world disintegrating. He stepped into the automobile and sat in stunned silence. Resignation. Thirty days. Ordered by the Navy Minister himself. Sudden tears welled.

Back behind the wheel, Albert turned toward him. "Herr Admiral?"

Then he quickly turned back to stare through the windshield.

"Eh? Oh, Hotel Brandenburger Hof, Albert."

As the automobile rolled into the early evening traffic, Kottenhoff stared unseeing at the busy sidewalk. *Resignation.* By a konteradmiral in wartime. Disgraceful, though he supposed he could plead illness. Perhaps this overpowering hatred of the airship actually was some definable form of illness.

How much does the damned informant know? Have I also ruined the life of young Reinhart? Alexia? Is there some way, any way at all to mitigate the impact of this calamity on them?

There is a way for me, of course. My old service revolver still lies in the attic, wrapped in oiled cloth, sealed in an airtight box.

26.

As Peter stepped into the control gondola of Kellner's aging L-3 class Zeppelin, Kapitänleutnant Hugo Kellner gave him an odd look. The airship kommandant's, craggy, beardless face looks more careworn, Peter noticed, than when I flew that training mission with him.

Kellner broke his penetrating stare and gave him a wan smile. "Welcome aboard, Leutnant. We fly together once again."

"But no longer as navigator, Herr Kommandant. I am now classified as an observer."

"And today with special purpose."

Peter frowned. Special purpose?

"I see you were not entirely informed," Kellner said with a little shake of his head. "We are to make landfall on the English coast at Harwich then follow the Orwell River to Ipswich and bomb the railroad car works in that city."

"A target tricky to find." What's behind this curious conversation between the airship kommandant and this temporarily assigned observer?

"Oberleutnant Bader, our executive officer." Kellner indicated a stocky, sour-faced officer standing aft near the radioman's work shelf. The exec and the hawk-nosed radio op look as unhappy back there, Peter noted, as our rudder and elevator men up here.

Kellner turned toward the bomb toggle array and began inspecting each of the switches. Without looking at Peter, he said, "Did no one explain the unusual part of this flight?"

"No, sir." Unusual part?

"We have aboard the experimental device Strasser has been ordered to test in combat."

Realization dawned. "The sub-cloud car."

Kellner swung back to him. "Now you are halfway to understanding. The geniuses who came up with this mission have left the crucial part to me to explain to you."

"Explain, Herr Kommandant?"

"There is an overcast fifteen hundred meters over tonight's target city, Reinhart. Above the overcast, our Zeppelin will be hidden from the ground. Perfect conditions to test the sub-cloud car in an actual attack. And as our observer, you will guide us over the target and report the bomb hits."

"From the damned angel basket?" Peter's heart leapt into his throat. He struggled for control. "My apologies, Herr Kommandant. It's just that I... that I –"

Kellner gave him a wry smile. "My sentiments also, Leutnant. But Befehl ist Befehl. An order is an order. Strasser has been ordered, so we are ordered. We will release the car shortly after we are above the overcast. You will be lowered on the cable beneath the overcast. Then you will direct us up the Orwell River to Ipswich where we will bomb our target – the largest factory on the south edge of the city. A maker of railroad cars and equipment. Verstehen?"

"Aye, Sir."

Kellner gave him a curious look. "Strasser himself has assigned you to ride the... angel basket. Why would that be?"

Strasser himself? My God, it's got to be the Kottenhoff thing.

"I have no idea, Sir," he lied and felt perspiration beading on his forehead. "A matter of luck?"

Kellner shrugged. "Go to your observation position, Leutnant. I will notify you when to climb into the hull and report to the bomb room."

Four hours later – four hours bucking the brisk westerlies over the North Sea – Peter watched the distant coast of England resolve itself into a gray rim along the horizon. As they drummed closer, Peter focused his binoculars on the predicted cloud layer, tinted rose by the setting sun.

Kellner ordered the engines' drone throttled back to a rumble with just enough thrust to counteract the headwind. The airship's forward motion died. At 1500 meters over the leaden sea, they hung unmoving, waiting for nightfall's concealment.

Forty-five minutes later, the glum-faced executive officer shouted, "Leutnant Reinhart! Up into the hull. Board the sub-cloud car. Stand by to deploy on the kommandant's order.

The idling Zeppelin's slipstream felt warmer than its usual chill at cruising speed. The access ladder's metal rings were slippery with condensation. Peter planted each upward step carefully. *The gloves helped. So did this mild headwind. Not much chance of being torn off the ladder by a mere 10-knot slipstream. But I'm afraid this is the easy part.*

He pushed up through the hatchway into the bottom of the narrow keel, knelt on the metal walkway, then scrambled to his feet. *Up here, engine noise is muted. I can hear this old crock's girder joints groan and creak. Those big hydrogen cells up between the framing rings look like they could be punctured with a toothpick.*

Forward, those are the bottom rungs of the ladder that go almost five stories straight up to the machine gun emplacement now installed by Strasser's order on all airships in the division. Which would be worse? Sitting on top of this thing with only a flimsy railing to keep you from sliding off into empty space? Or riding way below the Zeppelin in an angel basket hanging on a wire? Neither appeals to me, and the damned angel basket is waiting.

He grabbed the safety lines stretched along the catwalk and headed aft.

Ducking through a midship bulkhead hatchway, he stepped into the bomb room. Along the starboard wall, he eyed a row of ten 10-kilogram high explosive bombs and a row of a dozen or so smaller incendiaries. All were held in place vertically, nose down, over a sliding hatch in the floor.

But the most chilling sight in here is that thing hanging over a sliding hatch of its own. That four-meter-long duralumin teardrop with a little cockpit a meter behind the rounded nose. The sub-cloud car. Four small fins in the rear of the thing to keep it pointed into the wind. I hope.

Peter's stare took in the fully loaded cable drum mounted on a winch just forward of the car. From the winch, an impossibly thin wire threaded through a pulley system, then through a frame of slender girders, and down to a two-wire yoke shackled to the car fore and aft of the cockpit. What a rig! And it all depends on that damned skinny wire. I wouldn't send my worst enemy up – or down – in a contraption like this.

"You the lucky man, Leutnant?"

Peter tore his gaze from the sub-cloud car and joined the group of non-commissioned officers manning the bomb room. Two mates, a master's mate and a grizzled master gunner, surely in his 40s, who peered at him with a hint of sarcastic humor.

"Lucky?" This guy has to be joking.

"Ja, Herr Leutnant An army friend tells me their observers compete for the sub-cloud car assignment."

"Compete? Why?"

"Because once out of the airship, they can smoke."

"That thing might make me a smoker in a hurry."

Peter heard the Zeppelin's engines' mutter pick up. He glanced at the room's portside windows. Dusk out there. We're closing in on the English coast.

"Let me give you a hand, Sir." Despite his aged appearance, the master gunner practically lifted Peter in. Cramped in here. And this little seat is no armchair. Legroom for a midget. No instruments. No controls. Only a telephone handset with its wire snaking up to join the wire above the juncture of the yoke. One concession to comfort – that little celluloid windscreen about a hand span high.

He lifted the telephone hand set off its bracket on the cockpit's port side.

"Leutnant Reinhart checking telephone."

"You are coming through well, Leutnant," a voice responded promptly. Kapitänleutnant Kellner's voice. A direct telephone connection with the airship kommandant.

"We will make landfall and begin our climb above the overcast in approximately fifteen minutes, Reinhart. I will notify you when it is time to launch."

Launch? More like falling out of a tree, but the ground is a hell of a lot further away.

"All secure, Leutnant?"

With my head and shoulders sticking out of this glorified tin can on a string, how secure can I be? "All secure."

The master gunner stepped back several paces. "Wouldn't do, Sir, to be standing on the floor hatch when it opens up for you."

The engines accelerated forward and aft. The Zeppelin plowed through coastal air currents. Minutes ticked by. Beyond the bomb room's small windows, the fading light deepened into night. A single electric bulb illuminated the compartment.

The telephone grated. "Release car in five minutes," Kellner ordered. Then, in a softer tone, "Viel Glueck, Reinhart!"

Good luck, for sure. "Five minutes," he called to the waiting master gunner.

The gunner turned to the crew behind him. "Schnell, schnell. Smartly, now."

What kind of man am I? Peter wondered. Willing or only obedient? I'm already drenched in sweat. My legs feel like lead –

Beneath the car, the floor hatch slid open. The swirl of inrushing slipstream buffeted the angel basket. Gooseflesh rippled along his arms.

"We are making landfall over Harwich, Reinhart," the telephone crackled. "Will break out above the cloud layer in two minutes. Standby for launch."

Peter clutched the handset. Not much security in that.

"Launch sub-cloud car," the telephone rasped.

Peter nodded at the waiting crew. One of them threw a switch just above his head. The winch kicked in. The open space in the floor rose up, surrounded the car, then soared above it. As the angel basket (Oh, damn that nickname!) dropped into the night, the Zeppelin above him dwindled as a blank space among the stars. The stars disappeared. He could see nothing at all. The air was saturated with moisture. The car had plunged into the cloud layer.

Gray vapor rushed against the windscreen. Swirled in his face. The goggles steamed up, blinding him. He yanked out his handkerchief, jabbed at the lenses.

Abruptly the cloud layer soared upward. In the suddenly clear night, a scatter of lights dotted the black countryside far below.

"I am beneath the overcast, Herr Kommandant."

A dim glow on the horizon slowly resolved into a sprinkle of bright pinpoints.

"Scattered lights ahead, Sir."

"How far ahead?"

"Hard to tell from this altitude and still descending. Estimate twenty-some kilometers."

Still descending. How long could the damned cable be? At least 500 meters, he remembered Franz telling him.

He felt a jolt, and his heart flipped over. *The cable had snapped.* But he felt no sudden increase in the swirl of slipstream. The nose of the thing still pointed forward.

"You are at maximum cable length," Kellner told him. "We now take heading corrections from you to the target. Is Ipswich in sight?"

"A big cluster of lights now, about fifteen kilometers and some forty-five degrees to starboard."

"Where are you in relation to the river, Reinhart?"

"Directly above it."

"Then follow the river. The lights you are seeing must be Woodbridge and Martlesham."

"Then Ipswich should be dead ahead, Sir. But I see nothing there but black countryside. Is it possible –?"

"Follow the river, Leutnant."

"Sir, with all due respect –"

"Follow the *river!* Report when you manage to sight the not-small city of Ipswich. And, Leutnant, be aware that Ipswich may have reduced its lighting to avoid precisely what we are about to do."

"Aye, sir."

Dangling in space at the end of a 500-meter wire no thicker than a strand of spaghetti, Peter began to realize this might be close to an enjoyable experience. Surely a unique one. No sound but the gentle swish of slipstream. At this low altitude, the night air was almost comfortable. And he felt some pride in that he was now directing the airship's course. How ironic. Here I am dangling in this absurd car, alone over enemy territory and dependent on the crew in the bomb room out of sight far overhead. Yet this moment is the closest I have come to enjoying my airship service.

The scatter of lights drifted beneath him, not a city as he had thought. As it fell behind, he noticed the dull sheen of the river had strayed to his left. He pushed the handset button. "Five degrees to port, Sir."

Long seconds later, the car made a gentle leftward swerve. Back on course.

After two more corrections, he strained forward. A dull glow at least forty-five degrees to port was brightening. Surprising how far off course the damned river had led him.

"Sir, I'm sighting a large city quite a distance portside."

"Give me the course correction, Reinhart."

"Forty degrees, Sir."

"Forty? Are you certain?"

"Yes, Sir."

"Port forty degrees," he heard Kellner tell the helmsman. The slowly unrolling carpet of lights swung into position dead ahead. This was indeed a city-sized sprawl.

"Passing over the eastern edge of Ipswich," he reported. Within seconds, forward speed dropped to a near-hover. Oddly, the river passed through the city's north side. Hadn't the map displayed at assembly shown the river flowing through the middle of Ipswich?

"Herr Commander," he called, "Is it possible that we –"

"Can you see the rail car factory, Reinhart? It's the biggest building in Ipswich."

He scanned the lights beneath him. What was the problem with these people? London reportedly was blacked out every night, yet up here in Suffolk, they were behaving as if there were no threat at all. Their failure; his advantage.

Along the southern bank of the river, he noticed a large gray roof. No other building he could make out was nearly as big. That had to be the railway car works.

"Five degrees to starboard, Sir, minimum speed, and we should be directly above the target – if that is the target. I am not certain we –"

"We have no time for indecision, Leutnant. We are over Ipswich. The target is the largest building in the city. You will notify me when we are directly above that building. Do you understand?"

Peter bit back an angry response. "Aye, Sir. Over the target in two minutes estimated."

"All engines to idle," he heard Kellner order. Seconds later, the car's progress subsided to a crawl. The target drifted toward him, a large, flat-roofed factory dimly lighted by street lamps on its perimeter.

"Directly over the target in thirty seconds," he reported. "Twenty… ten… *Now*."

"Salvo bombs," he heard Kellner's voice over the telephone line.

Had anyone given thought to the risk of dropping bombs from a Zeppelin dangling a sub-cloud car? He stared up at overcast, ghostly overhead in the faint glow from the city's lights. Can't see the Zeppelin, but I hear the rumble of its engines up there.

Then he froze. That sounds like steam whistling from a boiler. God, it has to be the full load of bombs tearing past!

Sweating under his flight suit, he leaned over the side of the cramped cockpit, pulled down the goggles and brought up the binoculars. Nothing. Were they all duds? All misfires? Then directly below, a cluster of flashes. Fountains of flame and smoke. Now I can hear their thunder. A few explosions blossomed in the northwest corner of the building. The rest have torn up the street and whatever lies further on. Now there are pinpoints of fire in the darkness north of the target building. Our incendiaries missed.

"Northwest portion of the target hit," he telephoned, "and numerous small fires north of the target."

"Well done, Leutnant. We are turning east; then we will winch you up."

He heard the invisible Zeppelin's engines rev. The target area slowly rotated to port as the airship's speed increased. Beneath the car's blunt nose, the city rolled aft. Peter felt a rush of elation. We've done it, bombed a target unseen from the Zepp, guided by the sub-cloud car. We didn't flatten the target, but it's still a real accomplishment. The increasing swish of slipstream was reassuring. He sat back, folded his arms and grinned.

Then he heard a new sound in the darkness below him, a sound he heard last Christmas day. Never in his life had he felt so helpless. Somewhere much too close in this black night, he heard the rackety howl of an aeroplane straining for altitude.

27.

Peter's fingers clamped the headset. His chest turned to ice. "Herr Kommandant!" He struggled to control his voice. Calm. Clear. No panic. "I hear an aeroplane aft of the car. Climbing. Coming closer."

Kellner's voice crackled, "Distance?"

Peter twisted around. Nothing in the blackness, but the engine noise is getting louder. "Closer than a kilometer, I think."

He heard Kellner shout to the crew, "Maximum power, all engines. Retrieve sub-cloud car. Climb! Climb!"

Peter felt a surge on the wire. Up, Peter prayed. Up, up. But the aeroplane still came on. Get me out of here! The cloud layer doesn't look any closer. Aren't they winding me up as they climb? Turn that winch as fast as you can, you bastards. Is the drag of this damned thing slowing everything down?

A chill ran up his spine. Broke across his shoulders. What had Franz said? The army Zepp crews carry an axe. If they're in trouble, they can whack the wire. Cut the car loose. Just a rumor. An army rumor. This is the Imperial Navy. But God help me if the story's true, and that smirking master gunner does have an axe up there.

Because here comes the aeroplane! If I can't see him, he can't see me.

That guy's as blind as I am. He can slam right into me. Or hit the cable. Either way, I'm dead.

"Closing fast!" he yelled in the handset."

The aeroplane's blare overran Kellner's voice.

Now Peter spotted twin flares of blue flame. Side by side. Vertical flames straight aft and damned close. Were those machine gun muzzle blasts? I must be invisible to him, not a target. Oh! I'm staring at twin exhaust flares.

He grabbed the cockpit's edge and braced himself. Braced for the crash. The propeller slashing off the car's flimsy tail. The cable snapping. The hopeless free fall – Goodbye, Lexie. I love you…

Relief surged through him. The aeroplane's climb had drifted leftward, enough to miss the car –

The cable! If the Britisher hit the cable, it would rip into his wings, and they both would plunge through the night to smash into the English countryside. Again, Peter grabbed the cockpit's coaming. Now he was determined not to surrender to panic. If he were fated to die like this for the Fatherland, dann sollte es so sein. It was to be.

Not five meters to port, the aircraft roared past. Peter could make out its twin vertical exhaust stacks spouting fire above its upper wing. A biplane, probably one of their clumsy B.E.s. The pilot missed the car and the wire he surely never saw. Now he clawed upward above the car, surely intent on finding the Zeppelin that had bombed Ipswich.

Peter watched the exhaust flames dwindle far above him. Then wink out. Has the aeroplane's engine stalled? No, I can still hear its howl, lessened by distance. Can't see the exhaust flames, though. He's climbed into the cloud layer. Not seeing any Zeppelin exhaust flares below the overcast, the pilot decided the attacking airship must be above it.

"Herr Kommandant, the aircraft passed me and has entered the overcast."

"Understood, Reinhart. We are continuing to reel you – *Where?*" Kellner blurted to someone in the gondola.

"Aft, sir. Ten degrees to port," a scratchy voice shouted.

"Verdammt! Down! Schnell, schnell!" In Peter's handset, Kellner sounded close to panic. Then: "Engines full power. Valve hydrogen for maximum descent." The airship kommandant had ordered an emergency dive into the cloud layer.

The abrupt reversal from slow ascent to a frightening fast descent shot a cold wash through him. Peter hoped to hell the uninspiring crew on the bomb room winch didn't desert him now.

Overhead, he heard the stutter of a machine gun. Then another, that one with a faster firing rate. The aeroplane attacked. One of the Zeppelin's gunners is firing back. Not good up there. No better down here. If the Zepp goes down, so do I.

"I ordered emergency descent, damn you!" he heard Kellner shout, unmindful or uncaring of the open telephone line. "Into the cloud layer *now!*"

Some distance ahead in the countryside's black carpet, Peter spotted a pool of light. A farm? He watched it grow larger. A lighted field with tiny figures running – a playing field. It's growing larger. It should be passing below the car's nose, but its staying in position.

God. The Zeppelin's diving for the cloud layer faster than the winch is pulling me up. The playing field hadn't drifted past because I'm heading straight for it. Eyes glued to the fast approaching school grounds, he braced himself for disaster. Oh God, Lexie, if we could have had even one more day together –

The floodlit playing field whisked beneath him, not 100 meters below. He was still sinking. Then he was pressed into the seat. The Zeppelin had leveled off.

But not soon enough. Out of the night, a towering, even blacker mass loomed in front of him. With a shattering bang, the sub-cloud car plunged straight into it. Peter was thrown forward. The telephone handset flew out of his hand. His head slammed the windscreen. His vision dissolved into blinding flashes. Something twanged the forward yoke wire, screeched along the car's port side, then fell behind.

He slumped back in the seat. Feels like I've been hit with a hammer. He slapped his hand to his forehead, felt a long gash above his left eye. Blood, a lot of blood. He moved his other arm, his legs. Nothing seems broken. He yanked down the goggles, fumbled for the handkerchief, pressed to his forehead. The car's battered but still in one piece. And climbing. He looked down. Thank God, there are the white breakers of the coastline.

Then he heard an odd buzzing sound. What in hell is happening now? The noise is right here, in the car, just forward of the cockpit. One hand pressed to his forehead, he reached over the shattered windscreen with the other. I feel something there that shouldn't be there. Jammed under the forward yoke wire connection. A stick? He worked it free. Part of a tree branch. The English can have it back. No, wait. what a souvenir! A piece of the tree that had almost killed me. He set it on the rumpled flooring and picked up the handset.

"Herr Kommandant?"

"Reinhart! Mein Gott," Kellner shouted. "We thought we had lost you! A jerk on the cable, yet no loss of weight. What's happened down there?"

"I hit a tree."

"You hit a *tree!* Are you all right?"

"Bloody from a cut, damn it. But so far, not fatal." Uncalled for sarcasm. I'm trapped in a nightmare. "My apologies, Herr Kommandant."

"None needed. We have crossed the coastline, so there should be no more surprises."

"The British aeroplane, sir?"

"He lost us in the cloud layer."

"I heard the gunfire.'

"A few holes in one of the aft hydrogen cells. Our sail makers are patching them now."

As the Zeppelin drummed out over the dark water of the North Sea, the overcast thinned and fell behind. The battered sub-cloud car sped eastward beneath a dark canopy studded with stars. With a huge feeling of relief, Peter watched the silhouette of the Zeppelin growing larger above him. Minutes later, the car rose through the bomb room hatchway and jolted to a stop. Beneath him, the hatch rolled shut.

The master gunner stared, mouth agape. "Sweet Jesus, Leutnant. What have you done to the army's car?"

Peter was struck with a wave of bravado. "Send it back, Master Gunner. I have found it totally unsuitable for tree pruning. Now help me get out of the damned thing."

28.

"Sorry to keep you waiting, Leutnant Reinhart." Fregattenkapitän Strasser stepped into his office, closing the door behind him.

An apology from the Airship Division Kommandant, Peter marveled. Perhaps rumors of a contrast between Strasser's public brusqueness and private warmth are not as farfetched as believed.

"Sit, Leutnant. Sit." Strasser himself sat, abruptly plunking down behind his worn oak desk. Peter looked for a chair. The office was Spartan – the desk, three battered chest-high filing cabinets. He chose the chair near the map-laden table. The only brightness in the office came from outside: a panoramic view of the Nordholz airship launching and landing area, visible through a pair of corner windows. Peter could see the ground handlers out there walking Kellner's airship toward the Hertha side of the twin hangars.

"While you were having your forehead sewn back together, I took a look at the sub-cloud car." Strasser leaned back in his swivel chair. "Nose battered in, windscreen torn up, port side dented, two tail fins ripped away. Quite a ride, Reinhart."

"Yes, sir."

"What I want from you, while it's still fresh in your mind – well, I suspect such an experience will always be fresh in your mind – what I want is your frank opinion of the car's value to the Naval Airship Division. Your findings, good and bad. Then you can go to breakfast."

Does he really want my opinion? Peter wondered? Is he expecting me to support the damned sub-cloud car project?

"Beneath the cloud cover," he said carefully, "the observer has a view the crew above the clouds obviously does not. So using the car can permit accurate bombing in negative weather conditions."

Strasser's precise little goatee jutted forward, giving him a pugnacious look. "You sound like the salesman who sold the car to the army. I want the customer's findings."

Peter drew an uneasy breath. "There are some problems."

"Precisely, Leutnant."

"Hanging on its wire well below the airship, the car is a hazard to the airship. Besides the air drag slowing the Zeppelin, there are those hundreds of meters of suspending wire. Last night, the attacking aeroplane nearly flew into the wire. That could have knocked down the car and damaged the Zeppelin's bomb room. And, as I found out first-hand, in an emergency situation there is the possibility of the car's running afoul of objects on the ground, or the ground itself."

Strasser leaned forward, both hands flat on his desk. His expression looked grim. Peter's mouth went dry. Have I gone too far?

The Airship Division Kommandant sat back, peered briefly at the rough-planked ceiling. Then he said, "I believe the army can keep its exclusive franchise on that thing." Those intense little eyes again bored into Peter's. "Do you agree, Leutnant?"

Peter suppressed a sigh of relief. "Absolutely, Sir."

Strasser's piercing gaze persisted "One more matter, Reinhart: the reason you were in that angel basket. I received an order to put you there."

"An order?" Peter blurted.

"From Berlin. Have you any idea why?"

"No, sir." From Berlin? My God.

"Nor have I. That will be all, Leutnant. You are dismissed. And," he added, "there is no need to discuss this conversation with others. Verstehen Sie?"

* * *

Out in the cool morning, Peter picked up the piece of branch he had left at the corner of the administration building. Then he strode off toward the officers mess, thoughts churning. I told the Airship Division Commander one small lie. The order from Berlin has to be part of the unraveling of Admiral Kottenhoff's campaign. He agitates in Kiel. The vibrations reach Nordholz. Why else am I singled out for the hazardous sub-cloud car test? An experimental device. No instruction before the flight. An inexperienced handling crew. Happenstance or design?

The damned informant told *Berlin* about Kottenhoff? So does Berlin know about my part in it? Lexie's? Hauling all three of us before a court would be a publicity disaster for the airship program. Might even turn the public against the program. Better to discreetly "take care of" us... The admiral could be isolated in some remote outpost. For me, hazardous assignments until one of them proves fatal.

And Lexie?

He stepped into the officers' mess.

"Peter! Over here!" Franz sat with Ernst at a corner table near the entrance. "My God, Ernst, look at this guy. What in hell happened to your forehead Peter?"

"A 'dueling scar' for sure, Franz, but not from falling off a tricycle."

"Doing a little grounds keeping?" Ernst nodded at the piece of branch in Peter's hand.

He set it on the table. "Elm, I think. English elm. I picked it up over there last night."

They both stared. "Are you trying to tell us – Jesus!" Franz gasped. "Are you telling us the damned angel basket –?"

Peter felt a flush of elation. By God, last night I survived a really close one. "Gentlemen," he announced grandly, "I believe I made an historical first. I rode that rotten little angel basket through a treetop."

"Tell us, tell us," Franz pleaded.

"First I need a drink."

"I'll get it," Ernst scrambled to his feet. "Coffee?"

"Brandy."

He drained it in one gulp, banging down the glass. "We went in over a cloud layer," he began. Neither Franz nor Ernst said a single word. Peter wound up with a flourish. "And that, Gentlemen, is how the war came to Ipswich."

"And England retaliated," Franz said, "by swatting you with a tree."

Peter stood then had to grab the chair's back for support. Surely not from one shot of brandy. Sheer exhaustion. "I'm sorry. I'm too damned tired to eat. I need sleep."

The tree loomed out of the night, huge, with limbs made of grey rock. He tried to roll over the side of the angel basket, but he couldn't move. No escape. Helpless as the tree raced toward the speeding sub-cloud car – and hit him quite gently. Merely tapping his arm. Tapping, tapping...

He woke with a jolt. The insistent orderly of the day straightened. "Leutnant Reinhart, you are to report to Fregattenkapitän Strasser's office in fifteen minutes." The sour-faced young rating turned on his heel and strode out.

Peter sat up, groggy, still partly in the throes of that confused dream. Morning already? He checked his pocket watch on the table. Fourteen hundred hours. Same day, early afternoon. Haven't I already appeared before the Airship Division Kommandant? Why a second meeting?

He hurried down the hall to the latrine, splashed frigid water on his face, slicked down his hair then rushed back to the room to dress.

"Enter," Strasser's voice called when Peter tapped on his office door. Kapitänleutnant Kellner was seated in there with Strasser. The Airship Division Kommandant nodded toward the remaining empty chair. Mystified by this abrupt summons to reappear, Peter sat.

Strasser held up a single sheet of paper and glared at Kellner. "A Naval Intelligence report. You did not bomb Ipswich last night, Herr Kapitänleutnant. You actually shelled a bunch of oysters in a processing plant, some thirty kilometers southwest of Ipswich. Colchester, to be precise."

Dead silence from Kellner prompted equal silence from Peter. Strasser threw each of them a look that Peter found impossible to interpret.

"I realize it has not been history-making for an airship to attack the wrong target. But this was a test of a guidance device the army likes. Berlin hoped it would prove useful to us." He eyed each of them in turn. "I need your frank comments, miene Herren, concerning the navigational aspect of last night's fiasco."

Kellner cleared his throat nervously. "We made landfall at the common mouth of the two rivers, Herr Fregattenkapitan. The Orwell River leads to Ipswich, the Stour River toward Colchester. Unfortunately, Reinhart followed the Stour."

Peter resisted slumping in his chair. Kellner, you son of a bitch, you ordered me to follow the damned –

"This is not a fault-finding session, Kellner. It is an equipment evaluation. Reinhart, could you not see the problem from your position beneath the cloud cover and low over the ground?"

Peter sensed Kellner's quick glance but kept his eyes on Strasser. The Zeppelin's kommandant knew damned well Peter had questioned their course and had been told to stay on it. That was where the error was made – one of about 20 degrees – and it had resulted in their missing the target by 30 kilometers.

"Reinhart?" Strasser prompted.

Was the Zeppelin kommandant going to let his dangling observer take the fall? He knows damned well it was not my fault. Peter hesitated.

Then Kellner shifted in his chair. "Leutnant Reinhart questioned our heading, Herr Fregattenkapitän, "but I ordered him to follow the river he saw dead ahead. Unfortunately, it was the wrong river. The fault is mine, not his."

Peter breathed again. Thank you, Kapitänleutnant.

Strasser turned back to him. "You had no compass in the sub-cloud car?"

"No instrumentation at all, sir. And no light to see a compass if I'd had one. The angel bask – the sub-cloud car – may be of some use in army daylight attacks, but at night, it is of little or no use over unlighted countryside. In my opinion, of course, Herr Fregattenkapitän."

"And," Strasser said to Kellner, "from the vantage point of the Zeppelin, your thoughts on the effect of the sub-cloud car? Speak frankly, Herr Kapitänleutnant."

"There was the drag effect on the Zeppelin's airspeed. Only a few knots, but in certain circumstances, that could be critical. When Reinhart reported an enemy aeroplane in the vicinity, I knew it could strike the car or its suspending wire. We would lose Reinhart and also damage the Zeppelin."

"Your recommendation?"

"May I continue to speak frank –?"

"For God's sake, man, your recommendation!"

Kellner frowned. Peter held his breath.

Then Kellner said, "Screw that damned angel basket."

Strasser turned to Peter. "And you, Leutnant, as occupant of the car?"

"Kapitänleutnant Kellner has expressed it precisely, sir."

With a hint of a smile, Strasser nodded. "Test completed. Results negative. Thank you, Gentlemen. Dismissed."

Stepping into the muggy afternoon, Kellner again cleared his throat. "I'm afraid he has left the sticky part to me, Leutnant."

"The sticky part?"

"I suspect so. I have been informed you have been assigned permanently to my crew as our observer." As Kellner spoke, Peter thought he wore a look of relief.

Scheisse! Assigned to the last crew anyone at Nordholz wanted to be a part of.

"By Strasser?"

"No, Reinhart" Kellner said, his expression now one of puzzlement. "By Berlin." He glanced around. They were alone. "I trust you," he said quietly. Then he looked Peter straight in the eye. A man about to confess? "I need you."

29.

As he neared the intersection with the Hamburg-Hannover Road, Peter slowed the Ford. To the right, 130 kilometers south: my mother. To the left, through the city of Hamburg then a long pull to Kiel: Lexie.

When Kapitänleutnant Kellner welcomed Peter to his crew of misfits, he had wangled him a full week's leave. "You suffered a wound in combat, Leutnant. Convalescent leave is in order. And the summer's heat is knocking the hell out of our lift. There's not much flying anyway. So make the best of it. I will see you in a week."

Kellner, Peter discovered, was not the gruff airship kommandant he had first met in training. Over beers in the Officers Club one rainy evening, Kellner stared at his mug, then at Peter. "I'm a farm boy, Leutnant. A farm boy with a knack for machinery. Got sick of spreading manure when Delag needed apprentice Maybach engine mechanics. Took me two years to work my way into the control car. First as elevator man. Then helmsman. When the war broke out, I volunteered for naval airship service. Not many experienced airshipmen then. I was rushed into airship school then into an L-3 class Zeppelin as kommandant."

He paused for a long swallow of beer. "I'm talking too much. It's the beer." But he went right on. "I know I'm no Mathy. I've made mistakes.

The black sheep. That's why I get the, uh… crewmen the Division doesn't know what to do with." He reddened. "Not you, Leutnant. I don't know how or why you are on my crew. It's the only good luck I've had."

"I'm complimented, Herr Kommandant," Peter had said. But not inspired.

At the intersection, he stopped. I have to decide. The bandage is gone. The stitches are out. But I have this bright red scar from mid-hairline to left eyebrow. Mother would be horrified. Better to give it more time to fade. But I made this decision before I left Nordholz, didn't I? He swung the Ford left. For Kiel. For Lexie.

In Hamburg's sooty haze, he managed to become lost until he crossed a bridge with an impressive view of the harbor and its twin rows of huge sheds. To the west, he could see estates of the city's prosperous. As he drove northward along the Alster River, the stop-and-go traffic didn't agree with the Ford. The engine lagged, caught, lagged. If you're going to break down, Herr Ford, do it now. We are about to face 100 kilometers of not much between here and Kiel.

Then in lighter traffic, the tough little auto picked up smoothly. My thanks to Alois, chief of the Nordholz motor yard, and the few quiet marks a month I slip him to put in free-time hours on what he called Peter's "American tin."

Several kilometers north of the harbor, he swung east across the Alster, then north again. After another kilometer of dwindling streets, he drove into flat, sandy country. In just a few hours, I will be with Lexie. When I asked about hotels near her – started to ask – she shushed me. "I live in a house, Peter, a tiny one, a carriage house. But there is room for two of us." This was a dream. A whole week with the woman I love. What a way to forget the damned war. Or try to. Can I forget, even in Lexie's arms, my Berlin-directed assignment to Kellner's crew?

Hell, worry about that when I get to it. My concern now is finding Lexie's carriage house. He gunned the engine, and the Ford leaped toward Kiel.

At a crossroad in the tiny town of Neumuenster, a sign pointed left to Flensburg, straight ahead to Kiel. Fewer than 30 kilometers to go, thank God. This has been a long pull.

…Flensburg. I've heard that town mentioned. By Franz babbling about Delag's early days and Hugo Eckener's past. Eckener from Flensburg.

Heard it again, didn't I? The second time... The second time – Yes. I remember. My God!

Despite the late afternoon heat, a chill skittered through him. Was it possible? His mind raced. Admiral Kottenhoff had to be warned.

Or am I jumping to a dangerous conclusion? Suspicion is one thing. Proof is quite another. But will I be able to get proof?

Daylight had begun to fade as the Ford rolled into the outskirts of Kiel in sight of the harbor. Rumpled, dusty, with leg muscles threatening to cramp, he pulled to the side of the road to consult the hand-drawn map Lexie had mailed him. A light breeze carried the acrid smell of coal smoke as a battle cruiser slowly made way toward the Baltic. He stuffed the map back in his pocket, shifted the idling engine into gear and skirted the city's western edge. On a narrow lane just south of the Kiel Canal, he turned directly west.

He passed sprawling estates, lawns manicured, lights beginning to gleam in the large houses well back from the road. He drove by an expanse of woods. Just beyond it, behind a chest-high wall, a broad lawn fronted an impressive three-story mansion, red stone without a single light in any of its tall windows.

Exactly as Lexie had described it. And there's the gateway flanked by a pair of stone posts supporting wide-open iron gates. He slowed and turned into the gravel driveway. The drive rose gently to the mansion's entrance – then extended rightward toward a small fieldstone building in a copse of pines. The carriage house. Next to it, Lexie's blue Panhard! He pulled up beside it.

The carriage house door flew open. "Peter! You're here!"

Incredibly beautiful in a swirling, dark green skirt, pale green blouse, shoulder length auburn hair flying free – the most beautiful woman in the world.

She rushed into his arms, crushed her lips to his. Pressed her body to his.

"Mein Gott, Liebchen," he managed. "It's so wonderful to see you. I thought I'd never get –"

She pulled back. "Your forehead, Peter! What happened?"

"Banged my head during a flight." He decided to let it go at that. "Needed a few stitches. No lasting damage. A scar, probably. Will a scar bother you?"

"Of course not. But how –"

He waved her concern aside. "I'm starving, Liebchen. Might there be a restaurant in this rich man's wilderness?"

"Not tonight. Not for you... I have supper waiting."

"Now that's what I call a royal welcome!" He grabbed his bag from the Ford's floor, and they rushed arm-in-arm into the carriage house.

The front door led directly into a living room with a kitchenette to the left, a pine dining table and two chairs. Across the room, a sofa, a table with a telephone.

"For calls from and to the mansion?"

"It was, but when father made the arrangement, he asked Herr Manstein to have the outside line to the house extended here."

She pointed to the door at the rear of the living room. "Bedroom and bath back there."

"A bathroom in a carriage house?"

"When Pappi knew I would be living here, he talked Herr Manstein into it."

"My thanks to both of them. After ten hours in my bouncing American tin, I can use a wash-up."

"The estate belongs to the Mansteins," Lexie told him as they finished the Black Forest Torte she had made for him. "The family spends summers in America. New Hampshire, I think, where Herr Manstein owns a furniture factory. When the war started, he decided they would wait it out in America."

"I suppose he thought it would last only a few weeks, like we all thought. In a few weeks, it will be a year."

"With no end in sight."

"I'd never say that to our Airship Division Kommandant. Fregattenkapitän Strasser is sure he will put enough Zeppelins over London to make the English throw up their hands."

She stood and began clearing the table. "Is he right?"

"Would bombs falling on Hamburg make you want to give up or fight back? Here, let me help." He joined her at the sink, something his mother had never asked him to do, nor had he wanted to. But working next to Lexie, bumping elbows, was fun. When the last dish was dried and stacked in the overhead cupboard, she led him to the sofa. He slipped his arm across her shoulders and pulled her close.

"This is wonderful, Peter, But I… But…" She looked down.

"Say it, Lexie." He kept his voice gentle. "Whatever you want to say, it could never change the way I feel about you."

"I love you so, Peter. But… Sometimes I don't feel you are being open with me." She touched the slash on his forehead. "Can't you tell me how this really happened?"

"Just part of a Zeppelin crew's work," he muttered.

"Peter?" Her soft fingertips turned his head toward her. "That's just what I mean. You're treating me like a hothouse flower. I'm not. You know I'm not."

`"No, you're not. I'm sorry. All right. Nothing hidden from now on. I was part of a really wild test flight for what I consider a ridiculous device." And, careful to avoid overplaying his horrendous ride in the damned angel basket, he told her what had happened.

"What an incredible experience!" she burst out. "Terrifying."

The reaction I expected, he thought. But she seemed a little envious.

"Now," he said, "a question for you," he said. "If it's not too personal."

"Ask me anything, Peter." She smiled. "Anything at all."

"How on earth did you manage to find this little hideaway?"

"Oh. Through my father. I can't escape his dear helpfulness. Herr Manstein's factories use woodworking machines made by Pappi's company. When father learned the Mansteins were going to stay in America, he asked Herr Manstein if – well, you get the picture. I pay for electricity and telephone and keep an eye on the property. But nobody comes to a closed-up mansion. What I have is privacy. Which sometimes, to be truthful, is quite overwhelming. So I'm very happy to have you here, Peter. It is wonderful to have company at all, but when that company is the man I love, it is –" She grinned at him. "It's *daring!*"

"And it's getting late." He looked about the room and gave her a mischievous look. "Let's see. Where should I sleep? There's this sofa. There's the floor."

"Oh, stop it, Herr Prüder Mensch. There is the bed."

"Oh, you're right. There is the bed." Then he sobered. "Lexie, I think I said at the Blauer Adler we were taking a risk that could –"

With a finger to his lips, she silenced him. "I have visited my doctor in Kiel, Peter. There is no need to worry."

"Suddenly I don't feel tired. But I do want to go to bed."

"Oh, so do I, my love. So do I."

She was softly naked, her skin like satin against his. They lay side by side. Then he gently caressed her breast.

"Mmmm," she murmured. And nestled in his arms. "Love me, Peter," she whispered. "Love me. Never let me go."

30.

Peter awoke to the half-light of dawn edging the bedroom's curtained window. He lay on his back, Lexie snuggled softly against him, both of them gloriously naked.

"You're awake?" she whispered.

"I thought I'd sleep until noon, but I can't get the admiral out of my mind – even when I'm asleep. That's what woke me up. I was dreaming about it. Told him I knew who had reported his anti-airship campaign to Berlin, and he rushed at me like a madman. I was shocked awake just in time."

"Only a fantasy, Liebchen."

"Not altogether.

Her arm slipped softly across his chest. "Not altogether?"

"I think I do know who the informer is."

"Who?" she murmured absently as she slipped her leg over his.

"I'm not so sure you're interested in my detective work, Lexie."

"I am. I am. But at the moment, another interest is becoming much more compelling."

"I suspect I know what you mean, but the admiral –"

"Oh Lord, Peter, stop talking politics and pay attention." She loomed above him, her hair tickling his face as she bent down to meet his lips. "Let me conduct the magic this time, Love. Not the schottische –"

"Sorry. But it had been so long since we –"

"Oh, I enjoyed that dance, but now let's try a slow, dreamy pavane."

When he awoke the second time, she rested on an elbow, gazing at him. "So who do you think this informer is?" she asked.

"And a good morning to you, too." He chuckled. "You certainly are a woman of purpose. The challenge is to recognize which one when."

"Last night was not meant for an admiral's problems, but now tell me, who do you think is the sneaky... bastard who has put all three of us at risk?"

He looked at her in surprise.

"Well, he has. The admiral is despondent, you are assigned to an incompetent crew, and look at you!" She gently touched his forehead. "So who? That weasel, Moellendorff? Unreadable Leutant Krause? Who?"

He told her.

She was silent for long seconds. Then she said, "I hadn't thought of that possibility. But the admiral will insist on proof. How in the world will you convince him?"

"I have a plan."

"A plan? That sounds fascinating."

And more hopeful than reassuring, he realized. *I'll end up a genius or an idiot.* "A plan," he said, "that will cost us an evening together. Possibly an entire night."

"Now I'm not so eager to hear it. Breakfast first?"

An hour later, bathed and dressed, they sat down to cold cuts, cheese, boiled eggs, black bread and coffee. And a question from Peter. "Can you arrange to have the admiral join you for lunch somewhere out of the way? I think it best not to mention on the phone I will be there. Switchboards have ears, and with Berlin issuing orders on me –"

"And on the admiral, Peter. He was summoned to Berlin last week and came back looking as if lightning had struck him. He hasn't been the same man since. When I asked if I could possibly take this week off, he didn't even look up. Just waved his hand and nodded."

"This whole thing is getting too far out of hand for all of us."

"I'm not sure who knows what, but I am sure we have to prove to the admiral your theory on who has been the informer. So how do we do that?"

Peter stirred his coffee then clanked the spoon on the saucer. "I'll tell you how we might do it." And he told her. "So," he said, when he finished, "How do you think the admiral will react to this little project of mine?"

"I have no idea. Let's hope he'll go along with it."

And then hope I'm right. "Step one, my beautiful roommate, is yours. A call this morning to the admiral." He peered at her. "Why are you looking at me like that?"

Her emerald eyes stayed on his. "Because, my love, I know what a terrible position you are in."

"No worse than your own, Lexie."

"I'm a civilian employee, a naïve woman, I assume the press would put it. Ordered by my employer to deliver a series of reports from Nordholz. Or so a lawyer might put it. The publicity, though, could be terrible."

He studied her. Ever a woman of surprises, aren't you, Lexie. "I've never heard you say anything like that. You sound as if you are ready to distance yourself from the admiral. And from me?"

"No, oh no." She reached across the table to take his hand. "I'm making a comparison. A comparison of our situations. Mine is not as shaky as yours. You are caught between two opposites: an admiral who hates the airship service and a man –"

"Strasser. A man who is convinced the airship will win the war. And now," he shook his head in disbelief, "also caught by my conscience. It's telling me to warn the admiral about the back-stabber who has put all three of us in this mess."

She rose to carry their dishes to the sink. 'No, stay there, Peter. There's more hot coffee. I'll call Admiral Kottenhoff."

At the Café am Meer – an irony, because the obscure little café was several blocks back from Kiel's Schweden Kai, the strip along the waterfront – he and Lexie waited at a corner table.

"No navy people here," she said quietly.

"No admiral, either. He's late. Or maybe he's not going to show at all." I'm almost hoping he won't, Peter realized. I can be on the brink of making a total ass of myself.

"He's walking here from Procurement, Peter. That could take –" Her eyes swung to the entrance. "Ah, here he is now."

Admiral Kottenhoff spotted them, nodded and made his way among the sparsely attended intervening tables.

"He's in his fifties," Peter murmured, "but now he looks like an old man."

"Since the Berlin trip. And he's –"

"Guten Tag, Alexia. A surprise to see Reinhart here. Good to see you, Leutnant, though I have no idea why you are in Kiel." Then he looked toward Lexie and smiled. "Oh, I see. Sit down, Reinhart. Tell me why I am here."

Peter pulled his chair closer to the table and leaned toward the admiral.

"Your order, Sir?" The aproned waiter looked to be all of sixteen. Possibly the son of the owner, Peter thought.

"Lexie and I have ordered, Sir," he told the admiral.

"Reibekuchen. And a Pilsner," Kottenhoff said. When the waiter retreated, he turned back to Peter. "Well?"

"I am reasonably certain who our informer is, Herr Admiral."

Kottenhoff gave him an odd look. "Ja? Who?"

In a near whisper, Peter told him.

The admiral reared back in shock. "I find that very hard to believe, Leutnant. Do you have any proof? Any proof at all?"

"I have a plan to get that proof, Sir." A plan? Or just a stab in the dark? Too late to back out. And he told Kottenhoff what he wanted to do.

The admiral, stone-faced, heard him out.

Am I making a complete fool of myself? Peter wondered in the silence that followed. If he won't go along with this, then what? Are we to blunder on, with reports on all of it slipped to Berlin until we both are brought before a military court?

Then Kottenhoff asked, "Is that all you have, Leutnant?"

"At present, Herr Admiral. But I believe we can get proof."

"When?"

"Tonight, Sir. If you agree."

Kottenhoff compressed his lips, the perfect study of a superior forced to consider the improbable theory of a subordinate. Then he stroked a sideburn with a pensive forefinger. And surprised them both. "Worth a try, Leutnant. Now tell me how you got that wound on your forehead."

* * *

Precisely at 21.00 hours, Peter pulled the Ford into the parking area at the admiral's residence and twisted the door chime. A moment later, the door opened a few inches then swung wide.

"Good evening, Sir."

"Good evening, Albert. Is the admiral available?"

"I'll show you in, Sir."

The stooped houseman led the way to the library and tapped on the open door. "Leutnant Reinhart, Herr Admiral."

"Come in, Leutnant." Kottenhoff rose from behind his desk. "Come in."

Peter pulled a folded sheet of paper from his pocket.

"Ah, your sub-cloud car report. That will be all, Albert, unless the Leutnant would like some late evening refreshment?"

"No, thank you, Sir. I'm here just briefly."

"In that case, Albert, you may retire. I will see our guest out. Please close the library door on your way out."

Peter handed the paper to the admiral, who placed it in the desk's center drawer and flicked out the small lamp on the desk. Hastily written when Peter returned to the carriage house after lunch, the report was essentially what he had told Strasser after his nearly fatal ride in the angel basket.

"Sit down, Reinhart, over here near the fire."

"Just a few moments, Herr Admiral, then we must--"

"You really believe you are going to prove something with this little scheme of yours?"

"With luck, Sir." *God, have I actually said that? A feeble choice of words. This afternoon I was so damned certain about this grand plan of mine, but now I feel like a schoolboy sitting here with the schoolmaster – who, for all I know, is waiting for me to fall flat on my face.*

He stole a glance at the admiral, silent, his features deeply shadowed by the fading firelight. *That's not the face of the aggressive airship detractor I first met nearly a year ago. An old man's face now. A defeated old man. What had happened in Berlin?*

The admiral is staring into the fire as if I'm not here.

After long minutes, Peter suspected the admiral was waiting for him to act. He stood.

"Time to proceed, Sir."

Kottenhoff sighed then pushed out of his chair. "I shall see you to the door."

As Peter stepped into the night, he turned back. "I appreciate your willingness to go along with this, Herr Admiral. Let's hope for success."

"I am ambivalent, Leutnant. You can understand why."

"Yes, I do. Good night, Herr Admiral."

As the door shut behind him, Peter walked in wan moonlight to the Ford. He cranked the engine and drove off noisily. For perhaps 100 meters. Then he switched off the ignition. The Ford drifted to a stop on the road's sod shoulder. He waited a few minutes. Then, careful to walk on the turf, he stole back to Kottenhoff's looming residence.

Had the admiral remembered not to lock the door? Peter depressed the big brass latch. The door inched open. The admiral had played his part. In the darkened hall, Peter could make out the dying fire's faint glow in the library doorway. He ran his fingers along the wall on his right, found the entrance, and silently slipped into the dining room. He eased one of the chairs from the table and slid it along the carpet to the corner of the room with an oblique view of the library entrance. The chair creaked slightly as he eased down and stretched out his legs. No. That was too comfortable. He pulled his feet back and sat at rigid attention.

The house was dead silent. His back began to ache. He relaxed. Just a bit. Just enough to – A muffled sound froze him. He held his breath. Silence. Had to be embers collapsing in the library fireplace.

He breathed again. At the far end of the hallway, he heard a clock chime. Only 21.45.

Long minutes later, when the distant clock rang out ten measured strikes, Peter was becoming certain this melodramatic inspiration of his was turning into an embarrassment at best. A stupid stunt, for certain. I've talked an admiral – an admiral, for God's sake – into this craziness, based on nothing more than a coincidence that could mean nothing, and logic that could mean less.

Four notes down the hall. 22.15 hours, but it felt later than midnight. Not much sleep last night. Lexie was so… compliant. And wonderfully forward, too. Not a woman to spend her life in the kitchen. A good part of it in the bedroom, though. She will be a delight for the rest of my life. If there is any rest of my life. Depends on Kellner, doesn't it? I like the man, possibly because he recognizes his own faults. A navigator he's not. But he knows that. And his crew – my crew now. The misfits. I keep thinking that gang in the bomb room could have pulled the angel basket up a lot faster.

Just what are the chances of surviving the war in a hydrogen-filled flying whale? So far, the problems have been weather, accidents and ground fire against low-flying airships. Most flights, though, are scouting missions over water for the surface navy, though the public is told we swarm over England like flocks of eagles. The real story... real story...

What was that? Mein Gott, I was dozing. But I heard something, something sliding.

The dim light in the library doorway was no longer the ruddy glow of the dying fire. Now it was the pale yellow of an electric lamp.

Peter rose silently from the chair, stole across the hall. Then he stood in the library doorway, arms folded.

"Good evening, Albert. Have you found what you are looking for?"

In shirtsleeves, the admiral's trusted houseman straightened so abruptly his head banged against the desk lamp he had moved toward the open center drawer. His writing pad and pencil clattered to the desktop. Face ashen, eyes wide, he tried to slip a sheet of paper into the open drawer, the paper Peter had given the admiral.

"Too late, Albert."

The houseman stared at him.

"Nothing to say?"

"I – I'm only doing my duty."

"Your duty? For God's sake, you are betraying your employer."

"He, Sir, has been betraying the navy." Rebounding from his surprise, Albert slammed the drawer shut. "And you denounce me?"

Peter rushed to the desk, lunged across it. Grabbed Albert's shirtfront. Pulled him close. "You disloyal son of a bitch, you work for him. You're a servant, not a policy maker."

"I work for the navy," Albert shot back. He pulled free and straightened into rigid attention.

The electric sconces along the walls flared on. "You were right, Leutnant," A voice thundered from the doorway. "I am disgusted with you, Albert." Admiral Kottenhoff, a maroon robe over his pajamas, strode into the room.

"My apology for doubting your theory, Reinhart. The Flensburg coincidence seemed altogether too flimsy." He turned to Albert, standing stiffly behind the desk. "Is the Leutnant also correct in assuming you had some connection with your fellow Flensburg resident, Hugo Eckener?"

"My sister was his housekeeper until he joined Count von Zeppelin in Wilhelmshafen."

"Eckener hired you to spy on me?"

"Herr Eckener recommended me to Naval Intelligence," Albert said defiantly. "I work for them."

"Well, you just lost your assignment. You will leave this house at sunrise."

Albert's eyes drifted down – toward his pad on the desk.

"There is nothing in that paper of Leutnant Reinhart's that he hasn't already fully discussed with Airship Division Kommandant Strasser. Naval Intelligence can get it from Strasser if they wish, and you can get out of this house at six hundred hours tomorrow, Albert. Dismissed!"

No longer the subservient houseman, Albert stalked past them and out of the library.

"A God damned contract spy." Kottenhoff shook his head in disbelief. "You may have missed your calling, Leutnant. Naval Intelligence could use such talent."

"Thank you, Sir."

"But unfortunately your detective work has come too late."

"I am aware of that, Sir. The near miss with the sub-cloud car, the assignment to an inferior crew."

"Too late for both of us."

Peter was silent. The trip to Berlin. What had the navy's high command done to their controversial career admiral?

Kottenhoff sank wearily into one of the chairs near the fireplace. "I could do with a good stiff brandy, Reinhart. You, too, I suspect. There's a bottle and glasses in the dining room cabinet. Do you mind?"

Peter returned with the brandy to find Kottenhoff staring into the ashes of the dead fire. He put down the snifters and poured two generous ones. "Herr Admiral?"

"What? Oh, thanks." He took the glass and downed three quick swallows.

"Join me, Reinhart." He indicated the other chair flanking the low table displaying the ship model, then his eyes went back to the ashes.

In the uncomfortable silence, Peter sat on the edge of his chair, both hands holding his brandy snifter.

"I have been ordered to resign," Kottenhoff said abruptly. "At the end of this month."

Resign. A man in his early fifties who had spent most of his life in the navy. "I am truly sorry, Herr Admiral."

"My own doing. I was fully aware the navy did not appreciate criticism, surely not from one of its own. I was warned, by von Tirpitz himself. Expected a reprimand. Got one, from von Tirpitz himself. But I persisted. And now I am ordered to resign. By von Tirpitz. Himself."

Again, silence.

Peter's brain raced. If a career admiral is being pushed out of the navy in wartime, is my assignment to Kellner's crew the worst I can expect? And what about Lexie?

"If I may ask, Sir, have you any idea what may be done to Alexia?"

"With luck, she would simply be notified her services are no longer required. I will do what I can for her. Possibly have her reassigned out of Kiel, away from this mess." He looked at the floor and slowly shook his head. "I truly regret having brought both of you to this unhappy outcome. I can give Alexia an excellent reference, for what that may be worth from a disgraced employer. I believe I can do more than that for you, Leutnant. In the days remaining before I leave the navy, I should be able to have you reassigned to a naval command other than the Airship Division. As I recall, you had originally hoped for battleship service."

"Yes, Sir."

"That may be a possibility. I do have personal contacts, old friends I can call upon."

Peter's heart raced. A golden chance to get himself out of gasbags and into the surface navy. Off Kellner's disorganized and potentially lethal crew. He liked Kellner, but the rest of his crew would offer nothing but problems. Kellner was counting on him to make a difference. Kellner counting on him...

"Leutnant? It cannot be a difficult decision. As you, yourself, have pointed out, the airship raids have proved to be no more than pinpricks, if any find their targets at all. And the English are reinforcing their defenses every day."

Yes, they are, Peter knew. Yet, it suddenly struck him, that was something he had barely considered.

"That may be the real value of the Airship Division's bombing attacks, Herr Admiral. All those English guns, aircraft and men assigned to defense against our airships, all that is prevented from serving at the Front. By such logic, Sir, the effect of a few Zeppelins raiding could already be equal to something of a defeat for the English at the front lines."

Kottenhoff frowned. "Interesting rationalization, Leutnant. With some value, but at what cost?" His eyes held Peter's. "You haven't responded to my offer to have you transferred."

Am I hesitating because of my own little lecture on logistics, Peter wondered, or the memory of that hopeful look on Kellner's face when he told me of my assignment to his crew? Still, the possibility of battleship service...

"Your offer is much appreciated, Herr Admiral. And battleship service has been my intent all through my years at the Academy. And since."

"Good. I will see what I can do."

Peter hesitated, then inquired, "If I may ask, Herr Admiral?"

"Ask what you will, Reinhart."

Peter's voice faltered. Then he managed, "What will you do after... after –?"

"The end of my navy career? I haven't thought that far ahead. I doubt that industry would hire a disgraced, old admiral." He swirled the brandy remaining in his glass, stared at it vacantly. "A disgraced, old admiral," he muttered. Then he broke his stare and shrugged. "Of course, there's always the honorable way out."

Peter felt his heart pound. "Admiral, for God's sake, there has to be a better way –"

"No surer way, I'm afraid."

"After all you've worked for, it would be a tragedy, Herr Admiral."

"I'm so damned tired of fighting everybody – Forgive me. I'm..." He stood unsteadily. "I've got to get to bed. This has been a thoroughly exhausting night for body and soul."

"Promise me something, Herr Admiral."

"A leutnant demanding an admiral's promise?"

"Sleep on any hasty decision."

"And what do I get in return?" Kottenhoff asked with a wry smile.

"Your life, Sir?"

"I'm not sure I want what's left of it."

"I do, Admiral."

Kottenhoff's face softened. "I can't imagine why, but I thank you for that. May we both sleep well tonight."

31.

"The 'honorable way out'?" Lexie said as a small clock on the carriage house wall chimed midnight. "What did the admiral mean by that?"

Sprawled beside her on the sofa, Peter avoided her look. "You don't want to know."

"I do want to know, Peter. My leutnant has been depressed since he returned from the admiral's house. What is he hiding?"

Peter sighed. "To a military man, it means... ending it."

Her heart froze. "Suicide? Because his houseman turns out to be the informer, he's thinking of killing himself? God, Peter, we must do something."

"Do something?"

"Stop him."

He slipped his arm across her shoulders and pulled her close. "A leutnant zur see telling an admiral not to do something? An impossibility."

"Unless we could somehow do it indirectly," she said.

"Suggest something to get his mind off the indignity of forced retirement?"

"Write a memoir, perhaps. That's what Pappi keeps saying he'll do when he retires. Write a memoir."

"That's a good idea. The admiral would be free to write whatever –" He stopped. "No, that's not a good idea. We could find ourselves in print, and not favorably."

"Oh, Peter. You think he would actually expose what we've been doing for him?"

"Who knows what he'd write in the heat of being forced to cut his career short? Punished for opposing what he is convinced is a huge military mistake."

Nestled in the crook of his arm, she gave him an ironic little laugh.

"What's funny?" he asked.

"You realize we're wracking our brains for a way to save the man who made you a spy against your own service?"

"And made you a carrier of anti-airship information."

"And got you that scar on your forehead."

"And," he said softly, "he is the man who arranged for us to work together."

"And my falling in love with you," she whispered, her lips brushing his ear. "So how do we help this villain?"

"Through your father, possibly?"

She almost winced. *Nineteen fifteen, and women still are so damned suppressed. Pappi again. I've worked hard to become independent. Yet I have my job, my automobile, this carriage house, all thanks to Pappi. And now Peter suggests asking for his help with the admiral. How absolutely ironic.*

She sighed. "I will telephone him in the morning. Now let's... get some sleep. Last night was wonderful, but now I can barely keep my eyes open."

"Pappi? I apologize for calling you so –"

"You never need apologize for calling your Pappi, Liebchen. Even so early in the day. Do I sense a problem?"

"A problem for our friend, the admiral."

"I have already heard, Alexia. He has been ordered to resign."

"I should never expect to have such news sooner than you, Pappi. But please do not tell anyone what I am going to say."

Otto Tammler's tone sobered. "You have me concerned, Alexia. What's wrong?"

"It's the admiral. He has – He has threatened to... 'The honorable way out,' he called it. He is thinking of suicide."

"Mein Gott." After a long pause, Pappi said, "I understand your concern, Liebchen, but it should not be your problem. Let me think on it a bit. I promise I won't let him – or you – down."

"I'm so sorry to have to ask you –"

"Now, none of that, Daughter. What do you think fathers are for? My love to you, Liebchen. I will see what I can do for our friend."

"I love you, Pappi." And I can't ever seem to get free of your help.

"So how did it go?" Peter asked as she hung up the receiver and returned to their breakfast table.

"Pappi said he had heard about the admiral's forced retirement. And he sounded really concerned over how despondent he is." She spread a slice of black bread with the barely edible lard that passed for butter these days.

"Do you think he really will try to do something?"

"From my father, a promise is sacred."

"I know how you feel about asking him for favors."

"He likes me to ask. My problem is I don't like to ask."

"I understand that, Lexie. And I love you for it. For that and a lot more." He pushed back from the table. "Let's go find fuel for the Ford. It's getting scarce, I'm afraid. Then how about a stroll along the waterfront?"

The rest of the week, less one day, passed in a kaleidoscope of abandonment and passion. He had never felt as close to anyone as he felt with Lexie. But overriding it all was the foreboding of what awaited him on his return to Nordholz. Then, nudged by conscience, he tore himself away a day early to permit an overnight detour to Hannover.

They clung together the final moment of his final day at the carriage house. "I wish we could stay here together forever," Lexie murmured.

"So do I, Liebchen. But the war won't wait."

"The damned war."

His mother handled the impact of his still-red scar with more equanimity than he had expected. Perhaps because the romance in Hannover seemed to have deepened. "Am I about to gain a stepfather?" he asked his mother playfully? With Professor von Storch conducting a seminar in Braunschweig, Peter found himself speaking freely about his mother's and von Storch's relationship.

She actually grinned at him. "Only with your blessing, Peter."

"That you most certainly have, Mother. There's no need to ask. And the date?"

"The day the war is over."

"Mother, if you truly want to marry Horst, don't wait. The war seems to be lasting forever."

He left early the next morning, drove through rain squalls all the way back to Nordholz and pulled into the airship base late in the day, soaked. He had put up the folding canvas top, but without side windows, the Ford was no pleasure in wind-driven rain.

"So," Franz said with a leer as Peter changed into dry clothes, "how was – where did you tell us you were going? Oh, yes, Kiel. What were you doing there?"

"Personal business, Franz."

"Personal… Ah, your betrothed. You told us she works for the navy in Kiel. Himmel Herrgott, a whole week with her!"

"Mind your own business, you clod. Tell me what has been going on here."

"Let me see. Ernst is on another inspection tour, this one up at Fuhlsbüttel. There's a meat shortage at the Officers Mess –"

"I mean what about Strasser and his airship war?"

"Don't they have newspapers in Kiel?"

"I wasn't up there to read newspapers, Franz."

"I can believe that, you rascal. Well, the kaiser has finally removed restrictions on London attacks. Now everything's a target, except royal palaces and 'historic edifices,' whatever that means. As if our airship commanders are accurate enough to avoid them."

Peter pulled on his boots. "As if they can even find London."

"Strasser thinks they can. When word of the change came through from Berlin, he ordered a five-airship attack. Two of them from here. L-10 and L-11, with Strasser himself aboard L-10. Would've been three from here, but Kellner's crew screwed up on take-off. Pulled up too steeply and damaged the ventral rudder. That ship is still down for repairs."

"Kellner's misfits."

"Yeah, them. I heard a rumor you're being assigned to that bunch."

"That rumor, I'm afraid, is no rumor."

"You can't be serious!"

"I can and I am. You are looking at Hugo Kellner's replacement observer."

"You've got to be joking, Peter. What did you do to deserve that?"

Peter knew, or suspected he knew. But he said, "My wonderful work in the angel basket, I suppose. So Kellner missed out on the big raid?"

"Everybody missed out. L-9 out of Hage, was detached to bomb Hull, but they bombed Goole, thirty kilometers west of Hull. Wrecked ten houses, killed sixteen people, according to the Dutch papers. In L-15, Mathy turned around over the North Sea and limped back to Hage with engine trouble. The other airship from Hage and the two airships from here couldn't find London. Wenke thought he dropped L-10's load on ships in East London. Turned out he hit the Island of Sheppy, fifty kilometers east."

"A real fiasco."

"Gets worse. Von Buttlar thought we were over--"

"'We'?"

"I was in the aft engine gondola. Replacement for an ill engineering officer. Von Buttlar was assigned to hit Harwich. When he thought we were over Harwich. we got shot at – and missed, thank God. We dumped our bombs. Near Lowestoft, as it turned out. We were only 50 kilometers northeast of our target, and most of the bombs went into the water."

"Hell of a night, Franz."

"You still haven't heard the worst. The fifth airship on that raid, Peterson's L-12 out of Hage, never got near London. Wandered around until he spotted what he thought was Harwich. Dropped all his bombs and missed. They went into the water – not off Harwich, though. He was over Dover Harbor ninety kilometers south of Harwich."

"These are the weapons that are going to win the war?"

"Yeah, for which side? Dover artillery blasted away at him and got some hits. Two hydrogen cells. Peterson headed for occupied Belgium, but he didn't make it. The Zepp went down in the channel off Zeebrügge, stayed afloat and one of our torpedo boats towed it to Oostende. The English sent three floatplanes to bomb her. They all missed, and one was shot down. Then six more attacked, but all missed."

"That was damned lucky."

"Until luck ran out. The salvage crew got the control gondola loose and out of the water, then the hull exploded and burned. A great finale to Strasser's first raid under the new directive." Franz jumped to his feet. "Enough of that. You had anything to eat?"

"Since breakfast in Hannover, only a sandwich. Officers Mess must be closed by now. Maybe the Club will still have something."

"I'll go with you. I could do with a beer. And I still have to fill you in on the raid two nights ago. Another fiasco."

"Another?"

"Four Zepps. Wenke and von Buttlar from here were the only ones to reach England. Wenke dropped on Harwich. Von Buttlar couldn't find a worthwhile target and kept his bombs. Barely made it back here through one hell of a thunder squall."

"And Strasser hit the roof?" Peter closed the door behind them as they stepped into the hall.

"Nothing stops our fire-breathing leader. As soon as this weather clears, you can bet on another try to plaster London."

Halfway down the stairs, Peter heard Franz chuckle.

"What are you laughing at?"

"It just struck me that after a week in Kiel with your fiancée, now you can get some rest floundering around looking for London."

Twelve hours later, Peter was in the air and stunned by the morning's events. It all began with Kommandant Kellner's startling news that Bader, his sour-faced executive officer, had been transferred to Hage airship field, and was in training there for the position of kommandant of a new L-10 class Zeppelin.

"To ease the shortage of trained personnel, observers are assuming executive officer responsibilities in addition to their observer duties. That includes you." He paused. "You look less than delighted, Reinhart. Let me finish. A one-grade promotion goes with it. So, Oberleutnant zur See Reinhart, a wider stripe for your sleeves, and I will assist you through your first mission as our executive officer. A scouting assignment. We leave at oh nine hundred o'clock."

Now here he stood, shoulder to shoulder with Kellner in the control gondola's glassed-in forward section. When he came aboard, the helmsman and elevator man had given him the barest of nods. The radio operator was occupied with his Telefunken equipment and did not even look up. Apparently, the control car crew was not accepting his sudden ascendancy to exec officer with grace. Or there was no warmth among these guys in the first place. An hour into their west course over the North Sea, the helmsman, elevator man and radio op were still as readable as a pair of robots.

As they neared their assigned altitude, Kellner said in his ear, "Another tedious scouting flight. That's all this old gasbag has been flying since Strasser decided to send only the L-10 class ships on bombing missions. We're nursing an antique with a radio good only for short-range scouting. And there's never much of anything to scout close to the Frisians."

In the pleasantly cool late summer air at 1500 meters, they crossed Wangerooge the westernmost of the German-held East Frisian island chain. Fifteen minutes later, Kellner ordered the helmsman to bear a few degrees leftward to keep the islands in sight along the port horizon.

Peter sighed with boredom. Two hours out, in this brain-numbing first flight as executive officer. *The North Sea looks like a lake. Not a cloud in the sky. Just some haze ahead. Nice day for a picnic... Nice day to be with Lexie.*

He leaned against the bomb toggle console, lulled by the smooth grumble of the Maybachs into a daydream of her lovely lithe body, her – He shook his head. *No time for that. You're exec and observer. Observe.*

He noticed a deepening of the haze. He leaned forward. No horizon. Off to port, he could barely make out a distant island.

"Borkum," Kellner said beside him. "Last of the German Frisians, and the limit of our patrol sector. Helmsman," he called, "come about easterly to eighty degrees."

At the front of the gondola, the helmsman spun his rudder wheel clockwise. The ponderous airship swung slowly rightward in a long arc, the haze deepening as they turned further seaward. In an observer's reflex, Peter swept the haze-shrouded sea west as they turned. Nothing but the frustrating opaqueness of the –

"Herr Kommandant, what do you make of that?" He pointed ahead as the needle on the console-mounted compass inched past north.

Kellner grabbed his binoculars. "Where away?"

"Five degrees to port now. Something's down there."

"I see nothing, Reinhart. Not – Wait. Helmsman, new heading. Three hundred fifty degrees." Kellner pulled the suspended speaking tube's funnel close. "Engines to fast cruise."

With his binoculars glued in place, Peter watched the dark blob below resolve into a small ship. "Seaplane tender," he called to Kellner. "And it looks like she's launching one."

As they roared nearer, he could make out the wings of a floatplane beneath a crane aboard the tender. The faces of the deck crew gaped upward. As the airship rumbled closer, the floatplane splashed onto the sea's rolling swells. Blue and white rondelles with red centers marked the gray upper wing.

"British, Herr Kommandant."

"Bomb room, open the bomb door," Kellner ordered into the speaking tube. Much too late, Peter thought. Kellner grabbed the console's bomb release toggles. Then his hands dropped away. By now, the tender and floatplane were a half kilometer behind.

But still close enough for Peter to see the aeroplane's propeller become a shimmering disc. The crane's cable whipped free. A frothy wake grew behind the floatplane as it began its take-off run.

The flat thud of an explosion swung Peter around to stare at a burst of smoke dead ahead. The helmsman spun his wheel frantically as they plunged through it. The acrid tang of exploded cordite swirled into the gondola.

"Wait for my order, damn it!" Kellner shouted at the helmsman. "Hard aport. Hard aport. Come about."

As they turned back, another shell burst shook them. Peter ran aft and craned over the open starboard side. Where in hell were those shells coming from? Not from the tender. He'd been watching it when the first shell exploded.

Then he froze. As the airship swung ponderously away from the anti-aircraft fire, another far larger dark shape emerged from the haze.

"Battle cruiser!" Peter shouted.

As the airship completed its 180-degree reverse, a third, then a fourth shell burst at least 200 meters aft.

"They've lost the range," Kellner told Peter. "The tender is dead ahead."

"Where has the damned floatplane got to?" Peter scanned the sky forward. Port. Starboard. He rushed aft again, leaned over the starboard sill. There was the British aircraft, off the water now, its pilot's face a white dot, craning upward.

"He's still low," Peter called to Kellner.

No response. The kommandant, intent on bombing the tender, hunched over the bombsight on the center console, hands back on the toggles.

Peter glanced at the altimeter. Fifteen hundred meters. According to the recognition charts I've memorized, the floatplane looks like a Sopwith Schneider. Ceiling: 2300 meters, just a few hundred meters below our ceiling.

He stared back at the floatplane. Still well below. As he watched, two black objects fell from it to splash into the sea. The pilot had ditched his bomb load. Now his intention was clear.

"Climb!" Peter yelled at the elevator man, who stared at him, white as plaster.

"You heard me, climb."

"Five degrees starboard," Kellner ordered the helmsman. "Starboard, starboard." He whirled around to glare at the elevator man. "Hold your altitude. You had no order to climb."

"I gave the order, Sir," Peter told him. "The floatplane –"

A burst of machine gun fire rattled below them. Peter rushed to port, leaned over the side. The biplane, nose high, howled upward.

"Christ!" Kellner yelled. He reached for the bomb toggles, pulled. All four 45-kilogram bombs of their skimpy scouting load plunged downward. And missed the tender by at least 100 meters.

"Full power," Kellner ordered into the voice tube. "All engines, full power." He glanced at Peter then told the elevator man, "Maintain maximum climb."

After an agonizing delay, during which Peter heard a tinny confusion of voices from the voice tube, the Maybachs' tempo ramped up to full power. Now he couldn't spot the Sopwith. But he heard its yowling engine. Directly below them. Its machine gun yammered.

"He hit us!" the helmsman shouted over his shoulder. Peter peered forward. A scatter of small holes had appeared in the bottom of the hull where its upward curve began. Surely, hydrogen cells 15 and 16 had been punctured.

"Sailmaker forward. Bullet hole repairs," Kellner ordered. "Check the three forward cells." Holes in the bottoms of hydrogen cells were not critical, Peter knew, but holes in their tops let the hydrogen flow out.

They heard machine gun fire again, but this time, its rattle came from overhead.

Kellner's face went dead white. "Mein Gott, the damned Englander is above us."

"That sounded like a Maxim, Sir. Our gunner up on the hull. The Sopwith's still below, directly below. And our gunners in the aft gondola can't fire straight down."

"Then what in hell is our top gunner shooting at up there?"

"Panic, I think."

Kellner grabbed the voice tube to the gunner's platform. "What's your target up there...? You thought you saw something? Hold your fire, damn it. We could have hydrogen leaks forward. Your muzzle blasts will blow us all to kingdom come."

He glared at the altimeter. "Nineteen hundred meters. What do you think his ceiling is?"

"Twenty-three hundred meters, Sir."

"You sound damned sure of yourself, Oberleutnant."

"It's a Sopwith Schneider, Sir. It's ceiling is –"

"Twenty-three hundred meters. You're a walking encyclo –"

The Sopwith fired a third burst. Peter felt the gondola's metal flooring shudder beneath his boots. A scattering of slugs ripped upward, whined and pinged through the gondola and slammed into the hull above them.

"Anyone hit?" Kellner called. "Helmsman? Elevator man? Radio? You, Reinhart?"

Peter shook his head and peered down from portside. Here again comes the persistent Britisher. No hole to crawl in. Even if the gondola were armor plated, if the airship goes, we all go.

The Sopwith's climb steepened, but seemed to have slowed. As its machine gun began to wink again, the floatplane's nose abruptly pitched downward and the Britisher fell away.

"He stalled out!" Peter reported. "By the time he pulls out and climbs again, we could be above his ceiling."

The enemy pilot apparently had the same thought. Peter watched the

Sopwith plunge away in a long arc toward the tender, its pilot no doubt fuming at glory lost. Just as Kellner was.

"Ein Fiasko, Reinhart. Missed our big chance to sink a floatplane tender, and we return full of bullet holes."

"But no wounded, Sir."

"The only plus."

"There may be another. I saw the Sopwith drop a bomb load in the sea to come after us. His target could have been Hage or even Nordholz."

"A point, Reinhart. An interesting –"

A piercing whistle from the speaking tube cut Kellner short. "What is it?" he barked, then put its funneled end to his ear. "Ach, Gott!"

He turned to Peter. "Machine gun holes in cells sixteen and seventeen mostly repairable. What's not repairable is a two-meter tear in cell eighteen, the bow cell. Shrapnel from the cruiser's first shell did it. The cell has lost all its hydrogen."

"Yet we are still climbing."

"Yes, we are, Reinhart, but when we level off, we are going to be nose heavy. Landing could be a problem."

32.

As they droned eastward, Peter wondered why the elevator man was staring aft. Then he glanced over his shoulder at Peter.

"Down there, Sir. They've got a problem."

Peter leaned over the portside sill and raised his binoculars. The floatplane, possibly returning to the tender for a replacement pair of bombs, must have made a truly bad landing. A hundred meters from the tender, only the twin bottoms of its floats were visible. The Sopwith floated upside down as the tiny figure of its pilot flailed toward a small boat the tender had put over the side.

Peter rushed forward. "The Sopwith has crashed on landing, Herr Kommandant."

Kellner broke into a smile, all too brief. "Radio report to Nordholz, Oberleutnant. We have sustained damage from a floatplane attack and cannon fire from a British cruiser. The floatplane has crashed. We are returning to base. Our landing will be a problem."

Peter turned toward the shaken radioman, and then Kellner caught his eye again.

"Do not have him report we missed bombing the tender. Failed to get a shot at the attacking floatplane or were surprised by the cruiser. Christ!"

The kommandant grabbed the speaking tube. "Engine crews! All engines to fast cruise. "

Shoving the funnel aside, he told Peter, "That's for airspeed for elevator control. To keep the nose up. I'm dumping forward ballast, but God help us when we throttle back to land this thing."

As the radio operator went to work, Peter stared bleakly at the Ems estuary rolling beneath the stricken airship. This damned war our kaiser predicted would end "before the leaves fall" is in its second year – after one hell of a first year. From a green leutnant zur see trapped by an admiral's self-destructive obsession to an oberleutnant. Now I am second in command of an airship crewed by unreliables.

A year of uncertainty. Of guilt. Of terror. That damned ride in the angel basket. And one very bright, almost redeeming part of all this: Lexie.

As they crossed the coastline, the struggling Zeppelin surged upward through a strong updraft. We're doing well enough at fast cruise, Peter felt. But what's going to happen when we struggle to get this thing down without killing ourselves?

The town of Norden passed to starboard. Peter caught Kellner's attention and pointed at Hage airship field, visible a few kilometers beyond the town.

The airship kommandant shook his head. "We are returning to our own base, Reinhart. The problem is not staying in the air. The problem is getting safely on the ground."

Sixty kilometers later, they passed over the sprawl of Wilhelmshafen. Peter scanned the city's outskirts for an open area. An emergency landing with no ground crew? An impractical thought born of desperation. Kellner pressed on.

As the glittering bay of Jade Busen passed below, Peter was certain they were losing altitude. When Bremerhaven's smoky haze drifted by a few kilometers south, he eased forward to steal a look at the altimeter. Only 1000 meters now. Since leaving the Borkum Island area, they had lost a third of their altitude

He glanced at Kellner. Grim. Surely pondering his decision to pass by Hage.

At last, the familiar humped airship sheds of Nordholz lay ahead. Engines yowling, they flew nose high, but they were still sinking.

Kellner grabbed the auxiliary speaking tube to the gunner atop the hull. "Get out of there. Now. Down into the hull." He pushed that tube aside and seized the main speaking tube funnel. "Cut power to idle. Drop handling ropes. Jettison all ballast. Then brace yourselves. We are going in hard."

The engines' thunder faded to a grumble. The nose sank below the horizon. Almost twenty degrees below, Peter noted. His stomach felt as if he'd swallowed a lump of ice. At a hundred meters and dropping fast, they raced over the airship field's western boundary, the nearby sheds passing in a blur.

"Engines, full power for five seconds. Now. Now!" Kellner ordered. "Elevator up full." He grabbed the ballast release toggles.

The Maybachs burst into life again. Feathery streams of jettisoned water ballast burst from the stricken Zeppelin. The angle of descent eased. But only a few degrees. Grabbing one of the gondola's supporting struts with both arms, Peter watched the ground rush upward. To make matters worse, if that were possible, they were coming in downwind. The rushing ground became a green river, reaching up to drown them.

"Cut power," Kellner cried. But the engines kept hammering. He stared aft, letting the speaking tube swing free.

Peter took the funnel. "All engines stop." He kept his voice steady. "All engines stop." And the engines went still. Kellner stared at him. Then nodded.

The rushing river tilted upward. Then Peter heard the crackle and bang of breaking limbs and tree trunks. He was torn from the supporting strut. His flailing arms wrapped around the hull access ladder. Overhead he heard the screech and bang of tearing duralumin girders. The massive hull canted to the right, settled into the shattering trees like a stricken elephant.

The gondola smacked the ground with a bone-jarring thud, slamming all of them to the floor. But it stayed in one piece. Peter heard the hiss of escaping gas. Then silence, broken in a few seconds by the shouts of escaping crewmen.

"Anyone hurt in here?" Kellner's shaky voice. On the canted flooring, Peter struggled to his feet. Kellner pushed away from the control console, fell back against it, pushed free again.

"Reinhart?"

"I'm all right, Sir." With his handkerchief, he wiped his bloody hands. "Helmsman, elevator man? Radio?"

They were thoroughly shaken. Bruised, cut. But none appeared seriously injured.

"God, that was a rough one," one of the two grease-stained engine mechanics said as they clawed through the battered hatch from the engine room in the gondola's aft section. "Don't want to do that more than once a month."

"Or year," said the other.

"Out," Kellner ordered. "Everyone out. Fast. We're surrounded by hydrogen."

They fled through the gondola's access door, Kellner urging them along then stumbling out last. He scrambled to the edge of the woods, cupped his hands and shouted, "Everyone out, fast, fast. Assemble here on me."

He turned to Peter. "Bad luck followed by good, Reinhart, then bad again. We crash land, but the woods is a shock absorber. But, as you see –" He pointed to the top of the two-thirds of the hull that had remained out in the open. "She's broken her back. The least I can expect from Strasser out of all this will be one hell of a black cigar."

Peter and Kellner herded the straggling crewmembers into a group at the edge of the woods. "A head count, Herr Oberleutnant," Kellner ordered. Miraculously, Peter found all 16 of the crew, a gaggle of shaken men.

"Several broken arms," Herr Kommandant." A collection of cuts, sprains and bruises. One engine man may have a broken leg.

Then they were surrounded by the ground handlers, who were promptly herded aside to make way for the base's ambulance. The casualties were loaded into the ambulance as several trucks bounced through the growing crowd to transport the crew for evaluation by the medical officer.

"Kapitänleutnant Kellner and Oberleutnant Reinhart?" The enlisted driver standing by the door of a staff vehicle saluted. "I am to drive you immediately to Fregattenkapitän Strasser."

Kellner looked at Peter then rolled his eyes upward. "Sorry, Reinhart. Let's hope he stops short of a firing squad."

Strasser, narrow goateed face impassive, pointed Kellner and Peter to two chairs near his desk. Chairs? Peter had steeled himself for a fiery dressing down with them standing at rigid attention.

"Tell me what happened, Kapitänleutnant Kellner," their fireball leader demanded. "In full."

He listened impassively as Kellner blurted out a detailed report of the day's fiasco, a truly contrite admission of failure.

Strasser rose from his desk, projecting dominance despite his short stature. He clasped his hands behind his back and began to pace as he spoke. Slowly; both the pacing and his words. All of this, Peter knew, was a chilling preamble to what surely was about to be the blackest of cigars the Kommandant of Airships had ever laid upon an airship kommandant and his executive officer. *A true disaster to mark my first flight as second-in-command.*

"How shall I say it?" Strasser spoke as if to himself. "A Zeppelin destroyed as I watch. It roars into the woods and oblivion."

As Kellner was about to speak, Strasser silenced him with an upraised hand. "Say nothing, please." He swung around to pace back toward them. "Listen closely. For continued development of improved airships, the height climbers, it is essential that Berlin and the public understand the full worth of the Naval Airship Division. Now feel free to stop me if my summary of your report departs from accuracy."

Strasser's face remained impassive, but Peter thought he detected an odd glint in those penetrating eyes.

"As I understand it," the Kommandant of Airships said in an unusually conversational tone, "you were on a flight near the East Frisians when you sighted a floatplane tender about to launch its aircraft. Without hesitation, you attempted to bomb the tender, causing the floatplane to abort its apparent intention to bomb, I would assume, the airship base at nearby Hage."

Strasser reversed his pacing again and gazed upward. Like an author, Peter thought, seeking inspiration.

"As the floatplane climbed toward you, a British cruiser emerged from the dense haze seaward and fired at you, damaging the forward hydrogen cells. You fired at the approaching enemy aircraft, forcing it to stall, drop away and crash into the sea. Then, with hydrogen leaking, you managed to return to Nordholz. You made an emergency landing with a badly damaged airship without any serious injuries to its crew, though the Zeppelin was so severely battle damaged, it did not survive the landing."

He stopped his infernal pacing and faced them from behind the desk, both palms flat on its blotter. "Does that accurately sum up your destruction of an enemy aircraft, the near-destruction of its tender and your commendable and successful effort to save your crew?"

"It –" Kellner's voice failed. He tried again. "Precisely, Herr Fregattenkapitän."

"Good. Precision, by all means. That, then, is the report I will forward to Berlin. You will be assigned a replacement airship. But not another damned L-3 class. You will get an L-10. Dismissed, Gentlemen."

Out in the warm afternoon sun, Kellner's rough features wore a look of wonderment. "I don't know whether to shout with joy or just hope I don't wake up."

"Saved by political expediency, Sir. Strasser needs good news, not disasters." Peter cocked his thumb toward their crumpled airship, now crawling with salvage workers. "Don't be too flabbergasted, Herr Kommandant, if you get a medal out of that."

"I'll settle for the L-10 class replacement."

With two days remaining of his naval career, Erwin Kottenhoff slumped behind the desk in the library of his tomb-silent mansion. Without Albert to lay a fire for him, he had neither the need nor the inclination to do that chore himself. Not on what was about to be the final night of his now shattered life.

He lifted the Model 1898 Mauser pistol from its stained cardboard storage box and discarded its protective cloth. A collector's item now, the pistol had been a casual purchase from a Bremerhaven gun shop more than a decade ago. He had long forgotten why he had acquired the Mauser, nor could he recall having ever fired it.

He nestled the cylindrical grip in his right hand, pulled back the slide to cock it, released the slide, aimed the pistol upward and pulled the trigger. The crisp click echoed in the silent room. Perfect working order.

He reached into the storage carton to withdraw a box of shells. They were old, but kept dry all these years, they should be as live as the day they came from the gun shop's shelf. Live enough, anyway. He pulled back the slide again, inserted a single shell in the exposed chamber and snapped the slide back in place. Cocked and ready.

Cook Clara and Eva, the housemaid, had retired to their third floor lodgings. Would either of them hear the shot? Or would their first awareness of this desperation be a horrified Eva finding him slumped on the desk when she delivered his breakfast? A distressing thought. He hoped neither of them would be haunted by the false guilt of thinking they had done nothing to prevent this.

The honorable way out? Or the coward's way out? Too late to debate the philosophical aspects of blowing out my brains. This simply was a way out.

He raised the pistol. The mouth? God, I can't stand the thought of the front sight tearing out my teeth.

The temple.

Reinhart... Alexia... Guilt for them, too? But I am the guilty one. He placed the cold muzzle against his right temple. Steadied his trembling hand. Slipped his forefinger against the trigger –

Like a message from God, the phone jangled. He jumped. Good thing the trigger pull was in pounds, not ounces. Good thing?

A phone call at 21.30 o'clock? He held the pistol between temple and desktop, a tableau of indecision.

The damned telephone persisted. Would it continue its infernal racket until he steeled himself all over again and pulled the trigger? Or lifted the receiver and replaced it to break the connection? But would that deter this persistent caller from simply placing the call again?

With a groan of frustration, he set down the Mauser and put the receiver to his ear.

"Kotten--" He cleared his throat. "Kottenhoff."

"Erwin? Otto Tammler. How are you?"

How am I? For God's sake, I'm on the brink of shooting myself, Otto. That's how I am.

But he said, "I am well, Otto." Without much conviction.

"I, uh, have heard in a roundabout way, you are contemplating retirement."

Stop dancing, Otto. "That is correct."

"It has struck me that can be a fortunate turn of events, old friend. A fortunate turn."

"Fortunate?" What in hell was this man thinking?

"It happens I was talking recently with the procurement manager of one of my customers. He is leaving his present employer to accept a somewhat more lucrative position."

"Why are you telling me this, Otto?"

"Because it crossed my mind that with you about to become a free agent, so to speak, you could be just the man to replace him."

"As procurement manager? An admiral the navy has... A career officer who has apparently outlived his usefulness?"

"Is not procurement management precisely what you have been doing since the war began, Erwin?"

"That I cannot deny. What, may I ask, is the company your customer is leaving?"

"That, old friend, is why I know you should jump at this opportunity. The company is Gothaer Waggonfabrik A G, now in accelerated development of the Gotha G.II, the bombing aircraft our army intends to replace their airships, Erwin. To replace their airships."

Gothaer Waggonfabrik! The very firm that had hired Moellendorff's arcane services, which led to their anti-airship conspiring together. The firm whose bomber aeroplane could well replace the airship as the Fatherland's aerial attack weapon. My being forced out of the navy because of my anti-airship disdain frees me for employment by an anti-airship company? Divine providence?

"If you are interested in pursuing this opportunity, Erwin. I urge you to call Herr Hermann Mantz at your earliest opportunity."

Kottenhoff grabbed a pencil and scrawled the name and the telephone number that followed.

"Consider this seriously, Erwin," Otto urged.

"It is a most interesting proposal. I appreciate your bringing it to my attention."

"By the way, with your departure from Naval Procurement, my daughter will be faced with –"

"I will do what I can for Alexia, Otto. Rest assured. And my sincere thanks for your interest in my situation."

He hung up the receiver, reached for the Mauser again. Held it in both hands. For a long moment. Then he carefully wrapped it in its protective cloth and set it back in its storage box.

33.

"Before I..." Kottenhoff cleared his throat. "Before I leave, I want to thank you for your work, Alexia. Both here at the Procurement Division and on our other... project." Again, he paused. Project is my way of putting it, he reflected. More accurately, it has been a debacle for all three of us.

On this last day as an active duty admiral, sitting for the last time behind this desk, I'm finding it difficult to say farewell to this lovely, tall and remarkably competent woman. My faithful office aide. Aide? Accomplice is more like it. Accomplice in my conspiracy that has brought all of us down. Placed Reinhart in physical jeopardy. Cost Alexia her employment. Though that is something I can still influence.

"What will you do now?" she asked as he was about to ask the same of her.

He stood and faced the big window behind his desk. "I have been fortunate, Alexia. A position very much like this one but without the gold and brass is available in Gotha. I am accepting it. The Thuringer Wald will replace this view of Kiel Harbor, if indeed I have any window at all."

"I am delighted you have a new position, Herr Admiral." She smiled as he turned back to her.

"Sit down, dear girl. Sit down." He glanced at the clock on his desk. "In fourteen hours, 'Herr Admiral' will become simply 'Herr Kottenhoff,' a man no longer with stripes on his cuffs, now actually working to supplant the overrated airship with the far more practical bomber aeroplane of Gothaer Waggonfabrik A.G."

"You will be moving to Gotha?"

"I have already arranged lodgings there, Alexia. That will require me to close temporarily the house here in Kiel, of course. I have found new positions for the cook and housemaid."

"The automobile, Herr Admiral. What will you –?"

"'Herr Kottenhoff,'" he reminded her with a smile. "As for the Daimler, the navy has lost no time in reclaiming it. So I have purchased a new – well, new to me, since all automobiles manufactured now are destined for the military. I have acquired a modest but roadworthy Mercedes from a Department officer who has been transferred to sea duty."

"But you have no driver."

"My dear, I was not always a chauffeured admiral. You need not worry about me. But I have worried about you, which is why I have taken the liberty of making several telephone calls in your behalf. Especially after I learned that Leutnant Krause had submitted a request for your transfer from this office to his."

"Oh dear. Leutnant Krause."

"As I have deduced, Alexia. You should see your expression. So, should you be willing to leave Kiel, there is an opening in the office of the kommandant of one of the Navy's Ordnance and Mine Inspection Depots. A need for an assistant adept at shorthand and the typewriter, as you have certainly proved to be."

"Leave Kiel to go… where, Sir?"

"Cuxhaven."

"Cuxhaven?"

He was amused by her questioning look suddenly becoming one of realization.

"Yes, very close to Nordholz." A wave of sadness swept over him, and he turned back to the window. *Leaving this office, this place of punishment, is in itself a punishment. But that's mitigated by the opportunity I have engineered for her. And by the one she surely has engineered for me.*

He heard her rise from her chair. Then he was brought near tears by her gentle touch on his shoulder.

"Thank you, Sir," she said softly, "for your kindness."

He faced her, placed his hands on her shoulders. "It does not compare with the kindness you have done for me, Alexia." His lips brushed her forehead. "I wish only the best for you and Peter. May the war be over soon."

Hugo Kellner's wide-set eyes flicked around his and Peter's temporary lodging in the officers' quarters at Johannisthal airship field. Through their single window, Peter glanced southward toward the distant buildings of Berlin.

"Quite a surprise," Kellner said, "how quickly we have been assigned a new L-10 class Zepp. I'm told the Zeppelin works are rushing production on them to make way for prototype production of Strasser's height climbers. Our good luck. And already here we are for a week of transition to our new airship."

Sprawled on one of the small room's two bunks, Peter wondered whether Kellner was as elated as he sounded, or was he on edge? Just before they had boarded the truck that brought them here – a wearying drag through farmland and wooded expanses – Strasser had confirmed his new policy. Only L-10 class Zeppelins would continue to attack England. The few remaining L-3 types were permanently assigned to scouting duty.

With an early morning start, Peter and his airship kommandant had arrived at Johannisthal in mid-afternoon and had yet to settle in. The rest of the crew was to follow tomorrow. Then would begin the week of training on the new airship they were to fly back to Nordholz. The tight schedule would permit no chance to spend even a few hours in Berlin.

Kellner slipped off his tunic, sank on his bunk then laid back, fingers laced behind his head, to gaze at the ceiling.

"Are you as happy with this as I am, Reinhart? You haven't said much about it."

Peter turned from the window to sit on the edge of his bunk, hands on his knees.

"I'm happy we survived that landing last week."

"And happy with Strasser's version of our patrol's 'accomplishment.'"

"For sure." Peter thought a moment. "Though my ride in the angel basket was –"

"Worse. Time to be honest, Reinhart. I know my crew's work on the winch was not exactly – well, it was lousy."

"That's one way to put it, Sir."

Kellner sat up. "Damned right. To my order to reel you in, they responded like a bunch of schoolboys. I reamed them out, but I'm no Prussian." He shook his head. "I'll be frank with my new executive officer. I'm no adventurer, either. I'm in airships because I didn't want to spend the war in rain, mud and snow."

"No disgrace in that, Sir."

"I've always thought I was assigned to airship kommandant training because I was the oldest man in the group I volunteered with."

Peter found Kellner's burst of frankness embarrassing, yet oddly appealing. "You are underrating yourself, Sir."

"Let's drop the formalities when we are alone. Our new Zeppelin could kill us together, so it's 'Hugo.'"

"And 'Peter,' as well." He was finding Kellner quite human, though Strasser and the whole damned navy would frown on such informality.

"Good," Kellner said. "I've known I could trust you since that first time we flew together. That training flight when you knew I was lost almost in sight of Nordholz. You covered for me and I have never forgotten that, Peter."

"I only –"

Kellner waved him silent. "Be a mute priest while I am confessing. I am a lousy navigator. When navigation was made the airship kommandant's full responsibility, I was saved by all those scouting patrols in sight of land. If Mathy can't find London, how in hell was this flying farmer – that's what I was before joining the navy, a major grower of bread grains but a farmer—so how was this airborne farmer to find a target in the dark?

"I was counting on Bader, the exec you have replaced. Fortunately the order for my crew to bomb England had yet to come." He laughed. "But we managed to destroy our Zeppelin anyway."

"That's not the way Strasser saw it."

"Ah, but he was desperate for good publicity, not a story of a bumbling crew. Here's a test for you, Peter. How many errors did we make on that disastrous mission?"

An airship kommandant asking his new exec to criticize performance? Remarkable.

"Peter?"

"In my opinion, Sir –"

"'Hugo.' Please."

"In my opinion…Hugo, the first was my sighting the seaplane tender too late to drop our bombs on our first pass over it."

"Minor, compared to my preoccupation with the bombsight instead of ordering maximum climb as soon as we saw that floatplane. Next?"

"After we were hit, we might have landed safely at Hage while there may have been some hydrogen remaining in the damaged cells."

Kellner nodded. "Granted. And the final error was the chief engine man's failure to cut power just as we landed – plus my leaving the speaking tube to stare aft. You took over, but the delay put us into the trees."

"Which did absorb a hell of a shock, Hugo."

"But which resulted in major damage and the loss of the airship."

"So here we are," Peter said. "Praised by Strasser and about to receive a new, improved Zeppelin. Does the punishment fit the crime?"

"Good question." Kellner burst into laughter, the first time Peter had seen him truly laugh.

Then Kellner sobered. "I know my biggest failing. I've been so involved in flying the Zeppelin, I've let crew discipline slide. I'm not sure I'm cut out to be —"

"Hugo," Peter broke in, "I've been thinking about that. Now that crew efficiency is our problem, can you give me a copy of the crew roster — with photographs?"

Kellner looked at him with raised eyebrows. "As soon as we return to Nordholz." Then he pushed off the bunk. "Come, let's find out where officers can get something to eat."

The following afternoon, their crew arrived. The day after that, they all were in the air over the lakes north of the haze-shrouded clutter of Berlin, learning the finer points of L-10 class handling from a laconic veteran Delag Kapitän. At first glance, the only striking difference between the L-3 class Zeppelins and the new L-10 types was below the hull. No longer open gondolas, the control car and aft engine car were fully enclosed with sliding observation windows port and starboard. And the new airship had four Maybach engines in place of the older ship's three.

The hull, though, looked no different. A mere six meters longer and four meters fatter. Such apparently minimal hull increases, though, resulted in an almost 50 percent increase in hydrogen volume. "Greater lift, greater load," their flint-eyed instructor boasted. "More bombs."

And a bigger bang, Peter thought, if we catch fire.

With lift sluggish in the heated air of late August afternoons, simulated bombing runs were a challenge. But ultimately, Kellner, though frustrated by his generally uninspired crew, met minimum standards. Then they were on their way back to Nordholz, Peter reveling in the relative comfort of the enclosed car, its lack of buffeting slipstream and the relief of communicating with the control car crew at near-conversational level.

"Good news, Lexie?" At the hallway phone, Peter lowered his voice. No need for the whole barrack to listen in on this. "Can you hear me?"

"Yes. I called to tell you I'm leaving Kiel."

"That's good news? You're no longer working for Procurement?"

"I've been let go, Peter."

"I'm still waiting for the good news."

"I'm going to Cuxhaven."

"Cuxhaven?"

"Yes. I will be working for the Kommandant of the Naval Ordnance and Mine Deport there. So close to you, Liebchen. I will almost be able to see you just over the horizon!"

His heart leaped. "That is good news. When do you leave?"

"In minutes. I just finished packing. How about you, Peter? I haven't heard from you in days."

He decided to say nothing about the crash. She had enough on her mind.

"We just flew in from Kohannisthal," he said. "We now have a new L-10 class Zeppelin."

"A new Zeppelin? Is it safer?"

"It's faster." A little. "Flies higher." Barely. "And the control car –"

"Car?"

"No open gondola now. It's enclosed. Much more comfortable." Comfortable? "It's a better airship, Lexie."

And specifically designed to hit London. But no need to tell her that.

34.

From his cramped office on the second floor of the rambling Gothaer Waggonfabrick complex, Erwin Kottenhoff leafed absently through the morning's stack of acquisition forms. On this third day on the job, already the paperwork has become an avalanche.

Small wonder the company was so ready to hire me, he thought. My predecessor probably threw up his hands and found a plausible excuse to get out of here. I heard the man had been elevated to this office from simple inspection duties in the aircraft assembly area. Then he must have suffocated under the paper tide. But this former Admiral of the Imperial Navy is not about to be sunk by mere paperwork. Amazing the miracles a challenge can inspire.

He leaned back from the piled-up desk. The most difficult adjustment had been-- still is-- losing the impact of wearing a uniform, he realized. Gold stripes carried a clout my plain woolen sleeves never will. This dated suit from the back of my bedroom closet still fits, but I can't recall when I bought it, or why.

Kottenhoff gazed through his narrow window to the airfield beyond. A small tug pulled a prototype Gotha G.II to the distant downwind end of the factory's flying field.

Marvelous how things changed in just a few days. The navy reclaimed its Daimler. So much for his hope its ownership record had been lost. He was left stranded, but for only a few days, until he was offered the Mercedes. In the nearby city of Gotha, he was fortunate to find lodgings in a small hotel, comfortable and affordable, at monthly rates. In truth, he was happy to rid himself, if only until the war's end, of that lonely mansion where his life had essentially diminished to only two rooms, the library and his bedroom.

With a surprising sense of elation, he returned the Mauser pistol to the attic. From the distant end of the flying field, he heard the rumble of the G.II's twin Mercedes engines. Their big propellers spun into shimmering discs. The huge aeroplane trundled into its take-off run, picked up speed. The tail rose. The twin pairs of wheels bounced free of the aerodrome's turf and the massive bomber lifted into the calm September afternoon. Its roaring climb brought it past the factory buildings so close the glass in Kottenhoff's window vibrated. The bomber flashed past, its 25-meter twin wings supported by a forest of struts. The pilot and the fore and aft gunners leaned forward in their cockpits adding urgency to the lumbering bomber as it swept past.

Back to his paperwork, with a sense of justice. A crew of three compared to an airship's 16, even 20 in Strasser's proposed height climbers. And the Gotha could carry a respectable bomb load faster than an L-10 class Zeppelin. Range was another matter. The Gotha's radius of action was only 500 kilometers, but London lay fewer than 300 kilometers from Germany's coast.

Remarkable, Kottenhoff thought. By forcing my retirement, von Tirpitz has made possible my far greater contribution to the abandonment of airships. The Gotha bomber is obviously —

The intercommunication device on his desk buzzed. "Herr Kottenhoff," a woman's voice rasped metallically, "you have a visitor."

A visitor? he wondered. Who, outside factory management, could possibly know I am here?

"Who is it?" he said into the electric box.

"A Herr Moellendorf, Herr Kottenhoff."

Max Moellendorf, that shifty "industrial relations" operative? What in hell could he want?

As he heard a heavy tread clump to the top of the stairs just beyond his closed door, Kottenhoff tensed. What can I say to this man whom I so arrogantly and mistakenly ordered out of my house just weeks ago? As Moellendorf rapped on the door, Kottenhoff felt his jowls suffuse with embarrassment. No way around this. Face the music.

"Herein," he called.

The door swung open and big, blustering Max Moellendorf, sharp little eyes wide-set in his doughy Fatty Arbuckle face, walked into the office. Grinning, for God's sake, with his huge paw extended.

"Herr Admiral!" he boomed. "A pleasure to see you again!"

Kottenhoff sat dumbfounded. "I ... Well, I--" He clambered to his feet and took the proffered hand with an uncertain grasp.

"I have heard what has happened, Herr Admiral. Your retirement, then this." He swung his arm around the tiny office.

Kottenhoff, stunned by Moellendorf's effusiveness, managed to point him to the chair by the desk then sank into his own.

"A sad decision for you, I'm sure. Your retirement. But, my friend, what an opportunity opens for you now. The Gotha Bomb Dropper is obviously the wave of the future, the very near future. And you are part of it."

"Herr Moellendorf--"

"'Max,' surely for old time's sake."

First name basis? I think not. "It is for 'old times' that I owe you a most heartfelt apology."

"Apology? Oh, for that invitation to leave your house. Just part of the game I was playing, Herr Admiral."

"The game?

"Enlisting your help without telling you who I was working for. Not that it would have made any difference in what we were doing. I just felt a little deception would help ease your participation. Gotha, was — still is — developing an army aircraft, and you were navy."

"But I treated you most discourteously, and totally under a misapprehension."

"Who was the culprit who betrayed you, Herr Admiral? That is something I have not been able to find out."

"The man who was driving the car you dented, who met you at my door, who served you drinks."

"Albert? That inoffensive old man?"

"He was younger than he wanted to appear. Part of his 'cover' as a contract agent for Naval Intelligence."

"I'll be damned. I never would have suspected him."

"Nor had I. Until an astute young leutnant sur zee caught him red -handed. Ironically not a detective but an airship officer."

"Poetic justice, or so goes the saying. And speaking of airships, I'm here to give out a bit of information that surely portends disastrous consequences for the airship bombing campaigns, especially the navy's, now that the arny has cut back its England attacks. "

"To the point, to the point." Was this to be a Moellendorf-style bombast, or did the man actually have something?

"First, I must assure you that I am a businessman, not some kind of secret agent. But as a businessman who intends to pursue opportunity after the war no matter who wins, I have managed to keep open certain ... pathways of information on both sides of the Channel. And through these pathways, I have learned-- Let me put it this way. Does the name John Pomeroy mean anything to you?"

"Pomeroy?"

"An Australian inventor of sorts. In August last year, just a few days into the war, Pomeroy presented the British War Office a design for an explosive bullet. The War Office saw no need for such ammunition, and Pomeroy, discouraged by such shortsightedness, returned to Australia."

Moellendorf reached into a jacket pocket and withdrew a silver case. "A cigarette, Herr Admiral? I have taken up the habit to ease the nerves a bit." He offered the open case.

"Thank you, no."

"These are American."

"About Pomeroy?" Kottenhoff reminded his visitor. No end of surprises with this man.

Moellendorf crossed his legs, struck a match on his shoe sole and brought the flame to his cigarette. "Well, it has finally penetrated the English military minds that Pomeroy's ammunition could well be the answer to the 'Zeppelin menace,' as they term it. In the meantime, a J.F. Buckingham has devised a phosphorus bullet, and Royal Navy Commander F.A. Brock has conducted successful tests with his own explosive bullet design."

"And now?"

"Now the British Ministry of Munitions is conducting tests of all three proposed munitions. The results, I'm told, prove the explosive bullets will blow holes in airship hydrogen cells. The incendiary bullets will then ignite the escaping hydrogen."

Moellendorf puffed on his cigarette, exhaled a bluish cloud. "I trust you grasp the import of all this."

Kottenhoff frowned. "How accurate do you believe this information to be?"

"I would trust my source with my life. In point of fact, I already do."

Kottenhoff's eyes swung toward his window. Such ammunition could mean the end of the airship as a weapon, precisely the result he had sacrificed his career to help bring about.

In the distance, the Gotha G.II ponderously swung into its final approach for landing. An omen?

He turned back to Moellendorf. "What you're telling me could make me look like a prophet. What do you intend to do with this information?"

"I have just done it. I have told you. Do you think for a moment any highly placed officer in a position to react would listen to such information from this not overly respected citizen? Granted, I take opportunity where I find it. But I am a loyal German, and I leave this ominous bit of intelligence with you in the hope you still have Navy Department contacts who will listen."

Do I thank this man or curse him? Kottenhoff wondered. Or simply ignore him? Should his information be accurate, do I let events take their predictably tragic course, or try to warn the very service that cost me my career?

This same afternoon, Alexia, too, gazed out the window above her typewriter table in the headquarters section of the Cuxhaven Naval Ordnance and Mine Depot. Thanks to Admiral Kottenhoff, here I am, working for jowly, barrel-shaped Korvettenkapitän Ludwig Graber, the Depot's kommandant.

She had watched Graber's obvious resentment of such pressure fade during their interview as his Teutonic blue eyes studied her carefully arranged auburn curls, her little smile, her-- oops. The eyes, much warmer now, flicked back up to hers. In that instant, she knew she had the job.

Confident she would not be retreating to Kiel, she had already closed down the carriage house, not an easy decision. She was forsaking its conveniences and solitude for an uncertain future on the North Sea coast. But while regretting the loss of her Kiel sanctuary, she thrilled at Cuxhaven's nearness to Peter.

She sent a letter of explanation to Herr Manstein in New Hampshire. Since he had not charged her rent, there was no problem about that. She cancelled the telephone and electrical services, shut off the water supply, drained the piping. With all her Kiel connections disconnected, she found lodging in a Cuxhaven seaside boarding house, not fancy but pleasant enough, with an impressive seaward view. Inconvenient, though, for ... visitors. Only a few kilometers from Nordholz, she was concerned with only one "visitor." But the Blauer Adler Inn-- aah, that wonderful inn-- it, too, was only a few kilometers away.

Again she had been served by influence, this time not her father's, but Admiral Kottenhoff's. Perhaps for an ambitious woman, this was the way of the world.

Over the sea, she noticed, the sky had darkened. In the looming gray clouds, lightning flared. Another wet afternoon. Of the five I've been here, four ended in rain. And now the sky is hidden again by low hanging storm clouds.

What is that up there? She watched the gleam resolve into an airship several kilometers southwest. Making for the coast. With Nordholz not far from Cuxhaven, here came one of its airships, racing for home just ahead of the storm.

The bellying clouds above the descending Zeppelin flashed bright yellow. She stared. Hadn't that lightning bolt speared down at the airship? Then a chill rushed through her. A burst of flame had flared from the airship's nose.

Her hands flew to her face. She gasped in disbelief as the fire raced upward and the forward section of the huge hull dissolved in flame. The airship tilted downward, flame racing along its length as it slowly sank toward the sea beneath a plume of roiling smoke.

To her horror, Alexia watched a tiny figure fall free. Then another. Crewmen opting to jump to their deaths, rather than burn. The doomed Zeppelin followed them down to splash into the North Sea waves, burning fiercely, its pall of smoke rising into the onrushing storm.

She tried to cry out, but she was breathing so fast she choked. She heard shouts in the corridor outside her door. Without thinking, she burst into Korvettenkapitän Graber's office.

"Did you--" she gasped. "Did you see--?

He gaped out his window, telephone in hand. Then he swung toward her. "Saw it, Fraulein. I have Nordholz on the line."

He turned back to the window. "One of yours?" he asked into the telephone.

"Ach, the L-10 returning from patrol."

Alexia's heart thundered. Hadn't Peter told her he was the new executive officer on the L-10?

Oh, dear God!

35.

"Telephone for Oberleutnant Reinhart." The shout echoed down the officers' quarters' second floor hallway.

"Don't make a scene of it, Heinrich," Peter shouted back as he clomped to the top of the stairs. Could this call have something to do with that distant explosion to the northwest, the one the whole place had just been outside gaping at? The base was in an uproar.

Heinrich Holtz, a fellow executive officer on another airship, handed him the receiver.

"Oberleutnant Reinhart speaking."

"Peter! God, it's a relief to hear your voice..."

"Lexie?" She sounded near tears.

"I just saw an airship burn, Liebchen. Lightning hit it. A horrible, horrible sight.

"Then we learned it was the L-10, and you had told me you were assigned to the L-10, I was terrified. I was afraid you--"

"Lexie, Lexie, calm down. Please. I told you I was assigned to an L-10 class airship. Zeppelins built after the L-10 are called 'L-10 class.' I should have made sure you realized that. I'm so sorry."

He could hear her gasping.

"Lexie?"

"I'm all right. Just struggling to catch my breath." Then she must have turned away from the phone. "Yes, Sir. I will be right there." And back again. "I'm sorry, Peter. Korvettenkapitän Graeber is shouting for me. Much love."

"Lexie, when are we--" But she had hung up. So near now, but they had yet to see each other since she had left Kiel.

"Berlin calling, I presume?" Franz joked as Peter walked into their room. But his tone held a touch of derision, noticeable since Peter's sudden upgrade in rank and ascent to executive officer status.

"Lexie on the phone. Near hysterics. She thought I was aboard that airship."

"On Hirsch's crew? The L-107."

"She happened to be watching it when it blew. Said she saw a bolt of lightning hit the Zepp."

"My God, no wonder she was upset."

"I think we're all upset, Franz. One lightning bolt, and sixteen men are burned alive. Not much of a morale builder."

Franz plunked down on the edge of his bunk. "And just when it's beginning to look like we might actually be home by Christmas."

Peter sprawled on the window seat. "What prompts that kind of optimism?"

"Ernst, for one. Before he went off to Tondern for a week's administrative duty."

"Ernst optimistic? That's a new one."

"Said the Australians were getting nowhere with their useless Gallipoli campaign. We are still pushing east on a 1200-meter front from the Baltic all the way down to Romania, and we're several hundred miles into Russia. And," Franz said, "don't forget our new weapon on the Western Front."

"New weapon?"

"The poison gas, Peter. It has devastated the British and French, and that's where the war is going to be won. On the Western Front."

"That's what Ernst thinks?"

"Him-- and my brother Kaspar in Berlin." He frowned at Peter. "You don't look all that convinced"

"I remember something one of my Academy instructors said. He got away with it then. I wonder if he would dare say it now?"

"What? What did he say?"

" 'Germany plans to perfection, but at the critical point, sadly misses.'"

At the early morning officers' meeting four days later, Strasser strode in like a one-man thunderstorm.

Ernst, just returned from Tondern, nudged Peter. "What in hell do you think has hit him? A black cigar from Tirpitz himself? Or maybe we're all being stripped of rank and sent to the Western Front."

"I have no idea what's eating him. My crew hasn't flown since we got back from Johannisthal, so it can't be something his favorite misfits have done."

"Gentlemen," Strasser boomed as he began his aggressive pacing. "Last night, history was made. The first airship attack on central London. We have hit the outskirts, but this Zeppelin managed to bomb the very heart of the British Empire."

"So what's he so angry about?" Ernst whispered.

"Unfortunately, this accomplishment was achieved not by one of our navy airships, but by the Army's LZ 74. But," he added, his expression now almost mirthful, "the army did manage to botch its historical achievement. The LZ 74 had already bombed a bunch of greenhouses at Cheshunt in London's northern outskirts--"

Chuckles rippled through his audience.

"--so by the time the airship defied London's searchlights and cannon fire, one bomb remained. A small incendiary. History made, but effect wasted, gentlemen. And opportunity still beckons."

He turned to face them. "Tomorrow, we show the world how the German Navy can do the job. L-9 will attack the Skinners Grove benzol works on the north Yorkshire Coast. Not much glory in that. But Buttlar, Boeker, Kellner in his new L-10 class airship, and Mathy out of Hage will all attack central London. And with a lot more impact than one feeble incendiary."

This time, hearty laughs.

"Hit central London, gentlemen, hit it hard. Weather information at eight hundred o'clock tomorrow morning. Dismissed!"

September 8 dawned clear of clouds, but with ground mist dimming Nordholz. In the early autumn sun, the mist dissipated through the morning, and at 13.30, Buttlar's L-11 rose away. Fifty minutes later,

Boeker's crew, in L-14, rumbled westward. Kellner, ready and waiting, was ordered to delay lift off. Word had just come from L-11, barely over the North Sea. Engine problems. Buttlar was limping back to Nordholz.

Long minutes later, Peter, leaning against the control console, watched the stricken airship rumble inbound trailing a thin stream of black smoke, then settle in.

Close beside him, the radio crackled. "Mathy in L-13, departed Hage at 14.10."

Kellner turned away from the control car's forward windows. "Looks like we and Mathy are going to be Strasser's 'big' response to the army's London strike."

"Only two of us?" came a shaky voice from the portside observation window. Leutnant sur See Schwinn, a slim blond trainee, flying today as an observer.

"A signal honor, Leutnant," Peter told him with a wry smile. "Our opportunity for glory. "

"Make ready for lift off, Oberleutnant," Kellner ordered. Five minutes later, their sleek new L-10 class Zeppelin, with 1,800 kilos of bombs in its midship racks, rose majestically from the airship base. At 1000 meters Kellner leveled off. At 37 knots, they plowed west-southwest.

Past the Frisians, Kellner held course across 300 kilometers of the North Sea. After five dragging hours against a light but persistent headwind, Leutnant Schwinn, surprisingly alert, called, "Airship, forty degrees to port on our level, Herr Komnandant."

"That will be Mathy," Kellner told Peter. "His engines at idle, waiting for full darkness. Order our engines to idle, Exec. We, too, will wait. And you make our position as...

"Some thirty kilometers to sea north of Wells-Next-The Sea on the Norfolk Coast, Sir."

The pair of Zeppelins hung in the darkening sky, rapidly becoming invisible. This was the "dark of the moon--" the portion of the month when Strasser scheduled attacks on England. Just as total darkness fell, Peter spotted barely discernible pinpoints of flame to the northwest.

"Mathy underway, Sir. About five kilometers to starboard."

"All engines fast cruise, Reinhart."

Peter relayed the order to the engine crews. He made a point of addressing them by name. Having memorized the crew roster, he believed personalizing orders could instill a sense of real responsibility.

A tremor ran through the control car as the dual Maybachs beneath the hull's aft section and the two in the engine car aft compartment roared. In minutes, the sparsely populated coastline drifted 1200 meters below. Mathy steepened into a climb. Kellner followed. They bore inland then made the standard turn southward to approach London.

Peter marveled at the boldness of the English, who obviously had made no attempt at blackout. As the two attacking airships droned southward, the lights of scattered small villages glittered below. Stars above and stars beneath. Were it not for their deadly cargo, this could be a night for poetry.

A larger cluster of lights drifted past some 20 kilometers to starboard. In the glimmer of the dimmed and shielded electric lamp over the control panel, Peter studied the navigation map. Has to be Cambridge. He squinted forward. Is that a glow on the horizon? Yes. London. And so brightly lit, it's visible here, eighty kilometers north.

Through the next hour and a half, Peter watched the glow broaden then resolve into a carpet of lights. The kommandant at Cuxhaven, with jurisdiction over lights far inland, had ordered Nordholz blacked out since the war began. But fast-approaching London, having already been attacked, still sprawled defiantly lit. Apparently German Zeppelins were of little consequence to the city's officials. Both Zeppelins, Mathy well in the lead, had climbed to 3,000 meters. At 23.40 o'clock, with L-13 still northwest of England's capital city, Peter was startled by a line of five explosions beneath Mathy's airship.

"Checking his bombsight," Kellner decided. At the city's edge, a searchlight beam shot skyward. Then another. The two beams began to sweep the sky like a pair of uncertain swords, crisscrossing then swinging away. And finding nothing.

The barely discernible pinpoints of L-13's engine exhausts bore straight across London's center. Beneath him, Mathy left a succession of explosions that burst yellow against the lighted streets then resolved into a string of fires.

Now explosions began to flash in the sky below L-13's altitude but near enough, Peter noted, to force Mathy to climb toward the shelter of a cloud layer 500 meters above them.

The city, still brilliantly lighted, began to seethe into full response. The sky came alive with probing beams. "Twenty searchlights," Peter told Kellner.

"I count six fires," Leutnant Schwinn called, his voice high-pitched. "No, eight. No, ten. More, more!"

"Calm down, Leutnant," Kellner ordered. "Our turn now. Keep a sharp eye for aeroplanes, though I doubt they can reach this high."

"Aeroplanes," Peter heard Schwinn mutter. "God."

"Full power." Kellner sounded as if he were strangling. Peter relayed the order to the engine compartments, and he felt his rate increase. Dead ahead, the sky was alive with flailing searchlights. Antiaircraft shells flashed at their level. Engines howling, the Zeppelin surged forward. Then it slowed.

"What the hell is happening?" Kellner yelled. From the engine car aft, a voice grated over the communications speaker, "Problem with engine four. It just quit on us, Sir."

"Now?" Kellner cried. Then his mouth tightened. "Dead engine or no, we attack," Kellner commanded. "Maximum climb." The elevator man spun his wheel. The Zeppelin's nose tilted a few degrees upward. Peter glued his eyes to the altimeter. The needle refused to move.

"Damn!" Kellner grabbed Peter's arm. "Drop fifty percent of remaining ballast. Now!"

Peter yanked the ballast release toggles. The altimeter merely quivered.

"Drop all ballast."

More misty trails fell from the hull.

"We are finally climbing, Herr Kommandant,"

"Not fast enough, Exec. We are heading straight into the antiaircraft field of fire. And the searchlights are--"

A blinding glare burst through the control car's portside windows.

"Hard starboard," Kellner shouted to the helmsman.

The airship swung to the right, but the searchlight beam clung like an accusing finger. The shell bursts drew closer.

"We cannot survive that," Kellner muttered to Peter. We must come about."

"One-eighty turn, Kraemer," Peter ordered. Looking jolted by the use of his name, the helmsman spun the rudder wheel. For anxious minutes, the searchlight followed them. Then to their great relief, it fell astern and began to swing wildly behind them. In minutes, they passed beyond its range. Nose-high, struggling to hold altitude, the airship limped northward.

Kellner took off his visored cap, pulled a kerchief from his flying coat and mopped his forehead. His eyes caught Peter's. Was that a look of frustration, relief- or something else?

"With an engine out and unable to climb beyond the guns, we had little choice. You do agree, Oberleutnant?"

"Hard not to agree, Herr Kommandant." Turning tail had probably saved their ship and their lives. But they had failed in their mission

"We are not taking our bombs home with us, Reinhart. Not with a failed engine. We're barely holding altitude." Kellner peered down at the black countryside. "And we're not dropping them in some sheep pasture. The only reasonable target ahead is Cambridge. "

Cambridge? "What military targets are in Cambridge, Herr Kommandant?"

"We are no longer restricted to military targets," Kellner reminded him. "Give me a heading for Cambridge."

Peter bent over the map, then he straightened. "Herr Komnandant, if I could make a suggestion?"

"What is it, Reinhart?"

"A few degrees' course change eastward can take us over Great Yarmouth. The Naval Station there would be a far more valuable target than a cluster of Cambridge houses, Sir."

Kellner pondered a moment. Then he said, "Not bad, Oberleutnant. The heading for Great Yarmouth."

"Considering the eastward wind drift, I make it 30 degrees."

"Steer 30 degrees."

Peter relayed the order to Kraemer.

"You'll notice we are gradually losing altitude," Kellner said. "If we sink below 1500 meters, the bombs must go, wherever we are."

The race between bomb weight versus lift was a close one. Just past midnight, Peter spotted the lights of Norwich off to port. Great Yarmouth lay directly ahead. Then through a light ground mist, he saw the reflection of lights on water. The altimeter read 1650 meters as they rumbled overhead.

"Open bomb room ventral hatch, Shultz," Peter relayed.

"Salvo all bombs," Kellner told Peter a moment later. They both went at the console's bomb release toggles. Blinding flashes shredded he darkness of Great Yarmouth harbor. Over the engines' howl, Peter heard the rumble of multiple explosions.

"The Naval Station?" Kellner wondered.

"Couldn't tell. The explosions were so bright. But we did hit Great Yarmouth."

Kellner gave him a rare grin." Mission failed, then rescued?"

The English coast fell behind as they limped out to sea. A few minutes later, Peter heard the engine noise increase.

"I didn't order--" Kellner began, then was interrupted by a voice on the communication speaker.

"Engine four is now operating, Herr Kommandant."

"What was the problem?"

"A loose ignition wire, Sir."

A loose wire on a previously well-functioning engine? Peter wondered. Just as we are about to fly into antiaircraft fire? Then the engine picks up again when we are clear of the coast?

He stared at Kellner. The Kommandant's stunned expression told him they both realized the engine's return to life could be more damning than their having missed the primary target.

36.

A s the ground crew began to walk their Zeppelin toward the nearby Normann shed, Kellner and Peter stepped down from the control car to find Fregattenkapitän Strasser facing them. Hands on hips, head thrust forward, the Kommandant of Airships did not look to be a happy man.

They snapped simultaneous, heel-clicking salutes. Strasser gave them a perfunctory salute in return, then clapped his hand back on his hip.

"I just read the report you radioed after failing to reach heavily defended London, Kapitänleutnant Kellner. Engine trouble. I also read your subsequent message transmitted after bombing lightly defended Great Yarmouth, followed by the resumption of the disabled engine's full power. On the face of it, your flight was not in the medal-winning category, Gentlemen. Engine failure, then finally out of England, that engine's sudden return to life? Have you determined the problem, Kellner?"

"A disconnected wire in the engine's ignition harness, Herr Fregattenkapitän. When it was discovered a repair was effected."

"It was put back in place."

"Yes, Sir."

Peter came perilously close to rolling his eyes.

"You are to be commended, Kapitänleutnant, for attacking the Great Yarmouth Naval Base while impaired by the loss of an engine."

"Thank you, Sir."

Have we actually gotten away with this? Peter wondered.

"But you will determine precisely why that engine failed just as you were about to strike our most important target," Strasser barked. "And you will take appropriate steps to make certain such an incident does not recur. Dismissed!"

He spun on his heel and strode off toward the administration complex.

"He suspects something," Kellner muttered.

"Don't you?"

"By now, the crew is at breakfast, Reinhart. Find Master Machinist Mate Neubert and bring him to the Normann hangar. Now."

Ten minutes later, Peter, with Ludwig Neubert in tow, joined Kellner in their airship's cavernous, echoing hangar. The looming Zeppelin was crawling with maintenance crewmen replenishing hydrogen, water ballast, oil, and engine fuel. Kellner ordered two of them out of the aft engine car then Neubert and Peter up the short access ladder, through the car's forward gunners' area, then aft into the cramped space between the twin Maybachs.

"You will show us the electric cable that became disconnected," Kellner told Neubert, an angular man of middling height, his heavy eyebrows drawn in a scowl that turned down the ends of his thick mustache.

The master machinist mate reached over the portside engine and pointed at a cable connection. "That one, Sir."

"You are the one who found it disconnected?"

"Yes, Sir."

"Hours after that disconnection forced us to abort our assigned mission?"

"Y--yes, Sir."

"That strikes me as a long time for a master mechanic to locate and reconnect a simple loose cable."

"I w-was ... was preoccupied with--"

"Preoccupied? Preoccupied, for God's sake! How do you think the cable became disconnected?"

"Someone must have ... must have brushed against it, Sir"

Peter caught Kellner's glance. And he knew they were reaching the same conclusion.

"I will tell you what I believe, Neubert," Kellner said icily. "I believe you panicked at the sight of the antiaircraft fire over London. You grabbed that remote cable and pulled it free."

Neubert's face went chalk white. "Sir, I ... I--"

The man looked as if he were about to vomit. Peter took a step backward.

"I have no proof of such a conclusion," Kellner admitted. Then in a far grimmer tone, he told Neubert, "There will be no entry on your service record as to why you have decided to request a transfer from my crew. That transfer is hereby approved. You will report immediately to Personnel for reassignment. I do not want to see you aboard this airship again."

As Neubert, a man who had left his honor behind, walked out of the hangar, Kellner stood beside the engine car with his arms folded. He glanced around. They were alone. "We must consider this, Peter," he said quietly. "If word gets around that a crewman crippled his airship to avoid bombing London, the English will pounce on it like a chicken on a bug. Not to mention Strasser's reaction to such a cowardly act."

He shook his head slowly and let out a long sigh. "A difficult matter, Herr Executive Officer. I have dispensed with a crewmember who sabotaged our airship. But when he did so, he saved us from running straight into London's fully alerted anti-airship defense artillery."

He gazed at Neubert diminishing in the distance. "A difficult matter. I suspect you, an Academy man, might have handled this differently."

"I wonder. I'm sure all of us felt the same level of fear up there last night."

"But it is the difference in levels of response to that fear that matters, Peter. If I were a Prussian, I suspect I would insist Herr Neubert be hauled before a military court and then face a firing squad. His guilty stammer would guarantee that. But fortunately for Neubert, I am a Saxon."

As they walked toward the hangar mouth, Kellner shifted his gaze from Neubert to Peter. "Did you know the infamous 'Christmas truce' began in the trenches of the Saxon regiments? The Saxons and the Bavarians. The Prussians hated the whole incident as much as did officers at command levels." Together, they emerged into the late morning sunlight. "I am a Saxon," Kellner repeated. "And you are an Academy man."

"And I know at least one of my instructors there would agree with the Prussians and sentence Neubert to death. But that instructor never faced artillery exploding directly ahead of him in a hydrogen-filled airship."

"That's not an answer, Peter."

"It is an answer, Hugo. I think you were right."

Behind the wheel of his small Mercedes more than 12 hours out of Gotha, Erwin Kottenhoff was stiffly aware this was nowhere near as comfortable as being driven in the luxurious Daimler. Not that the Mercedes wasn't a fine machine. After all, Kottenhoff reminded himself, this also is a Daimler company product. The real difference is in my doing the work behind its steering wheel instead of sitting lordly-like in the Daimler's plush rear seat with the driving handled by Albert.

The subversive son of a bitch ... That still-rankling thought was quickly replaced by apprehension as Kottenhoff turned southward from the Hamburg-Cuxhaven route into the approach road to Nordholz.

Moellendorf's information, assuming it was accurate, has presented a dilemma of conscience. Should I simply say nothing and be vindicated when the new English ammunition begins to blow Strasser's Wunderwaffen out of the sky? The whole controversy, its negative side now almost exclusively my own, would conclude with my being correct from the beginning. But how many airship crews will die before Strasser becomes convinced his dream has become a nightmare?

How many good men lost?

I have been thrown out of the service to which I have devoted my life, Kottenhoff reflected bitterly. Who would fault my resentment? But how can I ignore the cataclysm Moellendorf assures me is about to erupt in British skies? A tragedy I can at least try to prevent.

He swallowed his pride and determined to confront Strasser personally. Yes, the starchy-sounding officer at Nordholz had telephoned back, Fregattenkapitän Strasser would see Herr Kottenhoff no later than 15.00 o'clock Tuesday, for no more than 15 minutes.

Now, on that appointed day, jouncing southward on the Nordholz approach road, Kottenhoff pulled out his watch. I set out well before sunrise, but the drive is taking longer than I thought. Only 20 minutes left before the damned deadline to reach Nordholz and find Strasser's office. Surely even such a precise man as he is, would allow--

At last, to his relief, he saw the humped hangars of Nordholz materialize on the flat horizon.

He was cleared promptly through the base entrance, apparently Strasser's office having notified the sentry of his impending arrival. Directed to a visitors' parking site, he found the Naval Airship Division's administration office nearby. Another nervous glance at his pocket watch sent him at a fast walk to the entrance. A fine way for a former admiral to behave, he told himself, but he didn't slow down. Told by the enlisted rank at the entrance to proceed straight ahead to the door at the far end, Kottenhoff strode between the twin rows of desks and at Strasser's private office door, rapped with a degree of authority he did not feel. Damn it. I'm becoming impatient with my own diffidence. I asked for this meeting, did I not? These plain jacket cuffs are the problem.

How I miss the reassuring shield of those konteradmiral sleeve stripes.

"Enter." The voice beyond the door carried all the authority Kottenhoff lacked. He turned the knob and walked in.

"Herr Admiral," Strasser rose with a tight smile. A shorter man than Kottenhoff had expected. "Welcome to Nordholz."

The honorary salutation helped. "Herr Fregattenkapitän," Kottenhoff responded with a touch of vigor, "I appreciate your making time to see me."

With that, they shook hands and Strasser indicated the chair before his desk. "My apologies for limited time, Herr Admiral, but war does not wait. You told my assistant you had information of considerable importance to me." He frowned then followed Kottenhoff's glance to the window behind his desk.

Near the distant hangar area, an airship slowly descended toward its clustered ground handlers.

"The L-11, Admiral. Returning from a scouting mission along the North Frisians." Strasser swung back to his visitor. "The purpose of your visit, Sir?"

Kottenhoff leaned toward him. "Are you aware of an Australian munitions expert named Pomeroy?"

"James Pomeroy? Yes, I am. Somewhere I have a Naval Intelligence report to the effect that he proposed an incendiary type machine gun cartridge to the British War Office just before the war began. I am also aware his design was dismissed as being unneeded. "

"At the time, Herr Fregattenkapitän. But are you now aware that the British are reconsidering Pomeroy's design, plus additional proposed anti-airship munitions, including an explosive bullet?"

Strasser's expression changed from one of patient forbearance to one of curiosity.

"How have you happened to acquire such information?"

"That I prefer to keep confidential, but I believe my source to be reliable."

Strasser frowned, then offered a wry smile. "Let me summarize what is happening here. The man known as Germany's most vocal critic of the airship as a weapon of war now appears before me with information from an anonymous source to the effect that the military airship is about to face annihilation."

"Herr Strasser, I must--"

Strasser held up a silencing palm. "This concerned fellow, who not incidentally has retired from the navy reportedly due to his antipathy toward the airship, now works for--" Strasser consulted a paper on his desk-- "is now employed by the company flight testing a competitor to the airship as a long distance bomber. I ask you, Sir, how much confidence would you have in such a man?

Kottenhoff fought back rising anger. "I am not here as a subversive competitor, Sir. I am here in an effort to save the lives of airship crewmen."

Strasser stroked his goatee "For the moment, and considering your former reputation as an exemplary battleship kapitän, I will set aside the possibility of a covert agenda. But even assuming the English were attempting to perfect anti-airship ammunition, bear in mind these facts: Only a few enemy aeroplanes can approach airship operating ceilings. When my new height climbers are put into service, they will easily soar thousands of meters above the maximum height attainable by any English combat aeroplane. What matters then the kind of ammunition they carry?"

"You cannot believe the enemy aircraft designers are not striving to increase service ceilings."

"I have no doubt they are. But in my opinion, lighter-than-air craft will always be capable of rising higher than any flying machine whose lift depends on a propeller to pull it through the thin air of high altitude. And consider this, now that you have committed your future to the heavy, lumbering bomber aeroplane. The airship has greater load capacity and far greater range. Your prototype Gotha is expected to--" Again Strasser consulted the paper on his desk-- "to have a radius of action limited to England's eastern coastline. My airships will shortly be capable of attacking any target in the British Isles. Any target anywhere, Sir."

He thrust back his chair and abruptly stood. "I can appreciate your concern, Herr Kottenhoff. But I am certain it is misplaced." He thrust out his hand, and Kottenhoff had no alternative but to rise and grasp it in a second perfunctory handshake.

"Thank you for coming," Strasser said. "May your career with Gotha be ... illuminating."

Dismissed, Kottenhoff realized. He compressed his lips, determined not to make a further fool of himself in Strasser's eyes as he walked back to his automobile, and paused. Should I seek out Peter Reinhart, the man I forced into the airship service to my own political purposes? No. I'm afraid I could not bear to face him now. He shook his head sadly for Peter. And himself. As he neared the parking area, he spotted another airship plowing inbound from the hazy coast.

"Poor bastards," he muttered. "Poor doomed bastards."

37.

"What a meeting that was," Kellner marveled as he and Peter walked from the officers' morning assembly into the chilly mid-September rain. "Strasser is a man possessed. After Mathy's big success on the eighth, he sends him out again on the thirteenth. They run into thunderstorms. The two airships with him turn back. Mathy pushes on until the guns at Harwich rip open two hydrogen cells, and he has to drop his bombs and come back the shortest way he can manage."

"Over Holland," Peter added. "And now the rain and wind delays are making Strasser more determined than ever."

"That, plus Von Falkenhayn's order to the army's airships on the twelfth."

"No more bombing of London city for them. Only the docks and harbor facilities."

"Strasser is obviously desperate to hit London hard before we face the same restrictions. So far, we're told to avoid only the northern part of the city. Where the poorer classes live." Peter pulled up his jacket collar and chuckled.

"You find that funny?"

"I find it crass, Hugo. In effect, we are told it is preferable to kill the rich."

"It's not class warfare. The northern quarter of London offers no worthwhile targets anyway. So the restriction is for public consumption."

"Whatever the hell it is, until the moonless nights return, we can relax and enjoy daylight scouting patrols, now that we have our replacement engine man."

"I won't mind serving as the 'eyes of the fleet,'" Kellner admitted. "Or at least as eyes of the minesweeper fleet. Should be as good as a vacation."

Not quite, Peter realized a few days later. Pushing through gloomy skies 1000 meters above the plodding minesweeper boats in the Helgoland Bight west of the Eider's mouth had become monotonous yet demanding. Amidst intermittent rain showers, visibility was capricious. Peter's eyes were soon as bleary and bloodshot as those of observer Schwinn, now assigned to their crew, and of Kellner himself. Scanning for the threat of an English seaplane or the machine guns of a torpedo boat seemed endless.

The hopeful aspect of these flights, Peter felt, is the tightening of crew discipline and effectiveness. Kellner seems uncertain how this is happening. I'm convinced it's at least partly the result of making both criticism and praise personal matters...

On October 6, an alert swept over Nordholz: Prepare to resume attacks on England. That announcement itself seemed to attract more of the chilly fall showers that had made the minesweeper patrols miserable. Despite Lexie's nearness in Cuxhaven, the on-again-off-again flying weather had kept Peter inescapably at Nordholz.

On October 13, the weather suddenly cleared. "Tonight, fortunately in the dark of the moon," Strasser announced at the morning meeting, "We will hit London hard. Four airships from Nordholz: Breithaupt, Boeker, Buttlar and Kellner. Two will join you from Hage: Peterson and Mathy."

In stunningly clear autumn sunlight, all four Nordholz airships cleared the base between 12.00 and 12.50 o'clock. Kellner's ship, the last to rise from the soggy turf, joined the other three west of the middle Frisian Islands. Engines idling just fast enough to hold position in the light west wind, they were joined 20 minutes later by the two Zeppelins from Hage, one of them Mathy's, the attack leader.

From its northernmost end, Peter found the line of six airships hovering loosely abreast to possess an unexpected majesty: massive grey bulls flaring golden as the setting sun emerged beneath a cloud layer low on the western horizon. As the sun sank below the blue rim, the line of golden bulls mellowed to orange. When the day's last light faded, the waiting Zeppelins turned ominously black, from beauty to beast. Their shrouded exhaust glows barely visible, they began to drum westward.

As scattered lights along the Norfolk coast drifted into sight, the radio crackled with a crisp command from Mathy: "Fly southwestward past Cambridge then due south to London, eastward on bomb runs toward the Channel, then northeast home." Simple enough, Peter thought. And overconfident enough to be heard by English antiaircraft defense radio monitors. We are as bullheaded about indiscriminate radio use as the English are about leaving their cities' lights gleaming.

"Car lighting to attack mode," Kellner ordered as they forged inland. Peter dimmed the car's interior lights to a minimum glimmer.

By the time they neared London, the glow of fires set by the preceding Zeppelins had turned the overcast red. The planned orderly procession of attacking airships had deteriorated into a confusion of individual runs across the city. Two distant Zeppelins on converging courses barely veered clear of each other. Searchlights swung in search of targets. Shells burst beneath the swerving airships.

They charged toward the melee. Then Kellner, to Peter's astonishment, abruptly salvoed their bomb load somewhere in the city's northeastern outskirts. Afterward, Kellner barked a new heading, the helmsman whirled his wheel and the Zeppelin howled for the coast.

Had they hit anything worthwhile? Peter wondered. A small concern in the face of our desperation to get out of range of London's searchlights and cannon fire. Had Kellner actually seen some worthwhile target down there? Or had he salvoed their bombs near enough to the city to be acceptable, yet far enough from defensive fire to let them turn away unscathed? As they rumbled toward home in the welcome darkness, Peter knew he would never ask that question.

Peering aft, he spotted at least a dozen fires in the city's sprawl and he noticed darting flares aloft, circling too fast to be Zeppelin exhaust flares. Aeroplanes! At least four of them. One, not far distant, straightened and began to climb-- toward a Zeppelin whose hull reflected London's newly kindled fires. As Peter stared, the airship tilted upward. The aeroplane's pilot apparently realized he couldn't match the Zeppelin's sudden ascent.

He broke away in a long descending arc, and Peter lost sight of him. Strasser would have felt vindicated: "Airships can out-climb aeroplanes."

By now, Kellner's airship rode in smooth night air well east of the defensive hornets' nest over London. In a few moments, they crossed the Essex coastline and bore steadily out to sea. Mates Meuller and Graber climbed down from the hull to relieve helmsman Kraemer and Weisinger at the elevator wheel.

"Go up with them, Sir," Peter urged. The kommandant's eyes were red with fatigue. "There are enough hammocks up there."

Kellner succumbed. "For an hour, perhaps. If anything—"

"I will notify you immediately."

Kellner nodded, then followed Kraemer and Weisinger up the ladder to the keel. As the control car settled back to homebound routine, Peter stood at the command console marveling at the irony. *A few weeks ago, I was part of an effort to get these things out of the air. Now I'm the acting kommandant of this one.*

He checked the compass. "Dead on course, Meuller." The relief helmsman gave him a pleased nod. "Graber, you are fifty meters low. Tighten up."

"Aye, Herr Kommandant."

I could get to like this, Peter decided. *In command.*

But for only 90 minutes. Kellner reappeared and insisted Peter himself now go fly a hammock.

The problem came after sunrise when they made landfall on the German coast southwest of Cuxhaven. They discovered the entire coastal area shrouded in ground fog.

"Can you see any sign of Nordholz in this mess?" Kellner's voice was tight with stress.

Peter moved forward to stand beside the helmsman, binoculars intent on the fog carpet rolling 300 meters below. *Where in hell was the tethered marker balloon that was supposed to locate the center of the landing area in a situation like this?*

"Spot anything at all?" Kellner asked.

"I'm hoping they've had the brains to get the balloon— There! There it is! A kilometer ahead, three points to starboard."

"I'm going to put us down right next to the thing," Kellner said. Then he shouted a barrage of orders to the engine crews fore and aft. The four Maybachs subsided to a dull rumble.

"Valve hydrogen cells eight and nine," he ordered Peter. The hydrogen toggles were slippery with cold condensation. Peter tripped the releases for the valves far overhead, and the airship sank into the blinding fleece.

"Ready on the ballast toggles," Kellner ordered, staring forward into white opaqueness. They were coming down hard.

Coarse turf loomed out of the fog, directly ahead and seemingly slanted upwards. "Nose up! Nose full up!" Kellner shouted at the elevator man. "Exec, dump all ballast!"

Peter had already opened the ballast valves on his own, and that apparently-- and miraculously-- turned their impending nose-first crunch to the turf into a surprisingly light jolt. They were down in one piece, close enough to the tethered marker balloon to make out its anchoring truck and winch.

The engines' idling faded away. The ghostly figures of the ground crew materialized out of the fog. Peter followed Kellner from the control car into the damp afternoon.

The chief ground handler snapped them a salute. "Congratulations, Herr Kommandant. You have spared us another search out in the flats."

"In the flats? I don't understand."

"That's where Kapitanleutnant Breithaupt has landed, Sir. Missed the balloon. We heard his engines fail. Then came the crunch of a bad landing." The muscular, mustached masters' mate shrugged. "He wasn't far off. We found him and walked L-15 back here."

Peter couldn't hold back a grin. Our misfits have landed dead center at our base while Breithaupt's vaunted crew had put down somewhere out there in the wasteland. Kellner caught his grin. "That, Oberleutnant," he said quietly as the chief ground handler trotted away, "is not how you looked when I dropped our bombs in London's outskirts —"

"With respect, Sir, our target was central London."

Kellner regarded him coolly, devoid of any readable expression. "Perhaps you failed to notice the target directly beneath us as we hovered on the outskirts. A factory complex, I believe, its stack pouring smoke. I concluded it was of importance to be operating at full tilt at midnight."

"My apologies, Hugo. May you have set back the English war effort."

That came forth with an unintended sarcastic undertone. Who do I think I am? Peter wondered! "Sorry, but I completely missed seeing that factory."

Kellner's voice dropped its brittle edge. "Before we face Strasser, I think we both can do with a beer-- or stronger. Come with me to the Officers' Club."

As they set off through the thinning fog, the sun glimmered through. But its weak glow carried an early winter chill.

Several days later, the results of the October 13-14 attack were posted in the assembly room. Breithaupt had set the record for the most people killed by one bomb: 17 on London's Wellington Street, as reported in London newspapers, then relayed through German Naval Intelligence. Breithaupt also hit the Inns of Court, Gray's Inn and the headquarters of the Belgian Relief Fund. Mathy had not fared as well. Thinking he was bombing the Victoria Docks, he had actually dropped on the Woolwich Arsenal, but with little effect. Under Boeker's command, L-14 hit the docks and an army facility, killing 15 soldiers. Peterson's L-16 missed London by 30 kilometers. He had bombed the town of Hartford, killing nine of its residents.

Kellner, it turned out, had severely damaged a meat packing plant northeast of the city, a seemingly meaningless accomplishment that prompted chuckles in Strasser's morning assembly, until he added the gratifying fact that the plant produced tins of "bully beef" for British frontline troops.

"My apologies, Hugo," Peter said as they stepped back into the raw mid-October breeze.

"Luck, Peter. They could have been producing window curtains, for all I knew at the time."

"The whole war is a matter of luck. Some good, some bad. Home by Christmas."

"Don't be a cynic."

"By now, Hugo, we all are cynics."

38.

Panting from his dash up the officers' quarters' steps, Franz rushed into their room and plunked down on the window seat. "Yesterday we lost one."

"Lost one? How?" Peter asked. "No airships were flying yesterday."

"No Zeppelin has flown a combat mission from here in the past two weeks," Ernst muttered, sprawled on his bunk. "Only a few scouting flights."

"It happened at Tondern up near the Denmark border. And the Zepp wasn't even flying. The brand new L-18 caught fire while a hydrogen cell was being filled. The fuel tanks blew. For more than an hour, L-18 burned to cinders. Killed one of the machinist mates and scorched seven of the ground handlers."

"These damned things are dangerous even when they're hibernating," Ernst said as he swung his legs over the bunk's side and sat up. "You two realize how many airships the navy has lost so far? Beginning with the L-1 back in '13, we've had seven of them crash in forced landings, or burn up in their hangars, or shot down by antiaircraft fire. That's almost a forty percent loss rate. Forty percent! God knows what the percentage will be if the English find a way to shoot us down with their aeroplanes."

"Height climbers, Ernst. Strasser's 'super Zeppelins.' They're supposed to out-climb anything the British have."

"Maybe you're lucky, Franz, now that you're a supervising officer for engine crews.

"You, too, Ernst. Personnel administrators don't fly."

"My headquarters assignment was ordered by Strasser. The damned paper flood is for the whole Division-- all seven airship bases to date. I'd rather be up in a Zeppelin control car, and my request for that still stands."

Slumped in one of the room's hard chairs, Peter yawned. "At least you're doing something, Ernst. The air crews wait and wait while this rotten weather refuses to break. A scouting flight now and then between storms. The one I was sent on two days ago was miserable. Almost no visibility. By the time we were in position off Borkum, the wind picked up when we got back here and we had a hell of a time landing."

"Didn't you tell us your fiancée had been transferred to Cuxhaven? Why are you moping around here?"

"I haven't been able to get any leave, Franz. Strasser keeps thinking the fog, rain, sleet and snow will disappear overnight as God miraculously clears the skies for him."

God did nothing for Strasser, but the next day, the persistently forbidding sky itself gave Peter the freedom he had been praying for.

"Gentlemen, we have a serious problem." Strasser's opening words jarred the assembled airship officers into dead silence. Though the Nordholz operations staff had its own kommandant, Strasser continued to address these meetings. His way, Peter decided, of personally participating in his airship offensive. This and his frequent self-assignment to combat missions. Now he has another complication in his ever-complicated airship program.

"This abominable weather." Strasser paced across the front of the room, hands clasped behind his back. "We have discovered it has had a devastating effect on our airships in their unheated hangars. The unusually high humidity has loosened the adhesive of the fabric stripping that seals the laced joints of the hulls' cotton panels. The continuous dampness is also affecting the gold beater's skin lining the gas cells. Therefore, despite possibly improved weather conditions, there can be no further flying until these problems are resolved." He turned to face his audience. "Questions?"

"Herr Fregattenkapitän," called a voice from the back of the room. "Any possibility of Christmas leaves?"

"That is the positive side of this infernal weather, Gentlemen. But use discretion."

The inn was jammed. When Peter strode in, he swept her up in a long embrace. Lexie nodded toward the registration desk and its beleaguered clerk, chubby-faced Helmuth.

"I'm not sure we can get rooms."

"We haven't waited this long only to be shut out, and I see our friend is on duty. Wait here while I test that friendship."

Hardly daring to breathe, she watched Peter greet Helmuth with a big smile, and felt hugely relieved by Helmuth's return grin. Peter transferred his billfold from one pocket to another with a significant glance at Helmuth. The pudgy desk clerk nodded, said something, and Peter scrawled in the guest registry. Then he edged his way back through the crowded lobby.

"One room available."

"One room? Did he--"

"Available to 'Oberleutnant and Frau Reinhart.'"

"'Frau', Peter, you didn't actually tell him--"

"No, that's the way he insisted on my signing the register. Otherwise, he feared he could face a problem with his superiors."

"With this place full of military men and their women, surely no one gives a damn how the register is signed."

"Possibly only our friend Helmuth."

In the sweet aftermath beneath their down-filled comforter, Alexia nestled in Peter's arms. The horrifying vision of 16 men burning to death in the collapsing L-10 had haunted her every day since. Now, she realized, I understand the comments I've heard about men in combat avoiding strong friendships that could be shattered with the next shell burst. If Peter were to-- I couldn't face it. I just could not.

What started as an exciting game has turned into something I never intended. Posing as a betrothed couple to cover our meetings here at the Blauer Adler was like play acting. Until... Until I fell in love with him. Now it's what I live for. The future-- if we have one? Marriage and children? Someday, but I'm not ready for a kitchen and nursery.

Not before I prove I can succeed without Pappi's help. He arranged for my job with the admiral. Gave me an automobile. Persuaded the

Mansteins to let me use their carriage house. But I want to succeed on my own. Not while the war is raging. After it's over. Maybe soon. The Russians are retreating. The Allies are leaving the Gallipoli Peninsula, wherever that is. The Cuxhaven Depot bulletin boards are full of positive news. What will I do when peace is declared? Will Peter stay in the navy? Will I...?

"Are you awake?" Peter murmured.

"Barely," she sighed. Then she felt his hand glide along her thigh. "But I'm awake enough."

And under his gentle insistence, her apprehensions again surrendered to passion.

The breakfast menu had been simplified. "Because of the war," said their waiter, a cadaverous white-haired man surely in his sixties. In fact, Peter noticed, the entire dining room staff now had an average age obviously beyond military usefulness. They settled on less than savory sausages, durable black bread, and barely passable coffee.

"I had hoped you could meet my family, Peter, but we never seem to have enough time. Oh God, how I wish this damned war would end!"

He reached across the table to touch her hand. "I'm so sorry, but you do understand. My mother would be devastated if I had leave time and failed to spend Christmas with her."

And, he realized with a pang of guilt, I'm relieved at not having to find out how successful I would be, posing as Lexie's "friend," rather than her lover. Surely Ingrid Tammler or even Otto would see through that. I'm not a coward in combat, but facing an irate father, who knows?

He glanced at his pocket watch. "Time to take to the road, I'm afraid. I'll be right behind you to the south turn-off at Hamburg, Lexie. And with luck, this sorry weather could get us back together soon." He grinned. "Strasser's misery is our delight."

"A year of failure," Professor Horst von Storch growled after he, Erica Reinhart, and Peter were seated at Christmas dinner in Hannover. His mother seemed as happily involved with Horst as before, but the art professor himself appeared burdened with war worry.

"Failure," he went on. "We have countered the British and French forces, but the Western Front stays where it was a year ago. A year! Huge losses, minuscule gains. Do you remember, Peter, our General Staffs of 1914 planned to win the war in forty days! Some prediction. True, the Russians have been given a push back with heavy losses, but they have millions yet to be put in combat. I remember an old saying, 'Russia is never as strong as she looks, but Russia also is never as weak as she looks.'"

"But the fighting stays in France, Belgium and Russia, none in Germany."

"Fortunately, Peter. But we accomplished more in the war's first few months than we have in the whole damned year since."

"Horst," Erika said gently, "it's Christmas. And Peter is with us. What more can you ask for?"

"Hope, Ingrid. A little hope. With men senselessly dying by the thousands to accomplish virtually nothing at all, I'm afraid we can ask for little more than hope."

39.

Peter raised his flight jacket collar and hunkered into its woolen thickness. At 2500 meters altitude with the control car's windows closed, he felt the chill.

Days of rotten weather visibly frustrated Strasser almost beyond endurance, but served England well. In the past several weeks, not one German airship had been able to forge through winter's dismal snow, rain and mist to strike the enemy's homeland. Not until yesterday. Nineteen sixteen's late January murk unexpectedly gave way to clear blue. Under Strasser's urgent order, 10 airships rushed into the suddenly hospitable skies at midday, January 31 – five from Nordhoz, including Kellner's, three from Hage, two out of more distant Tondern.

That impressive force, loosely assembled over the North Sea, was more than enough to rattle English coastal defenses as the skyful of bomb-laden Zeppelins bore westward. And at sunset, found themselves scattered all over the Midlands.

The problem was unexpected ground mist, dense as smoke, obscuring the countryside. Ten airships over the Midlands, but as darkness fell, Peter could not spot the exhaust pinpoints of a single one. With no visual references for wind drift, each plowed ahead on a compass course to its assigned target. Each kommandant relied on a compass course, and compass courses often proved to be less than perfect.

Experimental radio direction bearings had been deemed as helpful to enemy defenses as they were to the attacking airships. Now such guidance had been suspended.

So we are on our own, Peter told himself sourly, adrift over a sea of murk, but expected to find and accurately bomb the factories of Nottingham.

As he dimmed the control car lighting on Kellner's order, Peter was aware of the ever-present tang of engine exhaust, the musty smell of sweaty wool. Did the other four shadows in this gloom feel the same tightening of muscles? This shortness of breath? This cold apprehension?

With his binoculars, he swept the darkness below for nearly another hour. Nothing. Hopeless in this pitch dark – he craned forward. Was that the glow of a light? Several lights. A whole cluster of lights, hazy in the mist, but visible 10 degrees to starboard. A city! When would the arrogant English learn to completely black out their cities? This had to be Nottingham. Course, estimated ground speed and elapsed time from landfall checked.

"Nottingham, Herr Kommandant."

Kellner nodded.

Procedure called for altering course to pass a target, then coming about in a tight reverse to place the target on an eastward heading for the coast. Thus, any agitated ground defenses and enemy aircraft alerted by the bombing would be left behind.

Contrary to such sound attack technique, Kellner called, "Steer ten degrees starboard, helmsman. We attack now."

What? To Peter's surprised look, he said, "Visibility is so poor, we could lose the target in the turn."

Possibly, Peter agreed, but attacking while we're still headed west can give the English a golden opportunity to counterattack as we come about to head back east.

The dimly visible target swung dead ahead. Standing next to Kellner, Peter gripped the edge of the control console. From the corner of his eye, he noticed the elevator man throw a questioning look at Kellner, but their kommandant was absorbed in the approaching target.

Odd, Peter thought. No guns flashed down there. Did Nottingham lack defenses? Or were they putting too much faith in the thinning mist?

The city began to pass beneath them. Kellner nodded to Peter, and they toggled the entire bomb load. As they left the city behind, flashes burst among the scattered lights and grew into multiple fires.

"Hard starboard," Kellner ordered. The Zeppelin began its ponderous swing toward the homebound heading. Mission accomplished, and without a single antiaircraft burst. Odd, Peter knew. Where was Nottingham's defensive fire?

Then he leaned forward, raised the binoculars. Lights to the northeast, He felt hairs rise on the back of his neck. Lots of lights. What in hell is that?

A searchlight beam speared up, began to sweep the sky. An antiaircraft shell burst about a kilometer north. Then another, its flash temporarily blinding Peter.

"Nottingham." Kellner's voice. Flat.

"Then what have we bombed?"

Without answering, Kellner shouted to Wiesinger at the elevator wheel, "Full climb!" and levered the telegraph to the control car's engine section and the engine car aft to maximum power. Peter grabbed the console again as the Zeppelin clawed for altitude.

Nottingham. He shook his head in disbelief as they nosed through the cloud layer. A perfect mission, but the wrong target.

By late afternoon the following day, the reports from all airship kommandants were assembled. Nine reports, though 10 airships had been sent out. L-19 under Kapitänleutnant Loewe had failed to return to Tondern. Shortly after 16.00 o'clock, L-19's radioed request for a bearing had been picked up at Nordhoz. At 17.37 o'clock, Loewe transmitted a report of his attack on Sheffield. After one more location bearing request, at 18.41 o'clock, nothing.

Not until two days passed would the Airship Division be horrified by British newspaper reports. An English trawler had sighted L-19 in the North Sea off Flamborough Head – and had left the stricken crewmembers to drown. The trawler captain claimed he feared had he rescued the airship crew, the Germans could have taken his much smaller trawler crew prisoner and sailed to Germany. That was dismaying enough, but what infuriated the entire Airship Division was the Bishop of London's public approval of the trawler captain's decision to let the crew of "baby killers" drown.

40.

To Peter and the other officers this mid-February morning, Korvettenkapitän Strasser appeared positively buoyant.

"Again, Gentlemen," the Chief of Airships announced in his clipped phrasing, "We have proved the army's airship geniuses to be totally wrong. The first fiasco was our near-fatal testing of the army's so-called angel basket."

His piercing eyes bored into Peter's. "You, Oberleutnant Reinhart, were instrumental in proving the hazard of that contrivance far outweighed its usefulness to the Naval Airship Division.

"Now there has arisen the matter of the army's claim, resulting from their 'Cologne Trials,' that an airship cannot be easily seen at night by ground observers, even during periods of the full moon."

He paused in his pacing and faced his audience. "Last night, a clear night of full moon, Oberleutnant zur See Werner Peterson flew Navy Zeppelin L-16 across the Hage airship base. Four times at three thousand meters altitude. Ground observers clearly – I repeat, clearly – sighted L-16 on every pass. Furthermore, one of our Hage defense aeroplanes easily tracked the Zeppelin throughout those test passes, though the aeroplane could not be seen from the Zeppelin. So despite the army's conclusion that airships cannot be seen from the ground during nights of the full moon, the Naval Airship Division will not attack during those nights."Ernst leaned close to Peter. "Should make you glad you're not in army airships. And that he's such a good politician behind the scenes he can get away with defying the army's claim."

'That's reassuring, Ernst, but the other part of the Hage report isn't reassuring at all. Even with the full moon, no one aboard L-16 was able to spot the aeroplane."

As if to put upstart Strasser in his place, four army airships were launched February 20 under a brilliant full moon. Their targets: French-held railheads leading into the Verdun area. Intended to support the German Army's increasing forces, the attack proved Strasser right. French gunners fired an explosive cannon shell straight into one of the highly visible airships, and it plunged to the ground in flames.

But the impact of this lesson was promptly lost in the outbreak of a massive effort to exhaust French forces in a confrontation, designed not for victory, but for slaughter. The Battle of Verdun.

Too busy to gloat over the army's debacle, Strasser now was faced with an outbreak of engine failures. The navy's airship force was abruptly reduced to only three L-10 class Zeppelins and three older ones. On March 5, he managed to loft three airships toward England. Unfortunately, an incoming line of snow squalls had escaped the attention of German meteorologists. Barely over the North Sea, L-11 and L-14 were suddenly coated with freezing slush. Only with skill – and luck – did they make an about-face and struggle back to Nordholz.

In L-13, Mathy, the Division's most successful airship kommandant, forged through the squalls, though he also was beset with intermittent engine problems. At last yielding to those persistent mechanical failures, he jettisoned his bombs over the Midlands. With two engines now entirely out of operation, he limped toward his home base at Hage, but was forced into an emergency landing near Namur in occupied Belgium. Five days later, L-13 stuttered back to Hage. All in all, the March 5 effort had been an abysmal botch.

"The only good aspect of that mess," Kellner told Peter at breakfast when all reports had been complied, "is that we were not a part of it."

But they were a part of Strasser's next major effort against the British homeland. Each day for an entire week in late March, the Chief of Airships sent off a flight of airships to bomb English targets from the Scottish border to London. "Inspired, no doubt," Ernst claimed, "as the navy's counterpart to the army's now huge effort at Verdun. I wish Franz would get himself back here from Hage. I miss his brother's inside view of all this."

On March 31, the Naval Airship Division tried for London again. At midday, three Zeppelins lifted out of Nordholz and four rose from Hage. Kellner's crew was the third airship to rise from Nordholz into the pleasant afternoon. Strasser himself rode aboard Kapitanleutnant Alois Bocker's L-14.

Several hours outbound on "Route Black" toward London, all seven airships converged loosely. Under just-instituted radio procedure rules, none of the airships had transmitted take-off confirmations. High Command had at last realized that procedure had been alerting English defenses helpful hours before the airships' appearances over homeland targets.

Under radio silence, 10 kilometers west of the Dutch island of Vlieland, Kellner ordered a course to west-southwest. Without lowering his binoculars, Peter duly repeated the order to the helmsman.

Now Kellner peered intently to starboard. "What do you make of that, Reinhart?"

"L-9, Herr Kommandant. Seems to be having difficulty."

Some five kilometers distant, and low on the horizon, L-9 had visibly slowed.

"Reduce power to slow cruise, steer forty-five degrees to starboard," Kellner ordered, his own binoculars now intent on their Nordholz-based sister ship. "See anything amiss over there, Reinhart?" he asked as they drew closer to the faltering airship.

"Seems to be a loose bracing cable, Sir, swinging too damned close to the propeller in the control car's aft section." He strained forward, refining the binocular's delicate focus. My God! It just wrapped around the propeller shaft!"

They stared in disbelief as the whirling shaft wound in the dangling wire. The rear of the control car pivoted upward. Its 17-foot propeller tore into the Zeppelin's belly, high enough to slash into the hull's catwalk. A large piece of propeller blade flew out of the Zeppelin's top section and whirled away toward the sea.

"That had to rip open at least one hydrogen cell," Peter guessed.

"And there they go." Kellner's voice sounded flat, resigned.

L-9 nosed down in a long dive toward the water. Then the rear propellers stopped. Veils of water ballast erupted from the stricken airship's forward section.

"All hull crew aft," Kellner muttered. "All hull crew aft."The falling Zeppelin slowly flattened out its dive and wallowed on precarious even keel. The rear engines kicked back in, and L-9 began a wide swing back toward the German coast.

"Back on course, Exec, for London," Kellner ordered. Then in a lower voice, added, "For whatever awaits us there."

Whatever awaits us there? Peter glanced at him, but the Zeppelin kommandant had turned back to his flight instruments with no further comment. Peter returned his attention back to the sea, its surface darkening as late afternoon faded into early evening.

But he could not shake the impact of Kellner's remark. It sounded like a premonition.

Near midnight, the dim outline of the Holderness peninsula materialized in the gray void ahead. Kellner altered course south southeasterly to parallel the coast well offshore in the security of the seaward darkness. Lights visible landward seemed far more sparse than in previous attacks. Had the English at last begun to establish blackouts?

A few minutes after 02.00, Peter and Kellner simultaneously identified the dull sheen of The Wash.

"Steer one-ninety-five," Kellner ordered.

Two hours later, they determined London lay directly to starboard, though no vast spread of light confirmed that. Was it possible, Peter wondered, the powers-that-be down there had at last realized the value of a citywide blackout? Only a few scattered lights offered an indication that a city may be holding its collective breath down there. Or were they somehow passing well north of the city? Or even south –

Suddenly, the night was torn apart by dozens of explosions. Every antiaircraft cannon in London's defense ring must have cut loose.

"Climb!" Kellner shouted. "Maximum climb."

The engines roared. The nose tilted upward. In long minutes, they were well above the shell bursts. Peter swept the area beneath them, but his binoculars, brilliant with shell bursts, were useless. In the car's dimmed light, he turned to Kellner and shrugged.

The shelling abruptly stopped. That was odd. In the distance southward, Peter could make out the exhaust flames of another airship. Surely, British listening devices could now hear them both. Certainly, they would –

Then he knew. His scanning binoculars revealed a small flame, high and some distance to starboard, but moving toward them. An aeroplane's exhaust flame. The antiaircraft gunners had cleared the air for an aeroplane attack.

He pointed.

"I see it, Exec. And the damned thing is higher than we are." He shouted into the gunners' voice tubes, "Aeroplane, high to starboard, heading toward us. Keep your eyes peeled."

He turned to Peter. "We've got to out-climb that bastard.. Can't see anything in the damned blackout, but all that antiaircraft fire certainly tells us we're over London. Salvo all bombs. Now."

Peter jumped to join him at the bomb toggle array. Together they yanked all active toggles. Freed of the bomb's restraining weight, the Zeppelin surged upward.

But to Peter's dismay, the on-coming aeroplane tipped into a shallow dive and headed straight for them. He rushed overhead, a dark shadow against the gray of the night.

Kellner appeared mystified. "He didn't fire."

"Bombs," Peter guessed. "They know ball ammunition isn't effective, but one airship has already been bombed out of the air. That army ship over Belgium."

"If he tried that, he missed us."

"But –" Peter stared aft. "He's turning back toward us."

"Top gunner!" Kellner yelled into the voice tube, "be alert up there, damn it!"

They heard the rip of machine gun fire.

"So much for your bomb theory, Reinhart. The son of a bitch is firing at us."

"That was a Parabellum, Herr Kommandant. Ours."

"Top gun, report, report," Kellner shouted into the voice tube. He held the funnel toward Peter and they both were shocked by the gunner's garbled yell.

"He made a pass over us! I should have – Here he comes ag –" The rest of it was drowned in a long burst from the Parabellum.

"Where away, gunner?"

"Aft. Hard to see. Somewhere. There! Coming back! Christ! I can't –" He fired another burst.

"The man's scared blue, Reinhart. Can't blame him. But if that Britisher dropped anything, he missed us."

Kellner peered forward. "Damn! Here he's coming back, and we've got a top gunner in panic."

"I'm going up there," Peter heard himself yell. "With luck I could call down directions to confuse that bastard's bomb runs."

Before Kellner could respond, he slapped on his goggles, rushed up the hull-access ladder, shoved open the upper hatchway and clawed into the slipstream's blast. The impact plastered his trousers to his legs, flapped his flying jacket around the ladder's uprights, then the hatchway overhead was thrown open and a crewman reached down to help him clamber onto the keel catwalk.

A few meters forward, he gripped the rungs of a second ladder, this one towering straight up between bulging hydrogen cells 14 and 15 to access the top machine gun platform. The climb was equal to that of a six-story building, a scrambling ascent through the gloomy hull interior with its clankings and screeches of straining bulkheads and girders.

Gasping for breath at the top of the climb, he banged on the overhead hatch cover. The gunner yanked it open, and Peter pulled himself onto the incredibly exposed gunner's platform. The enclosed control car offered at least an illusion of protection, though machine gun bullets could easily slice through its thin walls and windows. Up here though, on top of the huge hull, all that stood between him and black oblivion was the spindly handrail. Which he grabbed with both gloved hands as the Zeppelin ploughed eastward toward the distant security of the English Channel.

The gunner, a short, wiry man apparently in his thirties, gave Peter a confused look. He shouted over the air rush, "Herr Oberleutnant? You? Up here?"

"To help you with spotting –"

"He's somewhere ahead of us." He flung out an arm in a wild arc. "Somewhere. Somewhere."

Peter grabbed his shoulder and close to the gunner's ear he said, "Steady, man. We're all counting on you."

Where was that damned aeroplane? He swept the darkness. Nothing. Wait... There – ten degrees to port. The tiny exhaust flare, drifting leftward, and climbing with them. God, we don't stand a chance in this deadly Katz und Maus game. Once that enemy pilot spots us again, all he has to do is bore in and – Hadn't he already done that and missed?

Attacked and missed. The exhaust pinpoint slowed in its arc then steadied. He's heading straight for us. Then Peter realized, with the oncoming aeroplane slightly higher than the Zeppelin, the enemy pilot can't see the exhaust flames of our engines beneath the hull. We can see him, but when he climbs above us for a bomb run, he can't see us until he's almost on top of us.

The oncoming telltale exhaust flame moved upward.

"He's climbing for another run," he told the gunner.

The man raised the Parabellum's muzzle.

"No!" Peter ordered. "Don't fire until he's past. Your muzzle flashes give us away." From its clamp on the railing, he grabbed the speaking tube. "Herr Kommandant, can you hear me?"

"Well enough," came the scratchy voice from 20 meters below.

"Standby, standby..." The aeroplane's exhaust flame dipped. "Hard aport!" Peter shouted.

He felt the mammoth hull lumber into a left turn. The attacker's exhaust continued in a straight path. Suddenly a shaft of bright light lanced from the aircraft, found nothing, winked out.

"Makes him a great target," the gunner cried.

"Hold your fire until he's headed away."

The aeroplane passed them well to starboard then began to swing port and starboard, its spotlight flaring intermittently. The Parabellum blasted a long burst – without any apparent result.

"You lost him, Gunner. But he's lost us, as well."

In frustration or lacking fuel for further passes, the enemy pilot dropped away in a long descent westward, his exhaust flame dwindling then disappearing.

"He has left us, Herr Kommandant," Peter reported. He heard faint cheers from the car far below. "Permission to stay up here until I am certain?"

"Granted, Reinhart. At your own discretion."

Peter raised his dangling binoculars and swept the barely visible horizon. He centered on an exhaust glow some kilometers aft. Oh, no! Not – Then he realized he had spotted a small group of several glows – another Zeppelin. And a tiny single flame descending toward it. That damned persistent Britisher?"

The aeroplane's searchlight flashed on, pinned the Zeppelin. Peter's powerful binoculars picked out the Zeppelin's large black-painted identification: L-15.

"Breithaupt's airship," Peter reported to the control car. "He's under attack."

Heart thundering, Peter watched the distant aeroplane's exhaust flame climb, turn. Breithaupt's top gunner fired long bursts, the muzzle flashes easily visible, pinpointing the airship's position. Three passes, but no aerial bomb explosions. Was the Britisher dropping the new explosive darts the Nordholz intelligence officer had mentioned at the last assembly? Whatever the persistent aeroplane was doing, it failed to produce any visible explosions or fire.

Minutes later, the fast-moving exhaust flame dropped away and faded from sight. Out of fuel or out of bombs, Peter decided. He grabbed the speaking tube.

"The aeroplane has broken off its attacks on L-15, Herr Kommandant. I don't see any sign of it or any others."

"Good work, Reinhart. Come back down."

In the hull's dark interior, Peter descended step-by-step to the catwalk, then down the short ladder into the control car. Weary from the long climb and descent, he welcomed its feeling of comparative though false security. Kellner acknowledged his reappearance with a brief nod, then turned back to the starboard windows.

"Breithaupt is sinking," he said over his shoulder. The aeroplane attacks may have ruptured several hydrogen cells without setting them afire. At the rate he's going down, L-15 cannot possibly make it back to Hage. Alter course to follow."

In the pre-dawn gloom, they watched the foundering airship jettison a trail of guns, ammunition and engine spare parts. At last, the coast passed slowly beneath the two airships. Kellner's dutifully following Breithaupt's ponderous turn to a northeast heading for home. But he didn't make it. L-15 sank lower and lower then plunged into the North Sea near a British lightship as Peter transmitted to Nordholz a report of L-15's loss.

Days later, he was to learn Breithaupt and his entire crew had been taken prisoner by several armed trawlers that tried to make the disaster complete by towing the barely floating Zeppelin ashore. But as dawn broke, the wreckage collapsed and sank.

Breithaupt's loss hit Peter hard. One of Strasser's most celebrated Zeppelin kommandants – one of the most experienced – had gone down. When would far less seasoned Kellner find his luck had run out?

41.

Day after day, for a full week, the Zeppelins from Nordholz roared low over Cuxhaven on their way west. From her tiny office, Alexia watched them drum seaward at midday. Then, often 24 hours later, she stared into the sky again as they straggled back home. Every day. Then early April soured into blustery rain and she heard no more Zeppelin engines. Relief. Peter was safe at Nordholz.

As if the rolling clouds and rain showers also signaled a slowdown in Cuxhaven Depot's work pace, Alexia was granted two days off. She arranged for a check-up of the Panhard by Rudi Mott at the Tammler factory motor yard, lunched with her father then rode with him to the family home in western Hamburg.

Now, after supper, while Pappi enjoyed an evening cigar in the glazed-in Wintergarten room, she sat with her mother on a sofa in the front parlor and found herself nervously picking at the sofa's heavy upholstery. She resolved that bit of fluster by folding her hands in her lap. I dread these mother-daughter heart-to-heart sessions, she admitted to herself. Mother is too perceptive. Able to get right to the heart of anything she's concerned about. I know I cannot much longer hide my love for Peter.

Ingrid Tammler's eyes lingered on her. Eyes spring-green in repose, but Alexia had always felt the deeper green of autumn when her mother felt concern. And at the moment, those miss-nothing eyes gleamed the dark green of a northern fir...

"I've been wondering, Alexia, do you have any... social life? Any social life at all?"

Alexia met her mother's gaze. *How closely I resemble her. Both of us tall, slender, auburn-haired with emerald eyes. Am I looking at myself, twenty-two years from now?*

"Alexia?"

"I do have what you call a 'social life,' Mother."

"Dances, parties at the Naval Depot? That seems unlikely. Perhaps in Kiel, but in Cuxhaven? It's so remote."

"I'm..." She hesitated to open this door, but it was inevitable. "I'm seeing someone, Mother."

Ingrid's eyebrows arched. "'Seeing someone.' Does he have a name?"

"Peter. Peter Reinhart."

"At Cuxhaven? A military man?" Ingrid's tone was offhand, but her eyes never left Alexia's.

"He is a Naval Academy graduate, Mother. An oberleutnant. His father was a career army officer on the General Staff."

"Where is... Peter – was that his name? Where is he from?"

"Braunschweig. His father is dead, but his mother still lives there."

"And Peter. He is stationed in Cuxhaven?"

"Not Cuxhaven. He is at Nordholz."

"The Zeppelin base?"

"He is the executive officer on an airship crew, Mother."

"Dear God!" Ingrid clapped a hand over her heart. "Do you know what your father thinks of the Zeppelins?"

"He is a good friend of Admiral Kottenhoff, who just left the navy because of his opposition to airships as weapons. I'm sure Pappi shares that view."

"And you, Alexia?"

"I am in love with a young naval officer, Mother. He happens to serve on a Zeppelin."

"In love? How far has this gone?"

Alexia felt her cheeks flush. "I... I don't know what you mean."

"Has he asked you to marry him?"

"No."

"Would you, if he asked?"

She looked down at her clasped hands. "I don't know." That is the truth. Would Peter agree to my having a career of my own? Would he expect me to settle for a hausfrau's life, subservient to my husband? Would he expect me to immediately become a bearer of children, my intent to be self-sufficient lost to dishpan and diapers? Do I love Peter that much?

"Alexia, a soldier in wartime--"

"He is an airship man, Mother."

"Men in the military, then. What is the saying? 'Eat, drink and be merry, for tomorrow –' "

"Mother! It is not like that. We truly love each other."

"So easy in wartime. Emotions in a jumble. Someone with kind words, a smile, a kiss or two –"

"Mother, please!"

"I'm only looking out for your –"

"I'm no longer a child, Mother. I'm a grown woman, supporting herself, working for the navy – and Peter Reinhart is the man I want to spend the rest of my life with."

Ingrid stared at her. Then that severe expression softened. She leaned toward Alexia, studied her face and reached out to take her hand. "I believe you do love him," she said softly. "I can see now, in your eyes. Oh, Liebchen, it can be a blessing. Or a curse. So much depends on him. Be sure. Be so sure. And never forget, Alexia – never forget who you are."

"Aha!" Ernst crooked a thumb toward their officers' quarters doorway. "The prodigal engineman returns."

There stood Franz, duffel bag in hand, grinning like a man just released from incarceration. "Home at last, such as it is. At least I won't have to put in eighteen hours a day showing green mechanics how to nurse the damned new HSLU engines all the way to England and back."

"We have trouble here with those damned new Maybachs, but they send you to Hage."

"Hage, Tondern and finally to Friedrichshafen, Peter. All findings went to Strasser, and he convinced Mercedes their HSLU version Maybachs need major modifications." Franz dropped his luggage on the floor and plunked down on his bunk. "So that's done, and here I am. What's been happening?"

"Reverberations from Verdun," Peter said.

Franz gave him a puzzled look. "I don't follow."

"Strasser finds his airship campaign against England eclipsed by the endless news about that endless battle. So he has been in a near frenzy to step up our Zeppelin attacks. It's a war for publicity as much as a war against the enemy."

"And the winner is...?"

"The only winners so far are weather and mechanical problems," Ernst told him. "Mathy nearly lost L-13 on March fifth. First, engine trouble forced him to land in Namur. Repairs kept him there five days, but he still limped into Hage with one engine dead. After that, we hit hard, every day for a week – from Edinburgh down to north London, but the weather was so lousy, not a single kommandant knew what he hit."

He turned to Peter. "Tell him about the March 31 raid. You were on that one."

"Seven Zepps head for London. Two turn back. One of them, L-9, because a bracing wire lets go, wraps around the control car's propeller shaft, pulls the car up to crash into the hull. A propeller blade rips through a hydrogen cell. I saw all that happen. So L-9 limps home, leaving us to face a damned British aeroplane that tries to bomb us in mid-air. Fortunately, we lose him in the dark over London. Blacked-out London now."

"You're too modest, Peter," Ernst said. "Our roommate here directed evasive maneuvers from the gunner's perch on top of Kellner's Zeppelin."

"Mein Gott, Peter! That should be worth an Iron Cross."

Peter shrugged. "Another incident in a month of odd incidents. The real problem is all this effort seems to be blowing up nothing more than a few houses and killing a handful of citizens. Most airship kommandants deliver glowing reports – all bombs on target. And they believe it until the English and Dutch papers arrive."

"And while that's going on, we keep hearing about the army's huge artillery barrages," Ernst said. "Nothing ever seen like them. But that battle has been going on since February. Two months of steady shelling, but no 'Big Push.' What in hell is really happening down there, Franz? You heard anything from brother Kaspar?"

Franz walked to the door and quietly shut it. "For God's sake, don't either of you breathe a word, or we'll all be in the soup, especially Kaspar. Verdun is a disaster and there's no end in sight. When the French pulled most of their troops out of the Verdun forts, our army decided it was a chance for a breakthrough. More artillery was put in place than we've ever used anywhere, and the French side was pulverized."

He shook his head in frustration. "The survivors fought like demons. The French rushed in reinforcements, so now it is down to a killing ground with obstinate general facing obstinate general. A matter of pride, I imagine. Falkenhayn versus Petain. Men dying by the thousands over a few kilometers of ruined countryside. And, Kaspar told me, Falkenhayn doesn't intend to win anytime soon. His purpose is to drag it out and bleed the French Army to death."

"While we struggle with maintenance problems," Peter said. "The Airship Division's performance can't come close to the dispatches from Verdun. Strasser must be chewing his nails down to his knuckles."

The apparent answer came quickly. On April 24, Strasser himself led eight airships in an attack on southern England. Kellner's Zeppelin, assigned a routine patrol mission, was not included, but there was no loss of glory in that. Over the Midlands, an unexpected and strong southwest wind forced the eight airships to abandon their London-bound course. In sudden mist then rain, the frustrated crews scattered their bombs anywhere, most notably on Dilham village.

"Forty-five bombs on a wide spot in a country road," Kellner snorted as he and Peter walked toward their Zeppelin's hangar two days later. "You saw the English papers. Result: one citizen dead of a heart attack. But now Strasser sees a chance for us to take part in an operation by the High Seas Fleet."

"That Irish thing."

"A rebellion, Peter. And the kaiser is supporting it by shipping in captured Russian rifles. Yesterday I heard that Admiral Sheer ordered several battle cruisers to make a diversionary bombardment on Lowestoft. And he's requested airships to scout the fleet's operations."

"One of them from here, apparently. I heard a lift-off sometime around midnight."

"L-6. Two others went out of Hage, L-7 and L-9. So we may get some favorable notice out of that. Fitting in a way, I suppose, since airships were originally meant to serve as the navy's 'eyes of the fleet.'"

A hell of a lot less nerve wracking than being shot at over London, Peter felt.

They neared the big hangar. "Let's make sure those hull fabric repairs have held up after our little tussle over London, Peter. Spot check them as if your life depended on it."

Which, Peter thought, it does.

42.

With a helpful tailwind on the evening of May 2, eight Zeppelins bore toward the northern coast of Scotland. As darkness fell, the widely spaced airships began their climb to attack altitude, hoping to soar above the reach of antiaircraft shellfire. The target: English battle cruisers reported anchored in the Firth of Forth.

Halfway through the climb, radio operator Mann handed Peter a revised weather report just received from Nordholz. The favoring tailwind was now an impeding south wind, bringing with it a low-pressure area with gusty rain. Decision to proceed lay with each airship's kommandant.

Kellner frowned. "No wind velocity given. No way to estimate drift. The chances of finding the Firth of Forth seem slim. We will try our luck on the Midlands. Helmsman, steer two-twenty."

As he and Peter were to learn later, all but two of their eight-airship group made such a southwestward turn. L-14 and L-20 – Bocker and Stabbert – pressed on toward the Firth of Forth. Neither got there. Bocker's Nordholz-based L-14 ran into rain then snow. Ice formed on the hull, and the Zeppelin lost a third of its altitude. Yet Bocker reported he dropped five bombs on warships in the Firth. Later reports determined he had flown over the Firth of Tay, 40 kilometers north of the assigned targets. His bombs plowed up a field 15 kilometers beyond the Firth.

Stabbert's L-20 out of Tondern fared even worse. Flying into sleet, the Zeppelin quickly iced up. Dumping ballast and some fuel tanks, Stabbert managed to stay airborne. Then he ran into heavy fog. Emerging from that, the wandering kommandant found himself over Loch Ness, now 200 kilometers from the intended target. Turning to a homeward heading, Stabbert spotted lights and dropped 17 bombs on what he thought were mine workings. But his frustrated bombardment damaged brightly lighted Craig Castle. His ill luck got worse, Peter would learn a week later. At the mercy of strong adverse winds, L-20 blundered over the coast of Norway to crash land in a fjord. Six of the crew, rescued on the water by fishermen, were to be repatriated. The remaining 10, including Kapitanleutnant Franz Stabbert, were under Norwegian military detention.

On this chaotic night, Kellner's crew fared better, but not well. As they fought the quartering wind in search of a suitable target – or any target in the finally blacked out English Midlands – Peter spotted a gleam of light a few degrees to port.

"Possible target at 170 degrees."

The kommandant raised his binoculars. "Ten degrees to port, helmsman." At the forward wheel, Kraemer put the Zeppelin's nose on what appeared to be a distant fire in the making. It disappeared behind low scud, then reappeared moments later, now a larger blaze.

"Another airship just bombed the target," Peter reported. "I can make out the exhaust flares."

As they flew nearer, he watched several more fires merge into an impressive conflagration.

"Our turn." Kellner bent over the console's bombsight, reached for the release toggles and pulled them in rapid sequence. "All bombs away."

As they flew directly over it, Peter scanned the growing fire but the glare blinded him. "Too bright, Herr Kommandant. I can't identify the target."

"No matter." Kellner wore a satisfied grin. "Two others found it worthwhile. So have we. A miracle in these infernal blacked-out Midlands. Helmsman, steer zero-nine-zero for the coast. We're going home."

"A moor, Kellner," heavy set Kapitänleutnant Alois Bocker called across the Officers Mess at breakfast two days later. His dark-ringed eyes showed a glint of humor. "You helped set fire to a moor."

Laughter swept the mess hall.

"I was led astray by L-23 out of Tondern, then Peterson out of Hage."

"Then came Kellner, out of luck!" someone shouted, prompting more laughter.

"The blind leading the blind," Kellner called back. "At least we cleared a lot of scrub land for somebody."

"'Heath bombing' Strasser called it," Bocker persisted. Then he returned to his sausage.

"Big joke," Kellner muttered to Peter. "Nobody hit the assigned targets in that attack, including Bocker. Ah well, I suppose we all needed a laugh. What happened to Stabbert, though, isn't funny. None of us had an easy time getting back here."

"What about those English ships? They were supposed to be one of the targets of that messed up attack."

"No more word about that, but early this morning L-7 from Tondern and L-9 out of Hage lifted off early to scout Horns Reef. A British seaplane was reported near Tondern. That means a British seaplane carrier was somewhere in that area."

A young leutnant zur see at the next table leaned toward Kellner. "Couldn't help overhearing, Herr Kapitänleutnant. Just before I came to breakfast, I was told L-9 had returned without spotting anything. L-7 is still out there somewhere."

And L-7 stayed out there – somewhere. In mid-afternoon, word reached Nordholz: L-7 had asked for a radio bearing some hours before, but had not been heard of since.

At 08.00 o'clock the following day, Peter stopped his meticulous polishing of his Ford's hood in the motor yard. Someone was shouting his name.

The orderly of the day rushed toward him panting, and saluted. "I was told you were down here, Herr Oberleutnant," the wiry little orderly gasped. "Your crew is to lift off immediately."

"Immediately? This early in the day?"

"Fregattenkapitän Strasser's order, sir," The winded orderly gasped for breath. "An emergency search for a lost Zeppelin."

Peter threw down his polishing rag and raced toward the officers' quarters. He threw on his flying gear, grabbed his binoculars and rushed toward the Zeppelin sheds.

Halfway there, he caught up with Kellner.

"We're ordered to search for L-7." Kellner was short of breath. "Not a word from Kommandant Hempel since he asked for a bearing twenty-four hours ago."

Out of its shed, the gray monster strained against the ground handlers' lines. They piled into the control car. Kraemer, Weisinger, observer Schwinn and radio op Mann right behind them.

"Did Tondern get a fix on Hempel's last transmission?" Peter asked Kellner.

"Off the Denmark coast, about thirty kilometers southwest of Horns Reef. That's where we're heading. And Strasser wants results. No one else has found any sign of L-7, so now it's up to us."

"Without a clue of what's happened."

A few minutes later – too short a time, Peter felt, for a thorough pre-lift-off check – they rose into the murky May morning.

Seven eye-burning, haze-obscured hours later, Peter felt as if he had personally viewed every square kilometer of the North Sea 100 kilometers east, west, north and south of Horns Reef. They had spotted nothing but the permanently anchored Horns Reef lightship – which radioed its crew had sighted no Zeppelin yesterday or today, except Kellner's, at the moment directly overhead.

With the clear sky fading into late afternoon, Kellner shrugged at Peter. "All we are going to get out of this, I'm afraid, is one of Strasser's mind-curdling scowls. Helmsman, steer 150 degrees. We are heading home."

Fifty kilometers southeast of Horns Reef, the passive sea abruptly churned into a froth of racing white caps. Peter almost lost his footing as the airship was buffeted downward, its nose high. An unreported weather front, Peter suspected, riding in fast on the south wind.

Weisinger whirled his wheel clockwise. The nose sank to level flight, then past level flight. They headed down.

"Elevator man, nose up, for God's sake!" Kellner burst out. "What is the matter with you?"

"The wheel is jammed, Sir," Weisinger shouted over his shoulder. "I can't move it."

Kellner stared at Peter. "Exec, see what –"

Peter leaped to the elevator man's side. "Come on, Weisinger. Together we can move this thing. They strained at the frozen elevator wheel. Then Peter shook his head. "Can't budge the damned wheel."

"Christ!" Kellner yelped. Then he pulled himself together. "All engines stop!"

Keeping his voice steady, Peter relayed the order. He glanced at the altimeter above the elevator wheel. The needle swept downward, passed the 1700-meter mark. They had already lost 300 meters.

"Drop forward water ballast, two breeches," Kellner ordered.

Peter yanked the toggles. A misty trail marked the airship's descent.

"All hull personnel move aft," Kellner called. "Schnell, schnell."

Peter glued his eyes to the altimeter. One thousand meters. Six hundred. Four. The sea came up fast. Weisinger wrestled with his damned wheel. Then Peter thought it moved. A little. A bit of hope? Was their plunge slowing?

Three hundred meters. The descent seemed to ease up a few more degrees.

Two hundred. But now Peter's boots no longer threatened to slide out from under him. He released his grip on the console.

The altimeter needle trembled at 200 meters. Then it held firm.

"Thank God." Kellner said. Through the tube, he called, "We've lost elevator control. Can you see what's happened back there?"

A few minutes later, the voice tube grated. "Masters Mate Hellmich, Sir. Through the inspection hatches under the vertical fin, I see the upper cable broke on the starboard elevator. From the engine car, they see the bottom cable's out of its sleeve. Portside elevator looks undamaged."

"Stand by, Hellmich." Kellner turned to Peter. "You heard all that?"

"I did, Herr Kommandant." He moved close to Kellner. "With your permission, Hugo, I'm going back there."

"Whatever they can do about the problem, it's a mechanic's job, not an officer's."

"Moral support, if nothing else."

"That could be all we have to offer. Go ahead."

Peter stepped to the hull-access ladder and climbed.

With the engines shut off, his rush through the keelway was in eerie silence broken by occasional clanks and groans of duralumin joints. He pushed through the empty bomb room then into the keelway aft. As Kellner had ordered, the hull crew had crowded back here, their combined weight helping to keep the Zeppelin in its still slightly nose down attitude. Peter made his way through the press of crewmen along the keelway to Masters' Mate Otto Hellmich, kneeling at the open portside inspection hatch.

"Suggestions, Hellmich?'

His full beard rippling in the breeze through the open hatch, the masters' mate stared up at him. "Herr Oberleutnant? Back here?"

"First-hand look at things, Hellmich. Any ideas?"

"Through the starboard inspection hatch, Sir, I saw that elevator is useless. Upper cable broke, bottom cable jumped its track. That's what's jammed the control wheel."

"What about portside?"

"Those cables are undamaged, Sir. It's possible we could disconnect the jammed cable and secure the starboard elevator in neutral. That should clear the control jam, and with luck we could make it back to base using the port elevator only."

"Do it."

"It means a work crew will have to go out there on the starboard fin. No safety net. It's a long fall."

"Get me the men."

To Peter's surprise, Hellmich grabbed his arm. "You can't, Sir."

"You're telling an officer –"

The man's eyes were pleading. "You must not, Sir. Because... Because we need you." His face went crimson. "We all need you."

With a half dozen men working precariously on the inoperative elevator, the temporary rigging dragged on for an hour while the stricken Zeppelin drifted slowly northeastward. Fortunately, the squall that had inflicted the damage proved to be an aberration. The repair crew, with only the damaged fin between them and a plunge into the sea, faced no more than a slight breeze.

At last, the exhausted crew crawled back into the hull. The hatch was secured.

Kellner was notified. The engines roared into life as Peter made his way back to the control car. Kellner gave the helmsman a revised southeast heading, then turned to Peter.

"Well done, Exec."

"I didn't do much, Herr Kommandant. The men did the work."

"You did more than you think. Masters' Mate Hellmich gave me a running account of what was going on back there and he sounded not like his usually surly self, but like a man inspired."

As night fell, the Cuxhaven coastline drifted below. Landing with only the portside elevator operational will be tricky business, Peter knew. But Kellner and I and this crew can do it.

Then it struck him. Our bigger problem is going to be Strasser's reaction to all this.

43.

Kellner stepped out of the Airship Division's Administrative Headquarters less shaken than Peter expected. More apprehensive, perhaps, than browbeaten.

The airship kommandant drew in a long breath, gazed up at the heavy overcast, then nodded at Peter. "Not quite a black cigar... yet. This time Strasser leaves us in suspense. He's waiting for structural and rigging experts from Friedrichshafen to conduct an investigation and submit their report. A matter of several weeks. And he's fuming about the meteorologists' latest prediction – this low ceiling, and rotten visibility with mist and rain expected to last through the rest of the month."

"In that case," Peter ventured, "might I do my worrying at a more amenable location?"

"Leave time? Strasser's investigators may want to interview you as well as me. But," Kellner added with a shrug, "knowing the navy, I don't expect them to appear for at least a week. In the meantime, with the blame of our scouting fiasco focused on me, I don't see why you can't seek a few days' 'recuperation' elsewhere."

He cocked his head and gave Peter a knowing smile. "She's in Cuxhaven, I understand. Oh, don't look so surprised. Word gets around. I'll clear you for several days, beginning tomorrow."

* * *

Arm in arm, they watched a trawler make its way through the mist-shrouded estuary toward Cuxhaven, its progress assisted by the ebb tide. Behind them, the lights of the Blauer Adler Inn glowed through the evening's haze.

How do I tell him? She wondered. How will he react? Oh hell, I'm just going to come out with it.

"Peter, I told my mother about us."

"All about us?"

"Of course, not all. But I think she guessed. As Pappi and I left to go back to the factory, her final words were 'be careful.' At the time, I thought she meant be careful about…" She gave Peter a facetiously coy glance. "But now I believe she was worried about where we are going with… this."

Peter gently turned her to face him. "Your mother has to be uneasy about a wartime love affair. But believe me, Lexie, I am not what she may be thinking – I'm not the cliché sailor with his, 'I may be dead tomorrow, so let's make love tonight' line. I'm in love with you, Lexie. If it weren't for this damned war, I would ask you to marry me tomorrow."

"Peter, I –" Her voice failed her.

"I'm the opposite of that slick-talking sailor. But it wouldn't be fair to have a wife worrying about losing her husband in a… In a –"

"But married or not, I worry about that now, Peter." She took his hands in hers. Then she wondered, had that sounded like a subtle proposal of my own? I didn't mean it that way. If he were to ask me to marry him, ask me at this very moment, what would I say? I love this man. And I love my independence, too. Am I willing to trade that freedom for a life tied to his? Am I being practical – or just selfish?

"When the war is over," he said softly. "When the war is over." He slipped his arms around her, gently kissed her forehead, cheek, then sought her lips. "We will marry when the war is over, Lexie," he promised, and kissed her again. "I want to be with you the rest of my life."

The rest of his life… "If that was a proposal," she said, "I absolutely accept." She threw her arms around him, kissed him with a passion she felt all the way to her toes. "Oh, God," she whispered. "It's absolutely time to go to bed." And for a few blissful hours, we can forget everything but each other.

* * *

The drizzling skies persisted two more weeks, then were cleared by a stiff southwest wind. No improvement for airship operations. Air and ground crews became sullen, grumping at the imposition of "make work" assignments. On one of those stand-down, blustery mornings, Kellner and Peter were summoned to Strasser's office.

"Your guess, Hugo?" Peter asked as they approached the administration building.

"I never guess when Strasser is involved."

So much for conversation. They entered the building, strode between the twin rows of desks and Kellner rapped on Strasser's door.

"Herein!"

The Kommandant of Airships stood at his window, shuffling a sheaf of papers. Which he tapped with a forefinger.

"The decision of the investigation into your control problem, Kapitänleutnant Kellner and Oberleutnant zur See Reinhart."

Peter tensed.

"A flaw in the control cable itself, Gentlemen. And a commendation from me on your handling of that emergency. Dismissed."

"I'll be damned," Kellner said, stepping back into the windy afternoon.

"A white cigar, Hugo?"

On May 30, the skies finally calmed. And on that day von Buttlar was scheduled to deliver to Nordholz the L-30, the first of a series of new six-engine airships with a 50 percent greater lift capacity.

"Quite an occasion," Kellner told Peter as they joined the welcoming party of airship officers and Fregattenkapitän Strasser out on the airfield.

"And there it is, Hugo." Peter pointed toward the south horizon where an airship appeared head-on, a growing silver orb.

The growl of its six engines increased to a roar as the airship neared Nordholz, then faded. L-30 began to settle. Rapidly.

"Too damned fast?" Peter wondered

"Indeed," Kellner agreed.

And, apparently, so did its kommandant. Silvery streams of water suddenly cascaded from the Zeppelin's ballast ports – straight onto the waiting reception party.

"I'm soaked!" Peter managed to gasp through his laughter.

"We all are," Kellner grinned, "including Chief of Airships Strasser."

The ground crew grabbed the landing lines, and L-30 settled in gently. The engines died. Red-faced Oberleutnant zur See Horst Baron von Buttlar stepped from the control car to confront a thoroughly drenched Strasser. Who amazed everyone with a bemused grin. "Herr Oberleutnant," he said, "you came in like a water wagon."

The applause was as much for Strasser's rare humor as it was for von Buttlar's stiffly emerging passenger: white-haired, white-mustached Graf Ferdinand von Zeppelin, the father of airships himself.

Strasser had his hands full. In addition to entertaining von Zeppelin, he informed his airship officers he had received an order from Fleet Admiral Sheer. Five airships were to escort the Grand Fleet as it thrust northward along Denmark's Jutland coast. Despite the urgency, the small armada, including two from Nordholz, was delayed by increasing winds that did not abate until the following early afternoon.

At 15.30 o'clock, the German fleet was intercepted by a British battle group near the Danish coast. What would be known as the two-day Battle of Jutland began. By late afternoon, German battle cruisers had sunk two of Britain's cruisers, *Indefatigable* and *Queen Mary*.

The scouting Zeppelins, however, spotted nothing. Persistent mist cut visibility to no more than five kilometers beneath a 750-meter cloud ceiling. As the frustrated first group of Zeppelin scouts rumbled back into Nordholz and Hage, another patrol lifted into the clearing night sky to continue scouting the same area. Among the four airships droning north from Nordholz into the clearing North Sea night was Kellner's.

"Course three-five-zero," Kellner ordered as they climbed past Cuxhaven into the black sky. "Exec and observer, be damned alert for any sign of gunfire."

Our kommndant states the obvious, Peter thought. Nerves. But who among the sixteen of us up here in this big target isn't nervous?

He stared starboard into the night's opaqueness as blacked out Cuxhaven fell behind. Did Lexie hear them rumble overhead then fade northwestward? She seemed delighted to be so near, but that nearness must bring her the sound of every Nordholz lift-off.

Somewhere ahead, a sea battle raged. But for Admiral Kottenhoff's manipulations, I could be on a battle cruiser under fire by English dreadnaughts. Which is worse? Down there with heavy shells ripping through battleship armor and the cold sea waiting for you? Or up here hoping no shell or careless crewman's spark blows the whole airship into flaming flinders? He shook himself back to alertness. Black sea. Black sky. Am I an airship officer dedicated to these gasbags? Still a civilian at heart, despite the Academy and all these flying hours? Or just a tired guy feeling sorry for himself? Fatigue and boredom at 03.00 o'clock in the morning are making me –

Everybody in the control car saw it – the scarlet flare of a huge explosion.

"Steer three four-zero degrees," Kellner ordered.

The Zeppelin swung toward the fading glow. An hour later, they could see nothing through the predawn mist below. Not until returning to Nordholz would Peter learn they had witnessed, at a distance, the British torpedoing of the venerable German battleship *Pommern*. It had gone down with all hands.

As dawn broke, everyone in the control car was astonished as the fog-shrouded sea 10 kilometers ahead erupted with muzzle flashes.

"Steady on course, Helmsman," Kellner ordered.

He turned to Peter. "Prepare to drop salvos of five bombs on my orders."

Antiaircraft fire began to pepper the sky dead ahead. To Peter's amazement, they plowed straight into it. Was Kellner desperate to hit something worth bragging about? "Now, Exec," Kellner shouted.

Peter toggled off five high explosive bombs. A moment later, their flashes joined the continuing bursts of wildly inaccurate gunfire in the swirling sea fog. Two more salvoes streaked down into the area of defensive fire. Are we hitting anything? Peter wondered. We are as blind as they are. Not one of the shells exploding all around us has come close. But I'll give Hugo credit. He took the chance.

"Break off, Helmsman," Kellner ordered as they passed beyond the field of fire. "New bearing: four-five-zero. We head for Jammer Bay."

An hour and a half later, Peter swung his binoculars along the distant northwest coast of Denmark – and froze.

"Herr Kommandant, a full squadron of ships in –" He consulted the map on the console. "Yes, in Jammer Bay. Twelve large ships. Heavy haze, though. I'm not sure…"

Kellner grabbed his own binoculars. "Steer parallel to the coastline, Helmsman. Well out to sea. Too much firepower in there for a closer look." He adjusted the focus. "British."

"Sir, I'm not so sure –"

"Not so sure about what, Exec?"

"About those vessels, Herr Kommandant. They look to be –"

"They look to be what they are, Reinhart. An attack squadron of the British Grand Fleet heading out of the bay, no doubt to attack Scheer's battle cruisers. Report to Nordholz."

"Sir, with all due respect –"

"Have Mann send the report, Oberleutnant," Kellner insisted.

"Aye, Sir." Peter stepped aft to the radio op. "Send: 'Sighted 12 apparent British large warships and number of smaller ships in Jammer Bay." He peered at Kellner.

"Send it," Kellner insisted, "Including our position. And add this: 'Clouds and haze make accurate attack impossible. We are breaking off.'"

Through the long hours back to Nordholz, Peter fought growing unease. Misfits. Are we about to be hounded by that insult again?

"Gentlemen, let me summarize the Battle of Jutland for you." For once, Peter noted, Strasser did not pace while he fumed. Facing his audience head-on this time, his fiery eyes raked across every officer in the room.

"In the late afternoon of May 31, Admiral Hipper's squadron sailed as bait to draw a far superior British force into battle with our main fleet. Making contact, Hipper sank three British cruisers. The enemy then retreated. Hipper followed – straight into Admiral Jellicoe's far more powerful fleet. In the two engagements, we lost one old battleship, a battle cruiser, four light cruisers and five destroyers. The enemy lost three battle cruisers, three light cruisers, eight destroyers and twice as many men as did we. On balance, a German victory. A costly one.

"But not a victory for the Airship Division. Just one of you made reliable reports of these actions. Just one of you. Korvettenkapitän Schutze in L-11 did manage to sight and report a group of British battle cruisers north of Terschelling. Fired upon, L-11 withdrew and lost sight of the British in the poor visibility."

Now Strasser began his pacing, almost a relief to Peter, tense in his uncomfortable metal chair. Kellner beside him, looking perplexed, whispered, "Why no mention of our Jammer Bay sighting?"

Thank God, no mention, Peter thought. But he said nothing.

"Not one of our airships saw anything of the sea battles. Kellner reported bombing a battle group that fired on him – bombing in the blind because of fog. No hits confirmed. Not one airship made any tactically useful sightings."

He stopped the damned pacing, faced them and raised a hand with forefinger pointing toward the ceiling. "Oh, yes, one of you did report sighting a major British battle group in Jammer Bay. Fortunately we did not forward that information to Admiral Scheer because we had been notified a German supply convoy had taken refuge in the bay while the Jutland engagements were underway."

Our own convoy. Peter fought the temptation to give Kellner a victorious look.

Strasser clasped his hands behind his back again and resumed his steady tread. "I realize visibility was minimal. But when you make sightings, for God's sake, make them accurately."

No one spoke, or stirred.

"There is a positive aspect to all this," he announced to everyone's surprise. "Admiral Scheer has somehow determined aerial observation was of some value during the Jutland... experience. He has advised me, and I quote, 'Airship scouting is fundamental for more extended operations.' On that happier note, you are... dismissed."

As the gaggle of officers dispersed into the gray morning, Kellner caught Peter's arm. "You were right, Peter. One day, I will learn to listen to you."

44.

"**A**dmiral!"

The cry echoed through the main Gotha hangar as Kottenhoff walked through it toward his office on his return from the factory's restaurant. With the army evaluating the prototype Gotha bomber, the factory was set to go into overtime production. Lull before the storm, Kottenhoff thought. So who is yelling for me?

As he glanced over his shoulder, a heavyset man panted up to him, his comedian's face contrasting with his serious black homburg hat. Moellendorf. Again.

"More of your insight on the war?" Kottenhoff asked coldly.

The company relations man looked about nervously. Several mechanics had just walked into the hangar.

"Not in here, Admiral." He nodded at the nearby side door and they stepped into the pleasant midsummer afternoon. Some meters short of the entrance to the company's two-story office building, Kottenhoff stopped on the gravel walkway.

"If you want privacy, this should suffice."

Moellendorf looked about. They were isolated out here. He cleared his throat. "Two items I trust you will find of value. As always, you understand, I cannot disclose my sources."

Such melodrama this man enjoyed.

"About the Pomeroy ammunition. I have it on solid authority, Admiral, solid authority, that the British Ministry of Munitions has had a change of heart – a change of brain, more accurately, concerning Pomeroy. The Ministry has taken delivery of a large shipment of Pomeroy machine gun cartridges and possibly similar incendiary ammunition. All of it three-oh-three caliber for Home Defense aeroplanes."

His little eyes squinted at Kottenhoff. "You did report my information on the Pomeroy cartridge to Strasser?"

"I did."

"And?"

"And he appeared unimpressed." Insultingly so, Kottenhoff recalled sourly.

"For God's sake. Unimpressed?"

"He is convinced his Zeppelins can fly higher than any British attack machines. Especially his much publicized height climbers."

"Which are still months from testing and delivery." Moellendorf shook his head in exasperation. "Perhaps this second bit of information I have acquired will shake him out of his damned complacency. Finally, this late in 1916, the English have managed to put into Home Defense service a new Sopwith aeroplane. It is said to offer a degree of performance that will make the sluggish B.E.2c obsolete."

"Specifically, Moellendorf?"

"A higher service ceiling than any previous design. Airships can climb faster but not higher. Your friend Strasser should find both of these revelations of importance to the Naval Airship Division. The courtesy of protecting your source will, of course, be appreciated."

Pondering the import of this information, Kottenhoff stood there in silence.

"I see you are impressed, Admiral."

"Have you told anyone in authority about these developments?"

"I informed my client here at Gothaer Waggonfabrik, of course. I leave further use of the information in your hands, Admiral." He tipped his homburg – quite flippantly, Kottenhoff thought – and strode off toward the automobile parking area.

In his secluded upper floor office, Kottenhoff stared through his narrow window at the empty airfield. The prototype Gotha G.II had taken off at 11.30 o'clock for another test flight, this one northeast to impress the powers-that-be in Berlin with Germany's first bomber aeroplane.

Would this damned war never be over? The Verdun lunacy grinds on, and now the British are launching a major offensive north of the Somme River. The need for our Gothas is more urgent every day. And now the English will use incendiary machine gun ammunition in their Home Defense squadrons. The Zeppelin bomber is doomed.

Damn Moellendorf, Kottenhoff thought bitterly. Every time I meet the man, he leaves me with a problem. A decision I hate to face. I could assume he is in error, or perhaps just reporting unsubstantiated rumors. But, damn it, the slippery bastard has been precisely correct every time. Presuming today's double bombshell is accurate, what am I to do with it? Face Strasser in a second insulting cold-shoulder conference? Herr Fregattenkapitän will be no more amenable to this disgraced has-been admiral than before.

Perhaps von Tirpitz himself? He terminated my career because of my rightful, damn it, my rightful anti-airship efforts. But von Tirpitz would consider this new information more of this misguided loner's anti-airship fixation.

Should I inform Peter Reinhart, the boy my clumsy efforts have put aboard the damned Zeppelins? But could Reinhart, a mere oberleutnant, convince Nordholz they face catastrophe? Perhaps I can do something for him personally.

Kottenhoff stepped away from the window and slumped in his desk chair. Would that be ethical? For me? For him? With the airship program about to face calamity, should I care about ethics at all?

Peter Reinhart... He reached for his telephone. Lifted the receiver. Hesitated. Should I transfer my problem to Reinhart? How would the boy explain his knowledge of new British anti-airship ammunition? Could he admit his source is the admiral thrown out of the navy for anti-airship agitation?

Kottenhoff's stomach roiled and his head began to pound. What in hell should I do? Nothing? Go back to Gotha's stack of purchasing forms and let events evolve? The Airship Division is about to face precisely what I predicted. This is my vindication, for God's sake. Why am I conscience stricken?

He drummed his fingertips on the desktop. Shook his head in frustration – and realization. Despite all I've been through, I must do something about this threat to navy men. God help me, my heart is still with them. Face it, retired Admiral Kottenhoff. You must once more inform Strasser, distasteful as that is sure to be.

He buzzed his secretary to place the call.

Moments later, she tapped on his door. "On your line, Sir. Not Herr Strasser, but his aide. A Leutnant Olbrich."

He picked up the receiver. "Admiral Kottenhoff here, Leutnant." Perhaps that would get him past this minion. "I must speak with Fregattenkapitän Strasser on a most urgent matter. Verstehen Sie?"

"The Chief of Airships wishes me to thank you for your interest, but his schedule is impossibly crowded. He is unable to find the time to fit you in. His apologies, Herr Admiral, but that is the situation here."

No time to "fit me in." Kottenhoff fought to keep his voice level and his anger muffled. "Will you at least convey a message, Leutnant Olbrich?"

"A moment, Herr Admiral, while I find a pencil."

Find a pencil? God.

"Ready, Herr Admiral."

And Kottenhoff repeated to this lowly aide what Moellendorf had told him twenty minutes earlier.

"'…and an improved attack aircraft.' Thank you, Herr Admiral. I will place this on Fregattenkapitän Strasser's desk at the earliest opportunity."

"Now, Leutnant."

"Thank you, Herr Admiral. Auf Wiederhoeren." And the starchy young aide broke the connection.

Kottenhoff banged his fist on his desktop. Dumkopf! But I have done my best, and that's all I can do.

He reached for his overflowing in-tray.

Peter scanned the dark waters 1500 meters below. August 19. Two years into the war that was to be won in a few months… Eight of us in the air before dawn. Eight crews in eight Zeppelins, all of us flying on Strasser's energy.

This day's plan was so secret the flight officers were warned not to leak it to any member of the ground crews, including officers, and to reveal it to their own flight crews only after lift-off.

Another North Sea scouting patrol, but this one far from the routine watch for occasional British ships, Strasser had briefed his flight officers at the late evening operational meeting, "Vizeadmiral Scheer, Kommandant of the High Seas Fleet, intends to bombard Sunderland on England's northeast coast. His covert purpose: to draw the British Grand Fleet in range of nine German submarines already lying in wait. You, Gentlemen, will report the location and course of the oncoming British ships."

Now Strasser's Zeppelins droned at fast cruise to their eight assigned positions along the English coast, a carefully planned screen of aerial observers alert for the movement of any enemy ships of war.

After five hours at fast cruise, Kellner had his airship in its designated sector of the Zeppelin screen, 100 kilometers east of Lowestoft, well down the coast from Sunderland. They were precisely on station, with all engines smoothly idling to counteract the eastward wind drift. All was well, but Peter was aware of two problems no one had voiced at the pre-mission meeting, or since. For one, the airship's radio had been picking up an unusually heavy stream of German naval transmissions. Any listener, including British radio scanners, could guess something unusual was underway.

The other problem, in Peter's estimation, was Vizeadmiral Scheer's conviction – expressed to Strasser, then through him to the airship officers – that a screen of Zeppelins along the English coast would surely protect the Sunderland-bound German force from surprise. An admiral during wartime assuming he was immune from surprise?

Within an hour on station, lowering clouds forced Kellner to a mere 400 meters above the rolling sea, with visibility further reduced by light haze. The discernible expanse of sea remained empty.

Another tedious patrol, Peter decided, with too much time for contemplation. Remarkable that I'm up here at all. From my Academy class report critical of the military airship to second-in-command of one. What an ironic outcome for someone who yearned for a battleship posting. If I defied Admiral Kottenhoff's "request" to serve as his confidential eyes and ears at Nordholz, would I now be aboard one of Scheer's overconfident battle cruisers – headed for Sunderland? Would I have found anyone as compelling as Lexie? Would I –

"Look sharp to two-seven-zero degrees, Exec." Kellner's voice jolted him alert. "What do you make of that?"

Peter jerked his powerful lenses westward and his body tensed.

"British destroyers, Herr Kommandant." He focused the binoculars beyond the destroyers. "And what appears to be an entire cruiser squadron bearing southwest at flank speed."

"Have Mann encode and transmit that to Nordholz for relay to Scheer, Reinhart. Time: 07.30 o'clock."

Radio operator Mann barely completed the message transmission when Kellner shouted, "Engines full ahead! Maximum climb."

His urgency was reinforced by the flat detonation of an anti-aircraft shell some 100 meters to starboard, but at their level. In seconds, the sky erupted with red-centered black shell bursts. One exploded dead ahead. They ploughed through its smoke, the acrid smell swirling through the open observation windows. Then, thank God, they rose into the obscuring clouds.

"Starboard ninety degrees," Kellner ordered. Whatever was developing below, they were out of it.

Until two hours later.

"British light cruiser, Herr Kommandant." Peter caught a glimpse of the three-funneled ship through a rift in the underlying clouds. "Heading southeast."

"Radio time and location, Exec."

Peter gave Mann the message to transmit to Nordholz for relay.

At midday, now flying just above low broken clouds, Peter was again jarred from the monotony of scanning an empty sea. A widely dispersed flotilla of destroyers and what appeared to be light cruisers had materialized along the horizon. At the same moment, Observer Schwinn cried, "Naval force ahead, Herr Kommandant!"

As they drew nearer, Kellner called, "Ours or theirs?"

The answer came as guns began to wink. Seconds later, the sky ahead was pocked with shell bursts.

"Maximum climb," Kellner ordered. Over his shoulder, he asked Peter, "Can that be the same force we came upon at 07.30 hours?"

Peter swept the sea below. "It appears to be, Sir. But now they are headed north."

"Radio for relay to Scheer: 12.30 o'clock, our location, enemy force, about 30 units on northerly course. We are being heavily fired upon."

Moments later, Mann handed Peter Scheer's relayed response. "Maintain contact. Report any course change."

Easier requested than carried out. The clouds thickened. Now Peter glimpsed the British ships through intermittent cloud breaks. Then a massive cloud towered above the broken undercast, darkening as they neared. In the boiling cumulus build-up, lightning began to flicker.

"Thunderstorm. Hard aport, Helmsman., Kellner ordered. "Take us around that damned thing."

Twenty minutes later, with the thunder squall falling behind, the cloud layer below had become opaque. Kellner looked at Peter with an expression of resignation. Dropping below the clouds would put the airship only 200 to 300 meters above any warships they might encounter. Fatally low.

"Six degrees down," Kellner ordered cautiously. "Slow."

When they broke out below the stratocumulus layer, Peter, Schwinn and Kellner himself scanned the sea, now disturbingly close. Not a single ship in sight. Relief and apprehension. Nobody to shoot at us, but –

"We've lost them," Kellner said, his voice leaden. "Report for relay to Scheer."

Two fruitless hours later, diminishing fuel left them no choice but to set a course for Nordholz.

After a late "breakfast-dinner-supper," Peter plodded back to officers' quarters. "A mess," Ernst blurted as Peter walked in. "A bunch of us crammed in the radio shack heard it all. A verfluchte mess. Too many reports from too few Zeppelins to cover the whole damned English coast. The best I can make of it is Scheer ended up chasing a small force reported to the south –"

"Reported by us, Ernst."

"Congratulations. That kept him from contacting the whole damned British Grand Fleet lying in wait to the west." He gave Peter a wry grin. "That just may have saved his butt. He never did catch up with the group you reported, and the idea of shelling Sunderland no longer made any sense. The submarine trap was never sprung. Your day of blunders just may have saved our High Seas fleet from disaster."

Peter slumped on his bunk. "I wonder how Strasser is reacting to all that?"

"I know how he's reacting. He was in the radio shack with us. He is more certain than ever that 'airships offer a certain means of victoriously ending the war.' That's a quote. And he's asking Berlin for four more Zeppelins to bring the North Sea force up to a total of twenty-two."

45.

With the army's acceptance of its two-engined bomber, the Gotha factory pounded with 24-hour urgency. Wing tip to wing tip, nose to tail, the big biplanes jammed the hangar. Almost a dozen more Gothas crouched beneath temporary weather shelters along the parking apron. Kottenhoff found the pervasive tang of fresh varnish exhilarating. These husky aeroplanes, not the fragile Zeppelins, might truly end the war.

At an upper floor hallway window of the office building, he paused to take in that panorama of parked bombers awaiting delivery. For the first time since the war began, he felt a sense of imminent victory.

In her cubicle outside his office, dumpy little Henni held out a sealed envelope. "While you were meeting with the production staff, Sir, Herr Moellendorf left this for you. He said he was in a hurry to get back to Berlin."

What now from ever-surprising Max? Kottenhoff walked into his office, shut the door behind him and sank into his creaking chair. He ripped off an end of the envelope and extracted the note from the self-styled "industrial relations" expert.

Sorry to have missed you, Admiral. One notable piece of news. Strasser has ordered four more Zeppelins to

fill out his goal of 22 assigned to the North Sea area airship bases for increased attacks on England. (I will appreciate your destroying this.)
Regards,
Max

Kottenhoff's caught his breath. Will nothing derail that goateed little fanatic? I did what I could and it cost me a career – perhaps a deserved punishment, to be objective about it. Defied orders to desist. Fortunate not to be thrown on the mercy of a military court.

But the real victims are Alexia and especially Peter. I managed to spirit her out of potential complications. But young Reinhart? I've failed him. Ordered him into highly hazardous duty to further my own prejudice. Sentenced a promising young officer to potential death in a lost cause.

He stared at the papers on his desk without seeing them. What have I done for him? What *can* I do for him? Friends in high enough places... Hermann Oberholtzer in Naval Stores? Peter counting uniform caps--I don't think so. Someone who had served with me in the old High Seas Fleet... Ludwig von Peltz! Had not Peter's first choice been battleship service? A choice I headed off. Perhaps I can work this out with old friend Konteradmiral von Peltz.

Fregattenkapitän Strasser swung about in mid-stride to face his morning audience of airship officers. Cold early autumn rain ticked the assembly room windows. Near the door, an officer without a Zeppelin badge on his jacket stood respectfully silent but his fingers drummed his thighs. A man, Peter decided, eager to speak.

They had sat through Strasser's comments on yesterday's aborted effort to penetrate the North Sea's soupy fog. They had heard today's weather report, which they all surely had predicted themselves while trotting here through it. Now Strasser nodded to the stocky, bearded Kapitänleutnant fidgeting by the door.

"In recent days, Gentlemen," Strasser said by way of introduction, "certain rumors have reached me concerning developments on the other side. I requested a report on those rumors." He motioned to the waiting officer. "Kapitänleutnant Stoltz, the Airship Division's Chief of Intelligence. Kapitänleutnant, you will report your findings."

Stoltz, a heavy man with the shoulders of a boxer, strode to the front of the room to face them stiffly, hands at his sides.

"Good morning, Gentlemen. I know my findings are not going to elate anyone, but at least you will know what you are up against. We have confirmation that the English Ministry of War has accepted three types of caliber .303 anti-airship cartridges. One, called 'Brock," after its designer, fires an explosive bullet intended to tear holes in airship hydrogen cells. The second new munition is termed 'Pomeroy,' again after the man who developed it. The Pomeroy cartridge, too, fires an explosive bullet. The third new cartridge we are aware of, 'Buckingham,' is an incendiary bullet to be fired with the explosive types. Its obvious purpose is to ignite the hydrogen released by the Brock and Pomeroy rounds."

"Mein Gott," whispered Kellner, seated on Peter's left.

"Silence," Strasser ordered. "Kapitänleutnant Stoltz?"

"One more item. We have learned the English are equipping certain Home Defense squadrons with an attack aeroplane recently developed by Sopwith. The Sopwith 'Pup.' Though its rate of climb is relatively slow – almost eight minutes to reach fifteen hundred meters – its service ceiling exceeds five thousand meters. It is fast and far more agile than the B.E.2cs you have been encountering. And it is armed with a Vickers .303 machine gun synchronized to fire forward, through the propeller disc."

Now the room was dead silent.

Stoltz turned to Strasser. "That is all I have for the moment, Herr Fregattenkapitän."

"It is quite enough, Kapitänleutnant. Thank you. Gentlemen, I want you to bear in mind you can out-climb even the new Sopwith." His penetrating eyes swept the room. "Dismissed."

Outside, Kellner said, "We can out-climb the damned Pup in a race for altitude, but if he climbs to 5,000 meters when he knows we are coming and waits for us, then what?"

In the Officers' Club, Ernst set down his empty glass with a thud. "That's number five. I think. I've lost count. I should be feeling pleasantly drunk by now," he told Peter "but I'm not."

"You're not?" Something, Peter decided, has been eating at Ernst all evening on this miserable day of persistent rain. The showers cancelled even routine coastal scouting flights.

"No, I'm not." Ernst shoved the glass away. "But I am finished drinking for the night." He stood, lurched over the table, caught himself. "Walk me back to quarters, Peter."

The early fall air held an unexpected bite. Peter raised the collar of his jacket and most unmilitarily thrust his hands in his trouser pockets. The airship field was dark, empty. In the moist gloom, the safety lights on the widely scattered Zeppelin sheds seemed to glow dispiritedly

Ernst stopped to gaze into the field's blackness. "I've been wondering..." His voice trailed off.

"Wondering what?"

Silence. Then he resumed his draggy pace. "Wondering how you feel about flying off in a gas bag that might not... might not come back." He cleared his throat. "I'm sorry. I have no right to ask something that personal. Sorry."

"I guess I feel like everybody else feels. I do the job I'm ordered to do. And we are all volunteers, so do we have the right to complain?"

They walked on a few moments, then Ernst stopped again. "Why did you volunteer for this, Peter?"

Why did I volunteer? Hell of a question. Of all the airship officers and crewmembers at Nordholz, I'm probably the only one who was *ordered* to volunteer.

"Why, Peter?"

"At the Academy, I pictured myself on the bridge of a battleship, or at least a heavy cruiser. Somehow, I got myself sidetracked into the airship service. Not such a bad choice, perhaps, when you think of all those big ships sunk in the Jutland mess." He peered at Ernst's frozen expression. "You?"

"I thought airships would be better than where I was. Bored to death in the Department of Naval Depot Inspectors in smoke-choked Wilhelmshafen. I was carried away watching the Zeppelins from the Wittmund airship base fly overhead. Sailing up there in clear open air had to be better than checking inventories of soap, mops and scrubbing brushes."

"From wharf pigeon to eagle."

"So I thought, but that was before Strasser decided airships could bomb England out of the war, and England began using the airships for target practice. Now they have bullets designed to blow up airships, and improved attack aeroplanes, and... and –"

"Ernst, get hold of yourself. This isn't you. It's all that beer talking."

"In vino veri... veri –"

"'In vino veritas,' Ernst. Wine, and obviously beer, brings out the truth."

"That's it. The truth. I was relieved to be assigned to ground duties here. I'm afraid I am a coward."

"But you trained for Zeppelins. We took some training flights together."

"That was before the London bombing began."

"And you told Franz and me just a few weeks ago you volunteered for flying duty."

"That's the only way I can stay in the flying officers' quarters and attend the assemblies, and –" Ernst's voice broke. He cleared his throat again. "And face you and Franz."

Jesus, Peter thought. "Let me ask you something. If your request comes through and you are assigned to a flight crew, what will you do?"

His voice almost a whisper, Ernst said, "I will... do as I am ordered. And," he added, "I will sweat."

They walked on. Then Peter said, "You're being honest with me. Let me be honest with you. I know damned well there is not a single airship crewmember here or at any other airship base who does not ask himself at every lift-off for a London attack, 'This time will I die in fire? Or from the long fall after I jump?'"

Ernst was silent until they neared the Officers' Quarters entrance. Then he said, very quietly, "Thank you."

46.

Weary from the long though uneventful patrol flight, Peter tossed his flying jacket on his bunk and slumped on the window seat. They had spotted nothing but the pale September sky above a few German torpedo boats cutting tiny wakes on the somber sea.

Franz flipped him a letter. "For you. Postmarked Gotha. Who do you know in Gotha?"

Peter studied the envelope. Only a stamp, postmark and his name and address. Who *do* I know in Gotha? He wondered. No one... Oh. Just one person there. Admiral – now Herr – Kottenhoff. He ripped the envelope open.

Sehr geehrter, Oberleutnant Reinhart:
You will no doubt be startled by this letter, but it has come to my attention an opening exists in the Department of Torpedo Service Inspection, located at Kiel. There is a position for an officer of your rank and abilities to supervise torpedo testing. I am confident you can be quickly qualified for this posting.

In my current situation, of course, I cannot directly recommend you. However, should you elect to take advantage of this opportunity, I am in a position to facilitate informally your acceptance by the Chief of the Department of Torpedo Service Inspection.
Please notify me at your earliest convenience of your interest in pursuing this matter.
Mit freundlichen Gruss,
Ihr,
Erwin Kottenhoff

The address following the signature was on a street in the City of Gotha.

Peter stared at the letter. This has to be an act of conscience by the man who put me here. Now the admiral offers me a way out. I appreciate his concern, but now I face –

"So?" Franz pressed. "Who is your secret admirer in Gotha?"

"What? Oh, just another navy man I worked with after I graduated from the Academy."

"Worked with?"

"Routine position. Clerical." For God's sake, let it go, Franz.

Some 'position.' Now here I am hoping like all of us I will survive the next bombing flight. And now the man who got me into all this finds me a way out. Can he actually do it? He did manage a refuge for Lexie. And now he offers one to me.

Five kilometers along the North Sea's low-level coastline west of Cuxhaven, Peter pulled the Ford off the sandy lane and stopped. He switched off the engine. They sat in silence.

"No airships flying over, headed to God knows where into God knows what." Lexie sighed, smiled. "I like this weather." The unrelenting low overcast kept Zeppelins in their sheds for days but liberated their crews for brief leaves.

Not a house, farm – or Zeppelin shed – jutted up from the flat, brush-studded countryside. The only sound this cool Sunday afternoon was the wash of waves a few meters from the lane.

"Peter? You haven't said anything since we left Cuxhaven."

"Oh, I'm sorry. I –"

"What is it, Liebchen?"

Should I tell her? Isn't it dishonest not to tell her? He swallowed uncomfortably. "Admiral Kottenhoff has sent me a letter."

"A letter?" She turned toward him, delicate eyebrows raised.

"He believes he can have me transferred from the Airship Division. To a position in the Torpedo Inspection Department."

He waited for her cry of relief. No more her feeling of dread when a Zeppelin flew overhead. No more the terrible suspense she had told him clutched her throat until the Zeppelins returned and he telephoned her to assure her he was back safe.

But she said, quietly, "Is that what you want to do?" Her eyes, though, seemed to implore him to accept.

He dodged her question. "Why would the admiral suddenly make such an offer?"

"His conscience, Peter. He is trying to do something for you to make up for what he did to you."

"If I accept an offer like his…"

"Peter, I will love you whatever you do."

"Even if I were to rob a bank so we could buy a house?"

She laughed. "Even if – but you would have to face Pappi. He once fired a man for stealing pencils."

"A lot of pencils?"

"Five boxes of pencils in five days. And a sharpener. Then he started on pens."

He opened the driver's side door. "Time for a walk, Lexie."

Hand in hand, they strolled to the top of a dune and watched the endless crump and swash of the shoreline waves.

I thought she would beg me to take the admiral's offer. Would that help me decide? Should there be any question? Why risk burning to death in a doomed airship when I can spend the rest of the war behind a safe desk? A man in his right mind would leap at the admiral's offer. The salt breeze ruffled Lexie's auburn hair as she peered far out to sea. Would not the decision be for her, not just for me?

Abruptly, she flew into his arms. "Hold me, Peter," she demanded, tears glistening on her cheeks. "Hold me tight."

At dusk, he wandered across the airship field. Alone. He needed solitude, an escape from the clamor of the Officers' Mess, the Officers' Club, and from the chatter of his roommates. The huge shed's double door had not yet been closed against autumn's capricious winds. A pair of engine mechanics walked past him with automatic salutes, which he returned in reflex. The Zeppelin towered above him; hectares of taut fabric stretched over an immense duralumin frame. Four powerful engines. Majestic. Kellner's airship. My airship.

Majestic if I don't think about its 19 cells pumped full of explosive hydrogen, waiting for an errant spark, an anti-aircraft shell – or a burst of explosive and incendiary English ammunition to blow the whole damned thing into flaming flinders.

Yet he had felt touches of magic in the long flights. Golden North Sea sunsets. The breathtaking sweep of clear blue on a perfect summer morning. A sun-touched undercast billowing beneath as the airship appeared to stand still in the crisp air of altitude.

The last few hands of the ground crew rolled the towering shed doors toward each other from their frames flanking the gaping entrance. Peter turned away – and found himself not alone after all.

"You, too?" Kellner said behind him. "I thought I was the only one who didn't look for answers in a glass of evening beer."

Together they watched the space between the doors dwindle to a crack then meet with a thud. The last of the maintenance crew filed out a side door and walked off into the evening's thickening haze.

"I hate the damned things," Kellner said. "But I'm proud to be an airship man. Proud of my crew. Our crew, Peter. They were culls from airship bases that didn't want them." He laughed. "Maybe I was, too. Never thought about it that way. But we've shaped up well. The work on that elevator failure. Your going up top to get Hansenkamp calmed down, then directing those evasive turns to shake off that English aeroplane."

"I only –"

"You only saved us, Peter. Look what happened to Breithaupt's ship that same night, maybe by the same aeroplane."

"You ever regret volunteering for airships?"

"Every time a shell goes off near us. But I get over it. It still beats mud and lice."

"Or a safe desk job, Hugo?"

"I don't know. I don't know what I'd do if I were offered one. I'd miss the crew. I would miss flying with you. Having you as Executive Officer has made a difference, Peter. To me. To the whole crew."

He chuckled. "Sorry. Didn't mean to get so personal. Come on, I'll walk you back."

"A letter to Lexie?" Franz asked the next day, another down day because of the dense haze.

"A letter to a friend, Franz."

"She's not a friend?"

"You know damned well she's a lot more than a friend." Peter tapped the paper with the tip of his pen. "Go back to your magazine. Let me concentrate."

> *Sehr geehrter, Herr Admiral:*
> *Your letter is most appreciated, and I have given it much thought. The life of a Zeppelin officer is surely not the career I had intended to follow my Academy graduation, and your alternative offers a more certain future.*

He stopped. His fingers were jittering. My future, if any, hangs on the next sentence.

...One day I will learn to listen to you. Kellner... *We need you.* Masters' Mate Hellmich... What others think of me matters. But what I think of myself matters most.

Do it, Oberleutnant.

> *I will not forget your kindness and concern in offering to work out an alternative. But after considerable deliberation, I have decided to remain in my present status.*
> *Again with much appreciation,*
> *Ihr,*
> *Peter Reinhart*

He sealed the envelope. Stared out the room's single window. The afternoon had darkened. Cold September rain ticked the glass.

He recalled Lexie's desperate embrace at the North Sea overlook. She knew what I would do before I knew it myself.

47.

"**D**espite our recent set-backs, airships will win this war," Strasser reassured his assembled airship officers. And that, Peter knew, was not just morale-building chatter. The Kommandant of Airships is obsessed with his certainty Zeppelins will inevitably blast the English into abject surrender. Had Strasser put forth his convictions from behind a desk, Peter suspected, his crews would now hate the man. But despite his position, he continues to join various crews on the increasingly dangerous attack flights.

The winds and rain of late August 1916, frustrated the Division's efforts to attack English targets on the 24th. Thirteen airships, with Strasser himself aboard the new six-engined L-32, headed westward into a stiff headwind. In mid-afternoon, six of the airships were fired on by British destroyers. Then in the clear night, cannon fire from a British cruiser slammed into L-13. The shell slashed through the Zeppelin midships, and exploded above it. Helped by the strong west wind, Kapitänleutnant Prolss was able to limp back to Hage.

The persistent wind scattered the rest of the optimistic armada. Five more turned back before reaching the English coast. Still at sea, Peterson in L-32 managed to hit an unidentified English ship off Dover. Then one of the two Schütte-Lanz types in the attack group suffered turbulence damage to its wooden girders. The creaking glue-potter headed back to Nordholz. Of the six remaining attack airships, only Mathy in L-31 and Peterson hit recognizable targets, though damage turned out to be mostly the destruction of residences. All in all, the major effort was a major failure.

"Glad we missed that one," Kellner confided to Peter. But they wouldn't miss the next massive attack.

On September 2, ever-optimistic Strasser launched another airborne armada; 12 navy airships, accompanied by four from the army. This will be the largest airship attack of the war to date," Strasser told his officers, "and the first time navy and army airships will work together against the same target."

To Peter's relief, the flight started well; an easy lift-off at 14.00 hours in clear weather. Then a strong wind sprang up. Hours later, the buffeted airship force struggled through rain and snow showers to approach the Suffolk Coast during a lull in the late afternoon's squalls.

Peter felt oddly elated. In a way, this is my first flight, my first as a true volunteer. Until now, I was rushed along by circumstance. The admiral's "scout." Then assigned to Kellner as punishment. But now, through rejection of the admiral's offer, I finally have some faith in myself." Waiting for darkness, the airship floats with engines idling. I feel an odd sense of… peace? Peace? With a bomb load waiting to be dropped on London?

He swept the sea to starboard. And spotted the exhausts of two airships reversing course in the face of a rain shower over there.

"Herr Kommandant –"

"I see them, Exec. But there are still fourteen of us heading to the target."

In near-darkness a half hour later, at 2000 meters altitude, they crossed the Norfolk coast. Now began the long grind southward toward London. The rain persisted, sometimes no more than a sprinkle, occasionally heavy enough to make it impossible for Peter to see anything beyond the control car windows. During a let-up in the pelting downfall nearly two hours later, he spotted lights ahead.

"Cambridge, Herr Kommandant."

Kellner ordered the standard 90-degree turn to port, and they took up the due south London attack heading.

An hour later they flew into an area of rain so heavy its weight on the hull began to force them downward.

"Drop one – no, drop three of our high explosive bombs," Kellner ordered.

Peter tripped the release toggles, and moments later, they saw the flashes below.

"Open country," Kellner decided. "A waste." He tapped the altimeter glass. "But now we're holding our own."

Thirty minutes later, Kellner tapped Peter's arm, "Look at that!"

Peter stepped forward, raised his binoculars toward the glow along the distant horizon. As they drummed nearer, it resolved into a forest of searchlight beams along the horizon.

"London, Exec. Waiting for us."

"I count twenty-nine beams Thirty – God! Must be forty or more searchlights. So much for blackout. They're daring us to attack."

In thirty minutes, they reached into the northern edge of an airborne maelstrom.

Searchlight beams swept past like seeking swords. Failing, thank God, to lock on in all this confusion. Peter watched three airships plow through a melee of exploding anti-aircraft shells. Searchlight shafts flailed desperately to pin them against the night. He heard the "pung" of exploding shells. Smelled acrid burnt powder. Then – Oh God? Peter spotted darting exhaust flames, the fireflies of death.

"Aeroplanes, Herr Kommandant. At least four of them."

"Climb to three thousand meters." Kellner's voice sounded parched. He cleared his throat. "Three thousand," he repeated, and stepped close to Peter. "Christ," he muttered, "we've never seen it like this. Find a target. Find a target so we can get the hell out of here."

Clawing for altitude, they plunged through the airborne fury, Peter desperately searching the city blocks below, now dimly visible in the searchlights' glares reflected from a cloud layer 500 meters overhead. With luck, we might reach the overcast before a shell burst or one of the searching aeroplanes finds us.

In the gray city, Peter spotted the Thames. They were about to pass over the East End shipping complex.

"Docks below," he called.

"Salvo all bombs," Kellner cried with no hesitation at all.

Together he and Peter yanked at the toggle array. Down went everything, their entire load of high explosives and incendiaries. Peter shook his head in frustration. As with every attack, careful planning had disintegrated into random bombing. Wild climbs for the safety of overhead clouds and an all-out rush for the coast.

As their bombs flashed among the waterfront buildings 2500 meters blow, a blinding searchlight beam washed past the control car windows, froze ahead of them, then swung back. Peter's heart seemed to stop. The beam flared past to starboard.

"Lost us." Kellner gave him a quick grin, and then leveled his binoculars portside.

A kilometer distant, three searchlight beams had pinned an airship against the black night. Its boxy control car and the large landing lines "finger patch" near the nose identified it. A Shütte-Lanz.

Peter squinted through his lenses. "SL-11. One of the army ships. Take a look below him."

Kellner adjusted his binoculars. "Aeroplane. But they should be able to out-climb him."

The Schütte-Lanz nosed upward. The aeroplane climbed with it, not gaining on the airship but keeping up in the climb. A dozen searchlight beams converged on the desperately climbing airship. The pursuing biplane flashed in and out of the locked-on light shafts. Then it leveled off.

"He's giving up?" Kellner rasped close to Peter's ear.

"Looks like a B.E.2c, Herr Kommandant. Its machine gun is fixed to fire upward."

The anti-aircraft shell bursts had stopped, clearing the sky for the duel in progress. Winks from the airship's dangling control car told them it was firing in defense The aeroplane passed some 200 meters beneath the airship, its upward angled machine gun sparking. Fine lines of fire lanced toward the airship.

"Tracers," Peter said.

"If he's making any hits, his ammunition isn't very impressive," Kellner said. "Now he's turned around for another run from aft."

As the B.E.2c enemy pilot completed his second pass beneath the airship, Peter craned forward. "See that glow under the stern? My God, Hugo, the glue-potter's on fire!"

Just forward of SL-11's tail assembly, brilliant flame erupted from the bottom of the hull. The fire swept along the keel then upward to wrap the faltering airship in a fiery embrace. With agonizing slowness, the airship began to fall. Brilliant flames erupted astern and raced along the hull.

How many crewmen in a Schütte-Lanz? They're all doomed.

Searing a scarlet trail against the night, the airship plunged down tail-first to flatten into a flaming pool. In the fire's glare, Peter saw the LS-11 had crashed near a small village in London's eastern outskirts. He shut his eyes. I wonder if there's cheering down there.

"Steer seventy-five degrees. Maintain climb," Kellner said, his voice flat. Peter pushed away from the window, repeated the order to Kraemer and Weisinger. He glanced at Kellner. Their eyes met.

"We just faced hell and got away," Kellner said. "And that isn't the first airship brought down by an aeroplane."

"But the first to be shot down in flames by an aeroplane's machine gun fire."

Kellner's expression froze. "Their new ammunition." He drew a long breath.

"Christ save us."

Peter felt his blood turn to ice. What I just saw was horrible enough. But it's just the beginning. The new English ammo against German hydrogen will change the war. If I had the chance to choose now, what would I tell the admiral?

48.

As the ground handlers worked their airship toward its shed, Kellner's crew walked off in silence toward the mess buildings. Except for Machinist Mates Graber and Mueller. They were unaware of Peter's presence close behind them. Or perhaps, he thought, they don't give a damn.

"Did you see it?" stumpy little Graber asked, peering up at taller Mueller.

Mueller glared at him. "Are you forgetting I was the other gunner in the engine car?"

"Well, it was a Schütte-Lanz, an army glue potter. Wooden framework."

"You think that makes a difference?" Mueller asked. "It was full of hydrogen. So is a Zeppelin. What the hell difference does a duralumin frame make?"

"You want a difference? I'll give you a difference, not in the two airships, but in the attack. That's where the difference is."

"Graber, I don't –"

"The glue potter was shot down by an aeroplane. An aeroplane, you idiot! Didn't you see that?"

"I said I saw it. Firing some kind of sparkly stuff. Tracers, I think."

"More than that. I heard the Brits have some new kind of ammo that sets hydrogen on fire. Now I believe it."

Muller kicked viciously at a dirt clod. "Scheiss!"

"Jesus! You think that's going to stop Strasser from –"

"Shut up, Graber." Mueller glanced around, spotted Peter. "Just shut up."

Peter slowed to let them pull ahead, and Kellner strode up beside him.

"We're going straight to the intelligence officer, Peter. We are eyewitnesses to what is sure to be a disaster for the Airship Division."

Peter looked up at the scatter of fluffy cumulus clouds against a backdrop of blue. The sky had seemed so benign when they had lifted off yesterday afternoon. Now even its brightness seemed ominous.

"How do you think it will affect Strasser?"

"I'm willing to bet you something," Kellner said, his square face solemn. "That glue potter blown out of the air won't discourage Strasser one little bit."

Peter glanced around then moved close to Kellner. "Doesn't it strike you that our chief of airships has become something of a… fanatic?"

Kellner shot him a quick look. "I prefer to think of him as a man of unshakeable resolve."

A few days later, word reached Nordholz that the army had canceled any further attacks on England. Shortly after that disconcerting revelation, a further calamity shook the Naval Airship Division. At Fuhlsbüttel, training airship L-6 exploded while its hydrogen cells were being replenished. A routine activity with a costly result. The flames spread to nearby sister training airship L-9. Both Zeppelins were destroyed and so was most of their shed.

Three airships in two weeks, but on September 23, Strasser ordered a 12-ship attack on England.

As they walked from the assembly room into bright sunlight, a thoroughly shaken Ernst told Peter, "Now, of all times, I find myself assigned as observer in a major attack."

"In a way, though, you're lucky. Only the four superzeppelins are to hit London. On Frankenburger's L-21, you're going over the Midlands. Not much antiaircraft fire there."

"But who knows where their damned aeroplanes are going to show up?"

"If I were directing English defense, I would concentrate all my efforts around London. That's the only target I could be sure the Zeppelins will hit."

"Makes sense, Peter. Makes sense."

He sounded a bit more confident, and when he boarded L-21 for its 13.00 o'clock lift off, Ernst looked back at Peter and managed a smile. A fleeting smile in a dead white face.

We all feel crawling apprehension now, Peter sensed. Volunteers for glory – with reality corroding the splendor.

At breakfast the next morning, Peter set down his coffee cup. "They're coming back, Franz."

They pushed away from the table to join the rush to the door. Even the hardened old hands hurried into the late September dampness to watch the return of the Nordholz participants in the 12-airship attack.

"L-23 settling in." Franz peered west. "We sent out three. Where's –"

"There's one." Peter pointed. "Coming in low over those trees."

The gray orb grew larger then turned to resolve into the familiar elongated hull of – Peter squinted, puffed out his cheeks, then let out a long sigh of relief. "L-21, Franz. Ernst has made it back."

Franz still stared westward "I don't see our third Zepp. It's one of the Thirties class. Bocker's L-33 superzepp."

"Give him time. He was one of the four sent over London."

An hour later, Ernst joined Peter and Franz at the Officers Club. Still pale, he opted for beer, not food, and his hand trembled as he set down his glass.

"It's all a matter of luck," he muttered. Skill doesn't count for much.

Peter glanced at Franz. One combat flight, and Ernst sounded near collapse. "Life is a matter of luck, old friend," Peter said. Meaningless, I know, but at least I said something.

"I heard what happened to Bocker," Ernst said, his voice lifeless. "Chatter from the crews after we landed. L-33 took an anti-aircraft shell 4000 meters over London. Lost altitude fast. Never made it out of England. Crash-landed near the coast. Then the Zeppelin caught fire. There's some hope that the crew got out then burned the Zepp to keep it out of enemy hands."

He held up his glass for a refill. "That's bad enough but L-32..." His voice faltered.

"What about L-32?" Franz pressed.

"I saw that one. From a distance, but I saw it. An aeroplane attack. The Zeppelin caught fire and just fell out of the sky." Ernst stared at the table. "A comet of death."

"You saw that?" Franz said. "You were supposed to be over the Midlands."

"Saw it from Colchester, where we bombed God knows what. A glow in the sky to the southwest. Sixteen men burning to death." He fiddled with his glass. "Luck. Christ!"

"You're a naval officer, for God's sake," Franz said close to Ernst's ear. "An oberleutnant. A combat volunteer."

"Easy for you to say," Ernst muttered. "You're not permanently assigned to a crew."

"Luck, Ernst. A matter of luck."

Undeterred by yesterday's loss of two airships over London, Strasser sent nine more Zeppelins back to England September 25; three 30s class superzeppelins to hit London, the other older six to bomb the Midlands industrial areas.

Three of the attack group turned back early, one of them returned to Nordholz scant hours after lift-off. "Damned engine problems. Again." Peter heard its kommandant mutter to his exec as they passed the cluster of off-duty airship crewmembers watching the Zeppelin's return. The kommandant was pale, staring straight ahead.

"Engine problems?" Franz wondered. "He looks like a man who just escaped execution."

"He's a wreck," somebody said behind them. "That whole crew's coming apart. Those poor bastards shouldn't have been in the air at all."

"Should any of us?" someone else asked.

Peter glanced at Franz. They both knew such a comment should have been angrily shouted down. On this late September afternoon in 1916, no one said a word.

That day's defiant attack disintegrated into a series of individual failures, though Dietrich in L-22 managed to inflict slight damage on armaments factories in Sheffield – plus major damage to Sheffield residences. Mathy, finding London's night sky lethally clear and cloudless, flew on to not-yet-attacked Portsmouth. There he ran into a battery of blinding searchlights and heavy, though inaccurate, antiaircraft fire. He dropped his bomb load presumably on Portsmouth, but according to reports incoming days later, he more likely bombed the English Channel.

"So the attack disintegrated into another night of confusion." Back in his favorite chair in the Officers' Club, Ernst lifted his glass. "To the gas bags. Long may they blunder – sorry – thunder."

"Shut up, Ernst," Franz muttered.

"Hell, everybody feels the same way." He swung his glass toward Peter. "'We who are about to die salute you.' Isn't that the way it goes?"

Peter pulled Ernst's arm down. "That isn't helping any."

"We are beyond help, my friend. Isn't it just a matter of time? Aren't we flying yesterday's weapons against tomorrow's? Nothing will help –" He stared upward.

"What's that?"

"Rain," Peter told him. "Rain predicted to last a few days."

"Only God stops Strasser." Ernst raised his glass toward the downpour pelting the roof. "That will help at least for a while."

Another stand-down. I should be as relieved as Ernst, Peter thought. Except for my promise to meet Lexie's parents when the weather grounds us again. Relief for everyone else; apprehension for me.

49.

In a tailored suit of dark green, her auburn hair free and hatless in defiance of convention, she was gorgeous. Peter resisted the temptation to take Lexie in a steamy embrace. Not in this alleyway behind the Tammler factory with the garage mechanics looking on. He restrained himself to a kiss on her cheek.

"This simple visit you've talked me into on the telephone is getting complicated," he teased. "How long have you been here?"

"Only a few minutes. I left Kiel at noon." She peered into the garage. "They're already working on my auto."

"Rudi!" she called, "Oberleutnant Reinhart is here."

A wiry, gnome-like man in soiled work clothes appeared, wiping his hands on cotton waste.

"Rudi Mott, Peter. He taught me to drive, and he's the best mechanic in Hamburg."

Mott's leathery pixie face crinkled in a pleased grin. "Herr Oberleutnant." He eyed the idling Ford. "American."

"But it's on our side now."

"I'll try to remember that. I'll drive it into the shop. Oil change, grease work. A good going over, Herr Tammler told me. Both autos will be ready when you come back."

As Mott pulled the Ford into the garage, a big, sky-blue Panhard Coupé de Ville pulled out.

"Good afternoon!" came a shout from the other side of the alleyway. A heavy-set man stepped out, sniffed the crisp fall air, slapped on a gray Homburg hat and rushed to them. Otto Tammler, Peter realized. Shorter than I expected, but definitely in charge.

Tammler kissed Lexie's cheek, grabbed Peter's hand.

"Oberleutnant Reinhart. Hell, Peter, if I may. Good to meet you at last. Alexia has told me so much –"

"Pappi! Please."

The Panhard pulled up beside them. A liveried chauffeur stepped out. All muscle and subservient, he opened the passenger compartment door.

"Alexia and I will ride in the back. Peter, you're up front with Hermann."

While Lexie and Otto rode more grandly in the enclosed rear seat, Peter decided in any seat, this is a far grander ride than in my chugging Ford. The glass panel cuts off conversation with Lexie and Herr Tammler, but that's just logistics. Enjoy the ride in this luxurious product of enemy ingenuity. But relax? God, I'm more apprehensive of this visit than I am boarding the Zepp for an attack.

He gazed down the long hood flanked by two spare tires already mounted on spare wheels. No sweaty roadside tire patching for this automobile. Off with the old wheel, on with the new, and off we go. He glanced at stolid, expressionless Hermann.

"Been with the company long?"

"Five years, Sir." No expression in Hermann's voice, either. Only the message: do not talk with the driver of this smoothly rolling company chariot. Peter turned his attention to the big lawns and setback mansions of the residential area they were now rolling through.

Minutes later, Hermann guided the Panhard into a graveled drive, and they rolled through a lawn neatly planted with groves of pines. The air was filled with their scent. Hermann pulled up to the entrance of a three-story gray stone fortress. The wooden-faced chauffeur dismounted and strode around to the left side of the Panhard to open the door for his company's chief and his daughter. As Peter stepped out with his small traveling bag, the big oaken door of the mansion swung open. No stately butler. Not even a humble footman. A tall – noticeably taller than

Herr Tammler – stately, auburn-haired woman trotted down the steps to embrace Lexie. Amazing, the resemblance of mother and daughter.

"Mother, this is Oberleutnant sur See Peter Reinhart," Lexie said in mock formality. "Peter, my mother."

I was relieved by Otto Tammler's informality, Peter remembered. Now I'm under scrutiny by Frau Tammler's cool green eyes.

"So pleased to meet you, Oberleutnant." She offered her hand.

He caught Lexie's grin, took Ingrid Tammler's cool fingers in his. Smiled. Clicked his heels. Made the customary pretense of kissing the back of the offered hand. "I'm pleased to be here, Gnaedige Frau." Well, I am pleased to be here... with Lexie. Maybe with Herr Tammler, too. But...

Hermann carried his traveling case and Lexie's into the house, then with a touch of his cap's visor, remounted the imposing Panhard and drove back down the winding gravel drive. No butler. No footman. There was, however, a rotund and excellent cook who served the four of them in the large dining room.

"Not my ancestral home," Herr Tammler told him, catching Peter's glance at the framed oils on the dark paneled walls. "And no Rembrandts up there. Some local artists. Landscapes I liked the look of. Liked the look of the house, too. Some poor soul had poured all his marks into it, then –"

"Otto," Frau Tammler broke in, "I'm sure Herr Reinhart is not interested –"

"Of course he is. Then, Peter, came a slump in the market. The auction block. I got a good –"

Peter caught Frau Tammler's frown.

"And so here we are," Herr Tammler amended.

"Otto, let the boy eat." But after a spicy potato soup had been served, the inevitable questioning began.

"Alexia tells me you are from a military family, Herr Reinhart."

Frosty and formal. I'll be gracious if it kills me. "My father was on the kaiser's general staff. He died eight years ago, Frau Tammler."

"I'm so sorry. And your mother?"

"She is well. She lives in Hannover."

"I understand you are a Naval Academy graduate."

And the smilingly expressed probing went on through a main course of Eintopf – with apologies for wartime stringencies, a fine red wine and a surprisingly lavish Rote Grutze dessert. By the time the meal was over, Ingrid Tammler had managed to extract Peter's family background, educational history and God knew what else, all gleaned with disarming smiles and a melodious voice. He had feared Kottenhoff's name would inevitably come up, but she had stayed clear of Peter's military experience. Thank God for that.

"And now," Frau Tammler said with a little chuckle, "why don't Alexia and I leave our two men to their cigars and brandy?"

Peter noted Lexie's eye roll. The inquisition wasn't over yet.

"Cigars and brandy," Herr Tammler echoed. "Let's go to my Herrenzimmer. An after-dinner brandy sounds good to me."

After wine at supper, I'm not eager for brandy, but... "To me, also, Sir."

Tammler led him two doors down the hall then into another impressive room. Beautifully framed oils – hunting scenes this time – contrasted with the dark paneling. A cluttered roll-top desk dominated the far wall. Four overstuffed armchairs flanked a low central table.

"This whole place is more than we need. We had hoped for a large family, but –" He shrugged. "That was not to be."

Peter nodded at a large painting over the desk, a hunter in safari garb aiming his rifle at a charging leopard. "You are a sportsman?"

"Only briefly, and now by proxy, I'm afraid. When I went into the machine tool business, I became a hunter of contracts and a stalker of inefficiency. Take a seat, my boy." He indicated the chairs at the low table, settled in one himself, and reached into a small chest nearby.

"Cigar, Peter?"

"No, thank you, Sir."

"You don't smoke?"

"I did, at the Academy. But it's prohibited, of course, aboard airships, and with the hydrogen being generated and cells being refilled at the airship field, not many of us light up on the ground. I've given it up."

"Understandable, understandable." Tammler selected a cigar from the chest and settled back. "Frau Tammler is not delighted by cigar smoke, but she is otherwise occupied at the moment." He struck a match. "No hydrogen here."

He puffed on the cigar until it glowed. "Ach, this lousy war. The battles grind on and on with neither side making any progress, except killing each other. Tell me something, Peter, what do you think of Strasser's insistence that the airship will win the war?"

How do I answer that? Peter wondered. "You have to admire his faith in what he is doing," he hedged. "And the airship campaign has tied up a lot of men and equipment in England that surely would be fighting us at the Front."

"True, true. But what about the cost? I'm told the army has stopped its airship attacks on England after one of its airships was shot down by an aeroplane over London. You are aware of that?"

"I saw it happen, Sir."

"My God. What a horrible thing to witness."

"Not exactly a confidence builder. The English are using a new kind of ammunition. It has made all of us –" He stopped. What am I saying?

"Apprehensive."

Herr Tammler has gracefully let me off the hook I was hanging myself on. "At the least."

Tammler slowly sent a cloud of bluish smoke toward the ceiling. "Well, it troubles me. Not only the Zeppelin campaign, Peter. The whole damned war. Thousands of young men killing each other. And Strasser pioneers a new grimness. I know his purpose is commendable – to force a quick surrender. But is he cowing the British, or just infuriating them?"

He paused, tapped his cigar ash into a nearby ceramic tray. "Sorry. I'm afraid my conscience is nagging; if you can believe a manufacturer of machine guns has one. I'd rather be back at producing machine tools for an industry bent on construction, not destruction."

He studied the cigar's glowing tip. "The war drags on and on. It's affecting all of us. 'Before the leaves fall,' for God's sake. What was everybody thinking? We are two years in with no end in sight." He shook his head. "Sorry. I'm just rambling. What I really want to say – Well, I don't know how to say it."

He watched Peter through a cloud of exhaled smoke.

"Lexie and I love each other, Sir."

Tammler chuckled and seemed relieved. "Yes, that's about what I had in mind to ask. You are certain this is not a... wartime infatuation?"

"It started that way. But no, it is a lot more than that."

"Marriage?"

"Only with your blessing, Sir. And Frau Tammler's. And only when the war is over."

Tammler studied him. "You think it would not be fair to her to have a husband aboard one of Strasser's… I don't know whether that's gallant or stupid, Peter." He puffed the cigar. "I've been lucky. Came of age between wars. Never called to serve." He tapped the ash into a porcelain ashtray on the table. "On the other hand, I never volunteered for service, either."

"But it was peacetime when you –"

"Were of military age? True. But Alexia tells us you are an Academy man. So you volunteered during peacetime. Now you're in a war. And I understand airship crewman is volunteer duty. So my hat's off. But I have a question."

"Sir?"

"You *both* have agreed to wait until the war is over?"

"Yes."

Tammler gave him a quirky little smile. "Surely by now you've discovered Alexia is not the traditional Fräulein who would easily become a traditional Frau. She dreams of a business career. Her mother tries hard not to deplore that." He leaned forward. "I find it admirable. To be honest, I think I see in her what I would have hoped for if I'd had a son." He settled back. "Never said that to anyone else. Never admitted it to myself."

"I admire her for that. I love her for that, Sir. I would never stand in her way."

"That is her ambition. What is yours?"

Hell of a question. "For now, to be the best damned Zeppelin Executive Officer I can be. After the war, to do well whatever the navy orders me to do."

"Even sea duty? That could strain the average marriage."

"Ah, but Lexie is no average woman."

Tammler grinned, pushed back his chair. "Join me in a toast to that, Peter. I have a bottle of Asbach uralt Weinbrand in the desk."

"I believe I will, Sir." Peter felt more than a sense of relief. I suspect I've not only passed the exam. I believe I've found a friend in the examiner.

50.

Back to reality. Over the North Sea, Kellner's airship and 10 more Zeppelins in loose formation fought gusty southwest winds. Peter eyed the thick clouds ahead.

"Unbelievable," Kellner growled in his ear. "Morale at rock bottom, the weather stinks, and here we are, heading into that." He scowled through the forward windows at the darkening sky. "That's not premature darkness, Exec. At this altitude, that has to be freezing rain."

At best an hour before we nose into that mess, Peter judged. Through the starboard observation window, he watched the sea drift past below, his thoughts elsewhere. Two days with Lexie. Wonderful but frustrating. Her kiss in the upstairs hallway. Sweet and lingering. Her glance down the hall to her parents' room. "Not tonight." Her decision. He felt again her soft fingers patting his cheek, as she slipped away into her room. He turned to the guest room, smiling. A naughty girl turned chaste at home.

Strolling the next day in the damp wood behind the house, retreating when rain began to patter the leaves. Checkers. We played checkers, and she beat me three games straight without crowing about it. A lesser woman would have let me win.

Too soon, we were heading back to the factory, now with me riding with Lexie in the enclosed rear seat and Herr Tammler perched up front in the open air with Chauffeur Hermann. Such seating insisted upon by Tammler himself. Something of a symbolic acceptance. I was elated.

Our goodbye in the alleyway. The hell with whoever might be watching from the garage. That long, desperate embrace. Her not wanting to let go. The muffled cheer from some daring grease monkey in the garage left her laughing through tears.

Then the lonely drive from Hamburg back to Nordholz, faithfully following Lexie's unmistakable Panhard until she pulled away with a farewell wave at the Cuxhaven-Nordholz intersection. Bouncing toward the airship base already feeling the depression that now seemed to penetrate Nordholz's every corner. "I dream of nothing but burning Zeppelins," I overheard one of our most veteran executive officers confess in the Officers' Club. A man in his cups, but no less apprehensive.

Peter forced himself back to the present. The only encouraging aspect of this hastily assembled October 1 attack was the presence of L-31, Mathy's invincible superzeppelin, and Heinrich Mathy himself.

As the threatening sky darkened into night, the widely-spaced Zeppelins made landfall over the English coastline, and once again, careful planning did not survive. Three Zeppelins – according to their radioed reports picked up by suddenly busy radio op Mann – promptly became lost and turned eastward, apparently hopeful at least of finding Germany again. Talk about black cigars.

Peter chuckled to himself, but only briefly. Kellner's airship abruptly nosed into freezing rain. Then it began to sink under the weight of quickly forming ice.

Kellner leaped to the ballast controls, salvoed trails of water. With all six engines roaring, they stabilized. Barely. The Zeppelin ploughed through low-hanging, roiling clouds. Then Peter caught a glimpse of multiple searchlights. What the Hell? That looked like London. They were supposed to bomb Norwich. Had they actually drifted that far southwest?

High over the darkened city, a half dozen beams converged on a distant Zeppelin, Peter clapped his binoculars in place. Looks like fireflies winking all around it.

God! Aeroplanes. To his horror, flame erupted midships. The fire began to brighten the overcast. And the doomed airship began to fall. Slowly at first, then faster as its hydrogen cells exploded in quick succession. Trailing white-hot flame, the disintegrating airship plunged into the ground. Low clouds began to drift in. Like a veil, Peter thought, to hide the agonizing deaths of 20 brave men.

He gripped the side of the hull-access ladder to control his jittering hands.

Kellner threw him an anguished glance. "That sure as hell isn't Norwich down there." And he ordered course reversal.

Fifteen minutes later they spotted through low hanging clouds and mist what might be – or might not be Norwich, Peter suspected. Down went their bomb load, and they made an all-out run for the coast.

"Who went down?" The exhausted crews of returning airships straggled through the late morning toward the mess buildings. "All Nordholz Zeppelins have come back. Who went down?"

By early afternoon, the word finally came from Alhorn. L-31 had not come back. "L-31?" Peter felt as if his dinner were about to come back up. "Oh, Christ!" he said to Kellner,. That's Mathy!"

Mathy! The unshakable master of Zeppelin attacks. Blown out of the sky in just minutes. The word rushed through the Officers' Mess like an incoming tidal wave. A great babble of voices. Then dead silence. Then someone said, "Shot down by aeroplanes, just outside London." More than one man abruptly shoved back his chair and strode, eyes fixed straight ahead, into the privacy of the depressing afternoon.

"Mathy," Peter repeated softly. My God, I saw the most experienced and revered Zeppelin Kommandant of the entire Naval Airship Division go down. Victim of the deadly new British ammunition. What hope is there for the rest of us? He threw Kellner a look and wondered – Am I as sheet-white as he is?

By breakfast time the next morning, the disheartening details came down from Naval Intelligence. L-31 had slammed down near Potters Bar just north of Greater London. The wreckage had burned for hours. Some meters distant, villagers came upon the body of Heinrich Mathy, half buried in the soft earth. Amazingly, he was still alive. But in moments, he died.

"Sweet God!" Ernst looked stricken. "What do you make of that, Peter?"

"He must have jumped."

"He jumped and left everyone else aboard?"

"Jump or burn. There was the only choice. What would you do? Pray and jump, or pray and burn?"

"Just shut up, Peter. Please shut up." Ernst reached for his coffee mug. His hand trembled so violently, he could barely lift it to his mouth.

October's fog, rain, persistent clouds and bad news hung like a pall over Nordholz. No one ordered to lift off. Strasser fumed. Until the 19th. Still noticeably shaken by the loss of Mathy, his close and revered friend, Strasser dispatched eight Zeppelins. Admiral Scheer again sailed to intercept the British Grand Fleet with Strasser's support, not including Kellner's crew. Peter felt disappointed, but shortly afterward, he was glad not to be part of it.

As radio reports began to filter into Nordholz, the whole operation evolved into a dismal fiasco. Engine failure. Defective propeller shaft. Blocked fuel line. Jammed elevator. Four of the Zeppelins pulled out of their patrol sectors.

"Scheisse, Franz," Peter muttered. "We don't need to be shot down. We're falling apart on our own."

"And the Fleet returns to port," Franz said, "leaving the other four Zepps out there with nothing to do."

Which did nothing to improve plunging morale at Nordholz. Every crewmember, Peter was certain, felt the impact of the unpredictable scheduling. Hours of stress during an attack flight then days of idleness to think about what had happened, and what very well could happen the next time. The possibility of suddenly ordered flights during unexpected weather breaks kept Peter at Nordholz. He telephoned Lexie, but the few kilometers separating them might as well have been a thousand. Then came November 27.

At noon, Peter was jolted by Strasser's adjutant shouting from the Officers' Mess entrance: "Break in the weather! Attack orders!" The red-faced adjutant consulted a list in his hand. "L-21, L-22, L-34, L-36. And Kellner. Lift-offs begin at 13.00 hours, latest."

Their targets were industrial works in England's Midlands. "We can thank God for that," Peter muttered to Ernst as they rushed from the hurried meeting in the Assembly Room. "No concentration of guns and aeroplanes anything like London."

"It doesn't matter." Ernst's face was chalk white. "I have a horrible feeling, Peter, about this... this –"

Peter clapped him on the back. "Buck up, Oberleutnant. We all have such moments. Look at that sun. We're going to have a beautiful night."

As the five airships from Nordholz and two from Ahlhorn and Tondern rumbled westward, moonless night descended on the North Sea. The sky began to glow with wavering wands of light. The Aurora Borealis. *An omen,* Peter felt as he stared from the starboard windows into the pulsating sky. *But an omen of what? I wonder.* Moments later, the soft rays began to fade, but the sky westward retained their eerie glow.

"Coast dead ahead, Sir," Helmsman Kraemer announced at 12.30 hours.

Kellner peered forward.

"Another Zeppelin just crossed the coastline some 10 kilometers ahead of us," Peter told him.

"That'll be Dietrich in L-34. You recognize our landfall, Exec?"

Peter studied the oncoming coastline and consulted his map. "I make it just north of Hartlepool, Herr Kommandant."

"And here we go. Steady on course, Kraemer."

Kellner barely got the words out of his mouth when Peter saw L-34 turn silvery bright in the dead-on accuracy of a searchlight beam. *Exactly like Mathy's Zepp lit up over London. God, not again.*

Dietrich's reaction to the searchlight glare was immediate. A string of bombs fell from his airship. *Planning?* Peter wondered. *Or Panic?* In moments, the darkened city below erupted in brilliant flashes.

"He's coming about, Sir."

"Smart man. They're wide awake and waiting down there," said Kellner as he checked the altimeter. "We're at four thousand meters. Looks like he's no higher than three. Could be a mistake on a night this clear."

Peter grabbed Kellner's arm and pointed upward, portside. "Aeroplane exhaust, sir."

"Christ! Just what we need. Full power turn to 130 degrees," Kellner ordered. They swung away from the prowling aeroplane, Peter holding his breath through the whole lumbering turn.

"Now parallel the coast five kilometers to sea," Kellner ordered. "Schwinn," he called to their observer, "be alert to starboard back there. Look for a possible target."

Staring aft, Peter watched the rapidly moving aeroplane. The exhaust gleam continued to streak westward. Then a brilliant shaft of light split the night ahead of it. Again, a ground searchlight found L-34 and pinned it against the cloud-strewn sky. In seconds, a dozen more searchlights pinioned the desperately fleeing Zeppelin, a perfect target for the aeroplane now lancing down in a long dive. A hawk after prey.

A red flare arched from the attacking aeroplane. A signal, Peter realized, as all the beams instantly went dark. Then the enemy pilot began to fire.

"Can't be a B.E.2c," Kellner said. "They fire upward. This one's shooting straight ahead."

"One of their new Sopwith Pups?" Then Peter's voice choked up. "He's... Dietrich's on fire!"

L-34, now almost some distance behind them, spurted a plume of yellow flame. As more hydrogen cells exploded, the massive fireball lit the night. The disintegrating Zeppelin took endless minutes to fall, nose-high, trailing a long scarlet plume until it crashed into the sea.

No one in the control car said a word. Endless minutes passed. Then Kellner broke the silence. "I don't see a single worthwhile target along this deserted coastline."

"Inland at The Wash?" Peter suggested. "We could hit Norwich."

"Possible, possible."

As the eastern horizon showed the first glowing rim of dawn, the 24-kilometer-wide mouth of The Wash loomed to starboard. Visibility was excellent – and dangerous. From their altitude, Peter could see all the way across the Norwich peninsula; could even make out another Zeppelin south of Norwich bearing seaward.

Then his grip on the binoculars tightened. "Herr Kommandant, look starboard at 140 degrees."

"Oh, God," Kellner breathed. "Enough. Enough for one night."

The distant airship showed a tiny stab of flame. In seconds, it blossomed into a brilliant rose. Then the Zeppelin began its death plunge.

"Christ," Kellner choked. "Two burned out of the sky. Two..."

Frantically, he searched the countryside below. "There, see those lights? That town. Steer for that town, Helmsman. Exec, we drop on it. Drop everything."

Peter moved close. "For God's sake, Hugo, it's of no military value whatever. A coastal resort at best."

"I don't give a damn," Kellner muttered, and he began yanking the bomb toggles.

51.

For long hours after their safe return to Nordholz, the crew did not hear a single radio transmission concerning L-21 or L-22. Jittery with exhaustion, Peter tried not to think of the ominous silence from L-21.Then word of L-22 came from Hage. From Hage?

"L-22 is a Nordholz-based airship, one of ours. What's L-22 doing in Hage?"

Setting down his barely touched potato salad, Franz offered only a perplexed shrug.

Then came the details: L-22 had been hit by antiaircraft shells near Flamborough Head. Two cells lost all hydrogen. Kommandant Hollander dropped everything that could be picked up or pried loose and limped across the North Sea to reach Hage for an emergency landing. The Zeppelin was repairable, but that was estimated to take at least a week.

"Bad news for the airship, good news for the crew," Franz said. Then his expression froze. "Oh Christ! Peter, that Zepp you saw shot down south of The Wash. That has to be L-21. Frankenberg's. Ernst was on that one!"

"God, Franz. You're right.

"With luck... With luck, some of the crew –"

Peter shook his head. "It went down on fire, Franz."

"Maybe when it fell low enough, he could jump."

"How low is low enough? It caught fire just under the overcast and burned all the way down." Peter had no taste for anything. He set down his fork. "Ernst knew, Franz. He knew. I remember when we left the assembly room, I said I was glad the target wasn't London. And he said, 'It doesn't matter. I have a horrible feeling.' He looked like a man walking to his execution. He knew."

Franz stared at his plate. "We all know, Peter. If we lose two or three airships on every attack, none of us will get out of this alive."

Peter shoved back from the table. Without a word from Franz, who had the good sense not to offer one, he strode from the Officers' Mess into the November chill. He walked onto the airfield, fast but aimlessly. Angrily. Yesterday's weapons against tomorrow's aeroplanes, ever faster, ever higher. Spouting ammunition designed to blow us out of the sky. We're targets as big as city blocks.

At the edge of the woods along the airfield's eastern boundary, he stopped. Turned back. Stared at the hulking sheds, the cluster of administration, mess and crew quarters buildings silent beneath low clouds racing before the cold west wind. All this for one purpose, destroy the enemy, praying not to be destroyed in the process. Only God's weather, Ernst had said, offered respite from this madness.

Ernst. A German officer who projected the aura of a British peer with his trim little mustache and bemused attitude. Someone at the Academy cautioned me not to make close friends in wartime. He drew a long shaky breath. Exhaled a frosty gust of resignation and walked slowly toward the officers' quarters. He and Franz would have to sort out Ernst's belongings for the orderly at Personnel.

On December 2, the solid cloud cover broke into scattered cumulus. The return of flying weather was predicted to be brief, but it offered the opportunity for Zeppelin patrols. During the period of limited visibility, the British were reported to have sent several light cruisers prowling the North Sea for a purpose as yet undetermined. They had been spotted by German torpedo boats that had promptly lost them in a snow squall. Now, with the skies more navigable, the Admiralty requested Zeppelin patrols, Kellner's airship among them – and the first to lift off at dawn this chilly day.

Almost immediately, they encountered fog. Great drifts of it obscured the sea, with only occasional breaks. Otherwise, Peter decided, this should be an easy patrol. Except... Except it didn't feel "right." Could this be how Ernst felt boarding L-21 for that fatal last flight? No! I don't believe in premonitions. This is just another routine patrol.

As if reading his thoughts, Kellner turned to Peter and shrugged. "Still more fog, damn it. Wouldn't you know? Helmsman, steer 260, parallel to the Frisians and 10 kilometers seaward. Exec, have Mann radio our position to Nordholz."

Every time we do this, Peter realized grimly, my stomach turns over. Our positions are transmitted in possibly compromised standard navy code. Such arrogance. No concern for enemy ears. German-speaking Home Defense listeners surely are hunched over their receivers, waiting to decode Zeppelin position reports. Tracking us with the help of our own radios transmitting in risky code for convenience.

He stepped back to Mann at his radio shelf and gave him the position figures.

At 1000 meters, they drummed west southwest. One hour of nothing but bad visibility. Two hours. Patrols over the empty sea were a pain in the arse, but better than a sky full of searchlight beams, antiaircraft bursts and now, God forbid, lethal aeroplane attacks.

The monotonous drone of the engines and the tang of exhaust, the control car's gentle rise and fall through occasional turbulence, all threatened to lull him into – He straightened, forced himself to continue sweeping the fog-patched sea with at least an attempt at alertness. He looked portside at Observer Schwinn. Got a shrug. Seven more hours of this monotony, interrupted only by an occasional climb into the hull for a long walk aft along the keelway to visit the head.

At last, they turned eastward to skirt Wangerooge Island on a homeward course. A totally uneventful patrol.

At that moment, a sudden flash and the flat "pung" of an exploding shell shattered the afternoon.

"Antiaircraft fire to port!" Schwinn yelled, his voice cracking in surprise.

Peter whirled around to see a gout of brown smoke whip past and fall behind. He snatched up his binoculars to sweep the fog layer below. Nothing. Or is that the dark bulk of a ship emerging from the swirling fog?

"Ship below," he called. "Light cruiser. English."

As the ship steamed beneath them, Peter saw two flashes from stern guns. "He's firing again."

"Hard to port," Kellner ordered. The horizon slid rightward as the ponderous Zeppelin began its left turn. To starboard, a flash. Then another. Two smudges dirtied the sky where they would have been without the abrupt turn.

Kellner grimaced in relief. "Thank God they can't elevate their big fore and aft turret guns high enough." Binoculars glued to the cruiser, Peter noticed something odd. "The forward turret, Herr Kommandant."

Kellner peered downward. "What is that, Exec?"

"Looks like a wooden platform over the two cannon." A sudden chill broke across Peter's shoulders. "I believe it's an aeroplane launching ramp, Sir. The report at assembly two days ago – The Sopwith Pup launches into the wind from a short makeshift platform. After the flight, the pilot lands in the sea to be picked up by the ship. The aeroplane is sacrificed."

"That report was unsubstantiated, Exec. I can't imagine purposely losing an aeroplane that way."

"Maybe they are only testing the platform down there. Or –" and he hoped to hell he was right – "they've already 'landed' their aeroplane."

Kellner paled. "Or is it a trap? The cruiser picks up our position reports, moves between us and the mainland. Hears our heading-home signal, launches the aeroplane. The pilot climbs, waits –" He grabbed the voice tube to the top gunner. "Hansenkamp, keep your eyes open up there. There may be an enemy aeroplane in the area."

"Look sharp, Schwinn," Peter ordered their young observer. "We can out-climb an aeroplane, but he may already be somewhere up there above us."

Now Kellner's, Schwinn's and Peter's binoculars probed the sky overhead until the curve of the hull blocked their vision upward. Not a sign of an aeroplane, thank God. Haze. Some wispy altostratus. After long minutes of sweaty anxiety, they settled down. Wherever the Sopwith had gone, if there was one, neither Peter, Schwinn nor Kellner spotted anything at all.

"With luck," Kellner said, "he's –"

A whistle shrilled in the top gunner's speaking tube. Peter grabbed the funnel. And heard a frantic shout. "Aeroplane straight overhead, sir! Five hundred meters above us."

Peter thrust the funnel at Kellner. "Aeroplane, directly overhead, five hundred meters."

"Has he spotted us?" Kellner shouted into the tube.

How could he not? Peter slid open the starboard observation window, leaned out as far as he could, but the hull's curvature still blanked out too much sky. He heard Hansenkamp's Maxim cut loose. A long panicky burst.

Kellner shoved the speaking tube back to Peter. "Can you do something about his damned tendency to panic?"

"Top gunner," Peter called into the tube, "Short bursts. Aim carefully. Short –"

"He's coming straight at me!" Hansenkamp yelled. The Maxim yammered again. And kept firing as the aeroplane plunged past them to port. The portside gunner in the engine car aft fired a quick burst. The enemy pilot leveled off some 100 meters below and began a steep climb.

"Nobody hit him," Kellner's voice was high-pitched. "Strasser is right. Airship guns are useless against an aeroplane."

With a Zeppelin moving at 50 knots and an airplane racing at perhaps 90 on different courses, Strasser had admitted the inaccuracy of defensive fire. That admission made, Peter suspected, to reinforce the need for his height climbers.

"I've lost him!" Schwinn cried.

Peter and Kellner swept the sky wildly. "There!" Peter shouted. "Swinging around behind us to starboard." Some 500 meters distant and at their level, the trim little khaki-colored biplane paralleled their course for a moment. Then it pulled ahead in a shallow climb and banked into a wide left turn.

"It is a Sopwith," Peter determined. "Single cockpit, gun firing through the propeller arc."

As the aeroplane banked back toward them, he lost sight of it behind the hull's forward curvature. Then Kellner yelled, "He's straight ahead, coming right at us."

He slapped the engine telegraph and shouted in the speaking tube. "Emergency full climb! Wiesinger, up five – no, make it ten degrees."

The oncoming enemy fighter climbed with them, then abruptly nosed down. "He's diving away." Schwinn looked like a man whose execution had suddenly been postponed.

"He's dropped down to get below our top gunner's line of sight," Peter told him. "And he's coming straight in to avoid the side gunners in the engine car. He's going to rake us from beneath, nose to tail."

The Sopwith's nose raised and the machine gun began flashing. Christ, Peter thought. Nowhere to hide. The forward windows shattered into a blizzard of flying fragments. Kellner clutched his throat, shot Peter a look of amazement then fell backwards.

Bullets ripped a half dozen holes in the floor and snapped through the control car's duralumin overhead. Glowing particles ringed the exit holes. Incendiaries.

Peter dropped to the floor to aid Kellner. Blood from his neck poured through the kommandant's gloved fingers and pooled on the floor. He stared at Peter wide-eyed. Then his eyes froze. His hand fell away. A jagged chunk of duralumin window framing protruded from Kellner's neck.

Kraemer, Wiesinger and Schwinn stared down at him. Peter shook his head. "Anyone else hit?"

"In the arm," the elevator man said. "Not too bad, I think." But Peter saw a slash in his right sleeve, and blood soaked his glove.

"Better let me take a look at that, Wiesinger," Peter said. "Schwinn, get on that elevator wheel with him. Hold the climb."

"The son of a bitch is making another pass!" Wiesinger said through clenched teeth. "If he comes in from the side, the engine car gunners will have a shot."

The engines howled at full blast. Schwinn and Wiesinger grimly held their steep climb.

Some 300 meters to port, the Sopwith drew even with them then began to pull ahead. They heard the top gun yammer again. The portside gunner in the engine car cut loose.

"Way out of range," Schwinn said. The observer looked disgusted, a kid spoiling for a fight. Overhead, the Maxim kept banging away.

"Out of his mind," Schwinn said. The gun went silent. "Or out of ammunition."

"Look at that!" Wiesinger shouted. The Sopwith had nosed down steeply, its propeller dead. "Hansenkamp got him."

"Out of range," Peter told him. "The damned aeroplane has engine trouble. Or he's out of fuel."

"Thank God for that." Schwinn looked down at Kellner's crumpled body. Blood was everywhere. The floor was slick with it. "He never had a chance."

Wounded arm dangling, Wiesinger, said, "Sorry for him, but now what?"

With a jolt, Peter realized he was now kommandant of this floundering Zeppelin. He set the engine telegraph back to cruise. "Schwinn, stay on that wheel and bring us level while I check Wiesinger's arm."

The elevator man pulled off the right sleeve of his jacket. The wound was an upper arm gouge, bloody, painful, but sparing bone and apparently any major blood vessel. "It doesn't matter, Herr Oberleutnant. What does matter is that our airship is still in one piece."

The speaking tube from the hull whistled. Peter grabbed it. "Herr Kommandant!" a panicky voice shouted. "We have a fire in the engine car!

52.

"How bad is it, Bitzer?"

"Fatal," the chief engine mechanic answered. "The engine car's fuel line was hit. An explosive bullet, from the looks of the damage. It's jammed the fuel cut-off valve. I wrapped the line. Can't stop the dripping. It's caught fire. Don't know how much longer I can –"

Behind the chief's rush of words, Peter heard shouting. He leaned far out the open starboard window and peered aft. A chill broke across his shoulders. He could see the glow of flame inside the engine car.

He rushed back to the speaking tube. "Any chance of repairs?"

"None, Sir."

"Then get everyone out of that car – your assistant, the two gunners, yourself."

"On the kommandant's order?"

'My order, Bitzer. The kommandant is dead."

"Jesus!"

"Cut off both engines, then get out of that car, up into the hull. Everyone goes midships on the keelway."

"Then what, Herr Oberleutnant?"

"Then, I –" Then what? "Do as you are ordered, Bitzer."

"Yes, Sir."

The aft car's hatch flew open, and Peter saw the crew begin to scramble up the hull-access ladder. Behind the stricken car stretched a thin stream of black smoke.

"God save us," Peter muttered. When he turned from the window, they all were looking at him. Kraemer. Mann. Wiesinger, clutching a rag to his right arm, left hand on the elevator wheel. A token grip. Schwinn, both hands on the wheel, peered over his shoulder. All of them waiting. The hatch to the engine compartment aft flew open. Engine man Marwitz stuck his head out, stared at Kellner's body. The control car is in shambles. Wiesinger's wound won't stop bleeding. The aft engine car is on fire. Time to run. Wiesinger lost his grip on the elevator wheel. Schwinn swung around, grabbed it with both hands. Looked down.

"The cruiser has launched a boat, Sir. They're picking up the Sopwith pilot."

Peter rushed to the starboard windows. Intent on the pickup, crewmen crowded the cruiser's bow. We're 1500 meters up, trailing smoke. They've written us off.

Time to run? No, God damn it! We're still in the air. Check the compass. We're drifting. Northbound.

"Kraemer, make a two-seventy turn westward."

The helmsman blanched. "Two-seventy, west, Sir? That could take us nearer that damned cruiser."

"Take us right over the damned cruiser, Kraemer. We are going to bomb those bastards."

"Aye, Sir!" Kraemer grinned. They all grinned. Marwitz ducked back into the engine compartment, slamming the hatch behind him. Peter ordered the remaining four engines – two aft in the control car and the two in the small twin gondolas amidships –to fast cruise.

Slipstream gusted through the shattered windscreen as the horizon rolled past. Northwest, west, southwest, south, southeast... East. "Course nine zero," Kraemer called. Peter looked to port. They had painted a loop of smoke in the crystal sky behind them.

"Target dead ahead," Kraemer called. "Herr Kommandant."

"Bomb room door open," Peter shouted through the speaking tube.

He squinted through the bombsight on the forward console. Kellner's job, but Kellner lies dead at my feet. Best guess... Best guess... The cruiser drifted toward them.

Finally realized what was happening. Machine guns began to wink on the stern. Small worry. We're out of range. He yanked the bomb toggles. Down went their patrol load: four 100-kilo high-explosive bombs.

One splash portside. Two close behind the cruiser's stern. And a brilliant flash on the enemy's stern. Probably not fatal, but damned satisfying. He heard cheers behind him, faced his crew with a grin.

Schwinn still peered down. "Antiaircraft gun firing near the cruiser's bow, Sir. "A lone shell burst well aft, and too low.

"Hold zero-nine-zero, Kraemer," Peter ordered. "Straight for Nordholz." The Brits will head home with a hole in their pride. We're headed home, but do we have any chance of getting there?

Peter took a quick look aft. Sweat broke out on his forehead. With Wangerooge Island well aft, their thin trail of smoke became a plume. The German coastline lay ahead. Ten kilometers ahead.

"Mann, forget the code. Report in the clear: 'Kommandant killed in attack by Sopwith northwest of Wangerooge.'" He paused to catch his breath. "'Fire in engine car. Estimated landfall five minutes. Ten kilometers south of Cuxhaven. Will attempt landing Nordholz. Oberleuutnant Reinhart.'"

He swung around to Schwinn and Wiesinger.

"Ten degrees down elevator." Grabbed the engine speaking tube. "Forward and midship engines full ahead. Now."

The stricken Zeppelin nosed down in a full power emergency descent. The control car floor slanted forward. Kellner's body slid against Kraemer's legs. God, Peter realized with a start, I've forgotten –" He grabbed the hull speaking tube. "Damage report."

"No hull damage reported, Sir," some crewman answered immediately. "We are lucky." Lucky. Kommandant dead. Engine car on fire. And we are roaring down, hoping to Jesus that fire will not spread to the hull with its 2200 cubic meters of hydrogen we dare not valve off.

Something... Something else I've forgotten. Our top gunner! Peter seized that speaking tube. "Hansenkamp! The engine car is on fire. We are going in fast. No time for you to get down in the keel. You have a parachute. Use it!"

"Jump?" Hasenkamp's distant voice, military protocol abandoned. Abandoned down here, too. "You said jump?"

"Your choice."

Silence. "Hansenkamp?"

A shadow whipped past the portside windows. "Someone is falling!' Schwinn yelped. Peter rushed across the car, stared down. Against the rushing sandy turf, a spread-eagled figure dwindled. A white disc blossomed. The only man on the crew with a parachute had used it.

They were going down fast. Peter shot another glance aft. The damned fire burned brighter, and the last man out had not closed the hatch. Tongues of flame lashed upward, dangerously close to the bottom of the hull.

"Altitude, Schwinn."

The observer-turned-helmsman stole a jittery glance at the altimeter above the wheel. "Three hundred meters."

"Call it every hundred meters." Peter peered ahead. Nordholz not yet in sight.

The ground's rushing toward us. Speed through the air more than 80 kph. We're in a flying disaster, shoved even faster by the strong west wind. We're going to flatten right into the ground. The flaming engine car will plough into the wreckage of 19 hydrogen cells. What can I do?

"Two hundred meters! Schwinn called.

Lexie, I never should have let you in for this –

"One hundred meters."

The ground raced toward them, a river of green and tan.

Helpless. Or maybe… "Kraemer, hard turn starboard. Ninety degrees."

"Crosswind?"

"Crosswind, Kraemer. We hit the ground crosswind."

Halfway through the turn, Peter judged the crippled Zeppelin was only 30 meters above the ground. "Schwinn, the elevator wheel is all yours. Level off, level off. Wiesinger, get over here."

His wounded arm dangling, the elevator man stepped to Peter's side.

"Stand by to pull this row of valve controls."

Wiesinger looked stricken. "Open hydrogen valves? We're on fire!"

"Do it when I tell you." The ground raced upward. "All engines, stop! Wiesinger, valve hydrogen. Now."

Hands flying, they both opened the valves for all hydrogen cells forward of midships. The ground leaped up, smashed into the bottom of the control car. Peter heard Schwinn and Kraemer hit the floor. The car bounced, crashed down again, plowed into the sandy turf.

"Hold, hold," Peter breathed.

Schwinn scrambled to his feet, checking himself for damage. Peter and Wiesinger had been thrown sideways but their grip on the valve controls had kept them on their feet. The hull began to tilt to port. The stiff crosswind was pushing it sideways, laying it over.

As he had hoped. With the forward hydrogen cells emptying, Peter prayed, the Zeppelin would stay down.

The control car began to tilt with the settling hull. Peter lost his footing and tumbled with the others down the sloping floor to crash into the portside wall. The creaking list stopped at about 45 degrees. In the car's compartmented aft section, Peter heard the two engine men scrambling for their exit hatch. A gabble of shouts rose outside as crewmen clawed out of the battered hull.

"Everybody still able to –" A blinding flash was followed by a thump that jarred the control car.

"Fire!" someone outside shouted.

Peter scrambled to his feet. Straddled the sloped floor and the portside wall. Lurched across the narrow car to the starboard windows. Looked aft – straight into a massive ball of flame engulfing the crumpled tail section.

Schwinn pulled himself up, staring. "The engine car fire. Set off hydrogen in the aft cell."

Another explosion shook the car. "Number two cell." Peter's voice cracked.

"Let's get the hell out of here."

The control car's exit was at the top of the slanted floor. The impact had sprung open the door, now dangling above them on warped hinges. "Schwinn, I'll give you a leg up, then I can boost Wiesinger, Kraemer and Mann up to you."

With Peter and Kraemer shoving from below, the young observer scurried to the exit. Then sweaty and fighting panic, Peter and Schwinn managed to shove and pull the wounded elevator man, radio op Mann and Kraemer out of the control car.

"Hurry," Schwinn shouted. Peter clawed his way up the slanted floor, grabbed Schwinn's hand – then stopped. Kellner. I can't leave him in here to roast. He dropped back.

"What in hell are you doing?" Schwinn yelled.

"The kommandant –"

"He's dead, for God's sake. You can't –" His voice was swallowed in the explosion of another cell. Peter felt the heat surge through the broken control room windows.

"Save yourself, Schwinn. I'm right behind you."

The metal flooring was almost too hot to touch as Peter struggled up its slope and grabbed Schwinn's outstretched hand then the doorway's edge. Schwinn jumped free. As Peter pulled himself through the exit, a tremendous roar deafened him. A searing blast of air punched him to the ground. He threw his arms over his head. Fire billowed over him then receded. The entire hull was aflame.

"Reinhart!" In the fire's thunder, he barely heard his name. "The car!"

As he shoved his seared hands against the ground and began to crawl out from under the tilted car, he heard the shriek of ripping metal. Melting in the flames, the control car slowly rolled over him.

His left leg was caught. A hell of a way to die. Pinned in the wreckage of the Zeppelin I commanded for less than an hour. Lexie, I'm sorry. So sorry.

Then the weight on his leg lifted. Hands grasped his shoulders, pulled him clear.

He looked up into Schwinn's stricken face, then to the straining crewmen heaving the collapsed control car up a few inches to free him.

His crew. Then he whirled into merciful blackness.

53.

Fragments are all I remember from the moment the control car pinned my leg to this awakening in... in a hospital room? Pain as hands pulled me free. More hands lifting me into a jouncing truck, I think it was. A clinic somewhere, with Lexie – Lexie? Bending over me, her fingers touching my forehead. A merciful dream to ease the nightmare? Then into another truck, this one with a cot. An ambulance? Across bridges into a city. Hands again, lifting me. But I remember nothing after that.

Until now. Here I am. But where?

Peter turned his head slowly, his neck aching with the effort. A blurry nightstand with a pitcher, a glass. Vision clearing... Not a ward; a small room with white walls, bare except for a framed photograph of Kaiser Wilhelm. A single narrow window. Tree branch just beyond its lowest panes. A branch with a single brown leaf. Cloudy day out there. Industrial buildings, and through spaces between, a busy harbor with more buildings on the other side. Hamburg?

"Ah, you are awake, Herr Oberleutnant." He turned his head away from the window. A tall white-uniformed nurse, haggard but smiling, stood in the doorway. "I am Nurse Brauer. Most unusual, I must say. Our military patients are assigned to the wards downstairs. Up here, only oberst rank or higher." She gave him a quizzical look. "Not oberleutnants. You must have influence."

I crash-landed a Zeppelin that exploded and burned into twisted duralumin and cinders. I have influence? Surely not Strasser's.

"My crew?" The words came hard, not much more than a whisper. "What happened to my crew?"

"Thirteen survived, Herr Oberleutnant. The newspaper says it was a miracle any survived."

Thirteen out of sixteen. Three dead. Kellner and two others.

"The paper said you are a hero of the Fatherland."

"The newspaper is getting desperate."

She walked to the bed, eyes alert in a tired face, placed a palm on his forehead. "How are you feeling today?"

"I'm not feeling much at all."

"That's the medications. You have burns on your arms and neck, fortunately not deep. But your leg –"

His left leg felt nothing. Did he feel nothing because there was nothing there to feel?

Heart thudding, he slid his left arm beneath blanket and sheet, ran his fingertips along his thigh and with a surge of relief, felt the hard edge of a plaster cast.

Nurse Brauer peered at him. "Better take some water, Herr Oberleutnant."

"My leg?"

"Water. Then if you like, I could bring you apple juice, lemonade."

"My leg, damn it!"

She lifted a pitcher from a small table beside the bed. "Doktor Feldmann will be here shortly. He will tell you."

"Peter?"

He woke from a half-sleep of vividly relived terror before the control car rolled on him. Kellner's stunned eyes on his as the kommandant fell. Then slam into the ground. The fleeting moment of relief that the hydrogen had not exploded. Then the great wash of fire. And the hands. All the hands –

"Peter?" A man's voice.

Eyes blurry, he blinked, squinted. "Doktor Feldmann?"

"No, son. It is Otto. Otto Tammler. Alexia's father." He stepped into the room. "She called me the minute she heard you had been injured. They had taken you and your crew, with burns mostly, to the military hospital in Cuxhaven."

Tammler shucked off his black, fur-collared great coat, draped it over the back of a corner chair, pulled the chair closer to the bed and sat. "I've taken some liberties, Peter, all in your behalf. Well, yours and Alexia's. I phoned your mother in Hannover. To reassure her, of course, and to get her permission, as your next of kin, to make some arrangements to your benefit."

"I'm not sure I –"

"Peter, I am a director on this hospital's board. I had you moved here to Hamburg, to this private room, and put under the care of Doktor Jakob Feldmann. He is one of the best surgeons in Germany. Your leg is severely injured."

"Herr Tammler, I can't let you –"

Tammler chuckled. "You are in no position to prevent me, my boy. If such priority tweaks your conscience, I am doing this for my daughter as well as for my future son-in-law. She will be here later today, with the blessing of her employer." Tammler smiled briefly. "An acquaintance of mine."

Friends. Perhaps not necessarily in high places, but in many places. Otto Tammler, not a man of impressive stature, was a man of impressive influence. If I were a man of excessive pride, Peter thought, I might resent this special treatment. But I am a man with a leg injury the nurse will not even talk about.

"I'm sure I don't merit all this, Herr Tammler, but I certainly thank you."

Tammler waved his thanks aside.

"My crew? Do you know anything about –?"

"Newspaper accounts say the kommandant was killed in the air attack. The crash and fire killed two more. A machinist mate and a sailmaker. A sailmaker?"

"They are aboard to repair tears in hydrogen cell fabric."

"Ah, I see. Amazing. Everyone else escaped with various degrees of burns, none fatal. Oddly, I thought, one man turned up in good condition some five kilometers west of the crash."

"Our top gunner. The only crewmember with a parachute. He jumped on my order."

"One parachute for 16 men? Incredible." Tammler sat back, frowned. "Let me tell you something in confidence, Peter. Military casualties are pouring in from the endless battle of Verdun, swamping hospitals already jammed with casualties from the Somme. The high command is keeping it quiet, but I've heard we lost 600,000 men killed, wounded and captured in the Battle of the Somme. And Verdun, still grinding on, could be worse. Endless injuries to arms and legs that require expert, intricate, lengthy surgery by specialists who all too often resort to amputation as an expediency. There are not enough Jakob Feldmanns to do otherwise."

He consulted his large, gold pocket watch, stood, patted Peter's shoulder. "Take heart, Peter. You have done your very best. Your mother and von – what was his name?"

"Professor von Storch."

"Ah, yes. They are on their way, as well as Alexia." At the door, he peered into the hall. "Oh, I see dinner has arrived. Come in, Nurse. Come in. I must go, Peter."

"Thank you for coming, Herr Tammler. And my thanks for all –"

Again, Tammler waved him silent. "For Alexia, my boy. And for you."

As he walked from the room, the nurse beamed. "Such a pleasant man. Perhaps a minister?"

"An industrialist, a maker of machines." Better than blurting: your minister makes machine guns. He picked at the paltry hospital food. Ate the boiled cabbage and beans. Couldn't manage the unsavory looking slice of unidentifiable meat. Sipped the tepid apple juice. He set the tray aside and lay back, eyes shut.

Kellner. Together we helped each other grow into responsible airship officers, sharing weaknesses and unsuspected strengths. Now he is gone. Ernst, near collapse but forcing himself into combat, gone. Burned to death – or had he jumped? – Over an insignificant English town. Franz, with his tricycle-inflicted "dueling" scar. Was he still flying or was he – Peter forced his thoughts elsewhere. Admiral Kottenhoff, who talked me into what had begun as a compelling game but led to combat duty I hated but learned to respect. Strasser, with near fanatical faith in his new kind of warfare, admirable in his conviction, but blind to the inadequacy of his weapons to accomplish it.

And Lexie. Whom I never would have met but for our heedlessly determined admiral. It was he –

Someone walked into the room. A tall, gaunt fellow with close-cropped white hair and a beard to match. The man removed his pince-nez glasses and cleaned the lenses with a kerchief he whipped out of his short white coat.

"I am Doktor Feldmann, Herr Oberleutnant, the surgeon who worked on your leg. How are you feeling?"

"Useless, Herr Doktor."

"From what I hear of your adventure two days ago, I believe you are a lucky man."

"The leg, Herr Doktor?"

"The leg was fractured in three places. I put it back together as best I could. It is not perfect. The damage is too great."

"I'm waiting." Peter bit his lip.

"Waiting?"

"For you to tell me I will never walk again."

"I never make such predictions to patients. So much depends on determination. With determination, you can progress. Wheelchair to crutches to cane. Up to you. However, I can tell you one thing that is certain. For you, the war is over."

"I heard that!" Lexie stood in the doorway, radiant in light blue, her auburn hair defiantly free, emerald eyes sparkling. She rushed into the room, brushed past the bemused doctor, took Peter's face in her hands and kissed him with far less decorum than might be expected in the presence of a highly respected surgeon.

"You are wonderful, Herr Doktor," she said as she straightened to face him.

"Wonderful?"

"You said the magic words. Did you hear, Peter? 'For you, the war is over.' Remember our promise to each other, Liebling, for when the war is over. I won't let you forget."

"A wheelchair, Doktor Feldmann tells me, Lexie. Then crutches. Then a cane."

* * *

It took him almost all of 1917, but in October he managed to walk into Hamburg's St. Petrikirche with no crutches, no cane. Only a limp.

EPILOGUE

From the industrial haze, the towering buildings of New York City began to emerge. Peter leaned over the outward slanted windows of the starboard observation promenade. America. Renouncing the old world for the new, he hoped, would prove to be a wise decision for Lexie, for 16-year-old Antje – and for him.

Twenty years since I rode Kellner's doomed Zeppelin with its dead kommandant into its crash landing. Thirteen men saved, but three dead. I thought I would never again set foot in an airship. Yet here I am, enjoying a totally unexpected exhilaration of flight: the purring engines, the majestic smoothness of lighter-than-air travel, the efficiency of the crew and the confidence of the passengers. History is being made this 9th day of May 1936. The world's largest airship, the 803-foot-long – I must think in American feet and yards now – the 803-foot long Zeppelin-built *Hindenburg* is about to complete its first transatlantic flight to the United States.

On the observation promenade railing, he put his hand over Lexie's slender fingers, turned to her and smiled. Not yet a hint of gray in that wonderful auburn hair.

"Look!" Antje cried. "The Empire State Building."

Peter's throat tightened. No, no, those oncoming biplanes aren't B.E.2cs or Sopwith Pups. They're the first Americans to welcome us. God,

I didn't expect that sudden wartime reflex. "For you, the war is over," Doktor Feldmann said two decades ago. But for those who experienced combat, the war is never completely forgotten.

Nor was his naval career entirely ended by his disability. After hours, days, weeks, months of therapy, after sweat, pain and struggle against frustration then the victorious limp down the aisle, Peter received not the expected release from service but orders to report "on detached service" to the Zeppelin Company in Friedrichshafen. He had wondered about financial survival when the navy axe would surely fall, and here was his answer.

Somebody up there... Otto Tammler? Kottenhoff? To his amazement, his benefactor turned out to be Strasser. The man who sent men to die, now, at least financially, saved one he had sent. The job: liaison between the navy and the Zeppelin Company. He and Lexie set up modest housekeeping near Friedrichshafen, and she surprised him. She determined to go back to work. "A secretary again?" he asked her.

"Not quite, Liebchen." An entrepreneur at heart, she began to build a service that supplied temporary secretarial help as needed. The clients paid her, and she paid her women, minus a modest fee." The project took a year to break even, and then Secretaries On Call began to post profits.

The war ground on, and in late 1917, Germany began to emerge as the possible victor. Strasser's pressure kept the Zeppelin Company in operation, but the company's management saw the writing in the sky more clearly than did Strasser. Attention shifted to building big bombing aeroplanes. With two other companies under Zeppelin license, Peter fell heir to coordinating all that, his predecessor having happily accepted a less wearing position at Zeppelin's subsidiary works in nearby Lindau.

Peter and Lexie moved into a larger Friedrichshafen apartment, and Peter soon developed an impressive ability to untangle administrative complexities. While the mighty R.V1s and Gothas hit England harder than the ponderous airships ever could, the war on the ground went more or less nowhere. On the Eastern Front, the Russians were disintegrating, but America had entered the war.

When American forces finally appeared on the Western Front in 1918, they quickly proved they could fight. The British and French were invigorated by this ally with thousands of fresh and aggressive troops, backed by mighty industrial muscle. By November 1918, the war was over for everyone. Germany, now fragmented with internal strife, was at the mercy of the Allies.

The Zeppelin Company hung on by manufacturing cookware while trying to find a market for Zeppelin airships. Peter adapted to pots and pans paperwork. Lexie managed to keep her secretarial service alive as Germany struggled to restore order, cope with the harsh Treaty of Versailles and rebuild the government as the Weimar Republik. The new constitution barely survived a spate of uprisings and galloping inflation.

Peter and Lexie lived on Peter's reduced salary and Lexie's hard-earned fees. Then in 1921, a glimmer of hope for the Zeppelin Company was born of tragedy. The British built the airship R R-38 for the U.S. Navy. During a test flight, R R-38 tore itself apart and plunged into the Humber River. Zeppelin Company head Hugo Eckener promptly secured a contract with the U.S. Navy to replace the lost R R-38. Peter was out of cookware and back to airship paperwork. The L-126, renamed Los Angeles, was delivered to America in October 1924. Thanks to that contract, the Zeppelin Company, Peter and Lexie financially survived.

The New Jersey coastline rolled beneath the *Hindenburg*, now cruising low and leisurely southward, past Atlantic City's bustling boardwalk with its grandiose hotels. Spring bathers dotting the beach stared up as the giant airship rumbled overhead.

What a contrast to the land we left, Peter thought, now a land of increasing regulations, brutally imposed by power-hungry men in brown uniforms. A Germany of growing resentment of Jews. Were it not for a superb Jewish surgeon, I could be sitting in a wheelchair dismally employed out of sympathy or not employed at all, not standing up here enjoying the view of May sunshine on peaceful American resort beaches.

After Peter left the Zeppelin Company following the delivery of the L-126, the years had not been easy. Despite the financial chaos of the 1920s, he turned down an offer from Otto Tammler, not relishing the inevitable "boss's son-in-law" stigma. Instead, he took a clerical job with Ebert Engineering, a manufacturer of construction equipment. Lexie struggled to keep her service afloat while coping with Antje"s birth.

In two years, Peter progressed to middle management. In four more, he was appointed a corporate vice-president. When Hindenburg was re-elected President of the Weimar Republic in 1932, the German economy was again in a slump. In the 1933 elections, the National Socialists emerged as the largest party in the Reichstag. They soon became known throughout the world as the Nazis. The next year, ailing President Hinderburg appointed Adolf Hitler the Chancellor. When Hindenburg died a few months later, Hitler assumed supreme power. Germany became a dictatorship in the grip of a spellbinding sociopath.

"With a hatred of Jews," Peter told Lexie.

"But we are not Jews."

He tapped his leg. "This was saved by a Jew, Lexie." At that moment, he knew they could not stay in a Fatherland that had become the property of a party built on brutality and hate. "We must leave," he told her.

"And go where?"

He didn't know where – or how, frustrations that gnawed for the next three years, then: "How is your English?" asked Ludwig Ebert, President of Ebert Engineering.

"Fair, I think. I took English as a second language in school and at the Academy. Why do you ask?"

"Because, Peter, we have bought an American company. Banner Construction. We need a dependable representative over there. For at least a year. The board has unanimously approved that representative to be you."

Selling Lexie's now-prosperous secretarial service was a hard decision. Leaving Nazi Germany was not.

The *Hindenburg* turned inland, leaving the coastline behind. "Lakehurst, Lexie. We're about to land in America." Landing lines dropped toward the ground handlers clustered on the airship field just ahead. The engines subsided to murmurs. Everyone on A deck headed for the twin stairways down to B deck and its exit gangways as the ground crew guided the airship to the stubby mooring mast. The largest airship ever built touched the New Jersey turf with a barely-felt thump.

Peter slipped his arm around Lexie's shoulders, drew her close, kissed her gently. "America, Liebchen." His other hand touched their daughter's shoulder. "We're here, Antje." He whispered in Lexie's ear, ""Here to stay until the Fuhrer is replaced by sanity."

After he, Lexie and wide-eyed Antje passed through Customs and emerged to claim their luggage, there stood a shiny black Packard. Its cheerful-looking driver waved at them.

"Mr. Reinhart?"

"Yes," he called in English. "Mr. and Mrs. Reinhart and daughter Antje. You are from Ebert Engineering?"

"That's me. Here, let me give you a hand with your stuff."

Heading toward the exit road, they rolled slowly past the looming *Hindenburg*.

He could not resist marvelling at its awesome presence, even felt a sense of admiration, an admiration tempered by the swastikas on its tail fins. But he could not shake a haunting feeling of apprehension. The mighty queen of the skies was lofted by the same hydrogen that doomed Strasser's grand strategy and Strasser, himself.

As the Packard swung onto the northbound highway, Antje pointed at the bright afternoon sky. "Seemöwen, Mutter."

"Seagulls, darling. You must use English now."

END

APPENDIX

STRASSER, STRATEGIC BOMBING PIONEER

Before Billy Mitchell, Bomber Harris and Curtis LeMay, there was Peter Strasser, history's first – and seemingly most unlikely – proponent of strategic bombing. Short in stature with pixie-like ears, wide-set piercing eyes, a dapper little moustache and goatee, he pioneered a new kind of war. His weapons were the most hazardous bomb delivery systems ever put in the air: huge, cumbersome, hydrogen-filled airships

Born in the Lower Saxony city of Hannover in 1876, Strasser began his remarkable military career by enlisting in the Germany Navy at age 15. He served on *Stein* and *Moltke*, two armed but not armored cruisers relegated to training status. On these converted training ships, teenaged Strasser revealed a talent for gunnery. But with ambitions beyond that of an enlisted man on sea duty, he enrolled in the Naval Academy at Kiel. He was commissioned a leutnant at age 19. Next came sea duty aboard a succession of five ships. One of them, the artillery training ship *Mars*, offered gifted young officers specialized instruction as gun battery commanders. Strasser's outstanding ability as a gunnery officer led to his assignment to the shipboard ordnance department of the Admiralty in Berlin. Though he was known for his wholehearted devotion to his assigned duties, he seemed to have wavered a bit when he volunteered for aviation duty in 1911. By then, he was a 35-year-old Fregattenkapitan, a rank equivalent to a U.S. Navy commander or U.S Army lieutenant colonel. His request lay dormant for two years until a tragic event catapulted him out of Berlin and into the air.

The man masterminding the updating of Germany's Navy, Grossadmiral Alfred von Tirpitz was no airship advocate until his sea captains began to recognize the scouting value of the "gas bags." That, plus the success of Germany's commercial airships and possibly a bit of pressure from Kaiser Wilhelm II, led to his change of heart. In 1911, the navy signed a contract with the Luftschiffbau Zeppelin Company for construction of an airship, navy designation L-1, delivered in September 1912.

On September 9, 1913, Zeppelin-built L-1 on its 68th flight was battered into the North Sea by a violent storm. Only six of the 20 aboard survived. Among those lost was Korvettenkapitan Frederich Matzing, chief of the recently formed Naval Airship Division. Two weeks later Matzing's successor was appointed: Fregattenkapitan Peter Strasser.

Initially, Strasser regarded his unexpected ascension to the head of the tiny Airship Division as something of a demotion. But characteristically, he threw himself wholly into his new assignment and quickly determined the airship's potential lay far beyond its current conception as no more than a flying observation platform serving the surface fleet. The disparaged "gas bags," he realized, could carry the war straight into the heart of the enemy. No desk jockey now, Strasser promptly arranged for airship flying lessons under the tutelage of Ernst A. Lehmann, captain of the commercial airship *Sachsen,* the Zeppelin-built airship operated by Deutsche Luftschiffarts AG – known to an enamored public as Delag, the nation's highly successful airship passenger line.

While Strasser learned airshipmanship in Leipzig in the hands of the man who would survive the coming war then die two decades later in the *Hindenburg* disaster, the navy's second airship, L-2, underwent flight-testing.

On October 17, 1913, near Berlin on its 10th flight, L-2 caught fire and plunged to the ground. None of the 28 aboard survived. Barely three weeks after assuming command, Strasser had no airships. He responded to this morale-crushing situation by pressing the Admiralty to temporarily employ passenger airship *Sachsen* as a naval training ship with Delag's Dr. Hugo Eckener and Ernst Lehmann in charge of flight operations. By early December 1913, the Airship Division was back in the air with *Sachsen* making frequent training flights under Eckener's direction. This potentially troublesome shared command between a civilian contractor and a career officer proved remarkably compatible, despite Strasser's reputation as a spit-and-polish military disciplinarian. Any on-duty lapse threatened to bring the offender before Strasser for a nerve-twitching rant, the navy's dreaded "black cigar."

Off duty, Strasser turned out to be a warmer personality, concerned with the well-being of his officers and enlisted men alike, and aware of their concerns. This off-duty personal warmth served Strasser well as he sold the tradition-bound navy a new kind of warfare with an unproven new weapon. Compared to Brigadier General "Billy" Mitchell in his effort to convert the tiny post-WWI U.S Air Service from a neglected auxiliary into a primary strike force, Strasser was more likely to schmooze superiors rather than antagonize them. Like WWII's RAF Air Chief Marshal Sir Arthur "Bomber" Harris, Strasser was committed to hitting the enemy's homeland, but unlike Harris, he was intent on military targets, not civilian casualties. Like the USAAF's General Curtis LeMay, Strasser could have been termed, "Iron Ass," concerning military discipline, but unlike LeMay, he neither wanted nor was technically capable of area bombing. All four officers were strategic bombing zealots, with Strasser possibly the most likeable off duty.

When World War I broke out in August 1914, Strasser had at his command a total of 12 officers and 340 enlisted men, among them only three qualified flight crews. His available offensive weaponry: a single airship, the Zeppelin-built L-3. His greatest asset was the Admiralty's realization that an airship could be built in a mere six weeks, compared to a cruiser's two-year construction time, a huge green light for Strasser. By the turn of the year, he had five airships and more than 4,000 officers and men, including 25 flight crews, at nine bases.

Now the dynamic little Airship Division commander determined to fulfill a pledge to personally fly on a combat mission every month. On January 19, 1915, he joined a crew of 11 aboard L-6 and headed for

England. Ninety miles short of the English coast, a crankshaft shattered, and L-6 was forced to come about and limp back to base.

Aboard L-7 on April 15, Strasser personally led a three-Zeppelin attack on military installations near the mouth of England's Humber River. This time, a powerful headwind forced the plodding Zeppelin to abort short of the target. Such unhelpful incidents with Strasser aboard led to his reputation as a bad luck "Jonah," an unfortunate catchword for the dynamic leader who was to build the Airship Division into the world's first airborne armada.

The June 1915 downing of a German Army Zeppelin by a French-built monoplane dramatized the peril in the low 6,000-foot service ceilings of Strasser's current airships. Modifications increased service ceilings to 13,000 feet. In December 1916, he informed the Admiralty a few more changes could raise service ceilings even further. This resulted in the high altitude Zeppelins the British termed "height climbers" with 16,000 to 20,000-foot ceilings. This ultimate class of Zeppelin-built combat airships left the British anti-airship forces defenseless until the last few months of the war when improved fighters could reach them.

In the meantime, Strasser continued his effort to fly a combat mission per month. In January 1916, he boarded L-11 for a nine-airship raid on England. His Jonah reputation was enhanced when fog obscured military targets and L-11 was forced to return to base with all bombs aboard.

Weather permitting, he stepped up naval airship attacks on English targets through the next several months. On September 2, he ordered what was to be the largest airship raid of the war. Twelve navy airships with four army airships rose out of eight bases and headed across the North Sea. The flaming loss of one of the army's airships near London heartened the British and proved a turning point in the army's lesser part in the airship war. German army airships did not attack England again, and the Army disbanded its airship service some months later.

Despite the flaming destruction of two training airships on the ground two weeks later, and the combat loss of two more a week after that, Strasser was undaunted – and promoted, to Leader of Airships, a second class admiral rank.

March 16, 1917, he ordered the first attack on English targets by the new height climbers. The raid cost the Airship Division its just-built L-39.

Blown eastward in a gale after dropping six bombs in Kent, the floundering airship was shot down by French anti-aircraft gunners. This was a blow to Strasser's efforts, but of greater portent was the shifting of German military aviation attention to the twin-engine biplane Gotha bomber in early 1917. The Gotha, though it carried about a third of a height climber's bomb load, required a crew of only three, needed no multi-man ground handling force, and was a much smaller target. And in the offing was the Zeppelin-built Staaken, an even more capable multi-engine biplane bomber.

The only advantage left to the airships was their far greater range. In the face of morale-crushing losses and the ascendancy of bomb-carrying aeroplanes, Strasser continued his airship bombing campaign – and his personal participation on combat flights. In May 1917, he was aboard L-44 when all five engines intermittently failed and the airship limped back to base with only one running at full power. Jonah had struck again.

The high altitude Zeppelins were now attacking at 20,000 feet, untouched by anti-aircraft fire, out of enemy aircraft range, and even higher than searchlights reached. Now they faced a new problem; the thin, fragile air at high altitude. Liquid compasses froze, control cables slackened, the compressed oxygen provided for intermittent whiffs was often contaminated, and crewmen declining to use it often collapsed. When liquid air replaced the original compressed oxygen, that problem was alleviated.

All to little avail.

On August 4, 1918, with the war obviously lost, Strasser issued an order for a five-Zeppelin attack on London. Strasser himself boarded L-70 to lead this first attack on England since April. At twilight, the Leader of Airships radioed his five airship commanders to attack. That was the last order he was ever to issue. An hour later, still at sea but nearing the English coast but apparently not yet at attack altitude, L-70 was shot down in flames by one of three patrolling Royal Flying Corps de Havilland D.H.4s. All 22 aboard L-70 died. The British recovered the bodies in 50 feet of water and buried Leader of Airships Peter Strasser at sea.

With his death, the use of airships as strategic weapons ended. There were no more attacks. In 51 airship raids (including several by army airships), 557 people on the ground had been killed and 1,358 wounded. The cost of damage to British property was estimated at a mere $7.5 million (U.S. equivalent). For those meager direct results, the German Navy had lost 389 Zeppelin crewmembers, a 40 percent death rate. Of its 73 airships, 53 were destroyed by enemy action or accidents.

The most significant effect on England's war effort was the retention of forces for home defense against the airships, thus prevented from serving at the Front. By the end of 1916, before the Gotha raids began, 17,341 officers and men were assigned to home defense, 12,000 of them in anti-aircraft units, the balance in 12 RFC squadrons totaling 110 airplanes.

The pioneer of strategic bombing died in the fragile weapon he had championed. But Strasser's concept of long-range strikes in the enemy's homeland lived on – with a vengeance.

Twenty-seven years later, Germany lay in ruins from strategic bombing.

END